MARC JOHNSON

WHAT ONCE WAS ONE

THE PASSAGE OF HELLSFIRE

BOOK 2

Fourth Edition, 2013

ISBN 978-0-9834770-7-5

Longshot Publishing

CHAPTER 1

I **STARED AT** the faded black words on the brittle page. All the letters blurred together until I lost focus and could no longer read what they said. I rubbed my heavy eyes. I knew I needed a break, but I couldn't stop now. This was the last day I would have access to Alexandria's library, and I had to find a spell, a secret path, a strategy—something that would get my friends and me safely through the monster-infested Wastelands and inside the spell-shrouded castle of the most feared wizard who had ever lived.

Not much to ask of a seventeen-year-old who had been a full-fledged wizard for no more than a month.

That whole month, I had been studying, doing my best to learn what awaited me in the Wastelands of Renak. My former master, Stradus, would have been glad to see me studying so hard. During my training, he'd had to nag or bribe me to keep me at my books. My face hardened and I glared at the book in front of me. The gap in my life where Stradus had been was still fresh and painful. He'd died protecting me, falling at the hands of the dark wizard Premier. The one I was going into the Wastelands to hunt down and finally defeat for good.

I flipped a page, almost tearing it. I flattened the page out before scanning it for any helpful information about Masep, Renak's old place of rule during the War of the Wizards, a thousand years ago. It was there I had to go to face Premier once more, bind his powers so that he would release his hold on the Wasteland monsters and no longer be a threat to the city of Alexandria or the lands of Northern Shala, which the city was sworn to protect. And this time, I would face him without my master at my side.

Premier was weakened, his powers temporarily broken by his defeat, but he was still dangerous. He had access to whatever secrets Renak had left hidden in Masep, and he still controlled thousands of the Wasteland creatures. But the biggest danger was his possession of the *Book of Shazul*—one of the most powerful and deadly books of magic ever created, and one that had corrupted Premier to his very soul. From what Stradus had told me about his one-time friend, Premier wasn't going to be waiting idly for me to come and get him. He would be plotting something, and he would want to strike back at the one who had defeated him—me. And I didn't have much time before Premier got his powers back. Another month and he would be back to full strength and just as dangerous as he was before.

I had promised Stradus I would capture that book from Premier, and I would. Stradus believed it was far too dangerous for any wizard to use, and it was definitely far too dangerous to leave in the hands of a wizard as evil as Premier. The problem was, Stradus also wanted me to spare Premier's life. I didn't know if I could do that. I wanted him dead.

I glanced away from the book, my gaze settling at the foot of a wooden bookshelf. The gashes and scorch marks from the battle my friends and I had fought here had been smoothed away and polished over, but I knew they were there. I remembered every elf and every dwarf who had died in this room at the hands of Premier's creatures, on the night he'd risen up with his hideous armies to take the city. The anger at their loss still burned in me.

I gazed around the room, seeing in my memory the broken shelves, fallen books, and shattered tables, and worst of all, the bodies of those who'd fought by my side. They'd given their lives to get Princess Krystal and me inside the city that night, and I owed it to them to make Premier pay for what he'd done. He had to be stopped. Even if it went against Stradus's wishes. If death was the only way to stop him, I'd kill him.

A small smile escaped my lips, thinking about how the Princess of Alexandria had danced a deadly dance with her sword, twisting and turning, slashing and thrusting. For each goblin, troll, or ogre she'd killed, another took its place. She'd been exhausted and wounded but she never quit.

I shook my head. The images of the battle disappeared and there were just scholars and scribes in the room, and my friends sharing my table and my research.

I closed my book. I wasn't finding anything here. I glanced at the empty spaces in the bookshelves, praying I hadn't destroyed what I needed during the battle. Even now, they were still cataloging and re-shelving the books.

I hadn't told anyone, but I was also hoping to find a way to help Alexandria. Krystal and her people had suffered—not just at the hands of Premier, but for their whole lives. Ever since the city was built, over a thousand years ago, their main purpose had been to protect Northern Shala from Renak's monsters to the north. All alone, for centuries, they'd held the border of the Wastelands, giving their lives so that the rest of Northern Shala could live in peace.

It was a wizard who had been the cause of this. Perhaps it was a wizard who could fix it. It would be the greatest gift I could give to Krystal—the chance to enjoy the peace her people had brought to the rest of Northern Shala. She had welcomed me into her city with open arms. Sadly, her people had not done the same.

I understood why. I was a wizard, the embodiment of those whose power had started the Great War that had torn the land in two and loosed the Wasteland monsters. Alexandria had been dealing with the mess wizards had made for a millennium.

I tried not to let the people's hostility and mistrust bother me. I didn't even tell the princess about it when we were alone together. She didn't need to know. I had tried to change people's minds by helping with the rebuilding, using my powers to make things easier. All I got were stares and whispers. The carpenters and blacksmiths didn't actively turn me away, but they didn't let me do much of anything, either. I finally gave up and settled on not using my powers. But even when I'd tried to help clean the library by scrubbing away the blood from the stone floor or sorting the books into piles, I got the same veiled looks and resentment.

I had eventually given up trying to get them to accept my help, and started spending more and more time in the one place where I could be sure I wouldn't run into any other people—Premier's tower.

During the time he'd spent in Alexandria as the king's advisor, before he made his move to take over the city, he'd taken one of the castle towers as his private living quarters and workroom. Cleaning out the tower and making sure it was clear of any leftover spells or traps was a way for me to kill time while the library was restored.

I also searched for any clues Premier might have left behind about what his ultimate goals were or what he planned to do next, but I didn't find any. I guess I shouldn't have been surprised. I'd only found out after he was defeated that the Premier here in Alexandria was only an avatar—that he'd been projecting his personality, power, and essence into it from his stronghold in Masep.

Once I was done cleaning it out, the tower also gave me a quiet place to practice my powers and meditate. I labored to access the powerful, frightening black fire that had allowed me to defeat Premier. For some reason, I couldn't. That both reassured me and worried me. I was afraid of the power rising up and going out of control, but I also wanted to be able to access it if I had to face Premier again.

The only person who would visit me in the tower was Krystal. It was one of the few places where we could be alone together. But she would never stay long. She had her duties to attend to, and after what Premier had done to her, I didn't blame her for not wanting to spend time in his private space.

I lifted a hand to my mouth, trying to stifle a yawn. I failed.

"Tired, lad?" Jastillian asked from the other side of the table. The weathered dwarf lowered the book he had buried himself in. His beady eyes shone with energy. He never tired of paging through ancient books.

"A little." I glanced at the sun outside the window, then back at him. The sun had reached its peak. Where had the time gone? "How do you always have more energy than me?"

"As much as I love exploring the lands the gods have created and digging for artifacts, researching is half the battle. And you know how we dwarves crave a good battle." He laughed. "Books like these transport me to faraway lands and times. If there's one thing I've learned from being a historian, it's that you must do your research."

"Hey, I found something interesting," Demay said. The young elf poked his head up from behind the huge tome he held. He grinned at us, his long ears twitching in excitement. Of the four of us, he hated being confined to the library the most. "This says that Renak used the Wastelands'...nexus?" He peered at the book again. "Nexus, that's right. He used it to fuel the spell that holds the Great Barrier. And according to the scholar who wrote this book, that's what's responsible for the barrenness of the Wastelands."

Jastillian, who had perked up at Demay's announcement, slumped back down in his chair. "That's just a theory, and not a widely accepted one. I've never seen any definitive evidence put forward to support it. The dominant theory is that the Wastelands are the result of the War of the Wizards and all the mana drawn from the land in its final battles. And, of course, those foul creatures lurking there."

"Maybe," Demay said. "But the Wastelands are growing—you know they are. Look, here's the border of the Wastelands when this book was written."

He laid it down to show me, and I looked at the map he pointed to. I was shocked. The book showed the border to be miles from the city wall. Now, the Wastelands ran right up to the city's northern edge. I turned to Jastillian. "Is this accurate?"

He looked at the map as well, and then flipped to the front of the book to see when it was written. "Aye, well, lad, I wasn't around then, so I can't say for sure. But even in my lifetime, the Alexandrians used to have farms north of the city, all abandoned now. The land's no good for growing any more. Still, the idea that anyone, even Renak, would do a spell that would result in such devastation would be...unbelievable."

Jastillian was right. As wizards, we had a responsibility to the world and those around us. I couldn't imagine even Renak purposely doing a spell that had the potential to erode the land on the scale of the Wastelands. On the other hand...I drummed my fingers on the tabletop.

"What is it, lad?" Jastillian asked.

"Well," I said slowly, thinking, "I don't know much about the kinds of enchantments used to create something as big as the Great Barrier. But I always wondered how the spell had survived Renak's death. When a wizard dies, any spells he has in place usually die with him. That's why it's so important for us to get to the White Mountain and secure it. Now that Stradus is gone, all the protections he put on the mountain and what's inside are gone too." I turned back to the matter at hand. "But if Renak powered the spell off a nexus, then that might explain it—a constant source of power. But a nexus draws its power from the land around it. A spell the size of the Great Barrier could possibly draw the mana faster than the land can replenish it."

Jastillian stroked his beard. "Fascinating. No scholars have ever put forth that theory."

I grinned. "I guess they never asked a wizard before." Which wasn't surprising, considering that, as far as I knew, Premier and I were the only wizards left on this side of the Great Barrier. My grin faded, though, as I thought about the implications. If I could bring down the barrier and restore the land, that could lighten the burden on Krystal's shoulders. The Wastelands would recede again, and the creatures with them. She and her people wouldn't have to worry about so many attacks.

"Jastillian, when you traveled the Wastelands, did you ever find the nexus, or hear of where it might be?" I asked.

He shook his head. "Sadly, no. It would be a great find if I did."

"Maybe it's in Masep," Demay said. "You said yourself you've never been there."

"Aye, but many went there after the war. I've never seen any records suggesting they found the nexus there."

"But—"

"Brother, please." The fourth person at our table, the elf Prastian, gently closed his book and laid it down on the small pile of others next to him. "We've been reading these books to get a better understanding of what we'll be facing in the Wastelands, and to find something that will help us get safely to Masep and defeat Premier. We don't have time for theories, however fascinating they may be. If you didn't want to be in here, you could be outside, sparring with Behast."

Behast was also an elf, but one who had been raised by dwarves, so his favorite thing was beating on people with his sword. Tired as I was, I'd rather be in here leafing through books than out there with him.

"I'm sorry, Hellsfire," Demay said, staring at me with his green eyes. "It's just I'm a little tired and I miss the forests."

I put my hand up. "It's all right. I'm just glad you three and Behast are brave enough—and foolish enough—to venture with me into the Wastelands."

Jastillian grinned through his thick gray and brown beard. "We wouldn't miss it for the world, lad. We have a chance to do what no other has done in centuries. Great songs will be sung about us. I can't wait."

"Me neither," Demay said. He pushed the book in front of him to the side. "It's far more interesting than reading these boring old books."

"We're coming along because Hellsfire needs our help," Prastian said. "He'll need our protection and our ears, plus Jastillian's considerable experience." His long, pointed ears twitched. Elves were famous for their hearing, and if you were worried about monsters sneaking up on you, it was good to have them at your side. And Jastillian had spent years traveling in the Wastelands, dressed in the skins of dead goblins to disguise himself from worse things.

The dwarf frowned. "I still think we should kill Premier. I would love to even the score, even if it wasn't my axe that did it. It's foolish to leave such a deadly enemy alive."

"I'm sorry, my friend," I said, wanting the same thing. "But it was Stradus's last wish. He said Premier would still be of use in the days to come. That he would play a part in my destiny."

Jastillian crossed his arms, frustrated. "I know. As long as we take the fangs off that snake by taking his book from him. I can't wait to see his reaction when you bind his powers."

We all shared a smile. None of us could wait for that. Premier had been nothing but pain and trouble.

"My biggest worry is I'm not sure how useful our goblin disguises will be as we approach Masep," Jastillian said. "There are too many creatures, and we'll have to get too close to them. It's why I've never been to the city or deep into the Wastelands."

We were silent. We'd had this discussion many times. Even though Premier was weakened and his control over the creatures loosened, there were still thousands of them. King Furlong had wanted to send his army to Masep, and it had taken many late nights of arguing in the council chamber to convince him that a small party was the better choice. The army's numbers were already diminished because of the recent battle, and they would have no reinforcement from the dwarves or elves. Neither Queen Lenora of the dwarves or King Sharald of the elves saw any reason to send their troops into the Wastelands.

A smaller group would have the advantages of secrecy and speed. I had tried to find spells or potions that would conceal us from the Wasteland creatures, but there were none to be found in my spell book or in Alexandria's library. The only option was to check Stradus's library and workroom in the White Mountain. There might be artifacts or weapons of power that could help us. Unfortunately, that was going to take time, and it could be dangerous.

With Stradus's death, the magic used to enchant and protect the White Mountain would have dissipated. With his safeguards gone, deadly creatures from elsewhere in the mountain could have found the caves where he and I had lived. I needed my friends' help in case we ran into them when we were there.

I hated the idea of taking more time to go through Stradus's library. Every day that went by meant that Premier was that much closer to regaining his power. If only King Furlong or Princess Krystal would allow me into Alexandria's magical archive. Over the years, they'd collected a legendary cache of magical artifacts, scrolls, and books, safeguarding them so wizards wouldn't misuse them. I could understand the king not wanting me to have access to the archive—he didn't know me or trust me the way Krystal did. But the princess? It hurt, after all we'd been through and after all I'd done for her, to have her turn me away as if I were another Premier or Renak.

I also needed to return to the White Mountain to finish off the binding potion for Premier. I had found some of the rare ingredients here, but the others could only be found in Stradus's garden.

"Hopefully, we'll find something tomorrow," Prastian said. "We haven't learned anything here that Jastillian doesn't already know."

Demay pushed against the table and stood. He stretched his short elven frame and yawned. "I need a break."

"Me too," I said, rising and doing the same thing. "Would you like to come with me to the marketplace?"

Demay nodded.

"Do you two want anything?"

Prastian peered at Jastillian, who shook his head no. "Thank you, but we're fine."

Demay and I left the library and walked the stone halls of the castle's keep. My heavy feet clattered against the floor, but Demay's light footsteps didn't make a sound. Demay greeted the guards we passed by. Their stony faces relaxed and they returned his greeting with a nod. Some of them even acknowledged me, which is more than I got from the servants who passed us. They edged by, not looking me in the eye.

The stone halls were decorated with great tapestries of dragons, Alexandria's symbol. Right before the exit into the courtyard, I lingered at a mural of Shala fighting Renak in the War of the Wizards. I ignored the sensationalized streaks of red and blue lightning shooting out of their hands, and concentrated on the background.

Shala stood on fertile ground, full of grass and lush trees. Renak stood in a barren and desolate place. Clearly, the builders of Alexandria believed that Renak had caused the Wastelands to be created. But how? I looked at Demay, still walking toward the courtyard, and wondered if the young elf could be right about the nexus and the Great Barrier.

I rushed to catch up to him and headed into the fresh air and sunlight. We walked by a giant marble fountain with a dragon on top, water pouring out of his mouth. My old friend Cynder, the dragon who had been Stradus's guardian and companion, always laughed when he saw it. According to him, no self-respecting dragon would spit water instead of fire.

I searched the castle grounds, hoping to see the giant red dragon. He wasn't in his normal, resting spot within the castle walls, next to his little shrine that the Alexandrians had erected to honor him. People constantly came to see him, giving him little carvings of himself, slabs of beef, whole chickens, and incense and candles. The people worshipped him, making him far more unbearable than he normally was.

We crossed near the practice yard, where a group of soldiers sparred with each other. Through the surrounding circle of people, I saw Behast fighting a Guardsman of Alexandria. Demay yelled to Behast, whose back was turned. Behast started to turn, and the Guardsman struck him, causing him to stumble and fall. Behast recovered and glared at Demay as we walked by.

"That felt good," Demay said and chuckled. "He does that to me from time to time to remind me not to be distracted in battle. He's made many an arrow fly wide."

We continued downhill, from the keep to the castle walls, making small talk. We greeted a guard named Jerrel, one of the few who was friendly to me. He smiled back and we went through the open gates and under the killing holes.

Only a month had passed since the battle, and the city was still being repaired. The buildings of Alexandria all had a uniform look to them. They were square and block shaped, built mostly of stone from the Daleth Mountains, with little in the way of unique designs or elaborate decorations. Krystal had told me it was because all of their energy went into the fight to keep the Wasteland creatures at bay. They had little time or patience for frills and ornamentation.

We wandered through the wealthier districts of Alexandria that housed the nobles, merchants, and craftsmen. These buildings were far nicer than in most of the city. They were large and spacious, with grass and trees between them, and almost all of them had guards and gates.

We left that district and came to the more common part of town. This part of the city needed far more repairs than the inner city. The fighting had been heaviest here. Premier's creatures had tried to hold the southern gates from inside Alexandria, against the allied army of dwarves, elves, and humans trying to liberate the city. The allies had broken through eventually, crusading their way to the castle. This area was bigger and housed more people, but there weren't enough skilled craftsmen to go around. They were just now getting the castle into pristine condition.

Fifty feet from us, a crowd swarmed around a tall woman—Princess Krystal of Alexandria. A few of her guards surrounded her, including the captain of her personal guard, Ardimus, and her close friend, Captain Rebekah, but she was never in any danger. The people adored her. She was looking back and forth between a piece of parchment in her hands, and a building that had its roof caved in. As I watched, she began giving the workmen orders about what she wanted done. They dispersed and when she turned, her eyes met mine.

As always, I became lost in the princess's enchanting violet eyes. The thumping in my chest increased, drowning out the chatter of the surrounding people. The air left my lungs and that inner fire within me burned brighter. It was only a moment, but she always made me feel that way.

She allowed herself a small grin and broke the eye contact.

I sighed, trying not to stare at her. I wished I could spend more time with Krystal, but we agreed that we shouldn't be seen in public together unless it was during a special function. Our relationship was a secret, both for her sake and her father's.

"Why don't you go to her?" Demay asked, jolting me out of my thoughts.

I looked down at the little elf and raised my right eyebrow. Did he mean what I think he meant? I brought my hand up to my face and wiped the little droplets of sweat away. I wanted to smack myself. I was a fool for letting my look linger for too long. I cleared my throat and asked, "What do you mean?"

"We elves have a saying, 'Heed the forest.' That means be mindful of your surroundings and listen to what's out there." Demay had a small smirk on his face. "We all know about you and the princess."

I stopped, and my back stiffened. "Have you or the others told anyone?"

He shook his head. "Of course not. It's none of their business."

I blew out a small stream of breath. I was thankful for that. I risked glancing back at her. "Things between us are...complicated."

"That's what my brother said too," Demay said. The elf was silent for a moment. "In time, I think you can change things. You saved the king, helped save the city—"

"From another wizard."

"From another wizard, and are going to make sure Premier is no longer a threat. You humans are overly emotional creatures, but you have short memories. They'll remember what you did for them lately."

"You think?"

"In time." He smiled at me. "Jastillian even told me they're writing a song about you in Erlam."

I laughed. "Really?"

He nodded.

I shrugged, allowing a glimmer of hope to seep into my mind. "I guess anything's possible then."

We resumed our walk and finally reached the market. Although it was crowded, with people pressing in on all sides, there always seemed to be a space around me and Demay. I knew it wasn't the fact that he was armed that made people edge away. It was the sight of my wizard's robes, and their fear of anyone who wore them. I sighed and strode on to the booth selling honey bread.

A little girl ran in front of us, carrying a huge loaf of bread. She stumbled and dropped the loaf.

I bent down and picked it up. I dusted off the dirt with my hand before handing it back to her. I gave her a smile and said, "Here you go, little one."

"Thank you," she squeaked.

"Would you like to take some honey bread home with you?" I asked. "We were just about to go to that stall right over there."

The little girl hesitated, but her face lit up when she saw the vendor and took a huge whiff of the smell of his delicious bread. She stared at Demay with huge eyes, her mouth hanging open. "You're an elf!"

He bent down and tapped her on the nose. She giggled. "That's right. Now do you want to come have a bite to eat with us? Our treat."

She nodded her head so hard it looked like it was going to fall off.

Before we could move, someone yelled, "Shawna! There you are. Why did you stop?"

Shawna put her head down in shame. "Sorry, but this nice man and elf were going to buy me some honey bread. You know how I love honey bread!"

"You can barely hold what you're carrying now." The woman reached down and took the bread from Shawna, cradling it in her right arm along with the dead chicken she carried." Her eyes widened when she saw me and she let out a tiny gasp. "Come on, Shawna, let's go."

"Are you sure you don't want us to buy it for you?" I asked.

"No, thank you," the mother said.

"Do you at least need help? We can carry those home for you."

"No, I wouldn't want to put you to the trouble."

"It's no trouble at all."

"No," she said sharply. "Let's go, Shawna."

Shawna pouted but walked alongside her mother. The woman whispered to her daughter in hushed tones.

Demay and I went to the stall and bought pieces of honey bread. But not even its sweet, sticky taste could cheer me up.

We went back to the castle to continue our studying and planning. There wasn't much left to do except to return to the White Mountain to find some answers there.

After dinner, I went to my room early, hoping to see the princess. My room was far away from Krystal's room, bordering on the servants' quarters. There was a small section of guest rooms there, but she had told me that it was where the less desirable guests were housed. The king might have wanted me there, but Krystal had chosen that specific room for a reason.

I was used to the smaller room, as opposed to the luxurious room I'd had when I first arrived. It was cramped, reminding me of my mother's longhouse in Sedah, the village where I'd grown up. The nicked dresser almost touched the bed when I pulled the drawers out. The bed could hold two people, but it was a snug fit. The small window gave me a view of the wall of a tower. At least the pillows were filled with feathers and the blankets made of satin.

There were secret passages throughout the castle and the city of Alexandria. This was one of the rooms that held one. The princess visited every night; no matter how trying her day was, she came. We talked, we cuddled, we did things that a man and woman would do. I loved spending time with her. She dropped her guard around me, knowing that she didn't have to be the Princess of Alexandria, as I didn't care about any of that.

I took off my boots and lay down on the comfy bed, staring at the stone wall in front of me, waiting for it to open and for the beautiful princess to come gliding out of it. During the past week she had been coming later and later, so I struggled to stay awake, but I was so tired I nodded off.

The soft scraping of stone walls woke me. The light in the room was almost non-existent. It was far later than I had expected—only a few more hours until dawn broke.

I magically lit the candles in the room, keeping the light dim, and rose to meet her.

She extinguished the torch in her hand and hung it in the gloomy tunnel. She walked inside my room and sealed the entrance. "Sorry I'm late. I should have been here sooner but I was caught up in something."

I stood in front of her and grinned, thankful that she had come anyway. I took her angled face in my hands. "It's all right. You *are* a princess, after all." I kissed her hard on her full, soft lips. She moaned and furiously returned it.

We broke the kiss, and as I looked closer, I was astonished by how terrible she looked. Her sun-kissed hair was in disarray and her eyes were ringed with dark circles. She yawned.

"Excuse me, it's been a long night," Krystal said, her violet eyes twinkling.

"And I have a feeling it's about to get longer." She grinned with anticipation. "But before we get to that, I have a gift for you. One I know you'll want."

I placed my hand against her waist and pulled her close until our bodies meshed together, the heat rising throughout the room. "And what could I want more than you?"

Krystal's face lit up and her face flushed red. "This." She held a scroll in front of me.

I let go of her and took the scroll, unrolling it to see what it said. I gasped when I realized it was a very powerful and ancient ritual. I stared at Krystal and opened my mouth, then shut it, wanting to finish reading before I asked any questions.

The ritual was the perfect disguise to allow my friends and me to venture into Masep. By using the blood of the Wasteland creatures, it would fool them into thinking anyone affected by the spell was one of them. To their eyes and noses, we would smell and look like them. But like all magic, it had a cost.

For the illusion to appear real, we would have to turn into those monsters. I would have to pull the dead creatures' souls from the afterlife and bind them to our own with blood magic. There was only room in one's body for one occupying soul; there was a chance those beasts could take control and we would be lost, or our bodies would die from the strain.

I sat down on the bed, lost in thought. In a month of research, we had found no other way. It was a risk I would have to take, but I would understand if the others weren't willing to.

"Where did you get this?" I asked, then frowned when I realized the answer. "That secret vault of yours?"

All tiredness in her face vanished. The lines in her face deepened and became stern. Here stood the Princess of Alexandria, hiding behind that royal mask of hers. I hated that judging, calculating, unemotional gaze where I couldn't read how she felt or what she thought. I much preferred the fierce woman who smiled and laughed and who showed how tired and frustrated she could be. That woman only appeared when we were alone—and not always then.

"I scoured for days, searching for information that would help you," the princess said. "It's similar to the way Jastillian disguises himself by wearing a goblin skin when he journeys into the Wastelands, except this illusion should hold up even at close proximity."

"Thanks for finding this, but if you had let me go through your vault, you wouldn't have had to search so late or so hard."

Krystal shook her head and grimaced. "You know I can't do that, Hellsfire. I have a—"

"Duty. I know. I've heard it all before."

The princess snatched the scroll out of my hand before I could stop her. She turned to leave, but I grabbed her arm. I didn't want her to go. Not because I needed the scroll or magic, but because I didn't want her to be mad with me. She gave me a dagger-like stare and I immediately let go.

"I'm sorry." I clenched my fists. "You're doing so much that I wanted to make things easier for you." My shoulders slumped and I sighed. "And I wish you would trust me. I care nothing for power."

Krystal took a step forward and held out the scroll. "I *do* trust you. That's why I'm giving this to you." Her royal mask melted and she glanced down at the ground for a moment as if she couldn't meet my eyes. "This may be the best spell I could find, but it's still very dangerous. You'll be binding another soul to you. You may lose your own in the process. I don't want that to happen." She gave me a sad smile. "I'm rather fond of you."

She might not be a wizard, but she understood the magic behind the ritual as well as its dangers. I was going to have to make sure my friends fully understood the dangers as well. They were all warriors—they understood risking their lives in battle. But risking their souls was something else again.

"You won't lose me," I said.

Krystal lifted her hand and rubbed my cheek. I nuzzled up against it. She gazed into my eyes, but said nothing. She walked past me and stopped in front of the bed. Unfastening her cloak, then the lavender dress that bound her, she let them fall to the ground. She slipped out of her thin smock. I stared at her naked backside, my eyes tracing the curves I had gotten to know so well over the past month.

She looked over her shoulder and a tantalizing smile passed over her lips. "Are you coming?"

I gulped and placed the scroll on the dresser. There would be time to memorize and study it later. Having it would cut down the time I needed to spend at the White Mountain to a day or two, reducing the risk of Premier getting his power back while we were in the heart of his stronghold.

But that was something to fret over later. Right now, I wanted to live in the moment and enjoy what little time I had left with Krystal. I pulled my robes over my head, followed by my tunic and breeches, and threw them to the floor. I crawled into bed on top of her and I brushed my lips upon her.

Krystal smiled, but it was a tired one. It had been a trying month for her, with seeing to her people and the rebuilding of Alexandria, yet she still managed to spend time with me and search for a way to help in my journey.

I rolled her over onto her front.

"Hellsfire, what are you doing?"

"Shhh."

I massaged her neck and shoulders, the tight, firm muscles loosening under my rough hands. The princess's breathing increased until she panted short, sharp breaths. I continued to stroke her for several minutes, taking pleasure in making her happy. Her whole body soon fell into a familiar stance, her breathing slow and rhythmic.

"Krystal?" I whispered into her ear.

She couldn't answer; she was asleep. I stopped massaging her and pulled the blankets over us. I wrapped my arms around her and she snuggled up against me.

I was happier in this simple moment than I had ever been before. I wished there was magic that could capture this moment in time, because I knew it wasn't going to last.

CHAPTER 2

BY THE TIME I woke up, the princess was gone. I rubbed the indentation her body had left in the sheets and inhaled the pillow she'd used, smelling her sweet scent that reminded me of lilac. I had never once woken up to see her there, and that always saddened me. For once, I wanted to see my sleeping beauty just as the dawn broke.

I dressed, then tucked the scroll into my purse next to my potions and snacks. I seized Stradus's broken staff and the urn with his ashes, depositing them into a bag with the utmost care. I pulled the drawstring and tied it off, making sure everything was supported before stringing the bag and purse across my body.

I ran into Jastillian, Prastian, Demay, and Behast at the entrance of the keep. We greeted each other and headed outside, walking to the spot where Cynder slept. It was well away from the walls, buildings, and even animals. There used to be a stock pen there, but Krystal had it moved. The dragon was curled up in a ball, much like a cat would be. However, a cat didn't snore loud enough to sound like it had dozens of bats trapped in its nose. Cynder's bright red, slumbering frame matched the sunrise from behind him. The sun shone on his body as if he were on fire.

While my friends had gotten to know Cynder over the time I'd been here, they still stared at him with glassy-eyed reverence. I used to live with him in the White Mountain and had known him far longer than anyone else. While he did once try to kill me, we were friends now. He was the only one who understood the things I had gone through and was yet to encounter.

My friends tried to wake Cynder by coaxing him out of his deep sleep with soothing and gentle words. That was never going to work, and neither was throwing a rock at his thick, scaled hide.

I strode to Cynder's head, next to the small shrine with carvings of wood and wax made in the dragon's image. Dried blood spotted the ground, no doubt from a meaty offering. Flies buzzed around small piles of rotting fruit and vegetables. The people should have known that he only liked meat.

I waved my friends away and screamed into his ear, "Cynder, wake up!"

His twitching tail flopped back and forth, but he still snored. I gritted my teeth, trying to think of a way to wake him up. We didn't have time for this. The rotting fruit gave me an idea. I picked up a brown apple and faced him.

"If you don't wake up," I said, "I'm going to pelt you with fruit until you do."

I put my right arm back, ready to throw the apple, when something smashed into me. It struck my back and splattered. Wet mush clung to the back of my neck like a damp spider web. My friends chuckled. I reached up and wiped the goo away, then turned around to see the end of a tail hovering above the fruit.

The dragon stopped his fake snoring and slowly opened his reptilian eyes, amusement dancing in them. The red irises burned like candle flame. He uncurled his body, stretched his elongated neck, and yawned.

"Little Hellsfire," Cynder said. "Still outmatched and outwitted by a far superior being. Will you never learn?"

I glared at him then ignited the fruit in my hand and flung it at him. He opened his mouth, exposing rows of pointy teeth. He swallowed the burning fruit whole, then smiled at me.

"I hate you," I said.

"You lesser beings are filled with hate."

"Are you ready?"

"I'm a dragon. We're always ready." Cynder lowered himself so we could all get on his back.

"Thank you for doing this, my friend," I said, rubbing his smooth scales. "I know how you don't like to give humans rides, as you've constantly reminded me that you're not a horse."

"I'm not doing this for you," he said, and snorted smoke. His red eyes settled on the bag with the urn, cradled in my arm. "I'm doing this for him."

I nodded.

The others climbed aboard Cynder. I handed the bag and staff to Prastian so I could scale Cynder's hide. He wore a malicious grin, no doubt considering whether or not to leap up and fly with me halfway on. He'd done that before, while I held on for dear life.

"Look," Cynder said in a low growl.

The princess stood near the edge of the soldiers' barracks, surrounded by Guardsmen. Krystal pushed herself past them so she could get a better view. She waved at us before disappearing again.

I climbed on Cynder, wishing she could have said goodbye in a more intimate way. It didn't matter. In a few days I would see her again, assuming all went well. I made sure my pack and purse straps were fastened across my body. I hugged Cynder's long, red neck.

"Make sure your weapons and supplies are secure," I said to my friends. "It gets rough up there in the cold wind."

"Ready?" Cynder asked. Holding on to his neck, I could feel his booming voice reverberating beneath my hands.

My friends nodded, and I said, "Yes. Cynder, if you please."

"Hang on, everyone," Cynder said. "You're in for the ride of your mortal life!"

The great dragon unfurled his wings, readying to take us back to the place where I first met him and learned how to utilize my powers and my destiny. Back to the White Mountain, where unknown dangers lurked.

CHAPTER 3

CYNDER DISCHARGED a mighty roar. Everyone around us ceased their movements and ogled in awe. Cynder basked in the attention before flapping his great wings. The fiery dragon rose into the air. He cleared the castle wall, causing those standing on top of it to duck. His hanging tail grazed a building's rooftop.

Cynder swooped over Alexandria, aiming southwest. The people of Alexandria were entranced by his flight, even though he caused complete chaos. Donkeys and horses panicked, threatening to run away. A cart of melons broke loose and spilled its cargo on the ground. A girl's skirt flew up over her head. Yet despite all the trouble Cynder caused, the people didn't panic or yell obscenities at him. However, I was about to.

"Cynder," I said. "Stop showing off!"

The great dragon finally rose away from the city. He puffed dark smoke and flew into it, knowing it would make us cough and gag. He flew faster, and my face felt like it was going to peel off. We rose until I was granted a bird's eye view of the landscape.

Cynder flapped his wings long and slow, decelerating his frantic speed. I took a moment to get used to the now gentle wind, ruffling through my hair. Birds scattered out of our way, Cynder blowing a stream of fire at those he deemed too slow. One bird narrowly avoided getting roasted alive. Deer in the forests below scampered away from the passing shadow, doing their best to hide in the dark greens.

The dragon rose until there was nothing but clear, blue sky encompassing us. I ducked my head behind Cynder's to shield myself from the blinding light as we continued our flight to the White Mountain.

It took us less than half a day to fly back to the place that had been my home. While I had learned how to use my powers there, I had also found something far more in Stradus. I smiled, thinking about him. I had thought he was a rather strange old man when I first met him, but then he became a teacher, a friend, and something I had never known—a father.

The White Mountain was so named because centuries ago, my former master had captured the winter around the mountain. While spring and summer came in the surrounding lands, the mountain remained in eternal winter, as if frozen in time. While some were brave enough to explore it, none ever returned. That was due to Cynder, Stradus's guardian. Stradus had stayed holed up in the mountain, studying references to the prophecies he'd once read in the *Book of Shazul*, waiting for me to fulfill my destiny.

I'd spent two years living in Stradus's huge cave complex at the top of the mountain. The last time I was there, it was to ask Stradus's help in the battle to save Alexandria from Premier and the Wasteland creatures. Even though I knew it wouldn't be the same without him, I still leaned eagerly forward for the first glimpse of my former home. But when I saw it, a shock shuddered through me. The White Mountain had transformed.

The slopes that were once smothered in cold, winter weather all year long were now splattered with spots of brown and white, as if a giant artist had dripped drops of paint on a canvas. As Cynder made a sweeping turn to land outside the cavern entrance, I saw a huge wall of snow break loose from an upper shelf, tumbling down the mountainside and crushing everything beneath it. The White Mountain was returning to its natural state, though it would take some time before there were enough trees and plants to support animal life. It had been centuries since the landscape was filled with warmth instead of winter.

Cynder twisted and swooped towards the entrance of the cave near the top. He settled on the ledge and lowered himself so we could all get off.

Demay walked to the edge of the ledge and peered up at the mountain. "What happened?"

"With Stradus's death," I said, "the magic's gone." I had known that would happen, but I hadn't really thought about what it would mean.

"Be on guard, little ones," Cynder said, gazing into the darkness of the caves. "While I am here to protect you, I no longer know what's inside."

Jastillian drew his axe and Behast his sword. Prastian and Demay readied arrows in their bows. I summoned mana, letting it hover near the surface of my body, where I could unleash it.

"I shall go first," Cynder said. "But once we reach the end of the outer caverns, you're on your own." Cynder was too big to fit into the interior rooms that had housed me and Stradus. "Hellsfire, make yourself useful."

I crept to the entrance of the cave. The wind howled inside and played havoc with my imagination. The black swallowed the incoming daylight. Without the torches that Stradus had magically kept burning, the only light came from this one giant opening. The White Mountain consisted of an extensive network of caves. Stradus never knew who built it, but he said he had encountered dangerous creatures when he first arrived.

I conjured my inner fire mana and spoke an incantation in the ancient language of Caleea. *"God of fire and god of air, please kindle the torches inside of here."* Little streams of fire flowed out of my hands. They danced along the sides of the walls, skittering around until they lighted every hanging torch in the cavern.

The darkness lifted from the caves. No monsters awaited us, but Demay and Prastian had their bows high and raised, aiming into the tunnels. Their ears twitched, searching for any unnatural sound. After a few tense moments, the pair lowered their bows and we ventured in.

As we marched inside, the hairs on my arms stood up. Stradus wouldn't be greeting me at the end of the trek with a warm smile on his face and a hot pot of tea. He was here, with me, his remains in the bag on my shoulder. Even though I had no idea what awaited me, I needed to go inside. Stradus must be laid to rest, and we needed to make the binding potion for Premier. My master had died to protect the world from Premier, and I had to finish his work.

I peeked up at Cynder, wondering if similar thoughts were going through his head. None of the others could ever understand. To them, the White

Mountain was just a cold and desolate place. There were times when I had trouble reading Cynder's reptilian face. This was one of them. He left me and continued to lead the way.

Part of me wished that Cynder had waited at the entrance. His loud footsteps reverberated throughout the cavern. While these sections of the caves were big enough to hold Cynder, he couldn't fly. If there was something in here, it would now know we were here. A wisp of smoke leaked from Cynder's nostrils. I might have been a fire wizard, but Cynder also knew how to create his own fire and could use it with deadly accuracy.

We split up into groups and searched the side tunnels. Behast was with me. His ears moved at every sound, mainly the dripping of the ice melting from the ceiling. Because of the way the torches danced and created shadows, I kept seeing monsters getting ready to jump out at me.

"I think I see something," Behast whispered.

He met my eyes and pointed ahead. I nodded and he vanished from my side, disappearing into the darkness and circling around to our target. Because of the fire cradled in my hand, if there was anything out there, it would be drawn to me.

I crept forward, my body tensing, wanting to unleash the magic I had built up. When I thought I was close enough, I pushed the fire in my hand forward, illuminating the area.

Behast leapt out at the exact same time and yelled, raising his sword.

We froze when we saw what it was. I grinned at the bones of a cow Cynder had eaten, trying my best not to laugh.

"Don't worry about it," I said. "Sometimes the light and the darkness play tricks on your eyes."

Behast glowered at the pile of bones. He sheathed his sword and stomped away. As he passed, I glimpsed a small smile spreading across his face.

We all met back in the main tunnel. No one had found anything. There were no signs of creatures or tracks, nothing that was out of the ordinary. We trekked down the rest of the long tunnel.

I sighed as my eyes traced over the stony walls. I had loved living here, but now there was a dead feeling. There was no life or joy—only the moaning of the wind and the constant dripping of melting ice. Cynder seemed to notice it too, as he stomped forward with his head hung low.

The cave ended with a human-sized doorway. Cynder plopped down and curled himself up into a ball. I expected him to say a quip, but he was silent.

The door to the room was open. The others stepped in, but when Jastillian got to the entrance, he stopped. He ran his hand along the edge of the doorway and bent down, squinting at it.

"What's wrong, Jastillian?" I asked.

"The design of these caves looks familiar. Did Stradus ever say who created them?"

I shook my head.

"It looks dwarven constructed, but we would not be this...sloppy," he grumbled. "I haven't read or seen any records of dwarves being in the White Mountain." Jastillian stepped through the doorway and waited with the others.

I went to Cynder and asked, "Are you all right?"

He opened one eye and grunted. "I'm fine. Go do what you have to do. I'll be here if you need me."

I turned to leave, then paused. "I miss him too."

"You would." Cynder's mouth twisted into a small smile. "Now go, and scream if you find anything."

I walked through the doorway, half expecting a magical detection web to flash with its presence. There wasn't one, of course. Stradus was dead and his magic with him. Webs were spells similar to what spiders wove, called so because of the magical threads used in their construction. They could be used to alert someone or keep something out.

I entered the small, comfy room and stared at the hearth. It was empty and cold, just like the room. The place wasn't the same without Stradus's guidance, his wisdom, his lessons, his presence, his magic. My eyes wandered around the room, remembering all the memories we'd shared.

My hands traced the wood grain of the stool where Stradus had once sat. He always seemed to have a kind and inviting face while we ate and chatted. I ran my fingers over the cold teapot on the table, grinning at how he always drank tea, no matter the time of day.

"Hellsfire," Prastian said, tapping me on my shoulder. "Are you all right?"

"Yeah, I'm fine. I'm…just remembering things."

I went to the closed door of Stradus's old room. While I had explored most of the White Mountain complex, there was one place I hadn't been in—Stradus's old room. He'd had a web around it that not even I could undo without him noticing.

"Everyone stay here," I said. "There's something I must do." I pointed to the open doorway at the other side of the room. "Don't go down there. We haven't seen any creatures, but they could be lurking there, and I don't want you to get lost in the tunnels."

They guarded the entrance while I disappeared into my former master's room. I pushed the wooden door open and it creaked in welcome. I had to light the torch in this room, since my fireballs couldn't go through the door. While the rest of the cave was cold, dank, and lifeless, my old master's presence was here. It was warm and inviting. I smiled at his ghostly embrace.

Stradus's living quarters were small and felt cramped because they were packed full of items. Open books and parchment papers were scattered on a desk. Candlesticks, wooden figurines, polished gems, an eagle's claw, a blue dragon's scale and even a feather or two had buried another table. I thought Stradus would have been a little cleaner than this because of how strict he was in his training and how clean his library and garden were.

Before I could see what else he had, a rush of magical energy emanated from the room. It closed all around me before it struck. I had felt that energy many times before when I trained with Stradus. The magical colors washed over me, then coalesced into a tiny ball. The ball zigzagged through the air until it reached the bed and dispersed upon a small wooden chest laid on top of it.

I cleared a spot on the desk and set down the bag with the urn and staff. I went to the chest, examining it for any magical traps. It would be just like

Stradus to have one, to see if I had learned his lesson about caution. There was none. I put my hand on the chest and opened it. Inside were two smaller boxes draped in magic.

The enchantment sparkled and sizzled around both boxes. The two different magics were very powerful for things so small. One box had the hint of air magic surrounding it, Stradus's strongest mana. The other one hummed with unknown magic. I reached for the one that reminded me of Stradus.

The moment I opened it, a brilliant flash of light blinded me. The magical aura around it disappeared. Swirls of tiny blue stars rushed out, orbiting me as if I were a flame to a moth.

"My dear boy," Stradus's voice said from the orbs of light. I jumped back, startled to hear my former master's voice. "If you're hearing me then I'm dead." The voice chuckled. "Don't be scared and don't grieve for me. It's as I've foreseen it." The voice turned serious. "You have a grave quest ahead of you, Hellsfire. I thought I would bestow you with my most cherished possession as a gift.

"Within the second box is a necklace forged from potanium, unbreakable, the strongest metal known to man. Attached to it is a jade hexagram. Its enchantment was cast from the most potent force in the world—love." The voice stopped and the lights dimmed.

The blue orbs flashed again. "Part of the necklace's function is to protect, yet there are also abilities it has that not even I am aware of. Like all magic, there is a drawback to it.

"The magic within will only work when the necklace is given to a person for whom you care deeply. It won't work for you alone. I've never had the opportunity to open my heart again and give it to another person." He sighed and the orbs stopped. A moment later, the lights spun again. "I know it will come in handy for you." The voice laughed and within the orbs, I imagined seeing Stradus's old, wrinkled, kind face, smiling.

"There is one last thing, Hellsfire," he said. "You know, you are not alone in this mountain. Those creatures I warned you about are very ferocious and dangerous. If you've not encountered them yet, you must reseal them behind the door you once tried to foolishly breach."

I nodded. There would be only one place they could be.

"Create the strongest web you can to keep the creatures out, and hurry, before they escape," he said. "And please be careful."

The light sped up around me until it became a solid blue barrier that entrapped me. "You've looked around my room and have seen the artifacts I've collected on my journeys, and the research I've done. I will leave them in your hands, Hellsfire. Some of these are mementos and trinkets of a once young man. Others are powerful tools that can be deadly. I would like for you to keep these things and study them, but if you have no place where you can keep them safe, you may have to destroy them rather than risk letting them fall into the wrong hands. I wish I could have turned them over to the Wizards' Council for safekeeping, but it seems that the Council, if it still exists, is forever lost to us behind the Great Barrier. So the choice and the burden are yours, my son."

The disembodied voice turned serious. "When you retrieve the *Book of Shazul* from Premier, do not look in the book. It'll…change you. I want you to destroy it, if you can. If not, make sure no one will be able to find it, or give it to Alexandria to safeguard. Something's wrong with the book. It corrupts people. It changed my best friend, Premier, and I'm positive it has altered others. There's a reason why Shazul was the mad wizard.

"Your destiny awaits you in Masep, Hellsfire. I have faith you will succeed—you *must* succeed."

The wall of light brightened the room with its blue aura. "I will always be watching over you, my son. Good luck, Hellsfire, and don't forget to bury my ashes in the garden. May the gods walk with you."

The magical light flew and funneled inside of me, filling me with a warm sensation as it strengthened my essence with Stradus's. I wheezed from the power that swelled inside.

Stradus must have had a vision of his death and prepared this just in case he died. I wished he was still alive. I could have used his help and advice and we could have retrieved the book together.

The room darkened without his spell. I gawked at the box, wanting to hear more of Stradus. When I realized there would be no more, I crushed the box in my hand and tossed it into a corner. I always knew I had to help people. It was something my mother instilled in me. Now that I had the power, there were far too many people to help, and along with it, a far greater responsibility. In the beginning, I wanted to learn to control my powers and I had. But now I had to do more than that. I had to learn how to not only carry a wizard's burden, but perform a wizard's duty.

I tore open the other box. The dull jade necklace sat there, its chain curled into a pile. The metal chain itself looked strong, but the jade hexagram looked frail. I sensed no magic from it. I put the necklace in my purse, knowing exactly who I wanted to give it to—and knowing that Stradus would have known, as well.

I took one last look around my former master's messy room and smiled as I remembered him. I gathered the bag with the urn and staff, leaving the room. There would be time to rummage through his belongings later. First, I needed to seal the door and trap those creatures.

"Did you find anything, lad?" Jastillian asked, pushing off from where he was leaning against the wall.

"None of you heard anything?" I said, staring at the elves with their extreme hearing. They shook their heads no.

"We tried," Demay said, his ears twitching.

Prastian nudged him.

"I mean, no, we didn't hear anything," Demay said. "We didn't even hear any of those supposed creatures down the tunnels."

A small smile passed over my face. It had been a spell for my ears alone. "Let's go. There's not much more to explore, but first we must go to the library so I can find the spell I need to create a web to contain those creatures."

I took point this time, and we moved silently through the halls. The hallway branched off and we ventured down the right-hand tunnel. After careful inspection of my old room and the exercise room, we found nothing. We finally arrived at the library.

The library was oddly dark. The torches I had lit were out. I started to step through the door when Behast seized my arm. He shook his head. The elves all had their ears pointed forward, hearing something. Demay pointed at the deep grooves clawed into the open door.

Jastillian pushed me out of the way and peered into the darkness, using his superior eyesight. His cheeks flexed. He couldn't see anything either. He turned to me and raised his eyebrows.

I understood. My friends braced their weapons. Jastillian and Behast were poised to strike anything that came leaping out. Prastian and Demay ached to loose their arrows.

I summoned my magic and ignited the torches inside. The library lit up. Our eyes and ears scanned the area. From the doorway, there seemed to be nothing unusual.

"Maybe they were once here, then left," I said.

"No, we heard something," Behast said.

"What did you hear?"

"A slight hissing sound, but I can't hear it now."

We crept into the room and the library's musty smell hit us. It emanated from the ancient books Stradus had collected throughout the years in his travels. He even brought a few with him when he came from Southern Shala. Shelves upon shelves lined the walls. There was a small reading table with a couple of candles on it, where I had spent hours reading books on faraway lands, history, and spells. It was a spell book that I needed now.

I was about to tell my friends what book I required when a loud hissing noise reverberated through my ears. Something collapsed from the ceiling behind me. I thought it was the mountain falling apart, but when I turned, a ferocious creature hissed at me.

The ebony-skinned creature was the size of a dwarf. Its ridged skin was like that of a reptile. Its small eyes were shut, but its big nostrils flared in my direction. It had knife-edged teeth and claws. The thing leapt at me before I could react, claws aiming for my throat.

An arrow spun and lodged in its throat. The creature flew and crashed against the wall, dark red blood coating it. Before any of us could react, four more beasts dropped from the ceiling and attacked.

In one swift move, Jastillian smashed his axe's hilt into one, stunning it, before swinging his axe into a side stroke, severing the thing's head. Prastian spun to the side, dodging the creature's razor-like claws. He saw an opening and sliced through the creature's tough skin with his sword. Behast wasn't quick enough to dodge the claws. His left forearm got ripped open in a huge gash. Behast used the moment to run his sword through the creature's gut with his right arm, impaling it.

Demay had no time to draw his sword before another creature sank its claws into the elf. He was the one who had shot the arrow into the first creature. I conjured my fire and hurled a fireball towards the creature on Demay. It caught the creature in its mouth, incinerating its face.

All the creatures fighting us were dead. We scouted the ceiling, thankfully seeing no more of them.

"Are you all right?" Prastian asked Behast.

Behast grunted as he tried to staunch the bleeding. "I'm fine. It looks worse than it is."

"Nonsense." Prastian tore a piece of his tunic off and bound the wound. Dark green blood soaked through it. "This won't be enough."

"There should still be supplies in the storage room," I said. "I'll go back and get them."

"No," Behast said. "We don't have time for this. There could be others."

"There are," Jastillian said. "They travel in packs." He glanced at the open doorway. "The others are sure to have heard these. Those piercing screams were a signal."

"What are they?" Demay asked. "I've never seen or heard of anything like them before."

Jastillian bent over one. He opened the creature's mouth and peered inside, running his fingers over its razor-like teeth. Jastillian held up a thin, strong arm and inspected the thing's hands. Its claws had retracted.

"These *things*," Jastillian said, kicking its body, "are a terrible secret my people have guarded since the time of the War of the Wizards. We call them *leshii*, meaning mountain dwellers. They reside deep in mountains, caves, and underground."

"Why have your people kept them a secret?" I asked.

"Remember when I told you how Eostar had a hand in convincing the dwarves to join Shala? Not all of the dwarves heeded his words. Some left, digging deeper into the mountains. Too deep. My uncle once said the dwarves changed because of the secrets they found; others believed it was their greed that did them in, and there were those who believed corrupted earth magic did it. Yet no one knows for sure.

"Time passed and we tried to make peace with those that left, but when we arrived to greet them they were no longer the same."

"Why didn't you warn others?"

"We've kept an eye on the places where the leshii dwelled and have exterminated a great many of them. We didn't know they were here. That doesn't matter now. The leshii are dead to us and we've vowed to smear their blood on our axes. Down to the last drop."

One leshii twitched. It sniffed, and although its eyes were closed, it gazed directly at Jastillian. "Traitorrr," it said in a whisper.

"What did you call me?" Jastillian shouted. He roared and raised his ancient and mighty axe. Bringing it down, he chopped the leshii's head off.

Prastian's ears pricked up. "I hear something. I managed to stop the bleeding for Behast, but we better hurry." He turned to me. "Hellsfire, how long will it take you to perform the spell?"

"Not long, but I'll need to find the book, then prepare the spell."

He nodded. "Jastillian and I will guard the door in case more of these leshii come."

I told them what book I needed, and then Demay, Behast, and I dispersed to search for it. We hurriedly read the titles on the spines of the books. Demay found the book and rushed it to me. I sat down and flipped through to find the correct spell. Everyone stood guard. The web required a potion and incantation to make it work. I reread to make sure everything was right, and practiced the motions with my hands while repeating the words.

After memorizing it, we backtracked and then took the left tunnel, heading to the garden. On our way, we investigated the practice room, the latrine, the storage room, and the spring, this time searching the roof of the caves. Thankfully, we didn't find any more creatures.

There was one final room to go to—the garden. After that, I could seal up the doorway and we could finally scrounge for something to help us while we were in the Wastelands. That, along with the binding potion, was the purpose of coming here. Everything else was secondary, even laying Stradus to rest. And I still had to tell my friends about the soul-binding spell Krystal had given me.

But when I opened the door, I stopped, shocked. Every plant in the garden was dead.

CHAPTER 4

THE EXOTIC AND WONDROUS plants Stradus had collected and cultivated over the years were no longer what they were. They had lost their color and life. Brown decay had set in, leaves withered and fallen, and the once soft ground was now cracked and brittle.

The garden had been Stradus's pride and joy, as if it were his child. He used to spend countless hours and years in his garden—growing, cultivating, and tending to the plants with his delicate touch. I kicked the hard ground, remembering the times when I would listen to him talk about the foreign lands he had traveled to obtain the seeds and bulbs of these exotic plants.

I reached out and a brown, dried leaf crumpled under my touch. I needed to make a potion to construct a stronger web. How was I going to do so without the garden? Without Stradus, the whole mountain was falling apart.

"I thought you said this was one of the most beautiful places you had ever seen?" Demay asked.

I sighed and said, "It was. Once."

"Can you do the spell or finish the potion without it?" Jastillian asked.

I shrugged my shoulders. "I don't know. I can do a weaker version of the spell, but they'll be able to break through if enough force is applied. The potion won't work. All the ingredients have to be fresh."

"I hear...whispering," Demay said.

Jastillian growled. "They come."

"Behast, stay here and guard Hellsfire," Prastian said. "We'll kill those in the tunnel and buy you time to make your potion."

"I can fight," Behast said, gripping his sword until his lime-green skin became even lighter.

"I know you can, but Hellsfire will need protection if a few manage to slip by."

Behast nodded and stood by the door. The other three vanished from the garden and into the hall.

I hurried, rushing from plant to flower, pushing my hands through the withered plants to find one or two that weren't completely dead. I dug up dried, dead roots. Most of the plants and flowers were so brittle, they disintegrated at my touch. I blew at the dust- sized plant particles in my hand, knowing it was useless to cook a potion with them.

I ran to the workbench, hoping that either Stradus or I had cut and left a few plants before we left. There were empty flasks, a grinding stone and pestle, but no plants. I slammed my hand on the bench, causing everything to jump, and said, "Gods damn it!" Of course, nothing would be out. Stradus wouldn't have left a mess and he would have made a point for me not to either.

One of the leshii's screeches broke through the door. I jerked up and stared at the doorway. Behast's feet etched furrows into the ground as he strained to go with the others and fight with them.

"You think they're all right?" I asked.

"Are you done yet?"

I snapped. "I can't do it without *healthy* plants."

"Whatever you need to do, you better hurry. From the sounds of things, they need our help."

Behast was right. We—no—*I* needed to do something. I was a wizard. I had all this power at my hand, yet I couldn't do anything. My inner fire flowed out of my hand, smothering it. Maybe it was best we grab what we could and leave now. We would have to come back with an army to clear out the White Mountain, and I would have to create the potion with ingredients elsewhere, if I could. Some of these plants were exceedingly rare. At one point, Stradus had known Sharald, the ruler of the elves. Maybe I could find the plants there.

I dashed to leave the room and help the others, but when I crossed the middle of the room, I stopped. Stradus's voice echoed through my mind. I don't know if it was memories or the orbs of magic, but it was clear as ice as sharp as a noble's tongue. He had told me to bury his ashes here, right now, despite all that was happening. I was going to do so now. There might not be another chance.

I set the bag down and ran to grab a shovel. The ground broke apart as I thrust the shovel into it.

"We don't have time for this," Behast said.

"Yes, we do. I'm fulfilling a promise." Our eyes met. "And I *always* keep my promises."

Behast grunted and kept his eyes on the doorway. I dug, flinging dirt everywhere, not caring where it went or even if bits of dirt struck my face. If this was Stradus's last wish, I was going to give it to him. When I finished, I took the urn and staff from the bag. I poured the ashes into the hole and then set the broken staff into it. I stared at the now clear globe on top of the staff. It used to swirl, filling with mana, when Stradus had it. The staff was carved into a snake and I once saw it come alive when Stradus fought Premier. It would move no longer. I heaped dry dirt into the hole before patting it down as best as I could.

"I'm sorry," I said. "I wish I could have buried you in your wondrous garden instead of this dead place. One day I'll use the knowledge you've given me and create my own garden in memory of you." I smacked my hands free of the dirt and said to Behast, "Let's go."

I focused on calling my magic to rise to the surface, drawing in the incredible power I was sure I was going to need to fight the leshii. But the place wasn't through with me yet. The earth bellowed as though a mob of leshii thundered down on us, demanding blood. But it wasn't leshii.

It was the garden.

Dead plants trembled and swayed. The dirt underneath my feet shifted and heaved as the whole room began to shake. I thought the ceiling was going to cave in, but it held firm.

Wisps of green mana swirled from the hole I had dug. It spread into the ground, sealing and erasing the cracks in the earth. Turquoise mana moistened and softened the ground with its water-based magic.

The magic dispersed throughout the garden, penetrating and reviving everything it touched. The plants twisted and ripened. Stalks and branches rose to their former stature. The faded colors darkened and deepened until the room became alive with vibrant greens and browns. The flowers reawakened, blossoming so that they painted the room. Familiar pinks, purples, oranges and yellows stared back at me and said their hellos. Reds blinded my eyes.

The shaking ceased. I gazed around the room, open-mouthed, at the garden restored to its former beauty. The scent of fresh flowers and plants tickled my nose. How was Stradus able to perform such magic after his death, just from his ashes? I hadn't known such a thing was possible. I realized then that life and death means more for a wizard—more than just the extended life Stradus had enjoyed. I bent down and grabbed a handful of dirt. I inhaled the scent of the fresh, soft soil, wishing I had Stradus's guidance. There were questions and I needed answers. But his presence would always be in this one spot for all of time.

"By the gods," Behast whispered, putting a hand to his mouth.

A leshii's body crashed in front of the entrance, interrupting our gawking. Behast pulled his weapon free and started for the door, then stopped and looked back at me.

"Go," I said, and motioned with my head. "Help the others. I'll hurry and prepare the potion."

Behast glanced to the open doorway. "I was told to stay here with you. If one of the creatures gets through, you may not have a chance to finish the potion."

I smiled. "Then don't let any of them through."

Behast nodded and left.

I yanked the dagger from my waist and ran around the garden. I cut the flowers and tugged out the roots from the plants I needed. I took more than was necessary, but there wasn't time to be delicate about it. I hated to waste materials, especially after what I had just seen and what Stradus had taught me, but my friends were out there fighting for their lives.

I brought everything to the workbench and tried to block out the sounds of battle—the grunting, shouting, screeching, dying. I shook my head free, trying not to remember when I fought in Alexandria.

I measured everything, then ground the ingredients with the pestle, hurrying to blend them all together. I dumped it all in a flask, poured in some water and heated it.

"Come on, come on," I said, rubbing my hands together, watching it boil and listening to the sounds of battle outside the door. They came closer, then faded, then moved closer once more. I was tempted to use my power to make the flame burn brighter, but Stradus had taught me not to. If I was off, I would have to start over and waste even more precious time. I ignored the mess I had made on the bench, wanting to scatter the extra petals, leaves, and roots to the ground.

The ingredients melted into a greenish, oozing liquid. I inhaled the scent of the minty liquid and knew it was done. I poured it into a flask, taking care to not spill a drop. I used my robe as a barrier while I carried the still-hot flask in my left hand and sprinted out of the room.

I ran down the hallway. At the end of it was an open door. Dozens of leshii funneled out of it. My friends held the line, doing their best to stop the leshii advance. Jastillian, Prastian, and Behast met the creatures with their melee attacks. From behind those three, Demay shot his arrows, piercing any leshii that crawled on the ceiling or got too close to the others.

They fought well, but my friends couldn't hold them off forever. Behast was injured and they had already been fighting for quite some time against an overwhelming force. Their movements slowed, and instead of giving inches of ground, they started to give chunks.

I conjured fire and wind magic. My body crackled with energy until an aura of fire surrounded me and the torches in the tunnel blazed hotter. A shield of air encompassed me, my hair and robes flapping as if I were in a storm.

"Everyone down!"

My friends dropped to the ground just as I released a torrent of wind and fire from my free hand. It funneled down the tunnel, burning and slashing at the leshii. They screeched in chorus as the skin peeled from their bodies. The sharp wind snapped at them like a wild animal, cutting and slashing.

I willed the spell to keep the burning wind from harming my friends. Yet it brushed against them, singeing their clothes. The fire pursued the leshii, heading through the open doorway and blazing deeper into the mountain.

I cut the fire off, gasping for air and feeling a trickle of blood drip down my nose. I wiped it away, along with the droplets of sweat hanging from my forehead. It was hard to create a spell that powerful and focus it to not burn the entire tunnel.

My friends rose. Demay brushed the soot from his tunic. Prastian soaked up the sweat from his forehead with his arm.

"Excellent job, lad," Jastillian said, smothering the small fire in his beard. "We weren't sure how long we could hold those blasted creatures."

Demay laid his hand on the now scorched, blackened wall and yelped. He blew on his hand and shook it. "That fire was a bit close."

"It's not over," Behast said. He closed his eyes and his ears twitched. "There are more coming."

We ran to the open doorway and peered down. The main stairwell split into other passageways. The caverns and tunnels were like the rest of the White Mountain I was used to, but far bigger. The cuts of the stone were smooth, but looked like they hadn't been maintained in centuries. A branching passageway's entrance had collapsed, the pile of rocks blocking it off. There must have been an entire city within the mountain, spreading to gods know where. The dwarves must have built it before they turned into leshii. I had lived here for a few years, thinking that I was in no danger and that the White Mountain was a comfy home. It was far more than that.

The sounds of the leshii grew, flickers of shadows creeping out from those passageways. More shades joined until their piercing sound of shrieks thundered closer to us.

Prastian grabbed a torch and tossed it down. The torch tumbled against the steps until it finally hit the bottom. The shadows merged together, moving and swirling like a basket full of snakes. There must have been hundreds of them. The leshii hissed and shrieked at the light. After peering up at us, they charged.

"I'm going to need more arrows," Demay whispered.

I flared the torch at the bottom. The leshii cried out in pain. I burned a few, but not enough, before they extinguished the light. I summoned more fireballs into the dark abyss, but it was like throwing stones into a well.

The creatures growled and screeched. Their collective voices sent chills throughout my bones, carrying with them the promise of death. The wave of leshii swelled as they clawed closer, scrambling on the walls, ceilings, and floor. The lure of live meat overwhelmed them and they climbed over each other, not caring that others in their way got hurt. One creature slipped and stumbled, and the tide of bodies surged over it, claws gouging its body.

"I'll need time to seal the doorway," I said.

"We'll give it to you," Behast said.

"Demay," Prastian said, sheathing his sword. "Draw your bow and help me."

Prastian and Demay stood near the doorway, bows at the ready. The elves took aim, drawing their bowstrings back. Behast and Jastillian guarded and flanked their sides.

"I'm not going to be able to help you while I'm in the trance," I said. "You're going to have to protect me. But try not to risk your lives needlessly. If you're overwhelmed, wake me and we'll leave."

They nodded. Prastian and Demay let their arrows fly. One after another left their bows and hit their marks. Arrows riddled the bodies of the deformed dwarves as they smashed into the ground, imparting one last shriek before heading to the afterlife.

I forced the battle out of my mind and stepped back from the fray. I couldn't focus on *if* my friends could hold the leshii off. I knew they *would*. They had to. I poured the green potion on my hands until it coated them, and flung the flask aside. I closed my eyes, slowed my breathing, and ignored the leshiis' shrieks and the iron blood smell of battle, leaving the world behind.

I visualized the doorway and began to weave my web. My hands moved in the intricate pattern I had memorized from the book. My fingers shot out in precise movement and my hands danced up, down, left, right, and zigzagged.

Webs were the strings that linked together all the elements of mana. I had to grasp that magical force and entwine them into the web I was creating. Those without magic couldn't see it, but there was a faint web growing in front of me. I strengthened it with the fire burning inside of me, along with my former master's strongest mana of wind, and pushed it out in front of me. The invisible web passed through everything and clung to the doorway, glimmering like the morning's dew stuck to a spider's web.

My trance broke, and the roaring chorus of the leshii hit me like a wall. Their high-pitched screeches burned into my ears. Agony? Or triumph? I couldn't tell. My hands were numb and throbbing, still covered in green goo.

Prastian and Demay leaned past the edges of the doorway, loosing their torrent of arrows down the shaft, their quivers almost empty. Jastillian and Behast were nowhere to be seen. When I went to the brothers, I saw Jastillian and Behast had forced their way down into the staircase. They fought back the swelling tide of creatures with brute strength, superb battle skills, and higher ground. Bodies piled up around them, and their footing threatened to slip in the blackening blood.

I gave a shrill whistle. "Fall back!"

Inch by hard-fought inch, the pair retreated. Jastillian covered their escape while the wounded Behast retreated. The dwarf killed another leshii, laughing and hollering. He seemed to enjoy slaying his people's mortal enemies.

Prastian used the last of his arrows to kill two of the creatures, creating a small window of opportunity for Jastillian. He turned and sprinted back towards us, pushing his muscles as hard as he could.

Behast had made it to the doorway, and we pulled him through. We yelled for Jastillian to hurry, but because of his age and heavy weapons, his feet moved as if through molasses.

A group of five leshii scraped their way to him, their sharp claws grabbing the stone and allowing them to gain speed with each passing moment. Prastian and Demay were out of arrows and I couldn't use any magic, lest the spell of the web I hadn't finished casting be broken.

The leading leshii leapt out, its sharp fangs and claws aching to dig their way into Jastillian's exposed back.

An arrow burrowed into its gaping mouth with such force the creature flew backward, tumbling into the leshii behind him.

"Got it!" Demay said with a triumphant smile, just as Jastillian flew past us. Behast flung the burnt door shut.

Jastillian had his hands on his knees, gasping for breath. Buckets of sweat poured from his head.

"Are you all right?" I asked.

He waved me off. "I'm fine. I hate running."

"Are you sure this will work, Hellsfire?" Prastian asked, glancing at the door. "The door's ready to fall apart."

"It'll work. The magic will keep them at bay, not the door."

The almost completed web shimmered like a crystal as it clung to the door. My friends held the door in place. There was no way to keep it barred, and the wood was already brittle from my earlier spell. My four friends held fast, straining their muscles against the incredible force of all the leshii tearing and scratching at the door.

I lifted my hand and spaced my fingers out. The mana I'd gathered for the web flowed around me, encompassing me. I transferred it to the drying potion on my hands. The green potion glowed in response. It flew from my hands and flung itself towards the door.

"Move!" I yelled.

They let go of the door and dove out of the way. Before the potion hit the web, I empowered it. A gust of fire poured out of my hands, forcing its way through the cracks, burning the creatures close to it. The web, potion, and fire all coalesced together like a polished candlestick. The green potion clung to the web and glowed, shining in all the colors of the gods before vanishing. The door and the web became one.

The relentless leshii pounded at the door. The old door held strong as the web reinforced it and made it immovable. My friends still cradled their weapons and stared at the door, afraid it might burst at any second.

"It's over," I said, gasping a deep breath and leaning against a wall.

"But what about the leshii?" Demay asked, still clutching his bow with a tightened grip. "Can they get through?"

"If they knew what was good for them, they'd stop."

I twirled my fingers and gestured to the door. A dark green light flashed through the cracks, deepening to a crimson red.

"They have one more warning," I said.

The web combusted into fire. An intense orange and red cascaded through the far side, illuminating the outline of the door. The heat radiating from it brushed against our skin. The leshii shrieked to the heavens one last time before the God of Death claimed their lives.

"What happened to them, lad?" Jastillian asked.

"They burned."

"Good."

One of the leshii on the ground squirmed. My friends readied their weapons, then lowered them when they saw the huge gash in its body and how it could barely move. The leshii's beady eyes stared at Jastillian. Such anger and hate seared into my friend. "Foolish...dwarf. You'll never...understand."

Jastillian spat and raised his boot. He stomped on the creature until its head caved in. Blood squirted on Jastillian's face, but he didn't care. He stormed off, leaving blood-filled footprints on the ground.

I left everyone there to tell Cynder what had taken place. When I stepped through the door, a stream of fire twisted and flew at me. My eyes widened, and I lifted a hand, parting the flame. It crashed against the cave walls. The fire stopped and the dragon smiled. Sulfur smoke billowed from his nose.

"What are you doing?" I asked.

"I was afraid you were one of those creatures," Cynder said. "Such annoying little things. Those screeches gave me a headache."

I glared at him. "What if one of the others came here?"

"I would have had a nice lunch. Now, aren't you glad you didn't get past the web a couple of years ago? That was such a bad idea you had. You could have been killed and we would have never found your body."

I raised an eyebrow. "*My* idea? It was your idea, you stupid dragon." I waved him off. "Some help you were. Couldn't even get your big head inside. We could have used you against the leshii."

"Leshii? Stranger name than yours. You did fine, little one. Stradus would have been proud. If you really wanted my help, I could have cleansed the caves with a stream of fire. That would have killed all those vile creatures."

"You would have burned everything inside, including us."

Cynder performed the dragon equivalent of a shrug by slightly raising his front foreleg. "I'm sure you would have shielded yourself and your friends." His eyelids flickered and he stared at the blood on my wizard's robes. "Now tell me what happened and leave in all the good bits."

I relayed to him what had happened, and then went to the spring to clean up. I finished the binding potion I had started in Alexandria, knowing it would be a few more days before it set. Instead of helping Jastillian and Prastian do more research in Stradus's library, Behast and Demay carried the charred leshii bodies out into the main tunnel. Cynder finally made himself useful and took care of those bodies.

I rummaged through Stradus's old belongings, trying to find anything of use for our trip to the Wastelands. Without knowing the origin or reason for the artifacts, I couldn't tell what they were used for. I didn't have time to research more than a couple of them. I scoured the library to look for a spell or ritual that could help in our quest, but I came up empty. I knew then that I was going to have to tell my friends about the soul binding spell.

Jastillian and Prastian found something useful though—a detailed map of Renak's tower in an old book. Etched into it were intricate markings of the way

Renak set up his place of rule. It showed us where his throne room was, the cells, the kitchen, the living quarters. We knew the tower might not still be like that, but it would be a good start.

I gathered everyone in the library and explained to them the magic the princess gave me and how I couldn't find another spell in Stradus's library that would work as well or get us as close to Masep as this. I outlined the dangers of the ritual until they understood the possible consequences.

They stood there, not looking at me or each other, as they gazed into nothingness. Questioning looks soon passed across their faces, and I knew it was only a moment before their emotions exploded to the surface.

"It's bad enough we'll be wearing those smelly little goblin skins, but now we can lose our souls?" Demay asked, bug-eyed. He glanced to his brother and thumbed his bowstring.

"Death happens to us all," Behast said. "But if these creatures take over our bodies, what will become of us? What if our bodies die and they're in control?"

"Then our souls will be lost forever," I said.

"Is there no other spell that could help us?" Prastian asked.

I shook my head. "I went through all of Stradus's books and couldn't find anything. There are no secret passageways to get us closer and no other spells to camouflage us. This is it."

"I'd rather go back to our original plan of getting as close as we can and fighting our way in," Demay said. "You're a wizard. The creatures should bow down to you or something."

"You knew it was dangerous when you agreed to go," I said.

"I know, but this is something else entirely. This wasn't what I expected."

I sighed. "I understand if any or *all* of you decide not to go. You've helped me enough already. I'll go alone if I have to."

Jastillian stroked his gray-spotted beard. "I'm with the lad. We dwarves have a saying, 'In for a chisel, in for a hammer.' This is our opportunity to do what no other has done in centuries. Great songs will be sung about us."

Jastillian smiled and clapped my back. "Plus, Hellsfire needs our help. Not even Shala and Renak fought alone."

Behast and Demay regarded Prastian. As the leader of the elves in the group, as well as the successor to Sharald, king of the elves, he was the one I had to convince. Whatever he decided, the others would follow him. Prastian didn't say anything. He had a thoughtful look on his face, but that expression faded as he walked right past me. My heart sank. I wouldn't have the elves—my friends—by my side.

Prastian sat down and studied the map of Renak's tower they had found earlier. "Well, what are you waiting for? We have a lot of work to do."

A frown passed over Demay's face. I worried he might not come, but then he said, "We're with you, Hellsfire. But please, I would like to keep my soul in *this* body."

"I'll do my best."

Behast nodded to me. "If we are to die, I would like to do so with my body under my own control."

I returned his nod. I smiled, glad to have their assistance. It was very dangerous and powerful magic Krystal had given me. I could see why she was reluctant to give me access to the magic Alexandria had collected over the years. If this was just a hint of what lay in there, what other secrets could their archive contain? I had to be careful for my friends' sake, if not my own.

I wished we could have found some more to help us, though. A potion, a powerful artifact or weapon, or a secret way into Renak's old castle. Seeing the gash in Behast's arm, the slight burns on Demay, and the anger in Jastillian's face, I thought coming here had been a waste of time. But then I saw the tranquility of the now-restored garden and how Stradus would always be watching over the White Mountain, and thought that after all he'd done, it was well worth it.

Before we left, I constructed webs on Stradus's room to safeguard his belongings, and on the library and the garden. Ones that required different passwords to enter.

After two days had passed, we finally left the White Mountain. When we departed, we took a couple of books with us that Prastian and Jastillian found of interest to them. I didn't take any of the relics in Stradus's old room. There wouldn't be time to study them before venturing into the Wastelands. Premier might not have his complete power back, but he would be expecting me, and he would be planning something. I was tempted to take a few and leave them in Krystal's hands, but I might never see them again.

CHAPTER 5

AROUND MIDDAY, we settled back down in Alexandria's castle and dismounted off Cynder.

Prastian bowed low to Cynder and said, "Thank you, again, Great Dragon. We are honored." The rest of them also bowed, but I didn't.

"Thank you, Cynder," Demay said. "I didn't know flying in the clouds could be so much fun."

"I prefer my feet on the ground," Behast said.

"I'm thankful for the gods' eye view of the world," Jastillian said. "It reminds me that the gods think differently from us."

"You should be so lucky," Cynder said and smiled. He stretched his long neck and peered into the distance. It took a moment for him to remember we were there. "It was an honor to get to know you all as well."

"I hope we can do it again sometime," Demay said, his green eyes filled with excitement.

Cynder didn't say anything, but swiveled his head and stared into the distance again.

"Come on, Demay," Prastian said, tugging on his brother's sleeve. "We've got preparations to make and Behast needs to be taken care of."

My four friends left, leaving me alone with Cynder.

"You're leaving." It wasn't a question, but a fact.

"Very perceptive. You've finally learned something from me."

I bit the inside of my lip and gazed up at the dragon. I had been worried Cynder was going to leave when he told me he wouldn't accompany me to Masep, no matter how hard I pushed him. I shouldn't have expected him to stay around, but I had. With Stradus gone, there was nothing to tie Cynder down anymore.

I laid my hand on his smooth, red scales. "Are you sure you don't want to stay? I could use your help."

"Of course you could. You're a weak human." Cynder grinned. "But no. It's time for me to spread my wings once again."

Cynder unfurled his wings, poising his body to take flight. My hand fell off him.

"Stay," I said, finding my voice hoarse. I cleared my throat. "Alexandria would worship you even more. They may even build you a statue. You're a symbol to them. You inspire them, especially after what happened with Premier. They would miss you...and so would I."

Cynder folded his wings and stretched his neck until his face came so close to me his sulfuric breath draped me. "I didn't know you cared, but you're not my type."

I clenched my fists. The stupid dragon was already making it harder. "Fine! I'll miss you, you arrogant, overgrown oven. Is it so much that I want my friend to stay? You're the only one who understands what I'm going through. Not even Krystal knows how I feel or understands the burden I'm meant to carry."

Long moments passed as neither of us said anything. Cynder stared at me and didn't move a muscle. Finally, he spoke. "You'll be fine, Hellsfire. You have friends who trust you and a woman who cares deeply about you. I can't stay with you any longer."

"But why? What else do you have to do?"

"There's an entire world out there. Why would I want to be stuck here with you?" Cynder snickered and smoke oozed from his nose. "I was Stradus's guardian, not yours. We'll always be friends. But if you tell any other dragons, I will deny it."

I chuckled. He was right. He wasn't my guardian and he had already done enough for me. "What are you going to do now?"

Cynder scratched his claws into the ground and flung a large chunk of soil. "I've already seen much of the world, traveling with Stradus." He sighed. "You know I can't go home until the Great Barrier falls."

I remembered him finally relenting and telling me the story of him and Stradus first meeting. How the youthful dragon helped the young wizard, and that because of it, Cynder was banished from his people. His people were from the far east, and if it wasn't for the Elders' punishment, Cynder would be with his people now.

"I will fly wherever the wind takes me," the dragon said.

"All right. If you change your mind, you know where I'll be."

"One wizard in a lifetime is more than enough, and besides..." His reptile-like face hardened until it became immovable—a serious look rarely found on him. He lowered his deep voice. "The path you walk is dangerous, Hellsfire. So much so that I think it's better for *my* health to stay away. There are times when you're going to want to quit, but you must stay your course."

I raised my right eyebrow. "What did Stradus tell you?"

"More than you'll ever know. What did Stradus used to say? 'Let your heart guide you and never give up, no matter how much you want to.' Maybe things will be as simple as that." Cynder smirked. "It's worked out well for you so far."

"Thank you, my friend."

Cynder lifted his snout and huffed a puff of smoke. He unfurled his long wingspan. "Prepare yourself. Next time we cross paths, it will be I who bests you, oh Chosen One."

"Aren't you going to say goodbye to Krystal or the king? I think you owe them that after you've eaten all their food."

"Hellsfire, when will you learn?" Cynder asked. "I am the greatest of all the gods' creations. I owe no one anything, least of all you puny humans." Cynder grinned. "I will give them something to remember me by. And who knows? They may see me from time to time."

Before I could say anything, Cynder launched himself into the air like a catapult. The eruption of wind staggered me and I barely kept myself from falling. Unlike all the other times when that maddened me, I smiled.

"Goodbye, you smoke stack." I waved as I watched him go.

Cynder swooped to the center of the city. He hovered in the air, flapping his wings. The mighty dragon let out an ear-shattering roar, pounding into the hearts of Alexandria's citizens. All the people in the castle stopped their work as Cynder mesmerized them all.

The red dragon flew higher, twisting and climbing until he became a dot. He blazed like a sun against the blue sky. I placed my hand above my eyes to negate the glare. Cynder's wings stopped and he dropped like a stone, his sleek body spiraling down.

"What are you doing?" I called out.

I worried he was going to crash into the city like a falling star. The guards standing on the castle walls pointed and yelled. Before he could hit Alexandria, Cynder heaved a trail of fire, moving his snout to shape it into a circle. He glided through it, lifting his body before he hit anything. I couldn't see over the walls, but I knew that backlash of wind caused people a lot of trouble.

"That egotistical dragon," I said and smiled, watching him as he flew into parts unknown. He did give Alexandria something to remember him by.

I walked back up the hill, heading back into the keep. Krystal had told me that her soldiers were going to gather the supplies we needed for the ritual, but a wizard always double-checked. I thought about how I couldn't wait to see her again, but I didn't have to go far to find her.

Krystal was standing near one of the buildings. Next to her were Ardimus and Captain Rebekah. Their awe-filled gazes were still trained on the direction Cynder had flown.

I greeted them, jolting them out of their trance.

"Hellsfire," Krystal said.

"Princess," I said and bowed.

"I was just coming to see you."

I raised an eyebrow. "You were?"

"Yes, I wanted a report from you about what happened in the White Mountain. I saw Behast's wounds." For a moment, her purple eyes filled with compassion and her face softened. She turned to her companions. "Leave us."

Ardimus departed, walking so he was out of earshot. When Captain Rebekah, walked by me she wore a smirk on her face.

I glanced from side to side and I suddenly realized we were alone. "Krystal, do you think it was wise to send them away?"

"Are you questioning my orders?" she asked with a playful smile.

She fell back into the shadows of the building and leaned up against a buttress. I went with her, disappearing from the view of any bystanders.

"I'm glad to see you're all right," Krystal said. "I was worried something might have happened to you."

I exhaled. "It almost did."

Her purple eyes darkened and her cheek muscle flexed. "Tell me."

I gave my report to the princess, telling her almost everything. I left out what Stradus said to me about my destiny. As much as I trusted her, I needn't worry her even more. As good as she was at masking her emotions, I could tell she was already distressed about me venturing into the Wastelands.

Afterwards, she said, "I'm sorry you had to fight the leshii. I'm just glad you're all right and that you completed the binding potion."

Her face became stoic for a moment. I knew she was still angry at what I planned to do. We, along with her father, had had many arguments about me killing Premier instead of securing a book they didn't believe existed and binding his powers.

Krystal ran her fingers along my arm. "I'm sure you won't need anything else except your powers and the help of the others in the Wastelands." She feigned a smile, but it was sad.

I knew she was lying, but I kept quiet.

"I've obtained the supplies you need," she said. "Unfortunately, my people had a hard time getting them. The Wasteland creatures are falling back from the surrounding area and the attacks have lessened since the battle."

"What do you think it means?"

Krystal narrowed her eyes. "Premier's up to something."

"You think he could be preparing for another attack? But how? He should be weakened after I defeated him."

"We'll ready ourselves for whatever may come, but it may be *you* who finds out first." Her eyes shimmered with a light sheen. In a hoarse voice, she said, "I'd send all of Alexandria's army with you if I could."

"I know you would, Krystal."

She turned to leave, as we had already spent too much time alone together, but I stopped her.

"I have something for you," I said.

"You do?"

I nodded. I reached into my purse and dug out my former master's necklace. I handed it to her. When she touched it, the dull jade mineral flared, the green light blinding me. The powerful magic shocked me, traveling up my arm until it sucked my breath away. My inner fire mana roared and blossomed, yet I didn't prepare it for a spell. The light vanished and the hexagram lost its life and color.

"What was that?" Krystal asked, putting a hand to her bosom. "It was incredible." She took the necklace and inspected it. "Where did you get this?"

"Stradus gave it to me. He said he once gave it to his beloved and now I'm giving it to you."

Her eyes met mine and she smiled. "You realize what this means?"

I shook my head.

"You don't know?"

"Stradus told me to give this to someone special that I cared about deeply.

There was only one person in the world I thought of—you."

Krystal brushed aside a lock of her sun-kissed hair and her whole face blushed. "You're sweet, but let me tell you what it means.

"Wizards used to have a tradition of bestowing magical gifts upon their loved ones. The gifts could be anything: a carved figurine, a dagger, a bracelet, a polished stone, or a necklace," she said, holding up hers. "I don't understand the magic involved or what could be done with it, but these gifts were very special because of the magic used in their enchantment. Some said it was the most powerful magic—and it's only given to the people they loved."

We were quiet as her words hung in the air. I cared a lot about the princess and while I had done a lot for her, I had never said those magical words. Neither had she.

I broke the silence. I didn't know how much I cared for her at that time. All I knew was that, "It's meant for you."

Krystal didn't hesitate to put the necklace on. The hexagram hummed and glowed in response, then went quiet. She grabbed a handful of my robes and yanked me in. Our faces were inches away from each other.

My eyes frantically looked around. "Krystal, what are you doing? Someone could see us." I should have pulled away from her, in case someone did, but I didn't want to. Her lilac smell rooted me to the spot.

She gave me a seductive smile. "We have a moment, hero."

The princess kissed me hard and with passion. I returned it, pressing my body up against hers, trapping her against the building.

She broke the kiss and whispered into my ear, "We'll have plenty of time for that later tonight, and I promise you I won't fall asleep."

Krystal nibbled my ear and I shivered. Her hand crept underneath my robes, dancing along my sides. She tickled me and I squirmed from my weakness. Krystal slipped out from between the wall and me.

"Come with me and make sure you have everything you need for tomorrow, Hellsfire."

I nodded, following her into the keep.

All of our supplies were prepped and ready to go. My friends and I went over our plans again and discussed things with the princess and her Guardsmen. We ate an early dinner, then dispersed to get ready for a long day tomorrow.

I went back to my room. I didn't have to wait long before Krystal came. Words weren't spoken as we tore each other's clothes off. Everything we had to say was spoken with our bodies, our hands, our mouths as we ravaged and devoured each other with an eagerness born out of desperation and fear.

I wasn't afraid of going into the Wastelands and dying. I was afraid of never seeing the princess again—of never holding her in my arms, of never again seeing how she laughed uncontrollably from that ticklish spot behind her right knee. It was that fear I was going to have to latch onto to survive my journey.

We stayed up most of the night, saying our goodbyes in that one special way. It exhausted me to do so, but she was well worth it.

CHAPTER 6

I STAND BESIEGED by the darkness as it consumes everything around me.

"Hellsfire," a voice from the darkness says. I turn my head in confusion, trying to pinpoint the sound.

"Hellsfire," the voice says in a mocking tone.

I realize it's not coming from a single source. The voice echoes and surrounds me, coming from the darkness itself.

"You will never get what you want, Hellsfire. If you continue on your foolish quest, you will lose that which you value most."

No. The princess reminded me I had a duty to do. I raise my arm. I summon fire to the surface. I free the fire from my hand to burn and dissipate the darkness, or illuminate what's there. I see nothing, but continue to shoot out fire. I turn until a ring of fire surrounds me, kindling the darkness.

He laughs and says, "Very well."

The fire burns with nothing to fuel it. The magic within the fire beats, matching my heartbeat as I await him. The flames swirl, rising higher like a pillar. They stop at my height and coalesce into a human form. The fire stops burning and the person becomes solid. I stare into his brown eyes. It's me.

"If you insist. I will see you when you get here." The impostor puts his icy hand forward. I ready my magic to fight him. His magic smashes past my defenses and he shoves me out of my own dream.

I cried out, waking up drenched in a cold sweat. I found my face buried in Krystal's chest.

"Shhh," she said. "It's all right, Hellsfire. You're safe." She hugged and cradled me while she stroked my hair.

"You're still here?" I asked, seeing it was only an hour or two until sunrise. "You're never here when I wake up."

"I know. I just wanted to experience it with you before you go."

"And?"

"It's nice."

I squeezed her tighter and nuzzled against her chest. "It is."

She pulled away, forcing me to look into her soft, purple eyes. "Did you have a bad dream?"

"It was...more than that."

"Tell me."

And I did. It was hard to talk about it, but once I did, I couldn't stop. The princess listened and didn't say a word until I was done.

"Can wizards communicate through dreams using some kind of spell?" Krystal asked.

"I don't know."

"Maybe Premier can and he's warning you to stay away because he's scared of you. After all, he did create an avatar and I didn't think such a thing was possible."

"Maybe." I shook my head. "It doesn't matter. Premier needs to be stopped so that he has no chance of harming you or Alexandria again. I'm the only known wizard in the land that can make that happen. I beat him before. I can beat him again." I found my voice surprisingly steady, even though I knew I had beaten him with Stradus's help.

Krystal intertwined her leg with mine. "Just be careful, hero. I don't want to lose you."

"I don't want to lose you either."

I lusted at her bosoms and my fingers slid across them. "A guy could get used to this."

Krystal laughed. "You wish."

I danced my fingers over her side. She squirmed in delight. I tickled my fingers on her body and she cried out in laughter, the beautiful musical noise ringing in my ears. She tried to get away, but the bed was small and there was nowhere for her to go. She couldn't do anything about it, or so I thought.

A pillow slammed into my face. Feathers scattered everywhere. She smashed it into me again, forcing me to stop. I plucked the pillow from her hands and threw it aside. I forced myself on top of her and pinned her against the bed, holding her wrists and binding her in place. I knew if she wanted to, she could easily wrest herself from my grip, but she made no move.

"I still have a little bit of time before I have to get ready and leave," I said.

Krystal's eyes sparkled. "Then stop talking, and let's make the most of it."

"As you command, Your Highness."

Afterwards, she left and I dressed and rushed to meet the others. We had a light breakfast of fresh fruit, bread, and cheese. We rechecked our supplies, loaded them on the horses, and made our way out of the castle to the northern walls of Alexandria.

Krystal and King Furlong waited for us, along with some of their soldiers.

"Your Majesty," I said and bowed.

"Hellsfire," the king said, nodding. "I came to see you all off and wish you well."

"Thank you, sire. We appreciate it."

King Furlong's blue eyes scrutinized me and his brow furrowed. I had seen him often during the time I was here. Because of the spells Premier had performed on him to gain the king's trust, I checked on him daily to make sure there were no lingering effects. The king's mind had been influenced by

Premier, allowing him to weaken Alexandria's defenses.

The king and I never talked long. He was always curt and direct. In the beginning, I tried to make conversation with him, at Krystal's urging. I wanted to see what I could do to help Alexandria or even just make small talk, to get to know the king. Those discussions never ended well. Eventually, I just gave up. Even though I'd saved his life and his kingdom, I felt I made him uneasy. I didn't know whether it was the fact that I was a wizard or that he knew I was seeing his daughter. I hoped it was the first part.

Furlong's eyes and face softened when he saw his old friend Prastian. "Is there any message you want me to relay to King Sharald?"

"No, sire," Prastian said. "I believe we have everything taken care of. Thank you."

"What about you, Jastillian? Any last message?"

"Aye. Tell my mother I expect great songs about us when we get back." We all laughed at Jastillian's words, but I knew he wasn't kidding.

"Maybe we'll write our own song about you," the king said.

Jastillian grinned. "We would be honored."

"Good luck to you all," King Furlong said. "May the gods walk with you." We all bowed to him. He folded his arms within his red and white robes and walked away.

A handful of Alexandria's Guardsmen and the princess waited around the horses.

"Patrols will be sent out every day to keep an eye out for your return," Krystal said. "For as long as it takes." She met my eyes when she said that.

Captain Rebekah said, "We'll ride with you until we reach the mountains and we'll depart there. My patrol will shadow you for a time in case you run into trouble."

"Thank you," I said.

Prastian and the others checked our supplies of food and water. I went to check the blood and skins I would need for the ritual.

A lone horse carried all the supplies. He could barely keep still from the rank smell that covered him. The horse bucked and whinnied, but a soldier held his reins in place. I had to breathe through my mouth and tried not to remember that I would be drenched in that smell. Five goblin skins were laid across the horse's back. Flies encircled him as if he was a carcass. There were six bags of blood. Five of them were marked with different numbers. I lifted a goblin skin and saw an identical number to match one of the bags. The sixth bag held a mixture of blood from all the creatures found in the Wastelands. I ran my hands over each bag, inspecting them for drips. The bags were secured tightly.

From the corner of my eye, I saw the soldier controlling the horse glaring at me. I wondered what his problem was, until I realized half of the soldiers there had that same look on their faces. Every time I moved to check the blood, their glares worsened.

"Everything's ready," Prastian said, walking over to me, forcing me to turn away from the soldiers.

"Me too," I said.

Demay had a look of disgust on his face and stopped when he was seven feet away. He pinched his nose. "That *smell*. There's got to be another way."

Jastillian slapped him on the back. "Don't worry, lad, you'll get used to it. Soon, you'll wonder how you lived without it."

"That's what I'm afraid of."

Krystal came over to us and said, "Good luck to you. All of you. Take care."

We bowed to her, then climbed on our horses. I gazed at her. There was so much more I wanted to say that I didn't get to say last night. I finally settled on, "Goodbye, Your Highness."

"Go," she whispered. "Come back to me."

I nodded.

As we rode out, I tried my best not to turn around. I knew that if I did I would see how much pain I caused her. I grasped the reins of my horse until they dug into my hands, leaving marks.

I finally caved in and turned when she was just a small dot. I thought she might have been gone by then, but she was still there, waiting for me.

Because of its location near the Wastelands of Renak, Alexandria wasn't the most fertile of places. Most of its farms were to the east as a large river ran there. But it could still support people. I hadn't been up north before, but I saw what Jastillian had talked about while we were in the library.

The land became brittle and hard the farther we traveled. The cracked ground became uneven with weeds and shrubs and gangly, leafless trees sprinkled about. Huge gray clouds blocked out most of the light. They seemed to never move, just hovered there despite the howling wind. That wind came from everywhere like a wild creature hunting in the night.

As we rode, I couldn't shake the feeling that we were being watched. From the corners of my eyes, I saw shadows flashing from behind boulders. A large branch wobbled, but when I turned my head, nothing was there. The longer we rode, the stronger the rotten, sewage-like smell became. It reminded me of the battle with the creatures in Alexandria. But there would be no escape here, and we couldn't kill them all.

An hour later, we arrived at the drop-off point. My friends and I got off our horses. The Guardsmen surrounded us, keeping us out of view, while we grabbed our supplies. The bags of blood were awkward to carry because of how the heavy contents swirled with each movement. I slung them across my shoulders. The smell reminded me of the animals I used to butcher for Farmer Andrick back in the days before I became a wizard. Except far more pungent.

With the soldiers surrounding us as shields, we took out our goblin skins. I draped mine over me, almost gagging from how disgusting it was. The slimy skin rubbed against my face and I shivered. While the goblin looked awkward on me, considering how tall I was and how short he was, I had an easier time of it than my friends. They might not have had to worry about their height, but their weapons got in the way. Prastian and Demay had hunchbacks because of their quivers. Behast and Jastillian weren't going to be able to draw their weapons with ease.

"Yuck," Demay said, and shuddered. His face paled to a darker shade of green.

"Don't forget to rub their innards on you," Prastian said.

Demay stuck his tongue out at his brother and everyone laughed. I stopped laughing when I ran the entrails and intestines over my face. Blood and slime clung to my skin. I bent over and gagged, almost heaving up my light breakfast. I kept going though, even smearing it against my black wizard's robe.

"It's not so bad, lad," Jastillian said, having no problem with the bits of entrails entangled in his bushy beard. "I remember when I first did this, I couldn't stop myself from puking. Now, it's no bother. Some of the creatures have an excellent sense of smell. This will help throw them off."

I shook my head. "I'd rather rub dragon's dung on me." Jastillian laughed and patted me on the back.

When I finished, I tied my food and water to my belt, making sure everything was secure. My back strained from how heavy it all was, but I knew it would lighten after the ritual and days of travel.

"You may not see us, but we'll shadow you," Rebekah said. "We'll try and take care of any large group of creatures that look to cross your path."

"Thank you," Prastian said.

"Good luck, all of you," Rebekah said. She stared at me. "Return in one piece. Don't make me give the princess bad news."

"I'll do everything in my power to make sure we all return in one piece," I said. "But if we don't return by the new moon then…" There were so many things I wanted to say to Krystal that I never had the courage to say. I couldn't tell the captain first. "Tell her…I'm sorry."

"I will do as you ask," Rebekah said.

"We'll take good care of him," Prastian said.

Rebekah nodded. "Fare thee well." She and her men sped away.

"We had better get a move on," Jastillian said. "We must reach the cave before night falls."

Jastillian took the lead and we followed. While walking through the alien environment, the elves and I constantly glanced around the bleak landscape. They had their hands on the hilts of their swords while I had my mana within a thought's grasp.

"I feel ridiculous," Demay said as he tugged the loose skin on his arm. "Are you sure this will work?"

Jastillian laughed. "To where we're going, no. But for right now, yes. I know where the dense population of creatures is. We'll be fine. I've traveled this area many times, and Rebekah and her people have cleared the area of creatures ever since the battle."

"I also need time to gather my magic," I said. "By drawing it from the land itself. I could have done it back at Alexandria, but incorporating the magic from the area where we'll be is better. And with this much energy, I have to worry about affecting people in the area. Here, there aren't any people to worry about." I also wasn't sure the effect the spell would have on us. It would be better if we were alone.

As much as I wanted to rest my weary feet, we barely stopped for any breaks. As the day progressed, the creatures became more visible. They were shadows no more. A pair of trolls lumbered near a boulder and an ogre chewed on a large piece of meat with the bone protruding from his hand. We had walked so long that I wasn't sure if Captain Rebekah and her men still shadowed us. If they did, we couldn't see them.

I couldn't even be of any help if we ran into trouble. I meditated and focused on gathering in as much mana as I could, in preparation for the dangerous ritual I had to perform. Gathering mana from the environment was difficult. While the creatures and small animals gave me some, the land itself didn't.

I tried to access the earth mana, but found the land damaged. In Northern Shala, the land greeted me in response, its mana racing up my arms. Here, it was like a dying heartbeat. I couldn't help but feel like I was crafting a candle with the wrong kind of wax.

I stared at Jastillian's back in front of me, his broad shoulders looking awkward as they shifted underneath his goblin disguise. The theory he had discounted was right. I might be a new wizard, but I could tell that something had drained the mana from the land, and a huge spell powered by a nexus seemed like the only explanation. The land shouldn't feel this...wrong.

I glanced back south towards Alexandria, then at the hard ground underneath my feet. The Wastelands was once a place of beauty, but it had changed and continued to do so. What would happen in the years and centuries to come? Would all of Northern Shala be touched by this blight? And since I was a wizard, with an unimaginably long life ahead of me, would I be forced to witness it?

I exhaled and stared ahead. I couldn't worry about that now. While I was a wizard, I wasn't a god. I had no idea how to fix an entire land. The only thing within my power was dealing with Premier.

I stopped taking mana from the land itself, drawing it bit by bit from my friends, the Wasteland creatures, the lizards that scurried across our path, the spiders that hid under rocks, everything. It was slow and tedious, but also safer. Eventually, the power built up, throbbing against my fingertips, aching to be released. Extracting magic and storing it inside you was a very unstable thing to do. My body could explode with magic at any moment, and I didn't want to waste it on an attack.

Jastillian said we were making good time. I felt it in my burning thighs. We climbed a small hill, but when we reached the top, we were shocked to confront a large ogre. Despite the elves' excellent hearing and the ogre's large feet and heavy footsteps, the beast seemed to emerge from nowhere. We froze, not daring to breathe or reach for our weapons.

The colossal creature was over fifteen feet tall. His long arms hung nearly to his knees, dragging a granite club the size of an elf, and his dark gray skin was the color of the ominous clouds overhead. Numerous scars were etched across his arms, peeking through the tattered brown rags he wore. The monster paused and glared at us. His big lips had been ripped away on one side, forever giving him a terrifying grin. His dark eyes burned with rage. He raised his club and unleashed a ferocious growl.

All the energy I'd gathered had been for naught. I was going to have to blast it on this brute.

"Cast your eyes down!" Jastillian whispered. "Make no sudden movements."

Jastillian made high-pitched screeching noises and danced around. The ogre growled again. I leaned back, feeling the hair on my body rise as his roar shocked my heart, praying that the ogre couldn't see past our flimsy disguises. Jastillian snarled back, stomping his feet. Jastillian then quickly bowed and lowered his head.

"Lower your heads," Jastillian said. "Now!"

We did as he said. The ogre stopped and stared at us with a thoughtful look on his face. He seemed to be weighing the desire to kill us against the trouble it would take. A low rumble came from his throat, but the ogre lowered his club. He walked away, continuing on his course.

"Let's go," Jastillian said, leading us in the opposite direction.

"What just happened?" Demay asked. "Why didn't he kill us?"

"In nature," the dwarf said, "animals puff themselves up to make them look bigger, or screech to scare off a bigger predator. I did the same thing here."

"But ogres are smarter than animals," Prastian said.

"Aye, but not by much. Just be thankful she wasn't hungry."

"She?" I asked. "I thought that was a he?"

Jastillian laughed. "No, lad. It's hard to tell the difference, but that was definitely a she."

"I've never seen such a huge ogre before," Behast said.

"Me neither," Jastillian said. "She's older and bigger than any I've seen, and she walks alone. That makes her extremely dangerous. Let's hurry before she changes her mind and decides she's hungry."

As darkness descended and more creatures woke, a shiver rode up my spine. I felt as if I was trapped in a sea of crazed predators, and I was meager prey. Bloodthirsty howls and screams raged through the night. In the distance, small armies of creatures crashed and fought against each other. We scurried to get out of plain view. Our makeshift disguises wouldn't last if any of them got closer than that ogre. Jastillian led us to a small cave in the side of an elevated plateau.

We stood off to the side of the entrance. Before we stepped in, the elves used their ears to scout the dark caves. Quietly, they motioned with their hands, saying there were four, possibly five goblins.

In complete silence, my friends took off their goblin hides and freed their weapons. They deposited the bags of blood and supplies on the ground. I watched over everything, keeping an eye out for any creatures in the area, while they made their way inside the caves.

Shrieks and screams echoed from the cave. I wanted to peek inside, but I needed to keep watch over our belongings. Without them, I couldn't perform the ritual that could get us into Masep, and my friends could handle a few goblins.

The goblins' noises ceased and Demay retrieved me. We carried all the supplies inside. Goblin bodies lay in impossible positions. Dark green blood oozed from their fatal wounds. The biggest goblin clutched his hand around a rusted broadsword.

I peeled off my disguise. The slime stuck to me like molasses. When I finally got it off, I was thankful that the air seemed fresher, even inside a goblin lair.

"Demay and Prastian, please prepare some food for us," Jastillian said. "Behast, would you help me chop off the goblins' heads and hang them outside? Lad, start preparing your ritual."

I nodded. The energy I had been gathering made my eyes twitch and the hairs on the back of my neck rise. It ached to be released. I stopped drawing in mana and meditated until dinner was ready, calming the inner storm trapped inside my body.

"Why'd you hang their heads outside, Jastillian?" Demay asked.

"To make others think this cave is being occupied by a couple of ferocious ogres."

"Why would that stop creatures from getting in?"

Jastillian laughed. "It means there's a mating ritual going on in here, and that things would get deadly for trespassers. There's nothing worse than interrupting a pair of breeding ogres."

We all chuckled.

"Will we need to rotate watch?" Behast asked.

"Aye, but there's only need for one person at a time. The heads will serve as a good warning for two days. No one would dare come in unless something far worse was outside."

After dinner, I started on the blood ritual, thankful to finally let the tempest inside my body out. The energy strained against my body, pounding to get out. I rubbed my temples and gasped for air. I had never held magic in for so long before. I'd cast powerful spells, but, like a roaring fire, they burned bright and were gone. Here, it was like carrying buckets of water across my shoulders for days. Magic wasn't meant to be stored like this with no outlet.

"Hellsfire, are you all right?" Prastian asked.

"I'll be fine as soon as I start the ritual."

"You don't look all right," Demay said. "You're glowing."

I was about to ask him what he was talking about, but then I glanced down at my hand. A faint glow encompassed it. I thought it was a trick of light from the fire, but when I moved my hand, it was still there.

"Let's get this over with," I said. I blinked, holding my eyes closed longer than I should have, and I nearly toppled over. "The sooner, the better."

Prastian was the first to volunteer. I painted a circle of blood around him from his slain goblin. The hard ground started to absorb the thick liquid. It didn't matter. The essence of the blood was all I required, and it would still be there, soaked into the ground.

I sat down in front of Prastian and handed him the goblin skin he had worn. "You're going to have to put on your disguise. Unfortunately, none of us are going to be able to take them off, otherwise the spell will end. And whatever you do, don't move. Understand?"

"What happens if I move?"

"Your spirit may be lost and I won't be able to recover it. Or worse, an unwanted spirit may inhabit your body."

"What kind of spirit?"

For a moment, I hesitated to tell him. I didn't want to make Prastian or any of the others nervous. But they deserved to know the truth.

"Dark spirits," I said. "I will have to journey beyond our realm to retrieve the goblin spirits we'll need. Other beings lurk in the place I will have to go. Beings that were never part of this world, yet would try desperately to cross over into this one. They're more mindless and savage than the Wasteland beasts and more cunning than you or I. Their desire to cross over makes them yearn like a desperate man dying of thirst, so they can wreak untold havoc on our world. With their knowledge and power and twisted desires, there's no telling what they're capable of."

Prastian's green eyes stared into mine and he nodded. "I understand."

I turned to everyone. "Don't interrupt me and disrupt the spell. That will cause more harm to both myself and Prastian. Even if it looks like something's wrong, or if we're under attack."

They nodded.

I turned back to Prastian. "Ready?"

"As ready as I'll ever be."

I sat cross-legged in front of him and closed my eyes. The energy I had been gathering hummed in a quiet tune no one could hear but me. I reached out to the two most elusive mana—life and death. The warmth of life and the cold touch of death brushed against me like standing in a cold breeze on a warm day. I balanced and intertwined them until they became one gray mana.

The gray mana buzzed and encircled me. I clutched onto it as hard as I could, lest it escape me. I manipulated its power to open a gateway and venture where few living had ever dared to go, and where all would go when our lives ended. My body collapsed and I blacked out.

My spirit crossed over to another world. I couldn't go into the afterlife because I still lived, but I could travel to a place between our world and the next, where the goblin could come to me.

Because of my living, mortal flesh, the boundaries of that place afflicted my soul. I froze as if my body had been dunked into the iciest lake in the midst of winter. I burned as if I were trapped in the Burning Sands, my throat parched from lack of water. I drowned, trapped in the ocean while it pulled me down.

Finally, I floated in the otherworldly void. A spectral, ghostly light surrounded me. I was staring at it, entranced by its beauty, when I realized I wasn't alone.

Those dark spirits I had warned Prastian of reached out to me, trying to tear me from the path and lead me to my own doom. One apparition enticed me with sweet promises of power and sex. Another specter lulled me with gold and riches. I ignored all the cries and songs. They had nothing I wanted.

The tunnel I drifted in brightened and shifted into horrific pictures. The dark spirits forced images into my head—my mother's head on the end of a pike, Krystal ravaged and beaten like an animal, dozens of people burning all around me while I fed the flames with my power.

No mortal eyes were meant to see what I saw, not even those of a wizard. I closed my spiritual eyes and mind, trying to shut out the ghostly lights before the images burned into my mind and I went crazy. Then I opened my eyes, looking only out of the corners of my eyes. The pictures continued to run, but I didn't directly look at them. My voice, imbued by magic, penetrated the veils of death.

"The essence that once resided in this skin, please hear me." I said in Caleea.

While the goblins couldn't understand the ancient language in life, in death they could. Even though I yelled, my call got lost in the loud jumbled tongues of the dead, the living spirits, and those in between. I was a single voice amidst a chorus. But since the spell was tethered to her body, she would hear me.

"I beg you to come back."

I waited in that place between worlds. The images ceased, but the light around me dimmed. Shadows surrounded me, coming over, trying to pull and tug at my spirit. They hoped to control me and use my body for their own purposes. They were fools. I swung my arm in a sweeping motion, propelling a blade of fire. It cut the insubstantial beings like a scythe.

The longer I stayed, the more attention I attracted and the weaker I became. A stronger entity would come—something that would take more than minor magic to fend off.

A small black hole materialized in front of me. I peered into it, believing the goblin spirit would come. Translucent green tentacles shot out from it instead, wrapping around my wrists. They yanked me towards the hole.

The hole grew bigger and an enormous, open mouth full of tentacles waited inside. The beast smacked its ghostly teeth in anticipation.

I cut through its bindings with magic and it roared. More tentacles shot out and latched onto me. No matter how many I dispersed, more came. Inch by inch, it reeled me in like a struggling fish. I stopped focusing on its tentacles and unleashed a torrent of fire into its mouth. It shrieked in pain, withdrawing all its feelers, burrowing itself back into its hovel.

I propelled myself away from the shrieking hole and flew in the ghostly tunnel, ignoring the cries and promises of the other spirits around me. When more holes popped up, I dodged those lest I be pulled in and have to cast more magic. I needed to conserve it. I had five rituals to perform.

I beckoned the goblin again, louder and with more force, even though I drew more dark spirits to me. I needed to hurry. The longer I stayed, the more I would be overwhelmed. And I worried about not having enough energy for myself and the others. There was far more at stake than I realized, and the spell scroll hadn't gone into detail about the dangers that lay in wait.

One spirit emerged in front of me, with more substance than the rest. Her form looked as if she still lived, making me realize that she was the one I had called.

In the void, her transparent blue spirit floated next to me with a hollow look on her face. I knew goblins were ferocious and savage fighters, but I wasn't sure how intelligent they were. Because of my friends' sizes, we had to use goblins. The ogres and trolls were too big. Anything with too strong a spirit might also take over, and goblins were one of the weakest of the Wasteland creatures, unless they were in large groups.

I grasped onto Prastian's mana, using it as a link so the goblin could see. "I give you a chance to live again by bonding your essence to the elf. Do you accept?"

Silence. I couldn't tell if she pondered her choice or if she even understood me. A dark tunnel formed around us as my spell started to fade, and began to collapse. The blood magic I used was ending. If I didn't leave now, I would be trapped here, my soul forever lost.

"I need your answer," I said, extending my hand to her.

Stradus once told me the dead would rarely say no to living again, even if it was only for the briefest time, but the goblin's pause made me think otherwise. She might not understand me. The exit back to my world dimmed. I had to go. I couldn't stay any longer.

As I turned to go, she took my hand. Together, we departed the land of the dead and journeyed back into the land of the living.

A flash of light blinded me. My eyes adjusted until they brought the world into view. Everything was tilted to the side, including Prastian's tense and worried face. I pulled myself off the ground and sat up straight. Thankfully, Prastian didn't move from his circle and the others didn't break it.

"Are you all right?" Prastian asked.

I nodded and in a hoarse voice said, "I'm almost done. Prepare yourself. This is going to hurt."

Prastian's body stiffened. He couldn't see the goblin spirit invade him. I smiled and let go of the tiring black and white manas. I worked Prastian's green mana, interweaving it with the spirit. Dipping my hand in the mixed Wasteland blood Rebekah had provided, I created markings across Prastian's forehead, cheeks, nose, and ears. Normally, I wouldn't do the ears, but elves believe that's where an elf's soul is, and this spell was going to bind to his soul.

"May the two essences combine and let those of this blood see only the outer skin," I said and took a deep breath. I was exhausted and still had a lot more work to do. "There. It's done."

"I don't feel any different," Prastian said. His green eyes shifted up and down and his ears twitched.

"You will."

Prastian's eyes suddenly bulged out. He squeezed his chest, gasping for air. The goblin spirit branched into Prastian's soul as the two became one. Prastian screamed. His body went taut, then collapsed on the ground. He didn't move for several long minutes.

"Brother!" Demay said, wanting to rush to Prastian, but Behast grabbed him. "Let me go! What's happening to him? Is he all right?"

Prastian's body shuddered. He slowly rose and his eyes were glazed over. He peered at his own hand as if he hadn't seen it before.

"How do you feel, Prastian?" I asked.

"Strange," he said sounding awed. "It's like having someone inside me with their cravings, thoughts, and feelings. It's amazing, yet scary. I'm—"

Prastian became quiet and his whole body froze. He didn't even blink.

I waved my hand in front of him and asked, "Are you all right?"

He didn't respond to me. I was about to reach out to his spirit to see if I had done something wrong, when Prastian leapt at me. He landed on top of me, slamming me to the ground.

Prastian lashed out with his fingers, slashing at my face, his own contorted in a vicious snarl. I summoned my magic to attack him, but stopped when I remembered who he was. I tried to get a hold on him, but he was so fast and strong and I didn't want to hurt my friend.

Behast and Jastillian seized Prastian, binding his arms in place. Prastian still struggled, snapping his teeth at them.

"What happened, Hellsfire?" Demay asked. "What did you do? What's happened to my brother?"

I touched the cut on my face, feeling fresh blood on it, and stared at Prastian. I leaned over him for a closer look, but when I did, it just agitated him more. "I'm not sure. He seemed fine a second ago."

I told the others to contain Prastian so he wouldn't squirm. I scooted over to him, placing my hand on his face. I forced open his eyes, peering into them. Through them, I reached out to Prastian's mana and saw his spirit deeply intertwined with the goblin's. That was good. That's what should have happened. The goblin spirit was overpowering the elf's, though. I sighed. I had no idea how to separate them without ending the spell or harming Prastian.

"Snap out of it!" Demay said, pushing me aside and shaking his brother.

Prastian didn't recognize him. He snapped his teeth snapped at Demay and struggled to break Jastillian and Behast's grip.

Demay slapped Prastian hard. The cracking sound rang in the small cave. Prastian ceased fighting. His frantic eyes settled onto Demay, and his pupils focused on his brother. "I'm all right now. You can let me go."

Jastillian and Behast glanced to me, and I nodded.

Prastian gave a small smile and brought his hand to his face where Demay had left a mark. "That was quite a slap you gave me."

Demay reached out and hugged him. "You needed it."

"I did. Thank you. Hellsfire, what happened to me? It felt as if she took control. I attacked because I recognized you all as a threat." Prastian paused and put a hand to his chest.

Behast shifted his body, getting ready to hold him again.

"It's all right," Prastian said. "Controlling her takes some...getting used to. You'll see. I *will* get used to it. We have to."

"Just let me know if anything at all changes," I said. "And if you feel any more outbreaks."

He nodded.

I exhaled and looked at everyone else. "Who's next?"

I was able to successfully perform the ritual on the rest of us. After each ritual, we were all on guard to see how the person would react. Everyone else's bodies seized up much like Prastian's did. Mine didn't. It could have been because I was a wizard, or even because I was human. Yet, I was bone-wearied.

By the time I was done, my head was throbbing and I could barely keep my eyes open. My chest tightened and I gasped for air. The room spun, and I couldn't stand, much less sit up. At least I had the goblin to keep me company, as strange as that sounds.

The goblin skin I wore no longer felt unnatural and weird. The flapping skin of the dead husk, which didn't even cover my ankles, was now part of me. The nauseating stench became my own scent and I was able to tell the difference between that scent and the others'.

As exhausted as I was, my goblin had lots of energy. He was a wild one. He wanted to roam the Wastelands now that he had returned. But underneath that excitement lurked pain. I didn't understand why. I drank a rejuvenation potion and rolled up in a corner, as I didn't have to take a watch. Even with the potion and the goblin's energy, I couldn't keep myself awake. With the second soul a part of me, I fell sound asleep.

I woke up refreshed the next morning, as the goblin's strength added to my own. He was just as eager to get on the way as I was. I needed his strength, because after performing all those rituals, there was no way in the Inferno I could go on without him. My magic wasn't strong, and I needed more time to recover. We left the empty bags of blood and departed from the cave.

As the days passed and our group inched our way closer to Masep, the number of Wasteland creatures increased even during the daytime. We were all alone. There were no signs of patrols from Alexandria, and we didn't expect them this deep into the Wastelands.

Jastillian didn't know of any more safe places, as we had reached the limits of his travels. We spent all our time outside, and we couldn't even make a campfire in case we attracted attention. Two of us were on guard at all times.

The good thing was that, with our new disguises, we didn't have to go out of our way to avoid other creatures, although Jastillian would steer us away when groups got too close. We all knew my magic was successful; we felt it. But when we looked at each other, we felt ridiculous.

Eventually, though, we ran into trouble and had nowhere to go.

A group of four loud humongous ogres stumbled our way from behind a rock cropping, cutting us off from our route. We didn't hear or see them coming until it was too late.

My heart nearly burst out of my chest, and I ached to scream. It wasn't because I was scared of the gigantic creatures. I had killed many before, but this time was different. The goblin smothered me with anxiety. I had to calm myself and not tremble because of him.

I glanced around, judging the ogres' distance from us and calculating how fast I could run northeast, deeper into the Wastelands where I would be safe with more of my kind. I shook my head. That wasn't right. This wasn't home. Home was in Northern Shala. With Krystal.

I stared at the others. They were having the same problem I was. Demay's left hand was shaking, and he grabbed it with his right to stop it. Behast snarled, drool dribbling down his chin, straining to attack. Prastian froze like a statue, his eyes glassy. Jastillian's lower lip quivered, and he couldn't even look at the ogres.

We needed to pull ourselves together. It didn't matter how big the ogres were or that they could kill and eat us without a thought. Then I remembered other goblins—friends—that had been slain by ogres, and I crumpled to the ground and put my hands to my head.

I clearly remembered hulking ogres ravaging goblins, pulling their limbs apart and smashing their heads in a frenzied bloodlust. My eyes widened as I thought of someone close—my lover? my wife?—no, *his* wife, dying. I was powerless as she was taken away from me and I—he ran away. Guilt and fear from that powerful memory threatened to overwhelm me.

I dug my feet into the ground. I wasn't going anywhere except to Masep. I had to make sure Alexandria would be forever safe from Premier. I had a duty both as a wizard and as someone who deeply cared for the princess.

I grasped my magic to soothe myself and him, but the goblin's panic and those flashbacks made it almost impossible. I rubbed my forehead and shook my head. I should have realized this was going to happen. Krystal was right. This spell was far too dangerous to be used. There was just not enough room in my body—or anybody's body—for two souls.

No matter how hard I thought or talked to myself, the goblin didn't understand that he was still dead and they couldn't hurt him. They could only hurt and kill me.

My friends broke the goblins' hold over their bodies, but their scared faces lacked the confidence and calmness I had seen them wear in battle so many times before. I was positive my own face was the same.

Since it took us too long to regain a modicum of control, the ogres had closed on us to where we could no longer run. We now had no choice but to fight, yet we couldn't get ready for it.

My friends couldn't free their weapons in time and my magic was unfocused. The goblins were too much to handle. My raging fire inside only fueled the terror. The goblin was as terrified of my magic as he was of the ogres. Our only saving grace was that the ogres didn't carry any visible weapons and the hunt wasn't in their eyes. It was like we were beneath their notice. My goblin was angry at that.

The leader of the pack stopped in front of Jastillian. He peered down, his large eyes settling on Jastillian, and I suppressed a shiver. He roared. We all jumped, and Demay tumbled and fell. Deep laughs came from the ogres. They pushed us aside and stumbled by. Their breath had a foul, tangy smell. I knew they were drunk, although it wasn't alcohol. Memories of a dark, thick, tar-like brew flashed in my mind. The same relieved look smoothed all of our grimy, blood-encrusted faces as the ogres departed the area.

It took us far longer to reach Masep than I liked, but it was necessary. We encountered more of the Wasteland creatures and we needed to learn to control our goblin spirits until we were no longer frightened of them. We were more at ease whenever we saw a group of goblins, but we had to contend with our spirits fighting to join them. When we passed by ogres and trolls, we avoided them, more out of our barely controlled fear than from them threatening to harm us. We still did our best to keep away from all large groups of creatures, so we ended up not traveling in a direct route to Masep.

The spirits took over at times. We couldn't fight them on everything. Even though the elves and I didn't eat meat, the spirits influenced us to consume things like grubs and worms, and we knew just where to find them too.

As time progressed and we reined the goblins in, they started to be helpful. They remembered caves to hide out in and places where ogres and trolls could be avoided. They were excited when they realized we were taking them to Masep. Whenever we talked about Premier, or even when I just thought about him, my goblin would clam up and I would shiver as if a cold knuckle ran down my spine.

I was able to keep my goblin under control by thinking about the princess and how warm and good she felt when she was cuddled up in my arms and pressed against my chest. She gave me strength even when we weren't together, and reminded me of what I had to do. I wanted to return to that and to her.

But it wasn't going to be easy. Renak's castle was going to be difficult to get into, even with the disguises. There was only one known way in and that was going to be guarded. We would be surrounded by thousands of Wasteland creatures, our bodies occupied by goblins we could barely control, and Premier would have to know I was coming for him.

According to my calculations, we still had a few days before Premier's power returned in full, and that was the only thing in our favor. But even a weakened Premier would be extremely dangerous.

CHAPTER 7

WE FINALLY ARRIVED at Masep. The five of us stood at the edge of a cliff, peering down into the place that was once the heart of Renak's operations during the War of the Wizards.

We were over five hundred feet above the ancient city. Masep was nestled into a huge crater with walls too steep to scale down. Small fissures had torn into the walls, creating gashes of jagged rocks. Steam leaked from those holes, blanketing the city in a low fog much like a morning's mist. Fifty feet away, at the south of the city, was the only visible way in. There was a dim light in and around Masep that seemed to have no clear source.

Other than that eerie light, darkness smothered this portion of the world like ash after a fire. Huge, black clouds hovered over the city. Lighting raced constantly through the clouds, and thunder cracked and boomed across the sky. The hair on my body stood on end as the magical power of the place brushed against my skin. So much energy buzzed in the air that even my friends felt it. The elves twitched their ears, and Jastillian turned his head as if sensing something.

I held my breath. It couldn't be Premier, could it? Could he be gathering in energy from the Wasteland creatures, using it to fuel his own? Could whatever dark secrets he'd unearthed from Renak have helped him restore his power? I tried to tap into the earth's mana. It was gone. Whatever disturbance I had felt near the border of Alexandria and the Wastelands was strongest here. It worried me that Premier might be behind all of this.

I shook my head. That couldn't be it. The magic was far too ancient and powerful for Premier to be responsible for. It was something else, something greater and more deadly than Premier. I hoped it was not something I'd have to deal with.

I followed the source of that power and found it underneath those dark, ominous clouds, at the far end of the city, at Renak's enormous tower. I had expected a castle much like the one in Alexandria, but the lone, rectangular tower was far more imposing against the bleak landscape.

A deep abyss surrounded the tower. There was only one stony walkway from the tower to the city, and it was blocked by a twenty foot gate. Guards stood at the entrance.

The tower had plenty of windows, but only a few still had shutters. One window had a broken shutter constantly flapping in the cool breeze. Gargoyles perched on the tower, the gray beasts watching the city. One gargoyle's head was missing. A few vultures circled over the city, but none of them dared to venture over Renak's tower.

I took a deep breath, knowing I'd have to see if my magic could permeate the building's defenses. If I could feel the magic from this distance, what would happen if I tried to directly access it with my own?

I had to find out if I aimed to go in there. I couldn't be like the vultures, afraid to venture near. The goblin in my head screamed for me not to use my magic, but I ignored him.

I summoned a tiny bit of mana, careful of Premier sensing me or the backlash from Renak's magic. I wanted to bypass the castle's magic and see if I could sense Premier. He could be anywhere in that building, but if he was gathering in magic, I would know. I closed my eyes, guiding my mana across the width of Masep. When I brushed up against the castle, the tower's magic surged and threw my own magic back at me. I yelped and bent over.

"Hellsfire, are you all right?" Demay asked.

I nodded, then put a finger to my mouth. I focused and used even less magic against the tower. It was like running my fingers over blades of grass, except that this grass would snap and bite my hands if I pushed hard enough.

My magic crawled against the tower, trying to be as unobtrusive as a summer's breeze. Even though the tower was physically decaying, the magical barrier Renak had created to keep his secrets was still strong after all these centuries. I couldn't get in.

I let go of my magic and gave up. We were going to have to go down there and get a closer look.

I stared down into the city below. Through that low fog, thousands of dark shapes scurried about. Trolls, ogres, and goblins stuck close to their respective races. With their gray, brown, and dark green skins, they looked like stones in a steam-filled bath. A vicious bath, as fights broke out wherever the colors clashed. We were going to have to navigate in those deadly waters.

I walked over to Jastillian and Prastian, who peered at the map taken from Alexandria's library. They chattered between themselves, looking down into the city and pointing. I told them I couldn't sense anything inside with my magic.

"That's all right," Prastian said, glancing up from the map. "We're having our own problems. The map is old and some of the buildings marked are gone."

"Aye," Jastillian said. "And what's left don't appear to be the same buildings as before." He leaned forward and squinted, using his superior eyesight in the dim conditions. "All I see are shanty towns and tents, and I doubt they contain the same things as they did before. This is just a small setback. We'll find a way in." Jastillian smiled and his eyes twinkled. "I can't wait to go into Masep and get inside that tower."

"You sound so...excited," Demay said, looking incredulous.

"We're about to do what no other has done in centuries. I've always wanted to come here. Think of all the information we can learn! And we'll be walking in history."

"No," I said. "We've got to be on guard." I glanced up at the black clouds, feeling the tingling magic stroking against my arms. They swirled with power. As Stradus once taught me, that power had to be used somewhere. "Something's wrong."

Jastillian crossed his arms. "I understand, but this is a once in a lifetime opportunity."

I nodded. "I agree. But let's make sure it's not our *last* opportunity."

"I can't see a way into the tower," Demay said.

"We need to get closer," Behast said. "And we need to do so without attracting attention."

"We have an idea," Demay said.

We all shifted our bodies toward him.

"Sorry. *I* have an idea." Demay clenched his fist so hard his hand paled, and he glared at the ground. "My goblin makes it feel like we're home. He wants to run off and be with others of his kind. It's getting harder to control."

The others nodded, but didn't meet each other's eyes. I also had a hard time controlling my goblin, but unlike the others, mine didn't want to run away to join his own kind. Mine wanted to run away from me whenever I used my magic. He was scared of my magic and of Premier. While he made it hard to control my own body, if I balanced it right, I could scare him into submission. But I also made it possible for his fear to overwhelm me.

"I say we let them," Demay said.

"What?" Behast asked.

"We give them control. We blend in and do as they would. We let them guide us into not making any mistakes. They've been here before, at least mine has."

"But there's only five of us," I said. "Without more, we're going to get into fights."

"Then let's find some," Behast said.

"It's not as easy as it sounds," Jastillian said, raising a finger. "It's a fair plan, but goblins won't allow just anyone to be in their group. They have different tribes. There are goblins with piercings in their bodies and others with cuts in their arms. We've shared the goblins' memories during the past few days; you know they were in their own group. It's how they were found and killed."

"Then what do we do?" I asked.

"We wait and watch."

"But we can't wait long," I said. "We've got to make it inside that tower before sundown."

"What happens then?" Prastian asked, looking back down at the creatures in the city.

"I'd just feel safer within the tower's walls then surrounded by thousands of these creatures at night." I glanced back at Renak's tower. "Not that we would be any safer in there."

We crept downhill, closer to the road leading to the gates of Masep, and hid behind a tumble of boulders, watching the unique cliques of creatures passing on their way into and out of the city. There seemed to be no guards—creatures were free to come and go as they pleased. The more I studied them, the more I could see the nuances to the creatures' appearances. It puzzled me at first, because I thought of them as nothing more than mindless animals—creatures I killed to protect Krystal and Alexandria.

A group of five trolls had iron bands wrapped around their forearms, while another group wore huge cloaks of goblin skins. That sight started my goblin spirit gibbering. Three ogres passed by, their ears and noses pierced, with a large piece of metal running from nose to ear. There didn't seem to be many goblins that were as plain and unadorned as we were. There were a few, but Jastillian thought it best we wait for a larger group.

"There!" Jastillian said. "That's our group!"

He pointed to a group of about thirty goblins. They didn't have any uniform marks and had a mish-mash of adornments, from piercings to scars. I didn't understand why he wanted to go with this group.

"But they're all different," Prastian said.

"Exactly. Some of the larger groups are together by force or by choice. If by choice, they're more apt to let others join their group. Remember, we must *act* like goblins. Be frightened of the other creatures, talk in a broken speech, and stay together. Allow our goblin spirits to guide us."

"But not too much," I said. "Don't let them take over."

They nodded in understanding.

We crossed the short distance and merged with the pack of goblins. A few turned a wary eye on us, but then returned to their conversations. The group looked exhausted. Deep bags were etched under their eyes, and scars and bruises covered their little bodies. Unlike most of the goblins we saw, these were armed with large swords, chipped from use, and wore dented battle armor.

The entrance to Masep slanted down into the city's bowl-like structure much like someone sticking their tongue out. Pieces of a once huge gate thrust out to greet us. The enormous hinges were rusted, and a large piece of broken wood swung from one side. Once through the gate, the shambles of a road became streets of broken stone. Just inside the city gates, the bottom half of a broken granite statue greeted us. I stared at its feet, reminded that Renak didn't just use these creatures to fight for him during the war.

Even though I had the goblin's memories and had overlooked the city from the cliff, Masep still wasn't what I expected. We followed the broken road, navigating the small camps populated by various creatures. They ate, chatted, and fought with each other. A group of four trolls huddled near a small campfire. A goblin fed her child a handful of grubs, and he greedily slurped them.

We strolled through their marketplace, gawking at the shops set up. They all looked eerily familiar. A lot of the stalls were constructed of nothing but rotted wood or scrap metal. The bigger and more popular ones, like the blacksmith's, were in the crumbled buildings that once housed Renak's people. We passed by an ogre roaring as he tried to get creatures to buy his roasted rats. A troll stonemason chiseled away hard rock, crafting clubs and other blunt weapons.

The creatures didn't purchase items with useless coin. They bartered with objects and food. They paid with entrails, the black blood dripping from their hands; scalps of human hair were traded, some even still attached to the top part of the head; wolf pelts were swapped; and the bigger creatures exchanged the swords and armor that wouldn't fit them, presumably from smaller creatures they had killed.

It shocked me that they were able to trade with one another and not fight and kill each other, despite small struggles breaking out all around us. At the stalls, they shouted and growled. They pointed their fingers, ogre and troll spittle flew everywhere, and goblins hopped up and down in anger. Even when the customers outnumbered the sellers, or were just bigger, they didn't kill them or even reach across and take what they wanted.

At the end of the market, we saw a strange sort of tavern. The sweet aroma of boiled blood seeped from it. The goblin inside of me was desperate to go and take a drink. My mouth watered at the thought of it.

I wiped the drool from my mouth and pushed away from the surrounding group of goblins. My feet sprinted me towards the tavern. Blood cravings seemed embedded into my mind, craving one last drink. I stopped and peered into the entrance. I patted my body, wondering what I was going to use to barter. I didn't have any meat.

My hands found a dagger. I pulled it out and gasped at how shiny and sharp it was. I couldn't remember where I got such a thing from. This was far too valuable to trade with. I could use it to kill more. I turned my head, seeing a small young ogre. If I could lure him away, I could kill him with this dagger. Fresh ogre eyes would do nicely and the rest I could keep for myself.

I had started stalking him when a large hand seized my shoulder.

"Hellsfire," he said.

Hellsfire? Who was Hellsfire? I gulped when I realized it was a dwarf. A dwarf wearing a goblin's skin! He befouled a goblin like one of those stupid ogres! I frantically glanced around. If a dwarf was here then those stupid humans could be here too. The others had to be warned. We had to—

Before I could raise my dagger, the dwarf grabbed my shoulders and shook me hard.

"Snap out of it!" he said, forcing me to look into his beady brown eyes. "Remember who you are, Hellsfire. You're a *wizard*."

My eyes widened. A wizard? I wasn't a wizard. I was a goblin and I was going to kill this dwarf and feed on him. Whatever was left of him, I could trade with and get that drink I craved.

I smacked his hands to free myself and lunged at him, aiming my dagger to bury it in his chest. The dwarf snatched my wrist and twisted it with his iron strength. I yelped in pain and dropped the dagger. I struck out with my free hand and went for his eyes. I didn't need the dagger. If I could wound him, then me and other goblins could kill him.

He snatched my hand and pulled, turning me around, my back facing him. "Snap out of it, lad," the dwarf said into my ear.

As much I tried, I couldn't break his grasp. I tried to ram the back of my head into his face, but he dodged it and yanked down on my hand. I squirmed in pain. Where were the others in my tribe? Why didn't they help me?

"Think of the princess," he said. "Remember her. Remember Krystal."

My back stiffened and I stopped struggling against him. "Krystal," I whispered. I wasn't a goblin. I was Hellsfire, a wizard. I summoned my inner fire to the surface and the goblin retreated in fear.

"Thank you, Jastillian," I said. "I'm all right now."

"You sure, lad?"

"Yes. You can let me go."

"Hurry. We've got to get back to the others."

We rushed back to the others and blended back in with the group of goblins. I apologized to them for what had happened.

"It's all right," Prastian said. "We understand. The control's getting harder to maintain." Prastian wiped the sweat from his cheek. "But we're almost there. We just need to hang on for a little bit longer."

I exhaled and focused on my fire and Krystal. I would get through this. I *had* to get through this.

We continued to use the large goblin group as cover. We had no idea where they were headed, but their direction took us closer to the tower. We knew we had to leave them at some point. Groups of four or five constantly split off, but others soon joined us. No one thought to question them.

"Stupid, ugly meanies," a new goblin next to us said, and snarled. "They think they better than us goblins. But soon we show them." He glowered at one of the trolls, but looked away when the troll roared back.

"You have problem with them?" Jastillian asked. The elves gave him a questioning look. They would have preferred silence, but Jastillian couldn't resist his curiosity.

"Of course!" the little goblin said, flailing his scrawny yet muscular arms. "Who not? In all attacks, we first to die cause there lots of us and they say we not smart or strong. But we never get weapons unless we steal or find or we lucky and he gives us. And we also food for others. Life no good. But we get revenge soon."

"In what way?"

"Come here," the goblin whispered. He grinned, exposing sharp, pointy teeth. We leaned in; the goblin spirit in me was equally curious. "We make big army and get weapons. We have goblin city and all tribes invited. You and friends come too. Take this." He handed Jastillian an old stone with strange markings on it. "Tell them great warrior, Kemek, sent you. You get in." His wide nostrils flared in pride.

"What's this?"

"Has password. We use rocks to spread word from tribe to tribe. You not read it?"

"Me not read."

"Me thought all goblins read our language even if they not read." Kemek shrugged. "It say…" He leaned in close and said something we couldn't understand in a high-pitched squeal.

"What?" Demay said.

"You not hear language either? You weird goblins." Kemek glared and sniffed us, keeping his hand on his sword. Jastillian didn't move as Kemek's nose came up to his beard. Kemek let go of his sword. "In this tongue, it mean as one, together, group. Like that. You say that and show stone and say me sent you. You get in. No problem."

"Where is it?" Prastian asked.

"It where sun falls and where half man holds sword." Kemek pointed northwest. "Where we were long time ago. Where we come from. It very far from here."

"Why you come here?" I asked. "To city."

"To get supplies and goblins for our city. Why else me come?"

"What about Premier?" Jastillian asked.

"Shhh," Kemek said, moving in quickly to cover Jastillian's mouth. "No say wizard's name. He hear us. If he discover goblin city, we dead. No hope for goblins. We can't fight magic men."

I raised my right eyebrow. Since Premier had the *Book of Shazul*, could he perform a spell like that, to hear his name when it was spoken in the city? Would he have enough power to do so? It would be such a focused and unobtrusive spell that it might be possible. Premier might know I was coming for him and be using such magic. We had to be careful against such a possibility.

I tried to access the goblin's memories about a secret goblin city. While the words Kemek said felt true, I couldn't remember any such thing. The goblin within not only wanted to learn more about this city, but ached to go there. I held him in check from asking questions, but just barely.

Jastillian struggled more with this as he palmed the rough stone in his hand, staring at the words. He opened his mouth but Prastian placed his hand on Jastillian's arm and shook his head. Jastillian put the stone in his pocket and nodded.

I wished we could learn more, because part of me worried that not all of the creatures were under Premier's control. This goblin city would have to have been formed long before Premier was weakened from his defeat. If the goblins were gathering, what was their purpose? And would they pose a threat to Alexandria? Krystal had to be told this.

We exited the marketplace and inched our way closer to the tower. The road to the tower was in better repair, but there were far fewer creatures on it. It was as if no one wanted to go near that place.

The goblins with us didn't intend to go to the tower. Instead, we crossed an open square, then cut through an alley. The goblin within was thankful that we weren't heading directly for the tower anymore. I had no idea where we were going, but we needed to break away. I glanced at the others, seeing the same worried expressions on their faces.

Kemek caught me staring up at the piece of the tower that peeked out from behind the buildings. He said, "Me know to stay away from magic. We tired of magic and big, stupid, ugly ogres and trolls." He growled and shrieked, "We want respect!" A chill went through my bones, and I growled with him. I shook my head and wiped away the spit dribbling from my chin. What was I doing?

"What wrong?" Jastillian asked Kemek.

"Me still mad. Many goblins die in great battle against smelly humans when fight human city."

"You heard about the battle then?" Demay asked.

"Yeah, me heard. Everyone heard about great battle. That also why me here. Don't care if others die, but why goblins?" We stopped and Kemek swiveled his head around, twitched his ears, and inhaled deeply with his long, pointy nose. "Me also heard rumor that more powerful magic man beat you-know-who. Didn't kill him, but wish he had. Tired of beatings on goblins and circle of death and all other things. No one seen ruler since battle. That why so much fighting lately."

"What's that?" Demay said, pointing to a creature no bigger than an oversized baby. It had moss-green skin, little wings, sharp claws, and a horn sticking out of its head. It briefly grinned at us.

"You not know what imps is?" Kemek asked. "Annoying creatures, but me still like better than ogres or trolls. Not wolves though. Hate big, ugly wolf packs. Imps steal and play jokes. Watch."

Four ogres stumbled out of a building, ducking their heads below the archway. They barked and laughed. On the roof above them sat a trio of imps. The leader of the ogres held out his polished club, and the others admired it. The imps swooped down and landed on the leader, who was easily ten times their size.

The three ogres surprised me by making no move to help their leader. Instead, they laughed at the little imps. Two of the imps grabbed at the ogre's eyes and face while the third dug into the pouch strapped across the ogre's body. The imp came away with a couple of eyeballs. He ducked the ogre's blow, climbed up the ogre, and hopped back on the roof. The ogre roared and glared at the imp. The imp stuck his tongue out before running away. The second imp followed suit, but the third one tripped on one of the ogre's massive boils as it scampered up his body.

The ogre seized that imp, squeezing him until his eyes bulged out and his head exploded. The ogre laughed out loud before taking a huge bite of the imp. He wiped the green, slimy blood from his face.

"Him slow imp," Kemek said. We all laughed with Kemek and my goblin spirit felt at ease.

A group of trolls lumbered up the road, shouldering between Demay, Behast, Kemek, and another goblin. He and his friends didn't care that we easily outnumbered them. They didn't even seem to notice we existed.

"Hey!" Demay said.

The troll stopped and dragged his massive square frame back towards us, his friends trailing him. He bent over until his disfigured face was within inches of Demay's. "Say something, little goblin?"

My companions shifted their goblin skins and reached for their weapons. My goblin spirit yelled to run. It was hard to resist him, but I dug my feet into the ground, preparing to back up my friend

Prastian nudged Demay.

"I didn't mean anything by it," Demay said.

"You sure talk funny for a goblin," the troll said. A low growl emanated from the troll. He sniffed around. "I should kill you for wasting my time."

"No!" Kemak said. "You leave goblin friend alone!"

The troll shifted his attention to Kemak, lurching over him. All surrounding noises stopped as eyes turned our way. "What did you say?"

"Me say you leave him alone." Kemek pushed the helm up his head, getting a better view of the troll. "You want fight, you fight Kemek!"

"You challenging *me*?" the troll asked. His eyes became blood-red and the veins in his square head and thick neck began to stick out, increasing to the size of small fingers.

I edged over to Jastillian and whispered, "What's going on?"

"A one-on-one battle, lad. That way, the fight won't get out of hand and involve the troll's friends and us goblins. While the trolls are bigger and stronger, we have numbers, and things could just as easily get nasty for them. Even if we lose, the winners will be weakened. Another pack might finish both of us off."

"I didn't know they had honor," Behast said.

"I don't know if it's honor, but they do have rules in their society," Jastillian said. "Keep still and whatever you do, don't interfere unless others interfere first."

"Yeah, me do!" Kemek said and yelled out a battle cry.

Kemek lunged toward the humongous troll, surprising him and toppling him to the ground. The troll got up and flung Kemek off him. Kemek landed on an imp and squashed him. Everyone formed a circle around them, yelling and cheering.

"Kill dumb troll!"

"Squash goblin! Squash goblin!"

"Kill each other!" an ogre said, and all the ogres standing around laughed. "And we'll eat you both!"

The troll seized the huge club hanging at his side and Kemek drew his battered, oversized sword. The troll swung his club, which was easily the size of Kemek. Instead of dodging, Kemek blocked the club with his sword, holding it at bay. No wonder his sword was so beat up. His two hands ground into the handle and his muscles pulsated.

I was surprised at Kemek's strength. I didn't know where he got it from, but his scrawny arms held their own. The two combatants growled and snarled, glaring into each other's eyes. The strain took its toll on little Kemek as the troll pumped more of his strength into his weapon. He was toying with Kemek, sporting a malicious grin as he did so. The goblin warrior looked like he was going to lose. How could a lone goblin stand up to a troll? My heart went out to him.

In a skillful move, Kemek stopped struggling and gave ground, allowing himself to slip under the massive club. The club whizzed by him, grazing against Kemek's helm. The troll stumbled forward and tripped. Kemek seized his chance. He ran behind the troll and hopped on his back. Kemek stabbed his sword through him, over and over again until the troll plummeted to the earth. The troll yelled in agony, the dark, thick blood flowing from his body.

The troll tried to use his long reach to swat Kemek off him, but it was futile. Kemek raised his sword, giving one mighty roar, and rammed his sword through the troll's neck. The troll fell limp. All of the surrounding goblins yelled in unison, including us. All the non-goblins turned their backs and dispersed. The trolls took one last look at their friend and left. The goblins all moved towards the carcass, diving on it like vultures.

"Well fought," Behast said, and nodded.

"Me show trolls that me mighty warrior! Me sore though." Kemek stretched his neck and rotated his arms. "You guys want first bite after me?" He pointed to the deceased troll and his mouth salivated.

"No, we ate already," I said. My stomach churned. Not only because of how gross it would have been to eat raw troll flesh, but because part of me wanted to dig in.

Kemek shrugged. The goblins around us had hungry eyes, but waited for Kemek to eat first. "We *all* great warriors in city, not just me. Like to see you there."

"Maybe you will," Jastillian said, stroking his dirty beard. "Maybe you will." By the way his eyes gleamed, I knew he would go one day.

Kemek turned and dove into his dead opponent. The other goblins followed suit. They savagely tore apart the troll, ripping chunks of flesh out of the wounds he'd suffered from Kemek. Some didn't even bother to tear the flesh apart, just used their sharp teeth to bite off pieces of the troll.

"We had better be on our way," Behast said, his face paling to a light green.

"And this time, please don't anger anyone else, Demay," Prastian said.

"Hey, it wasn't my fault. *He* bumped into *me.*"

We left the feeding frenzy and traversed the streets back toward the tower. We skittered up against the side of the old buildings, trying to avoid everyone. We didn't want to get into another fight. Without the larger group I felt exposed. Other groups that would have avoided the larger group, made it a point to force us out of the way. It was as if they craved another fight because they knew they could beat us.

We didn't merge with any other goblin groups, but began to shadow one group after another to make it less obvious there were only five of us. Slowly, we angled our way closer to the tower.

"That was an enlightening experience," Demay said.

"Enlightening?" Behast asked. "That's not what I would call it. I still wouldn't hesitate to kill a couple of them if the situation warranted it."

"Most of the goblins I've seen are cowardly and follow whoever's in charge," Jastillian said. "But Kemek and his band are different. I've got to go to that city the next time I go on an expedition. I'll need you to perform your ritual again."

"Are you sure? I have no interest in venturing deep into the Wastelands again. You'll be without my magic and you could lose control."

Jastillian peered into the distance. His tiny nose scrunched and he nodded. "I've thought about it and it's worth the risk. Just like it was worth coming here. If I die here or there, I will have seen and done what no other historian has." A huge grin was plastered on his face.

"If we survive this, I'll do what I can."

An imp peeked out from under a rusted scrap of metal. He cradled a small shard of it in his tiny hand. His neck stretched forward as his eyes ran over us.

"Why's he staring so intently at us?" Demay asked.

"Oh no," I said. "Imps aren't normally found near Alexandria, right?"

"No," Jastillian said.

"Then when Rebekah and the others got blood for us, I doubt they got any imp blood. Without any imp blood in the ritual—"

"That means they can see us!" Behast said.

The imp continued to stare at us, scratching his little horn. Soon, he dropped his mouth and shook his head. His hand trembled.

"You…you…you not goblins," he said in a high-pitched voice as he backed away. "You—"

Behast kicked the scrap metal aside and reached for the imp. The imp sliced Behast's hand with his shard of metal, but Behast just grunted and ignored the pain. He plucked the shard from the imp's hand and threw it away, lifting the little creature high into the air. The imp struggled, flailing his arms, but he couldn't break Behast's brute strength. Behast squeezed until the imp's tiny head popped off.

"That takes care of that," Behast said, throwing the imp's limp body away. A goblin picked up the body and took a bite. Behast tore off a piece of his tunic to wrap around his hand. "Let's avoid any imps and any other creatures that aren't located near Alexandria. We might run into something more…fierce."

I stopped and stared at the goblin munching on the imp, wondering if that was necessary. Meeting Kemek, hearing my goblin spirit within, and seeing Masep up close made me realize that the creatures lurking within the Wastelands were more than just monsters. They were people. Monstrous and very strange people, but still people. I had to remember that when I had a choice about killing them. I wanted to get back to Alexandria and tell Krystal of this. What would she think? She had been trained her whole life to think of them as the enemy.

We finally made our way to the tower, stopping twenty feet from the only visible entrance. We stood out, having nowhere to blend in. It stood alone, on a rocky island in the midst of an abyss, and none of the creatures dared to approach it. A spiky gate, twenty feet high, blocked the only pathway across. Two ogres and two wolves guarded it. With my wizard's sight, I could also see an eerie black, electrical energy emanating from the gate, designed to kill or injure those that would try to pass through uninvited.

Many magical secrets must be buried in the tower. While I was scared of what I would find in there, a part of me was also excited.

"I don't see another way in," Prastian said.

I shook my head. "Me neither, and the gates are fortified by enchantments. Looks like we're going to have to figure out a way to get past the guards."

The ogres were completely encased in shiny red armor with wicked spikes. It wasn't dented, worn, or rusted like the armor most of the creatures in the city wore. The ogres stood at attention, scanning the occasional creature that passed by. Their huge longswords were unsheathed, points resting on the ground in front of them. They kept both hands on the pommels, ready to attack at a moment's notice. The wolves, twice as big as normal dogs, were attached to metal posts with thick chains, long enough to allow them to cover all the ground in front of the gate. They barked and growled at everyone who came near.

I glanced up at one of the tower's open windows. Was Premier watching us even now from one of the shadowed alcoves? I looked back down, past the barking wolves and the ferocious ogres. I couldn't worry about that now. First, we had to get past these guards.

We were all quiet, trying to figure out how to get inside, as the low mist swirled around us. None of us could come up with any idea. It was getting late. I didn't want to be camped out here with no protection, surrounded by thousands of creatures under these black clouds. There had to be a way.

I clenched my fists and bit the inside of my lip, but it wasn't me who came up with a plan. It was the goblin.

His fear nearly made my knees buckle. A memory of him watching as a group of goblins were summoned and escorted into the tower flashed in my mind. He had worried that it was going to be him and his friends. Premier's voice had boomed from the tower. Two hours later, the whole of Masep was chilled into silence as Premier's pet ogre, Baal, hung the goblins from one of the windows. Their flayed bodies flapped in the wind, entrails dangling from their sliced abdominal cavities. They were meant to serve as an example of what befell those who displeased Premier.

I wrapped my arms around me, shivering from that memory. But the memory of Premier's disembodied voice emanating from the tower gave me an idea. I told the others of my plan and they agreed with it.

We shuffled up to the gates and kept our heads down. I took a deep breath, forcing myself to ignore the frantic yelling of my goblin spirit. He wanted me to sprint away as fast as I could. He thought the same thing would happen to him as had happened to those other goblins, even though he was dead. Goblins never went into the tower. Ogres, yes. Trolls, occasionally, but never goblins unless they did something horribly wrong.

I dragged my feet forward, remembering my duty. I summoned the wind and prepared to use a little trick Stradus had taught me. It wouldn't require much magic, so hopefully Premier wouldn't detect it. I recalled Premier's smug, arrogant, voice as clearly as I could. The memory made me dig my fingernails into my hand. I could never forget his voice, nor what he had done to Krystal, to Alexandria, and to Stradus.

"The little runts have come to die," one of the ogres said, bearing down on my friends with his sword raised. The ogres sported malicious grins.

Before the ogres or wolves could tear us apart, I bowed my head so no one could see my mouth, and muttered, "Let them pass." Everyone heard Premier's voice coming from the direction of the castle.

"Master?" the ogres asked. They lowered their swords, confused looks on their faces.

"Let them in and be quick about it!" I said, the voice booming along the stone bridge. The few creatures in the road stopped and gazed towards the castle. Gradually, the entire city fell into silence.

The ogres put aside their swords. It took their combined strength to open the gates, the hinges creaking loudly. They each grabbed one of the barking wolves, holding them back as we passed by. The wolves howled and snapped at us, their ears pressed against their heads. The spell I'd used had contained no wolf blood, and they could see and smell us as we really were. At least they couldn't communicate with the ogres. At least, I hoped they couldn't.

"We'll soon be seeing their bodies strung up for the vultures to eat," one of the ogres said, and laughed.

I took point as we prepared to cross the wide, ancient stone bridge, ready to scout for any other magical safeguards, and to be the first line of defense if Premier or another guard peered out of one of the windows and saw us coming. Before starting out on the stone bridge, I stomped down hard on it, concerned about how secure it was. It was wide enough to carry carriages, horses, and whatever other monsters Renak had dreamed up, but the bridge looked like it had lost its war with time. Cracks raced under our feet and the edges of the bridge had chipped and fallen away like someone had taken a chisel to it.

A wave of vertigo overcame me as I leaned over and examined the precipice underneath the bridge. The endless darkness at the bottom of the abyss wasn't an empty void. Great power beat like a heart. I extended my wizard senses to see if I could tell what it was. I couldn't. The only thing I knew was that it was intense. The sound called me and I swayed. I leaned farther out to get a better look, to understand it better, even though all I could see through the fog was blackness.

A firm hand seized my arm, pulling me back before I could fall over. "Are you all right?" Prastian asked.

I exhaled and put my fingers to my temples. "I'm fine." Although I wasn't. My head throbbed as the magic from beneath tugged at me.

I thought it might be a trap Premier had set, but the magic was far too ancient to be his doing. What I feared was that Premier could tap into that power.

We started over the bridge, which held despite the cracks and pits. The closer I got to the tower, the more residual energies came from it and caressed me. Would it harm me, like it had from the outskirts of the city when I tried to peek in? I glanced back at the ogres guarding the gates. There was no turning back now. We couldn't leave and none of us had found another way in. I clenched my fists and focused on the princess, trying to remain calm. The tower's magic crawled over me, and I braced myself for whatever might come.

Now that I was inside the gates, the magic didn't harm me, but it did open my eyes to what the tower really was—a focal point for magic such as I had never seen. It glowed. Waves of rainbow colors swelled over it. It was no longer a drab, black tower of death. It was beautiful, and even calmed and awed the goblin inside of me.

"Amazing," I said. The jewel-like shimmering light had me nearly in a trance. I couldn't stop staring at it, straining my neck to see its entirety.

"What do you see, Hellsfire?" Prastian asked.

Demay gulped. "Traps?"

"No," I whispered. "The tower. It's not as drab and gloomy as you might think. It's...beautiful. It's a shame you lack the eyes of a wizard."

They shook their heads, unable to grasp the unbelievable sight we walked into. I tried to focus. Even though it enthralled me, I had to be on guard against the ancient and powerful magic that hid inside. If the gate's enchantments were still active and the tower shone because of all the magic that was conducted here, what other enchantments could still be working?

Premier had access to all of that. He might not have his own power, but that might have made him more dangerous. I couldn't underestimate him. If only Stradus was still alive to help me. But because I had gotten Stradus killed, I had to be the magic against magic. Alone.

CHAPTER 8

COMPARED TO THE outside of the tower, the inside was dead and drab. The powerful, glaring residual magic I'd felt outside was no more. No Wasteland creatures were to be seen as we huddled near the entrance. We peered around, not moving more than a couple of steps from the doorway.

We stood on a tattered and faded carpet in a cavernous entry hall, with numerous openings off it. Wind howled through the empty corridors. The top half of a banner, high above our heads, had come loose from the wall and swayed back and forth. Sconces along the stone walls held half-burned candles, but they weren't lit. The little light in the room came through the windows, revealing tiny dust specks swirling through the air.

I ran my finger across a nearby wooden table. A thin film of dust coated it. This was unlike Premier. Back in his tower in Alexandria, Premier was unusually fastidious. Even when that bastard had dissected an ogre for displeasing him, he didn't make as big a mess as anyone else butchering an animal would have. If Premier had let the castle go to this extent, what did it mean?

According to Kemek, Premier hadn't been seen in a while, but he could be anywhere in this gigantic place. I stared into one of many empty, darkened corridors. He was here and he was hiding, but where?

"Can you elves hear anything?" Jastillian whispered.

Their ears twitched about and they cocked their heads from side to side. I held my breath for several tense moments. The elves shook their heads.

"I don't see anything either," Jastillian said.

The map from Alexandria's library may have been out of date, but the one from Stradus hopefully wasn't. It showed us that Renak's old throne room was near the top of the tower, and with any luck, Premier would be there.

My friends studied at the map, discussing any corridors and passageways where an ambush could lie in wait. Just because we didn't see any creatures right now, didn't mean that there weren't any hiding upstairs. I let them handle that; I had to pay attention to more than the conventional traps.

I extended my wizard senses, searching for any signs of magic, no matter how faint they were. I ran into a couple of problems.

There was a haze of magic lurking inside Renak's tower, lingering like background noise. Premier could use that to mask any spells until it was time to spring the traps.

Also, the more I listened, the louder grew the faint beating noise I had heard outside. It tugged on me, filling my very being. Even my friends' voices began to drown in it. I looked down at my feet, trying to see through the stone floor. Whatever it was, was down there, and very powerful. Could it be the nexus Demay had found reference to?

I had a hard time focusing on other, possibly more intrusive magic because of it. It worried me that Premier might be accessing all that power. Could it be a spell that he was working on right now? Or was it an enchantment worked into the very construction of the tower?

I told my friends about it, worried about where to start first. If Premier was in the middle of a ritual, he was probably below, at the source of the power, and we needed to stop him as soon as possible. If not, he was probably in the throne room.

Prastian said, "It's your decision, Hellsfire. We'll search in whichever direction you want to go first."

I glanced to the right, seeing a staircase that led upstairs, and then to the left, seeing one leading downstairs. If I made the wrong choice, it could be disastrous.

"We'll go up," I said. "The power feels too different from when I fought

Premier. It probably isn't him." I searched their faces, wondering if they would ask the question I feared. Would magic cast through an avatar be different than magic cast without one? They didn't ask, and I would find out.

Behast and Jastillian drew their weapons. Prastian and Demay restrung their bows and nocked arrows in them. I summoned my magic and took the lead as we ventured into the tower.

I scanned for any magical traps. Behast and Jastillian flanked my two sides. Demay and Prastian fell in behind.

We slowly crept our way through the tower in complete silence. In the hallways, unlit torches hung on the walls. As much as I wanted to, I didn't dare light them. But without them, the tall ceilings were lost in shadow. I worried that archers or other Wasteland monsters could lie above, waiting to entrap us. I let my magic senses guide me, while Jastillian used his heightened eyesight and the elves their powerful ears.

The silence in the tower bothered me more than anything else. I had gotten used to being in Alexandria with its bustle of guards, servants, and nobles. They rattled trays; they coughed, laughed, and joked; conversations were whispered, and swords and armor clanged as they walked. Here, it was dead quiet.

But it was far from empty.

It felt as if the tower's eyes were upon us, watching us every step of the way. I couldn't shake that feeling, no matter how many desolate rooms and empty corridors we searched. Every turned corner and every opened door, I expected something to jump out and attack us. Nothing did, but that feeling of being under observant eyes never left. I worried that it was Premier and that he had created a spell to watch us, but my bones knew it to be the ancient tower itself. We stalked the place in silence, but I didn't know if we were the hunter or the hunted.

Most of the rooms were stark and bare. There were so many rooms that Premier didn't need to use them all. We didn't see any signs that Wasteland creatures stayed here. From what we had learned, Premier preferred to keep them outside. He didn't care about the creatures; he only used them, the way one uses a knife for bread.

Down one of the hallways, we came upon a broken mirror. Shards of it littered the floor, and a tiny trickle of dried blood was stuck against the frame. Had someone been attacked here? Or had Premier destroyed it in a fit of temper?

We climbed five stories of stairs before reaching the top. I rubbed my hands against my aching thighs. According to the map, there were only a handful of rooms on the top floor. We gathered near the stairs. At the end of the long, darkened hallway were the closed double doors to Renak's old throne room. The torches weren't burning in this corridor either. If Premier was here, he would likely have lit them. But we had to make sure.

I closed my eyes and quieted my mind, digging past the residual magic of the tower and the beating magic at the bottom. I stared at the door at the end of the hall and felt it with my magical senses. Premier was there. His magic was very weak, weaker than the centuries-old magic in the tower, but I knew his magical signature. I had experienced it when he fought me and killed Stradus.

"He's there," I whispered, pointing down the corridor.

"Are you sure, lad?" Jastillian asked.

I nodded. I reached into my purse and fingered the binding potion. Premier wasn't going to do this peacefully or quietly. I needed one shot to throw the vial at him.

"Then let's go," Prastian said.

I continued leading the way. We searched the first three rooms, wary of any surprises. Those empty rooms didn't reassure us, and neither did the quiet. Sure enough, when we stepped in front of the fourth room, the torches along the walls exploded into flame. The magic was brief and ferocious, but it was enough to temporarily blind me. I stumbled, reaching out with my arms.

"Look out!" Behast yelled. He pulled on my robes, then pushed me out of the way. I slammed into the wall just as a granite club passed where I had been.

An ogre wearing full gold-tinted body armor rushed out of the open doorway and blocked our way. A helm masked his face, but from his size, I knew it could only be one ogre—Baal. The one who had carried out Premier's orders when he was preparing to attack Alexandria. He seemed to be the only creature Premier trusted. If the ferocious creatures outside knew Premier was weakened, they might attack him, but Baal was protecting him.

Prastian and Demay drew on the ogre and loosed their arrows. The metal-tipped heads pinged off the ogre's helm. They aimed once more, trying to find an opening in the ogre's armor. Baal didn't let them. He raised his club and attacked.

Jastillian and Behast recovered, blocking Baal's path and facing off with him. The pair of veteran warriors engaged the ogre, thrusting and parrying in a deadly dance. Because Behast was raised and trained by dwarves, the pair fought well together, never getting in the other's way. They tested the ogre's defenses, attempting to find an opening. Even though the ogre possessed superior brute strength, he didn't force it like most of his kind. Baal took his time, feeling out my friends' abilities. Behast and Jastillian tried to circle around Baal in the wide hallway. The ogre cut them off, using the stone wall and his huge club as stopping points. Prastian and Demay continued to shoot arrows, but they merely glanced off his armor.

I brought my mana to the surface, getting ready to use it on the ogre, when I saw the shimmering aura around the armor with my wizard's sight. I cursed. The armor was enchanted against magic.

"I can't use my magic against him," I said, lowering my fire-encased hand. "He's shielded against it."

"And we can't penetrate his armor," Prastian said, peering down his bow's sights. "He's too well protected. We're just wasting arrows."

"There must be something we can do," Demay said.

I stared at the ogre's armor. My magic couldn't get past it and the arrows needed to be precise to slip between the ogre's plating while he moved. Maybe if I combined the two?

"I have an idea," I said. "I'll guide your arrows so they'll get past Baal's defenses. Get ready."

The brothers nodded.

"Jastillian and Behast, move!" I bellowed. "Now!"

My elven companions let their strings go. Behast and Jastillian leapt out of the way as the arrows spun into the air and flew towards them. Time slowed as I focused on the arrows. I reached into the air mana, pulling it within me until I felt the hallway's air move. Each footstep, each body shift, each swing of the sword disturbed the air. I honed in on the air around the arrows, feeling the ripples of their flight. I tightened the wind around the arrows until I wrestled it under control, forcing them to go where I wanted.

Baal swatted one arrow, shattering the spell and the arrow. When his arm swirled to hit the other one, I spun it around. The arrow glided over his club and twirled down. I pushed, driving the arrow into the opening in the back of his knee where the plates were forced to part.

Baal howled in pain and black blood seeped from his wound. He backed off, dragging his right leg. Jastillian and Behast renewed their attack against their wounded opponent. Baal continued to fight, switching to a defensive stance. The ogre started to yield ground.

Prastian met my eyes, and I nodded. I drew in more wind as the elves loaded another arrow.

"Enough!" a voice yelled. Baal froze in place with his club held high. Jastillian and Behast stopped but didn't lower their weapons.

At the end of the hallway, the double doors were now opened. A figure clad in shadow-colored robes leaned against the partially open doors with both of his hands outstretched. He had his hood pulled over his face.

"Premier," I said, narrowing my eyes at him.

Prastian and Demay aimed their bows at Premier. The ogre stepped to the side, blocking our view with his massive frame, but giving Jastillian and Behast a clear shot at him.

"Baal, come." Premier turned around and disappeared back into the room. Baal followed on Premier's heels, never turning his back to us.

Prastian and Demay lowered their bows and we rushed to Jastillian and Behast.

"Are you both all right?" I asked.

Behast nodded.

"Fine, lad," Jastillian said. "How about you?"

"I'm all right." My shoulder was bruised from when I had slammed into the wall, but I pushed aside the pain, staring into the room where Premier had disappeared into. He had left the doors open. An invitation? Or a trap? "Be careful. We don't know what other surprises he may have for us. He might be weakened, but there's nothing more dangerous than wounded prey."

Before we entered Premier's chambers, we checked the last two rooms along the corridor lest any more surprises leap out at us. One of them contained crates. We looked inside one, seeing supplies of food. I led the way, cloaking myself in mana, readying myself to use it at a moment's notice. There was no longer any need for secrecy.

Just inside the room, we stopped. I let my magical senses search for any other hidden magic, keeping one eye on Premier.

Renak's throne room was stark, yet clean. A stone workbench stood off to the side, underneath one of two windows. Apparently Premier used this room for many purposes. The workbench was clear except for a pestle and grinding stone. Could Premier have been concocting a potion? He wouldn't need any magic for that.

There was also a small wooden table with a chair and a half-full glass of dirty water on it. At the end of the room was a smooth, marble throne. Premier slumped on the throne, not looking up at us as we approached. Baal stood at Premier's right hand. His helm and armor from his wounded leg sat on the floor next to his feet, along with his club. The arrow in his leg had been snapped off until only a tiny piece stuck out.

"I underestimated you, Hellsfire," Premier said, his voice rough and coarse. Labored breathing came from under his hood, but I still couldn't see his face. "I knew you would be coming, but I expected you to rally the troops, risking thousands of lives to finish me off. And you flying on your dragon like the stories of old. That would have been the heroically foolish thing to do."

I took a tentative step forward, struggling against the goblin spirit. He screamed at me not to go anywhere near Premier.

"Instead, you utilize a powerful and subtle spell to blend in with the creatures," Premier said. "I'm surprised and impressed."

I took another step forward and said, "I don't care about impressing you, Premier. I came here for a reason."

Premier ignored me and said, "But you didn't take everything into account." He lifted his head, revealing his face. The whites of his eyes shone against the red and black ridges of his face. His skin had been peeled back and scorched. All of his hair was gone.

"What happened to you?" I whispered. That couldn't have been me, could it? Could my spell have traveled through whatever had linked Premier and his avatar?

Premier narrowed his hate-filled eyes and smiled. "*I* control the Wasteland creatures, boy. *All* of them."

As soon as he said that, I realized my mistake. I tried to rip off my goblin skin to end the spell, but it was too late.

Premier expelled his stored-up magic. It burrowed its way into my soul, twisting itself around the goblin spirit. Premier seized the goblin, commanding him to freeze. I clutched my chest and fell over. My friends dropped their weapons and collapsed.

Premier leaned forward. "You shouldn't have come here, Hellsfire. After I kill you and your friends, Alexandria will fall. I will burn the city to the ground. I want you to remember that *you* were responsible for the princess's death. You left her all alone without any protection." Premier sat back and snapped his fingers in the air. "Baal, finish them."

The ogre heaved his heavy weapon. I struggled to break free from Premier's spell, but the goblin wouldn't allow me to. He was terrified and resigned to his fate, though sad that he had to obey Premier. He didn't want to. He didn't care for Krystal or Alexandria, but he hated the wizard's enslavement of his people.

No, I wasn't going to let this end here like this. I had to fight for Krystal and my friends.

My inner fire bloomed, brushing aside the goblin's compulsion to obey

Premier, its heat burning away his spell. Premier grunted as he tried to strengthen his spell. He couldn't. He *was* weakened and my magic began to overpower his. This must have taken the last of his power. I rose and faced him.

"Baal, finish him quickly!" Premier said, panic in his eyes.

Baal raised his gigantic club. I lifted my arm and shot out fire and wind, engulfing him. His enchanted armor protected him from most of it. The flames bounced off his armor, hitting his exposed head and leg. I aimed my attack toward his unprotected areas. He shrieked in pain, dropping the club and spinning away to the side. Baal smothered the flames from his head and leg and snarled. He glanced back down at the helm, knowing that if he could reach it, there would be nothing I could do to stop him before he killed me. Premier's spell still made it hard to react. It wasn't completely gone. I didn't have time to finish burning the spell.

I pointed my hand toward Premier. "Make a move and he dies."

Baal's eyes shifted toward Premier. Premier stared at me, seeing if I was lying. I wasn't. Premier sighed. "Enough, Baal."

I pumped more of my power into myself, letting the fire combat Premier's spell. I stood straight and flexed my hand. His hold on me vanished and the goblin was no longer scared of him, but of me. I reached out to Premier's magic and burned away the strands he used to immobilize my friends.

My friends broke free and picked up their weapons. I never took my eyes off Premier as I talked to my friends. "Are you all right?"

"We're fine," Jastillian said, stepping up next to me.

"What happened?" Behast asked, flanking my other side.

"He used his magic to control the goblins within us," I said. The magic I felt inside Premier was empty. "But he can't do it anymore." I narrowed my eyes at him. "He's powerless and weak."

Premier glared back at me. I wanted nothing more than to kill him. I didn't understand why Stradus wanted him to live. What part did Premier have to play? If only Stradus hadn't been dying, and had more time to explain to me. Premier had threatened to kill Krystal, he'd tried to kill me and my friends. The world would be a far better place without him in it.

I patted the binding potion in my purse. Taking his powers might not do any good. The knowledge the centuries-old wizard contained made him far more dangerous than a normal person. It was probably best that I bind him anyway, but first I had to get the book back.

"The time for disguises is over," I said.

Premier wheezed. "Agreed. The five of you look more ridiculous than I."

I kept my eyes on Premier. "Behast and Demay, please wait with me until the others break their spells, in case Premier tries something. Jastillian and Prastian, when you take your skins off, be careful. It's going to feel like the gods are ripping your soul to shreds."

Jastillian and Prastian peeled off their goblin coverings. The magic in the ritual exploded, shattering into stars only Premier and I could see. They howled in ferocious pain. The transparent goblin spirits burst from their chests until they separated. They floated back to the afterlife with glazed and empty faces. My friends leaned over, gasping for each breath.

When they recovered, my friends took their places to guard Premier and Baal. I shed my own goblin. My heart wrenched in pain. I toppled over and my teeth clenched while the sweat poured off me. Because I was a wizard and felt the magic more keenly, it was far more painful for me than my friends, and I screamed in agony. From the corner of my eye, I saw Premier reach within the sleeves of his wizard's robe.

He pulled out a small vial. I clenched my fist, trying to get a hold of myself and summon up my magic. I couldn't move. I had a hard enough time not convulsing in pain from the goblin's spirit being yanked free. Premier gave a smile of self-satisfaction before throwing the vial at the ground in front of me.

Jastillian and Demay pushed me away as the glass vial shattered. A gray smoke rose from it, covering the pair until it forced its way in through their noses and mouths. They clutched their necks, falling to the floor. Their bodies quaked. Before Baal or Premier could make a move, Behast blocked Baal's path and Prastian had an arrow pointed at Premier.

I finished ripping the skin from me. I stared at the transparent goblin spirit in front of me and I found myself thinking I was going to miss him. He'd taught me a lot about the goblins and the Wastelands, more than I ever thought possible. He waved goodbye before journeying back into the afterlife. A blinding light overtook him and he was gone.

I gagged, then retched from my own stench. Without the goblin's essence to influence my sense of smell, my grimy body reeked.

"Hellsfire!" Prastian said.

I rushed to Jastillian and Demay. Their bodies stopped quivering and I worried that they were dead. Slowly, their chests rose. I leaned in close and heard their shallow breathing. I placed my fingertips on their necks and their pulses were weak and fading.

I glared up at Premier. "What did you do to them?"

He stared at them intently and stroked his chin with his burned hand. "I'm not sure. That potion was designed to kill human wizards. I have no idea what the effects will be on a dwarf or elf, but it should be fascinating to watch."

I raced to Premier and my hand closed around his throat. My anger at what he had done flowed outward until the fire heated my hand. I squeezed, causing the closed wounds of Premier's throat to reopen. Premier struggled to move but I increased the pressure, my fingernails digging into his skin while I held him in place. Anger, then pain, radiated across his face. The aroma of burnt pork flooded my nose. He was going to pay for what he'd done to my friends, to Stradus, and to Alexandria. To the Inferno with Stradus's request. Premier deserved to die!

I released my fingers. Premier gagged for air. I needed information from him before I killed him.

Premier wheezed and coughed. He cleared his throat and rubbed it with his hand. "Wise decision, boy. If you had killed me, your friends would have died."

"They're not going to die?" Prastian asked.

"Not yet."

"Then cure them," I said. "Or I *will* kill you."

"You're going to kill me anyway."

He was right. After what he had just done, he had to die. I had already made that decision. But I had to make him believe I wasn't going to kill him. I had to do something I wasn't very good at—lie.

"I didn't come here to kill you, Premier," I said.

Premier cocked his head and stared at me for several long moments. He smirked and said, "I almost believe you."

"It's true. Stradus didn't want me to kill you. He wanted me to spare your miserable, wretched life, and in return, I want the *Book of Shazul*."

He gasped and recognition gleamed in his eyes. "You came here for the *book*?"

I nodded. "Save my friends and give me the book, and I'll let you live."

"Give me your word as a wizard, and I'll do what I can."

I glared at him. "Save them now or I'll kill you where you sit."

Premier's mouth pursed. He got off the throne and forced me aside. He bent down to Jastillian and Demay and opened their eyes. They were glazed and empty. Premier pried open their mouths and peeked inside. He leaned over to hear their breathing, then felt their foreheads with the back of his burnt hand.

Premier moaned as he moved his body back onto the throne, as if his bones ached. "Your friends are fine." He gave me a taunting smile. "For now. They're in a coma-like state, but after three days, they will die. I *can* cure them with another potion."

"Then do so," Prastian said.

"Why should I? You're going to kill me anyway, especially when I tell you I don't have the book."

I gasped, and my eyes widened. He didn't have the book? Impossible. This was a trick. It had to be. "Don't lie to me."

"I have no reason to lie to you."

I had no choice. I pulled out the dark blue vial from my purse and held it up. The dim light from the window gleamed off it. "Help my friends and tell me where it is now or I'll bind you. Then I'll throw you outside and feed you to the goblins, trolls, ogres, and wolves. I'm sure they would love to get their hands on you when they realize how powerless you are."

Premier slammed his hand on the throne. "I told you, I don't have it!"

"Then help my friends." I was going to have to search the tower after I bound or killed him. I couldn't trust him to be telling the truth.

"No. You'll kill me or bind me after I'm no further use to you."

"Then what do you want?" I asked.

He smiled. "Only one thing. I want the Great Barrier to come down. If you value your friends' lives, you will help me."

My breath vanished. *He* wanted me to help him bring down the barrier? How was such a thing even possible? I shook my head. I hadn't come here for that. I came to get the book back, and so far I'd failed and gotten my friends hurt in the process. I looked through the window, staring at the black clouds. Stradus would be disappointed in me, and so would Krystal and King Sharald. I'd let them all down.

"Bring down the barrier, Hellsfire," Premier said, "and you will find the book there."

"What is it doing there? Stradus said that you had the book."

"I did...once." He curled his hand into a fist. "It was deliberately stolen from me. I was ambushed!" His angry eyes glared past me and into the past. "I spent years trying to find a way into Southern Shala to retrieve the book and exact my revenge." He seemed to remember I was there and glanced up, his eyes meeting mine. "The book has a will of its own and digs into your soul and mind, boy. You don't want to go anywhere near it. It took me awhile to admit that the stories of Shazul's book were true." Premier sighed. "But bring down the barrier, and that's where you'll find the book."

"If such a thing were possible then why haven't *you* brought down the barrier?"

Premier's eyes were as cold as the White Mountain. "I haven't lived this long by being foolish. I'm a cautious wizard and to bring down the barrier will require more than caution, experience, or even power. It will require...will."

I clenched my teeth. I couldn't trust him, and I didn't even know what he was saying. Will? I glanced back at my friends' still bodies. They were dying. I didn't have anything to save them, and I didn't know what kind of potion Premier had used. If he could save them, I could deal with him afterward. I fingered the binding potion in my hand.

"You have my word, thrice times, as a wizard," Premier said. If a wizard gave a wizard's promise, they were bound to do what they said. If not, their powers would decay over time until that task was completed. "That I will save your friends *after* you bring down the Great Barrier." He gave me a crooked smile. "Assuming you survive. This is also for the good of Alexandria."

That caught my attention. "What do you mean?"

"You must have felt it when you entered the Wastelands. Renak's spell is drawing power from the land itself. It's dying, Hellsfire. Soon all of Northern Shala will look like this desolate place." Premier shook his head. "He was a fool for doing such a ritual in the first place." He smirked. "Stop this and the princess will love you for it. Otherwise, in a thousand years Northern Shala will be another wasteland, and it won't stop until it engulfs the entire land."

I ignored Premier and focused on Demay. The little elf was right. The barrier was the problem. Jastillian would be excited to learn that if he were still conscious. I still didn't know what to do. I looked to Prastian for advice. He stared back at me, giving me a subtle cue that it was my decision alone, even if it meant his brother's life. Premier couldn't be trusted, but I had no choice.

This wasn't what I wanted. Although I had known we could be killed coming here, it still hurt to see my friends in pain and on the verge of death because of me. I wanted to fulfill Stradus's wishes because the *Book of Shazul* was too dangerous to leave with Premier. What would another person do if they got their hands on it? Even if I brought the barrier down, Southern Shala was vast. I had no idea where to start. I could go to the Elemental Council, but they might not believe me. When Stradus had tried, they hadn't believed him either.

There was also Krystal and Alexandria. The land could start to heal itself and be restored. It might be too late for the Wastelands to be what they once were, but if I could stop the slow blight now, I should. I was a wizard and I had a duty to the land, to the people, and to magic. I stared at my motionless friends. And I had a duty to them. They trusted me enough to go with me on this foolish quest.

I remembered Stradus's words from the mountain. When he spoke of my destiny in Masep, I thought he meant it was about retrieving the book, but it might have to do with bringing down the Great Barrier. If I succeeded, I wouldn't have to worry about my destiny and could live my life as my own—as a man should.

My left cheek flexed and I ground my teeth. "I want your word that you'll cure them whether I fail or succeed."

Premier smirked. "Wise, boy. Very well. I will cure your friends even if you fail."

"And I want your word that you'll leave Alexandria alone. Now and forever."

Premier's icy stare bore into me, then he motioned to Demay and Jastillian. "You're willing to risk your friends' lives for her?"

"Yes," I said without hesitation.

Premier snorted. "Of course, you would. Very well, I give you my word as a wizard thrice times that I'll cure your friends if you attempt to bring the Great Barrier down and that I will leave Alexandria alone *if* you succeed."

"But—"

"Do not push me any further, Hellsfire. This is as far as I will bend."

I groaned, then remembered the potion. When this was over, I was going to use it on him. I couldn't unleash him into Southern Shala without some way of keeping him in check.

"Why do you even care about the barrier falling?" I asked. "You don't care about the land. You only care about yourself."

Premier shrugged. "True. I don't, but you do. Remember that. My reasons are none of your concern."

I nodded. "You have a deal. But cross me and—"

He waved his hand and gave me a disgusted look. "Enough with the threats, boy. You've made it perfectly clear." Premier clapped his hands. "Baal, show them to the empty room at the end of the hall. Take the dwarf and elf there, get them all some food and water, then dispose of these...things they wore. After that, I'm going to need you to get me some supplies." He smiled at me. "I have a potion to brew."

Baal bowed. "As you wish, Master."

The ogre picked up Demay and Jastillian and slung them across his broad shoulders. Prastian and Behast looked uneasy at the ogre carrying them. They lowered their weapons, but didn't put them away. Baal's heavy footsteps led us out of the throne room and to the room near the staircase. Baal gently laid the pair down, then left.

Prastian rushed over to Demay and checked his brother. "Do you think Premier will keep his word?"

"He has to if he values his magic and his life." I sighed and stared down at Demay. "I'm sorry about your brother. He and Jastillian saved my life."

Prastian put a hand up and shook his head. "We all knew the risks we took in coming here."

"How do you know Premier's not lying about the book?" Behast asked, his arms crossed. "We can't trust him, and I don't like this business of bringing down the Great Barrier. It's another trap. He could have done it himself if he desired."

I cracked my knuckles. "I know, but I have to save them."

"Are you sure you should bring down the barrier, even if it's possible?" Prastian asked.

I looked at Demay and Jastillian, "But what about—"

"You mustn't let their lives or our lives influence your decision. There's a bigger picture here. If you succeed, things will irrevocably be changed. People will see it as new opportunity for both sides. Opportunity that may end up in bloodshed. We have no idea what's waiting for us down there except that there's far more magic there than here. And there's still Alexandria."

"What about Alexandria?"

He looked at me with calm eyes. "This might ease things between Alexandria and the Wastelands. There may not even be a *need* for Alexandria. And what's a soldier without a war?"

I stared at my friend, letting his wise words sink into my head. Prastian was right. There were going to be so many repercussions no matter what I did. If I succeeded, the land would be forever changed. People would be allowed to finally go to where no other had gone in a thousand years. If I failed, Premier would return to Alexandria and destroy those who had beaten him.

I had no clue what to do. But I remembered how *wrong* the land felt. How it was dying beneath our feet and would blight all of Northern Shala given enough time.

I took a deep breath then said, "I have to do this. It's more than saving our friends' lives or even Alexandria. Premier wasn't lying about the land dying. If the barrier isn't brought down, all of Northern Shala will be turned into one giant wasteland. If you could feel what I feel, you would understand. I'm a wizard and I have a duty. If there's a chance I can correct Renak's mistake, I should."

Prastian gave me a small smile. "I may not be able to feel or do the things you do, but whatever you decide, I'll back you."

"We both will," Behast said.

I smiled. "Thank you, my friends." I reached into my purse and took out the binding potion. I handed it to Prastian and said, "You're the fastest out of all of us. I need you to use this when Premier tries something, whether I succeed or not. And he *will* try something."

Prastian nodded. "I'll keep my ears open."

"What are we to do with Demay and Jastillian?" Behast asked. "We can't take them with us and if we leave them here, more harm might befall them. Premier might have another one of his creatures take them hostage."

"We could hide them," I said. "In one of the other rooms or in another part of the tower."

"No," Prastian said, his voice firm. "We can't afford to lose them in the tower. We're not important to Premier. We'll just have to hope it stays that way."

"It's your call," I said.

Baal returned with some old blankets, stale bread, dirty water, and stiff rags. He placed the supplies down and turned to leave, but I stopped him.

"Why do you serve Premier, Baal?" I asked. Having gotten to know goblins during our journey here, I wanted to know more about the ogres Premier favored. There might also be a chance to turn him to our side. "He doesn't treat you well."

The large ogre paused, considering this. "My master isn't bad," he said in a deep voice. "He keeps me well fed and away from the fighting outside." He shrugged his massive shoulders. "I have no choice."

"Premier's powerless. You have a choice now."

"I'd be the first ogre in a long time to have one," he said and left.

We cleaned ourselves up, trying our best to get rid of the stench, dried blood, and slime that permeated our clothes and skin. We even cleaned up Jastillian and Demay. We all needed a bath, but it would do. We ate and while little was said, there was a current of nervousness running through the room—far more than what we'd felt in coming to the Wastelands.

We left the door to the room open so we could see into the hallway. We rotated guard watch in case Premier tried something.

I was thankful when my turn at watch came. I could barely get any sleep, thinking of Premier. Premier might finally acknowledge that I was a wizard, but I would never be considered his equal. By him or by me. He had centuries of experience and controlled the Wasteland creatures. I was still finding my way. I only believed him about the Great Barrier and possibly bringing it down because of what my friends had said earlier, and from what I experienced when I touched the land. But there was something Premier wasn't telling me. With his power and experience, if he wanted to, he could have already brought down the barrier.

Since I was in the tower, the power thrumming through me was getting harder and harder to ignore. I didn't know if the source of it was danger or a warning. I couldn't investigate because I still had to worry about my friends and Premier. Knowing Premier, he would lead me right to it.

I had no idea what was in store for me or how I was going to bring down the Great Barrier, but I knew I had to do it for my friends and for Krystal.

CHAPTER 9

WE WANTED TO wake up before Premier, but he beat us to it and came early the next day. Baal had taken off his armor and didn't have his club. He wore tattered brown rags with his wounded leg wrapped in one of them. That eased my apprehensions slightly, as I didn't have to worry about Baal attacking us and being shielded from my magic. But as I stared at his monstrous size, I realized he didn't need those things. The ogre was a formidable opponent on his own.

Premier's eyes gleamed as he stood near the doorway of our room, waiting for us to get ready. He had an eagerness about him. I couldn't tell if it was from the fact that I could possibly bring down the Great Barrier, or more that I would be out of his way and possibly get killed.

"I hope you're ready, Hellsfire," Premier said, clasping his bare hands together. "It's going to be a big day for you."

"Where's the potion?" I asked, trying to stifle a yawn.

"It'll be a day or two before it's ready."

"My friends could die in a day or two."

Premier sported a malicious smile. "Then you'd better not dally."

I grimaced, but he was right.

My friends and I made sure the slumbering Jastillian and Demay were comfortable, draping blankets over the pale pair.

Prastian bent over Demay and said, "We'll be back, little brother. Stay safe."

We left the room and closed the door. Premier shuffled along, leading us deeper into the depths of the tower. Baal limped alongside Premier, holding the torch. My friends and I walked behind them.

Although most of the tower rooms had windows, there were none in the corridors. In the light of Baal's torch , shadow monsters crawled on the walls, preying upon us.

As we descended lower, things worsened. In the distance, I could hear the sounds of metal chains dragged across the stone floor. My back stiffened, wondering if I was imagining things. I glanced at my friends, but they didn't seem to hear anything wrong, even with their elven hearing.

I shook my head and we continued our descent. When we passed by one level, an overpowering stench whisked past my nose. I covered my mouth and gagged, nearly hurling the contents of my stomach on the floor.

"Hellsfire, are you all right?" Prastian asked.

I peered up at him. "You don't smell that?"

"No, what—"

"What's that?" Behast asked, drawing his sword.

"There's nothing here," Premier said.

"Don't lie to me. I hear something." His ears twitched and he stared toward the end of a branching hallway.

I leaned forward, looking at Prastian for confirmation. He subtly shook his head. Suddenly, his ears perked up. I was about to ask him what he heard when the sound of a whispered conversation dug itself into my mind. The sound grew louder, and I spun around, trying to pinpoint where it came from. Prastian freed his sword, and I summoned my magic.

Premier chuckled at all of us. "You don't understand."

"What is it, Premier?" I asked, glaring at him.

He stared at me for several seconds, then looked away. "Very well. When I first arrived at this place, the tower was alive—still is. You've seen its magical aura, I'm sure. Some might say this place is haunted by magic and memories of a depraved era and a foolish war. Even you elves must have felt it—the sensation that you're constantly being watched. The deeper we journey into the tower, the stronger, it'll become."

Premier paused before speaking again. "Ignore what your ears, nose, and eyes show you. They can deceive you. But be warned, not everything in this place is shadows and dust."

"What else is there?" Prastian asked.

"There are things left over from the War of the Wizards, little elf. Terrible things. Things *I* never would have thought of." Premier rubbed his temples. "I remember when I first arrived here. I found a hidden and locked room, more of a prison cell. When I broke it open I found a disgusting lump of meat, or what I thought was meat, though there were no insects crawling over it, which I thought was odd. When I came closer, the pile of meat rose.

"Its body twisted as it grew, bones snapping into place until it was a hunched creature in the shape of a man. It reached out with its arms, dragging its body towards me. It was immune to any magic I cast, nor could I control it as I do the Wasteland creatures."

"How did you defeat it?" I asked.

Premier stopped and turned to face us. The torch's flames danced across his face. "Who said I did?"

Premier resumed leading us. "Let's not dally anymore, and cease your incessant tongues. Or you may attract unwanted attention."

We continued our trek in silence, traveling throughout the gloomy, haunted tower. The closer we got to the bottom, the more the powerful magic called out to me, its beating worming its way into my mind. I closed my eyes, trying to drown out the drum-like noise. I couldn't.

I put my fingers to my forehead and performed a practice exercise. I focused on my inner fire, letting it burn bright. The fire's crackling noise succeeded in driving back the noise, but only a little. The raging drums became a soft roar.

Were we going to that place? Was that where the nexus was? Was that the reason why the Great Barrier was still up? Nexuses weren't supposed to be like that, but I had never heard of one powering such a potent enchantment.

With each passing floor, the pain sensation worsened. I stumbled and crashed into a brick wall, barely stopping myself from falling over. Blood dripped from my nose.

"Hellsfire, are you all right?" Prastian said.

I wiped away the blood and stood up straight. "I'm fine." I stared at Premier. Why wasn't he having the same problems I was? I didn't expect the others to feel anything because they weren't wizards, but Premier was. Was he just used to it, or could he not feel it because of his lack of magic?

"Premier, where are we going?" I asked, stopping as we got to another staircase.

"Don't worry, we're almost there. Just a few more floors to go."

"No, now!"

He turned around and gave me that cold, impatient stare of his. I was getting tired of that look. His eyes widened when he stared at me. "What's wrong with you?"

"I don't know. Where are we going?"

"To the nexus."

"*The* Nexus of the Wastelands?"

He nodded.

"Why do I feel this way?" I narrowed my eyes at him, because my vision was starting to blur.

He cocked his head. "I...don't know. That's never happened to me. Maybe we can sort this out when we arrive, if you think you can manage it."

"I can if you hurry."

Three more floors and we finally reached the bottom of the tower, deep underground. Near the staircase was a heavy stone double door that could easily fit a giant—if any of them still existed. Protection wards crawled over the doors, their glistening shine reflecting like a bubble.

"This is it," Premier said, patting his burnt hand on the door as if it were a pet.

I peered up at the door. The beating sound in my head grew louder and I could barely stand or see straight.

Baal didn't hesitate, moving to open the heavy door. I studied him to see what the wards did to him. He grimaced, but I couldn't tell if it was from the wards or the weight of the door.

When Baal opened the door, an intense light blinded me, and I lifted my hand to cover my eyes. The power and warmth radiating from it was overwhelming, crushing my spirit. In a strange way, it also comforted me. The noise I had been hearing from outside the castle ceased. The light lifted it. This was it. This was what I was meant to find.

Premier smiled, amusement on his scarred face. "This is the nexus of the entire Wastelands, the reason why Renak settled down and built his stronghold here." He motioned with his hands. "Come, let us get a closer look."

"Wait." I stared at the wards they couldn't see. "What about the protection wards?"

Premier stepped inside the bright room. "They're perfectly harmless. See?"

I looked at Baal, seeing that he didn't join his master. I had a hard time reading his face, but he seemed hesitant, as if he were waiting for something.

"The wards are there for a reason," I said.

Premier cocked his head, then smiled. "Very well. I was just seeing if you were paying attention. These wards are harmless...to you and I. This chamber was designed for only wizards to enter."

"Why not others?"

"That's what you are going to find out."

I stared at Baal, remembering his hesitation about entering. "Can others enter?" It would be safer for my friends if they were out here, but I needed them to back me up when Premier made his move. And Prastian was the one with the binding potion.

"Yes, it's possible for them to enter with a simple protection spell that I can teach you." Premier sighed and shook his head. "When are you going to realize that you're a *wizard* and you're better than these lesser beings?"

"I wouldn't have beaten you and your army or gotten here without these so-called lesser beings."

Premier smirked. "You must not rely upon them. They are a weakness of yours. Elves and dwarves live longer than humans, but they will still die before you do." He smiled. "Unless, of course, I kill you first."

"Just show me."

Premier taught me the incantation to counteract the wards' barrier. I memorized the spell and performed it on Baal first. Stars of energy sprang from my fingertips and showered him, a protective, magical layer solidifying around him.

"Go," I said to Baal.

He looked to Premier and only moved when Premier gave a nod. The ogre went into the bright room, and the wards reached out to him. The bright light grazed him, but because of my spell, it didn't touch him. The wards curved around his body, encompassing him in a thin aura. I waited a few moments, but nothing happened.

I hurried and performed the spell on my friends. Together, we went in. The wards reacted to me, stretching from the door, twisting and weaving through the air. I lifted a hand and let them caress my finger. A soft sensation overwhelmed me, but it didn't threaten or harm me.

In the center of the large chamber, a huge diamond-shaped beacon of light glowed and hovered.

"Amazing," I whispered, staring at it. "So this is what I felt outside the tower."

Premier turned away from the nexus and stared at me, studying me with those intent eyes of his.

I ignored his gaze and focused on the nexus. Each time it pulsated, I felt the small piece of sun illuminating me with its warmth and power. It hypnotized me and I slowly reached out to it, wanting to take its essence to my very core.

"Baal!" Premier said.

Before my friends could react, the ogre wrapped his arms around me and lifted me into the air, stopping me from going inside. My feet hovered above the floor.

"Let go of me," I said, drawing in magic. Now that he was without his armor, I could strike back at him with as much force as I wanted to.

"You fool," Premier said, motioning for Baal to drop me. "Wizards should be more careful, Hellsfire. Stradus should have taught you that."

"He did."

"Let me explain before you let your impulses and the power of the nexus over take you again. I've found one of Renak's old journals, and through the tattered and faded pages, it told that many people have gone into the nexus, but few have returned. Those that have returned were either crazy, or an empty vessel." He pointed to the light. "And it's in there *you* will have to go, Hellsfire."

"Coward," Behast said, his muscular arms crossed over his chest. He never took his small eyes off of Premier. "You don't even go in there yourself."

Premier chuckled. "Hellsfire aside, wizards don't rush headfirst into things they don't understand. And you need to understand what the nexus is."

I relaxed my clenched hand. He was right. As much as I wanted him to hurry up for the sake of Jastillian and Demay, it was required of me to comprehend the Wasteland Nexus, and I could only do that with Premier's help.

"I didn't know you could go into a nexus," I said. "I thought it was just a focal point of magical power in a given area."

"It is, but it's also much more than that. This one goes somewhere."

"Where?"

"That is the one question I cannot answer." Premier paced around the bright nexus. "The answer might have been in the pages that were missing, or Renak might have left it out altogether." I couldn't tell if Premier deliberately held back information, or if what he spoke of was true.

"How do you know this nexus has anything to do with the Great Barrier?"

"Finally, you're starting to ask the right questions." Premier smiled. "The journal also spoke of it. If your historian were here, he would tell you of the theories surrounding the construction of the Great Barrier. This is the only one that's correct."

"What's inside?"

He shook his head. "I've never been in there and before I discovered Renak's journal, I didn't think it was possible. All nexuses may end up in the same place, or this may be unique. You may be in there for hours or days."

"Days? I don't have days. My friends are dying."

A sly smile played across Premier's face. "Then I'd hurry if I were you."

I walked over to Prastian and Behast, who guarded the door. They were as far away from the nexus as possible.

"You have until the end of the week before Premier's powers return," I said. "Keep that in mind."

"We will," Behast said. "Come out alive."

My eyes met Prastian's. "You know what to do."

He nodded. "Be careful, Hellsfire."

"You too. You have far more to worry about than I." I glanced at Premier from the corners of my eyes. I wished I had something more to give them.

I left them and went back to the nexus. I stared into it without blinking, wondering what I would find inside.

"Premier," I said in a sharp voice, never looking at him. "Remember your promise."

"Your friends will be cured. I gave you my word on that. As for your precious princess, you had better succeed." Premier flexed his magic. It wasn't much, but it was there and it was strengthening. "Otherwise, I'll give her my regards."

I bestowed an icy glare upon him as my fire magic bubbled to the surface. The flames encompassing my hand ached to destroy him. I could have killed Premier now. He was no use to me anymore in bringing down the Great Barrier, but if I killed him, my friends would die.

I secured my purse's strap and took a deep breath, forcing the flames aside. Premier might not have any honor, but I did. This would be settled between us after I returned from the nexus. And I *would* return. Nothing was going to stop me from seeing Krystal again.

I stepped into the light, not knowing where it would take me.

CHAPTER 10

CHILLS COURSED THROUGH my body, rippling it with goose bumps. My skin burned red and the pressure against my head made it feel as if it were about to explode. I gasped for breath, the air escaping my lungs. Each of the six elements of magic surged through me.

To combat the sensation, I conjured my magic to encompass me. It grounded me from the nexus's onslaught with its tremendous strength, shielding me against the harsh rain of magic. I pushed against the spell of the nexus, my fire burning bright. I was able to breathe again and my head lightened.

The nexus opposed me, assaulting me with its power. Its barriers lashed against my fire, attempting to extinguish it. My magic strained as if I were trying to move a mountain. The nexus's barrier held fast and firm. My anger fueled my fire until I became a shooting star, shattering the nexus's barrier.

As I passed through, I collapsed and blacked out.

I found myself lying on the ground, and struggled to open my eyes. There was fog all around me, lit with a dim blue light. I groaned and forced myself up on wobbly legs, head spinning. I glanced around, trying to find my bearings, but I could barely see past the encompassing fog.

I stared at the ground beneath my feet. It reminded me of the Wastelands, hard and dry. I kicked until a chunk gave way. I bent over and grabbed it. It was rough and coarse, and lacked the freshness of fertile earth, nor did it contain bugs, worms, or any sign of life. I threw the piece of dirt away. This wasn't real.

I waved my arm up and down. Afterimages of it hovered, and I remembered. I was in the Nexus of the Wastelands and I was here to make sure Premier cured my friends, to help Northern Shala, and bring down the Great Barrier. But first I had to figure out how.

I summoned air to part the fog. But when I touched my magic, that was when the nexus greeted me. That was when *he* greeted me.

"Welcome," an eerie and familiar voice said, coming from the surrounding mist. "I've been expecting you."

"Who are you and what do you want?" I asked.

His laughter rang in my head. I spun in confusion, looking for something tangible to fight.

"You can't comprehend what I want or what I represent," he said.

A low growl erupted from my throat. I grew tired of people underestimating me. I was a wizard now. My hands reached out and flame flared through the thick fog, melting it away. A circle of fire burned around me, protecting me as it always would.

The mist didn't cross the streams of fire. It coalesced and drew into itself, revealing a bleak landscape beyond. Barren brown layered over monstrous mountains in the distance. The blue light never revealed its source. If there was one, it hid much like the sun at day's end.

The mist grew thicker and darker. It rose, growing limbs and legs so it could take a human shape as tall as me. Its density grew until I could no longer see through it. Burning red and orange flames ignited in its eyes. Bones materialized, then muscles and flesh emerged. Black wizard's robes sprang from nowhere, and the form became solid and real. He had his hood up. I summoned my magic, ready to battle him as I peered into his fiery eyes.

The shadowy figure stepped through the burning flames surrounding me. He stopped no more than five feet from me. I flinched as he pulled back his hood and his eyes lost their fire. It was me.

"Don't be so surprised, Hellsfire," the doppelganger said. He even had my deep voice.

"Impossible."

"It has been many centuries since a wizard last came here. None have survived. I wonder, will you be any different?"

"What are you going to do to me?" I asked.

"I would never do anything to harm myself." He laughed. What disturbed me was that it was so malicious. I'd never laughed like that. He soon stopped himself and focused his brown eyes on me. "I do like your name, Hellsfire. It's very inventive. I wonder how accurate it is, though?"

This was the second time he'd said my name. How did he know so much about me while I knew so little about him? I had to think. I focused not on my breathing but on his. How real was he? The fire around us died and disappeared. My muscles loosened and I reached out into the nexus and whatever stood next to me.

I expected a life force, a trace of mana, a soul, anything. I got nothing. He was as hollow as a drum. It reminded me of when I first met Premier, when he used an avatar to fool all of Alexandria.

My lips tightened and I said, "You're not me. You're nothing."

"Excuse me?"

"I said you're not me. I can sense that whatever you are, you are *not* me."

"Very good," he said. I stared at the evil reflection, trying to remember that it was not who I was or would be. "I'm not you. I'm the ghostly essence of a wizard who once ruled the lands—a man of unequaled skill. I'm the one who raised this very tower, the one responsible for the Great Barrier, and the one who has forever changed the lands. I am—"

"Renak!" I took a step back.

This couldn't be possible. He was dead. Dead! He had been gone for a thousand years. Shala had defeated him in the final battle. I stared at the phantom. If there was one wizard I was afraid of, it would be Renak. This ghost could have knowledge of that and use it against me.

"You're not Renak," I said. "He's dead."

The phantom's eyes flashed. "It's immaterial. Believe what you wish."

It didn't matter who he was. If I had to fight this ghost, I would soon know if he was Renak or not. It would explain why no one had brought down the barrier.

Renak weighed me with an intimidating gaze. His eyes and body didn't waver. He stood straight with his head held high, reminding me of King Furlong, Krystal, and others who ruled. Yet I knew I had never looked that way.

I reached out to my magic, cloaking myself in it. No matter who or what he was, I wasn't going to back down from him. I had to help my friends and Northern Shala. I couldn't let anything or anyone stand in my way.

"I don't care if you truly are Renak, you're not going to stop me from getting what I want," I said. My body tensed. We stared each other down. I wasn't going to make the first move.

Renak smirked and folded his arms inside his robes. His eyes shone. "Believe me, I am and I will."

I shook my head. "You're not Renak. He died centuries ago."

Renak nodded. "True, but like all magic, the Great Barrier required a cost. I was it. A part of my essence was to remain here. Renak wasn't at his best when he fought Shala."

"Why would he do such a thing? He had a war to fight."

"All questions must be submitted in writing," he said in a hushed tone. Renak allowed himself a small smile. For a moment, I forgot who he was and grinned back. The warmth on his face vanished, replaced by a deep pain.

"My heart was already gone," he said. "What did it matter if I was to lose a part of my soul and be trapped here?"

"What happened?" I asked.

"I lost the shine of life, my wife."

I didn't say anything. That would be terrible. It hadn't even occurred to me that he might have had a wife. The stories never mentioned her. Did he have a son, daughter, a best friend? All I knew was the wizard Renak from the stories I had heard growing up, but he was also once a man.

The emotion in his face disappeared and Renak became stoic. "But enough of the past. I'm glad to finally see a wizard again. It's always interesting to see how well a wizard fares when he sees his own soul."

"Soul?"

Renak raised his right eyebrow like I would. "Did you expect to fight a monster? Monsters can be defeated, lands conquered, armies destroyed, and enemies killed, but the true question is, can one stand against himself?"

"It can be done, Renak."

"Everyone eventually breaks. You just have to know how to break them, and that is how I designed this place. I am the guardian of the Wasteland Nexus. I was left here not only to ensure the Great Barrier rose and stayed, but also to see it fall." He cocked his head and stared at me. "I wonder, are you the one?"

Renak swept his arms and beamed like a parent proud of his child. "The nexus feeds off a person's fears and desires, their wishes and dreams. Everyone falls to those sooner or later. After all, everyone who comes through is only a mortal. Can you name me someone who's been able to stand against all of that?"

I said nothing, racing through my memories. I thought of the people who were closest to me: my mother, Stradus, Krystal, Cynder, Prastian, Jastillian. They were each strong and had been through their own trials, but I wasn't sure if any of them could qualify at the scale Renak meant. But there was one heroic person who came into my mind. One person who I aspired to be like now that I was a wizard.

"Shala," I said, my voice a whisper. "Shala did, otherwise how could he have beaten you?"

Renak glared at me. His eyes burned bright with fire, despite the cold stare he unleashed. The embers within danced with anger. "What do you know, foolish boy? You weren't there. History has been unkind to me. If only people knew why I did the things I did, maybe I would be considered the hero. But they never understood.

"*I* was the one who brought peace to what you call Northern Shala. The area was a lawless, savage, and harsh land until I came. I did what no other could or would not even the precious council."

"A peace without freedom," I said. "is no peace at all."

Renak opened his mouth to reply, but then thought better of it. The fire in his eyes extinguished and sadness overtook them. "What do you know? You're young. You know nothing of what awaits or what took place before. You know little even of the power you possess. Your limited view of the world may yet be your undoing."

He smoothed his black robes. "But we don't have time for this. Are you ready, Hellsfire?"

I cleared my throat, barely getting the word out. "Yes."

"If you succeed, you may be considered the hero I never was." Renak grinned in joyful anticipation as he approached me. "Then again, you may bring a far worse fate to your land."

"What do you—"

Before I could finish, he waved his transparent hand through my head.

I screamed in nauseating pain. My brain and soul exploded as they were pulled from my body. Incoherent memories raced through my head and my mind spun in a whirlwind.

All the while, Renak laughed and laughed.

CHAPTER 11

I VOMITED WHEN I came to. I wiped my mouth and stood up. How long was I out? Were the others in trouble? Did Premier get his power back? I expected to see Renak and my own mocking face, but I was alone again.

I gasped when I realized where I was. I was near my home town of Sedah. The pond outside it rippled with a cool breeze. A small forest encircled me, blocking the day's sun. The ground beneath my feet felt soft and full of life, unlike what I had endured in the Wastelands. I danced my fingers and tickled them on a fern. It *felt* real. But was it?

I inhaled the light air, admiring the way the sunlight reflected off the water. I picked up a pebble and tried to skip it across the pond. It sank with one bounce and I laughed. I always felt at peace here, which is why I'd named it "Peaceful Pond." This was my one place of contentment growing up.

I shook my head, trying to remember how I had gotten here. I wasn't near my hometown of Sedah. I was...in the Wastelands of Renak and I had...something to do.

"Hellsfire," a gentle voice said.

I spun around in confusion, but I couldn't see the source of the voice anywhere. It sounded familiar.

"Hellsfire," she said again, and this time I recognized it.

"Mother?"

"Hello, son," she said from behind me.

My mother strolled out of the forest, appearing before my eyes as the young beauty men once fought over. Her long, lush auburn hair wrapped around her body. There were no wrinkles around her tender smile or on her forehead. Her green eyes were renewed with life.

"What are you doing here?" I asked.

I was cautious as the younger version of my mother glided towards me. It had been years since I last saw her. I missed her so much. She had sent me away to learn to control my powers, but she could never have foreseen what would happen to me. I had so much to tell her.

I couldn't get rid of the haziness in my head. There was so much I didn't understand about the nexus or its magic. If it was possible to go inside one, what else could it do? The rational part of me wanted to deny this, but another part of me yearned so much for it to be real.

My mother came closer and my body caved in to her open arms. She hugged me, and it was as warm and gentle as I'd always remembered it. It *was* her. She was my mother. She looked different because of the magic of this place. Because...I couldn't even remember the name of wherever I was. It didn't matter.

It had been so long since I'd last seen or heard from my mother that I laid my head on her chest and whimpered.

"I'm so glad to see you," I said. "It's been so long and I've been through so much. The things I've seen and done..." I sniffled in her arms, remembering the battles, the death, the destruction. The fear I felt, and the worry of what would happen if I didn't succeed. There was so much I wanted to get off my chest that words failed me. All I managed was, "It feels good to be with you again."

"I know, Hellsfire," she said, hugging me tightly. "It's good to be with you too. There's someone here I want you to meet."

I gazed into her loving green eyes. She swiveled her head in another direction. A shadowy figure approached from behind one of the oak trees. I let go of my mother and turned to face the mysterious visitor.

"Hello, Hellsfire," a man said.

"Who are you?"

"You know who I am."

He unsheathed a beautiful dagger from his belt. It was the one my mother had given to me, and she had received it from her husband. I reached to my waist and my dagger was gone. My mother let me go and moved over to the man. She wrapped her right arm around him and leaned into him.

"Father?" I asked. I had never seen my father before. He died a hero in the Burning Sands before I was born.

"Yes, Hellsfire," he said, and nodded.

"How is this possible? You're dead."

"Remember where you are. Anything's possible here."

But I couldn't remember. I rubbed my hand against my head. My mind was blank. The harder I tried to think about it, the more my head hurt. I took a step closer to see his face, but I still couldn't make him out. The shadows draped his face.

"Hellsfire, you've been given a chance," my mother said as she snuggled up against my father.

"A chance?" I wiped my sweaty palm against my pounding head. "A chance for what?"

"A chance to be with your family," my father said. "To get what was denied to all of us. We can be together." He placed his firm hand on my shoulder. His dark brown eyes had the same look to them as mine. Yet no matter how close he was, I couldn't make out his face.

"I...I..." I tried to say no, ask why or how, to formulate some kind of words, but my dry mouth wouldn't let me. There was only one phrase that stood clear in the canvas of my mind. Something I had wanted since I was a child. "I want nothing more than to be a family." My mind eased from the pain the moment I said that.

"Then let's be one, son."

My parents embraced me. The heavens surrounded me, radiating with love. The stress and tension melted away. I was finally free. There was no more responsibility, no more worrying about the future, about my destiny, about things far too big for only one man. I cried, but they were tears of joy.

"Come on, son," my father said. "Let's go."

"Where are we going, Daddy?" I looked up at him. He was a giant. My small hand was palmed in his.

My father lifted me up, putting me on his shoulders. He pointed to a bright light through the trees. The tiny star was a short distance away. It reminded me of something—something I had seen before, but I couldn't remember what. I let go of that thought, rocking back and forth on my father's shoulders, smiling at being on top of the world.

"We're going over there so we can be together," he said.

"What's over there?" I asked.

"A special place."

"Let's go," my mother said as she grabbed my father's free hand.

We walked to where we would become a family. I giggled and laughed while riding my dad's shoulders. The grass around us stood up straighter and the flowers bloomed to their fullest. I even heard the sounds of birds off in the distance.

The bright light mesmerized me and the love and joy of my parents comforted me. I was no longer going to be alone.

I looked back down the path we'd traveled. The scenery and light had disappeared, replaced by darkness. There was something I was forgetting. No, not something, someone important and special to me, but I couldn't remember who.

That didn't matter now. I turned my head away from it and towards the bright light. The warmth from it was intense, but not dangerous. I stared at the light and it reminded me of a glistening gem. Not a gem, but a crystal.

"Krystal," I whispered.

Just as we were about to enter paradise, a powerful and beautiful image of the woman I cared about more than the world ripped through my head. If I vanished with my family, I would never see Krystal again.

I yelled out in pain, putting my hands to my head. My father put me down. Memories of Krystal and all the time we had spent together flooded my mind. They clashed against the hope and joy of being with my family again. They became a relentless storm, threatening to make my head explode.

"We've got to do something!" my mother said, reaching for me. I tried to go to her, but my body wouldn't obey. It kept squirming and twisting.

"Son," my father said in a calm voice, "if we go to the light, everything will be fine. I promise."

I glanced up at my father, wanting to speak. I couldn't because of the pain.

The two conflicting thoughts hammered me. I wasn't sure I could survive it until Krystal said, "Hellsfire!"

Her word exploded the fire within, burning my mind and soul. They shredded my entire being, altering my body to what it once was. I remembered who I was and what I was supposed to do.

"I'm a wizard," I whispered. I rose and faced my parents.

"Come with us," Mother said. "Please." Her green eyes brimmed with tears.

"Yes," Father said. "We can live happily ever after."

My heart yearned to be with them. I wanted so much to be a family and have that which was denied to me. "I want to...but I can't." My shoulders slumped and I could no longer meet their eyes.

I had to live in the present and not be lost in something that couldn't be, no matter how real it seemed. I was a wizard. I couldn't disregard my responsibilities to the world. That's not what Stradus had taught me—or my mother. I had to help my friends and I couldn't leave Krystal behind.

I tried to meet my parents' gaze. "I'm sorry, I can't go with you."

"Why not, Hellsfire?" my mother asked.

"There's...a girl."

"Who?"

"The Princess of Alexandria."

"Ah," my mother said. She paused as she considered her words. "You realize you may never be together. She's a princess and you're a wizard. Her people may never accept you."

I sighed. "I know. She has a duty and is out of my league, but—" I looked into my mother's eyes. "I still have to try."

"That's my son," my father said, and smiled. I returned it. "You must care for her a great deal, Hellsfire."

"I do."

"Good."

"There are also some things I still have to do."

"Then you do them," my father said. "You do what you have to. I'm sure we'll be together again. One day." He walked over to me and handed me his precious dagger. "Hold on to this. You're going to need it like I once did."

"What do you mean?"

He smiled at me. "Don't worry about it now. I know you'll make me proud, son." He settled his hand on my shoulder and touched his forehead to mine.

My voice drowned in tears caught in my throat.

My mother leaned in and kissed me on the cheek. "Goodbye, son."

The stinging tears dripped down my face as I watched the two go into the light. They turned and smiled at me before disappearing. Everything around me vanished and shimmered out of existence. There was no more pond, trees, flowers, or even light. I was all alone in the void. All alone to face my destiny. I collapsed to the ground, the darkness overtaking me.

Screams and yells rattled in my ears, jolting me awake. The landscape of my home was gone, replaced with the bleakness of the Wastelands. I staggered up and gasped at the sight of my friends.

Prastian, Behast, Ardimus, and Krystal battled against a behemoth monster as gigantic as a fifteen foot tree. Its multiple, thick arms fought with unnatural quickness, dodging and blocking their blows. Its six eyes moved independently and locked onto each person like a lizard. The reddish brute even hurled beginner elemental spells, flinging fireballs similar to mine.

What were they doing here?

"They came to save you," my doppelganger said, appearing next to me. "Unfortunately for them, none of them are wizards, so they had to fight a creation of my own."

I stared at my friends, trying to decide if what Renak said was true. I shook my head to clear the fog. Their movements were so fluid while they handled their weapons. The sounds of battle that resonated were so real.

"No, this isn't real," I said.

"The two elves are already protected by your spell and the man has his enchanted chainmail," Renak said. "As for your princess, you underestimate how much she cares for you, and she has the blood of Alexander in her veins."

"What does that mean?"

Renak stared at the creature and the battle while anger rippled through his face for the briefest of moments. "Stories have basis in truth, Hellsfire, but over time that truth becomes distorted. Yes, Alexander may have sided with Shala in the fight against me and a dragon carried him, but he wasn't the ordinary man the stories have painted him. He was a magical...anomaly. He was able to do things with magic, despite lacking his own power. I was never able to find out more—or maybe I did, after this ritual." His eyes settled on me for a long moment before looking back at the battle. "Should you really be focusing on things long ago, or more current concerns?

"Time flows different in here, Hellsfire. Not much has passed for you, but plenty has passed in the outside world. The elves took care of that wizard who's squatting in my tower, but they had no chance to escape Masep without you. This princess of yours got tired of waiting." Renak put a thoughtful finger underneath his chin. "I do wonder how many people died in order for her to enter the tower?"

I couldn't trust Renak. I couldn't trust for this to be real. He was responsible for the war, the Wastelands, the Great Barrier and the spreading blight. But what if he was right? I stared past him to see my friends fighting.

Krystal led the fray, not wanting to back down. For a moment, our eyes met and my heart knew it to be her. I had gotten lost in those enchanting eyes many times. Magical or not, there was no way the nexus could imitate her eyes. I left the copycat and rushed to help Krystal and my friends.

I ran as fast as my long legs could carry me. I reached the battle just as the creature puffed out a long stream of flames. I raised my hand, halting the fire.

Krystal blew a piece of loose hair out of her face and gave me a small smile. I knew that smile. It *was* her. "Thank the gods I found you in time." She raised her sword and parried one of the monster's arms, cutting it. It bellowed in pain.

I guarded her flank while Ardimus defended her other side. Behast was in front and Prastian was behind us, shooting his arrows at the monster. A few had pierced its thick hide.

I summoned my magic, unleashing a torrent of fire and flame. The creature held its arms together, blocking its face. A dull sheen of magic glowed around it. When I stopped the fire, it smiled. It was unharmed.

I gathered in more mana, readying myself to strike with a harder spell, when the creature turned its head towards me. Its yellow eyes flashed and it spoke in a strange, foreign tongue. Its spell breached my defenses and I cried out in pain. I toppled to the ground, a surge of agony coursing throughout my body. It bound me into place and I couldn't move.

"Hellsfire!" Krystal said.

The monster grinned and renewed its attack.

"Princess," Ardimus said, "Guard Hellsfire. We'll keep the creature occupied."

Ardimus and Behast held off the creature with their swords while Prastian tried to find a weak spot with his bow.

Krystal knelt down and leaned over me. "Hellsfire, what can I do?"

I couldn't answer. I accessed my magic, trying to cast it, but my body stiffened. I sought to cry out against the pressure on my spine. Yellow sparks of magic sizzled around my body. I latched onto my fire, pushing past the pain, using it to combat the monster's magic. I motioned with my eyes to the princess.

She nodded. "I understand." She laid her hand gently on my heart. "I didn't come all this way to lose you, hero."

My fingers twitched. My magic had begun to overwhelm the creature's, but I needed more time.

"I'll buy you time," she said.

I wanted to tell her not to, that the others would take care of it, but I couldn't. I screamed in pain as my muscles fought against each other. I was useless. As I struggled to recover, I could only watch in horror as my friends battled Renak's beast.

The creature distracted Behast, fighting him with its multiple arms and keeping him off guard. Behast struck the creature and dark red blood oozed from it, but it didn't matter. Within another fist was a huge fireball. The creature let it go, the magic consuming and burning the elf.

Prastian's quiver was empty and he drew his sword. He charged the monster in a blind frenzy. He dodged the beast's spells and claws. Running up the creature's massive arm, he leapt about to strike its eyes, but it opened its mouth and spewed a massive fireball, incinerating Prastian.

I cried out, reaching toward them. My arms moved, but I couldn't yet rise. I fueled my spell with more magic. In response, the creature's own spell renewed its furious attack, electrifying my body with a powerful and painful glow. I struggled to sit up, wanting to stand. They needed my help and I wasn't going to let them down.

Ardimus had enchanted chain mail, protecting him against magical attacks. The beast's magic bounced off of him. Ardimus sliced through one of its fireballs, shattering the spell.

The creature sacrificed one of its hands, plucking away Ardimus's enchanted scimitar. Ardimus drew a dagger and swiped at it, but the tiny weapon wasn't enough. I could only stare in horror as it grabbed hold of Ardimus by a leg and an arm. The creature heaved on his limbs and the hardened warrior shrieked in agony as his body snapped in two.

Krystal screamed as she saw her protector fall to the ground. My power crackled at my fingertips. I staggered up, letting my rage burn away the creature's magic. The flame encompassed me until I burned like the sun. I stumbled forward and yelled out Krystal's name, warning her to stay away. I would deal with this creature myself.

Krystal dropped her sword and retrieved Ardimus's scimitar. She used the heavy sword as best she could, deflecting the beast's lunges at her and cutting it. It roared in pain, unable to heal its wounds. Krystal chopped off one of its hands and in return, it sliced off her hand.

She screamed and dropped Ardimus's sword, but didn't slow down or show fear as blood gushed from her wound. With her only remaining hand, she drew her dagger. The creature grinned in anticipation and swiped at Krystal. Its razor claws sliced into her, leaving huge gashes in her side. She spun and fell, her clothes overflowing with her own blood.

"No!" I yelled.

I limped along as fast as I could, dragging my numb right leg and arm. I stopped trying to fight the spell, instead using all of my power against the monster. My body stiffened and started to slow down as the thing's magic renewed itself.

Before it could bring down the killing blow, I conjured as much wind as I could and blew it at the monster. The wind sliced off its claws and it stumbled backwards. I used my momentum and more air magic to force it to the ground before I barreled into it.

My body froze again, but not before I unleashed all of my magic into the creature's gaping mouth. I poured the raging fire into it until its red body could take no more. Its spell on me collapsed. I rolled off it and felt its body threatening to explode.

The fire ate the creature from the inside. It burned, and its huge body collapsed in on itself until there was nothing left to fuel the fire.

Krystal's body twitched and I crawled over to her.

"Hellsfire," Krystal said. I strained to hear her weak voice.

"Shhh, don't move. I'll try to heal you."

I placed my hands on her blood-soaked clothes. The blood was so cold and sticky and she so pale. I turned my head aside so I wouldn't focus on how badly hurt she was. I reached out to the white mana. It was elusive to me at the best of times, but I couldn't get more than a flicker here. I didn't have enough time to gather in all I needed and I was exhausted after warring with that creature.

"Damn it!" I said. "Come on!"

But all that came was the roaring fire. I stifled it, not wanting to hurt her. As powerful as it was, it was useless here. My fire couldn't heal her. I took off my black wizard's robe to staunch her wound. My robes soaked up far too much of her blood.

Krystal struggled to raise her remaining bloody hand to my cheek. I nuzzled into it, my face becoming smeared with cold blood. "Why didn't you save me?" Her violet eyes, always so full of life, dimmed and her hand went limp. Tranquility passed across her face.

I cradled her dead body in my arms. She was right. I should have saved her. I should have saved them all. Despite having all this power at my fingertips, I was powerless.

I sat there for a long time with her body against mine. Her sweet smell was gone and her body was so stiff and icy. I pulled away from her, staring at my lifeless friends, their bodies forever motionless.

I thought about leaving the nexus. So many people had died on this quest of mine. It was all to fulfill my former master's last request and retrieve a book. I now understood why Stradus had locked himself up in the White Mountain. It wasn't only to wait for me. It was to hide from the pain of being responsible for people's deaths, and all the burdens of being a wizard. What would life be like now, without her?

Could I do what Stradus had done and hide from everything? More importantly, should I? I brought nothing but death and destruction to those around me. I wasn't Shala, who had mastered the white mana of life. My ability was with fire. It burned and destroyed.

I sat in the nexus for what seemed like hours. My arms were wrapped around Krystal and I stared at her lifeless body, dark thoughts playing through my head. I had no idea what to do and there was no one I could share my thoughts with as I had with Krystal.

Krystal's open eyes stared through me. I gazed within them and even though I found no life, she seemed to be telling me I had a duty to finish. She would have finished it if our roles were reversed. That's what I'd learned from her. I was going to finish this. I was going to find the *Book of Shazul* and heal the land, even if it wouldn't shine as brightly without her.

I kissed her on the forehead. There were so many things I wanted to say. So many things I should have told her while she was alive. I opened my mouth to tell her now. I closed it, realizing it would do no good.

"I'm sorry I couldn't protect you," I said, staring at the ineffective necklace I had given her. I pulled it from her neck, wanting to bury it in Alexandria, since I couldn't afford to take her body with me. I put the necklace on. "I'll do my duty, princess. For you and the others."

I gently laid her back on the ground and closed her eyes. I took my blood-soaked robes, rose, and walked away. I was going to defeat the nexus and Renak and be done with this place. If possible, I was going to give that wizard a second, more permanent death.

I paused and turned around, taking one last look at my fallen friends and my heart. I left them, journeying deeper into the Nexus of the Wastelands. It wasn't long before he appeared.

"Renak," I said in a whisper.

"Hellsfire."

I barely lifted my head to stare at the reflection. Those brown eyes were devoid of all emotion. The man who had sacrificed his soul because of his lost love was gone. All that was left was this phantom.

"What do you want, Renak?"

He cocked his head as his intense eyes studied me. Finally, he spoke. "Given up?"

I took a deep breath and met his eyes. "No. They're not going to die in vain. You're going to tell me what I have to do to bring down your barrier and end your destructive spell. Too many people have died for this."

"One more thing and you're done," he said.

"What is it?"

"You have to get by me."

My body tensed and my hands tightened around my robes at the thought of fighting the legendary wizard, but then I remembered my friends. "Very well. You've killed Krystal and my friends. You deserve to pay for what you've done."

"I wasn't the one who failed them." He pointed. "*You* were. I'm not going to let you bring down the barrier. I can't. I wasn't created to allow you or anyone else to."

"Then let's end this."

"As you wish."

The environment around me shifted and changed. The landscape brightened, with a warm midday sun shining overhead. Tall, soft, green grass sprang from underneath my feet, and a cool breeze brushed against my cheeks. I found myself wearing my wizard's robes, now cleaned of Krystal's blood, but my necklace and purse were gone. I glanced back to see if my friends were still there, and that's when he attacked.

An earthquake rumbled and a fissure opened up, racing towards me. Jagged rocks burst out from it, and Renak shot them at me. I barely had enough time to summon a defense and force the rocks to part around me. I leapt out of the way before the ground swallowed me whole.

I raised my hand and released the flame inside me. The fire didn't get more than a few feet before Renak countered with a windstorm. It blew out my fire and soared towards me. I softened it, but the wind sliced into my face and hands.

Renak tripped up my feet with earth magic, then conjured fire of his own. A giant wolf made of flames snarled and raced towards me. I tried to stand, but Renak kept me off balance with the shaking ground. I scrambled backwards to get out of the way, but the wolf leapt at me with wide jaws, trying to devour me whole.

I seized control of the magic within the beast. It froze in midair. Renak was a master wizard, but his specialty was with black mana. Mine was fire.

I turned the beast around and it growled at Renak. I poured more magic into it and it exploded in size. It ran towards Renak, but he bombarded the wolf with rain and wind. I willed it to hold form and rose, pouring more of my magic into it. I might not be able to beat Renak, but his own spell could.

Renak halted the wolf when it was a foot away from him. He used the same magic I used, seizing the fire mana within to control the beast. The heat singed his clothes and body, but he didn't flinch.

The ancient wizard started to regain control of the beast. I used my own magic to rip the ground apart, flinging pieces of rock at him. He ignored the smaller pieces and the blood trickling down the side of his head. He didn't seem to feel any pain as I forced the wind to slice into him. His concentration was incredible, showing no signs of losing his hold on the magic.

I focused only on the fiery wolf, forgetting the other magic. Its paws reached out towards Renak and its jaws snapped, but it never touched him. Both of us tried to control the creature, but in different ways. Renak had a calm expression on his face while the sweat dripped down mine.

The beast began to turn its head towards me. Its raging eyes showed its longing to feed on me. I wouldn't be able to stop it if Renak was able to fully control it. I had gambled too much on strengthening it, and was still tired from battling his earlier creature.

I thought of Krystal and of my friends' deaths. If I failed here, it would all be for naught. Renak might have been a calm wizard, but I wasn't. I let my emotions seize and enrage me, remembering Krystal and how she died because of me.

I journeyed to a place I've only been to once. I wasn't sure if I could control it or what it would do to me. The power always threatened to overwhelm me. That no longer mattered. Renak had taken the one thing in my life that mattered and he would die a second death because of it.

I embraced the wolf and the fire that composed it. The fire wolf rippled, burning brighter, hotter, and darker. The beast became fueled by black flames and it attacked Renak. Renak's face was full of surprise. He couldn't stop the beast—it opened its massive jaws, swallowing him whole. The creature flared hotter as Renak's body blackened like the flames. The wolf exploded with such force it knocked me off my feet.

Even though the beast was gone, the dark, powerful magic beckoned me. I was tempted to give in. There was nothing for me now that she was gone. My anger at letting her get killed fueled the fire, threatening to overwhelm me. I was about to release it in an uncontrollable rage, unsure if I could ever bottle it up again. But then I thought once more of Krystal and my friends.

The grief doused the fire. The sorrow and the spell had taken so much from my body. I collapsed, my face pressed against the broken ground, with bits of grass and dirt as a pillow.

When I opened my eyes, the scenic view was gone. The void had returned, along with the muted blue light. I got up. Without Renak, what was I going to do now? Had the barrier fallen?

"Hellsfire, what an appropriate name."

I spun around to see Renak there. I readied my magic.

He put a hand up and said, "Calm yourself. I'm not here to fight you. You already beat me. Congratulations, Wizard Hellsfire."

I didn't drop my guard. Not around him. "Has the Great Barrier fallen?"

"Not yet." Renak waved his hand. A bright light emanated from above, illuminating a table with a simple wooden chest on it.

I walked to it, always keeping my eye on Renak. I bent over, examining it without touching it. I wasn't about to fall for a trap or get caught by surprise this time.

I stared at the chest. "What do I do?"

"Open it, and after all these years, the Great Barrier will finally fall."

I raised my right eyebrow, sensing he was holding something back. "But?"

Renak disappeared and reappeared beside the table. "There are two things. As I said before, I put the barrier up to keep something from happening, *not* to cut Shala off from his resources. I had this entire area at my disposal, as well as the creatures. In time, I would have beaten him."

"What's in Southern Shala you're so afraid of?"

Renak scowled. "Afraid is the wrong word. During the war, one of my followers warned me of a great imbalance. She said that the cycle that had been in place since magic first formed had been upset, and because of it, the world is in danger. I didn't listen to her at the time. I was so caught up in the war that I had forgotten my duty as a wizard."

He sighed and placed his hands on the chest. "I did end up remembering my duty. Unfortunately, because I waited too long, I couldn't stop it; I could only delay it."

"But what's down there?" I asked. "What could threaten the world?"

"Wizards today, and even during my time, have forgotten our history, why we exist, and where we get our powers from."

"Everyone knows we get our powers from the gods," I said.

Renak gave me a sly smile. "True, but it's not for the reasons you may think, and it wasn't always like that. There's a war between the gods, Hellsfire. I didn't believe it at first, nor do I fully understand the reasons why, but it is happening."

"You're telling me *you* stopped a war between the gods? *You* who created the Wastelands and enslaved the creatures there and caused the Burning Sands?"

I blinked and Renak appeared in front of me. "I would take care how you speak to me."

My gaze met his, but after a few moments, I looked away.

Renak backed off and continued talking. "The gods' war is of no importance."

"But you just said—"

"Neither side has gained the upper hand. That works to our advantage. If one side ever does, it will be disastrous to all of magic, and to our very world. But an event happened to change all that. The sides had been tilted in favor of one, throwing the scales out of balance."

He was quiet, letting his words sink into my head.

"Why should I listen to you? My friends are dead! Krystal is dead! All because of you and your accursed nexus!" My fire boiled to the surface. Nothing mattered without her. He was going to pay for what he had done.

Renak didn't make a move to stop me. I felt no magic rising up within him. In a calm voice he said, "Your beloved princess and your friends are alive and well."

I halted my attack. In some stories, Renak was named the Great Deceiver, but he was far more complex than that. Would this be one of those stories?

"How can I believe you?"

"You can't. But the moment you step out of here, you'll see them alive again, except for the princess who's not here."

I calmed myself, letting the magic I had gathered dissipate. "All right. I'll listen to you. Do you know what caused this imbalance?"

He shook his head. "I was on the right track, but never found out who or what it was. If only I had listened to Lyria earlier."

Renak might have been right, but he also might have been lying and his point of view was skewed. He wanted the barrier up, and he might lie to me.

"A lot of time has passed since then," I said. "Maybe it's gone."

"No. You don't understand. The gods' war never ends. The disturbance might have merely taken a different form after all this time."

"Or what if it had been defeated? Much time has passed since you last walked the earth."

"Perhaps." He didn't look as if he believed it. "If it hasn't been dealt with, you would have to deal with it, as it would be your responsibility now as a wizard."

I walked to the chest and stared at it. I had no idea what to do. If I did nothing, the land would slowly turn into a wasteland. If I brought the barrier down, I would have to deal with the imbalance Renak talked about and the ramifications from a reunited land.

"I've made my decision," I said. "Your spell's destroying Northern Shala. I have to stop it while I still can. Otherwise, my children and children's children won't have a future."

"And what about what I told you?"

"I can't worry about that now."

"Oh?"

"But I promise you, if my friends still live, I will look into it." Even though I didn't want to, I had a duty. Renak might have remembered his when it was too late, Premier might have shunted his away, but I wasn't going to. If my friends were dead, I couldn't let them die for naught.

His dark eyes studied me. "Even though you're young, I believe you may be the one."

"Is there anything more you can tell me about this threat?"

"You'll be able to sense how wrong the magic will be, and it will be powerful."

"Is that it?"

"Lyria once told me, 'The brightest light sometimes casts the darkest shadows.'"

I stared at him blankly.

"She was a seer. They're always a strange bunch because of the things they're able to see. It can drive a person crazy. I believe she meant the threat will be hidden, but it can't hide forever. There will be a time when it must reveal itself. If you can, find it before then and strike. Destroy it and the land will be safe."

"I'll do my best," I said. "Southern Shala is a pretty big place. I'll also tell the Elemental Council about it. Maybe they'll be able to help."

"I wouldn't count on them," Renak said. "They didn't help me when I needed it."

I placed my trembling hands on the chest and was about to open it when Renak vanished and re-emerged right behind it. His face was intent as he stared at it. He wanted so much for his spell to stay intact, but I had defeated his nexus and him. He was just the ghostly essence of Renak, bound within his limits.

"You may leave now if you like," Renak said, waving his hand. A bright, diamond-shaped light materialized.

"No. The Great Barrier shouldn't be. You're killing the land, Renak. I'm bringing it down. Now."

"Heed my words, Hellsfire."

I nodded. "I will."

Renak's sharp eyes stared at my hands and the chest. This was it. I took a deep breath before I lifted the latch. The chest creaked as I opened it. A bright, white swirl of light rushed out of it. It enveloped me inside and out, filling every part of my body with warmth and comfort. The light shifted and changed, becoming black. I shivered from its icy touch. With each breath I took, the air around me was frosty.

"Something's wrong," Renak said.

The streaking light left me, heading for Renak. It consumed him and he faded in and out of existence.

"What is it?" I asked.

"The spell's been changed." He wasn't disturbed by his flickering appearance, but by his magic. "The wizard in my tower. He's altered it somehow."

"What about the barrier?"

"It's down." Renak stared at his fading hand. "If only I had more time to deduce what is different. Hellsfire, be careful of this wizard. He's crafty. Deal with him quickly, then heed my words. The land is in grave danger."

The most feared and powerful wizard the world had ever known was carried out on a black beam of light, vanishing.

I hesitated, terrified of what I would find outside. If my friends weren't there, then it meant what I saw in the nexus was true. I still had to worry about the threat that lingered to destroy the land. But first it was time to deal with Premier.

I had no time to think about it, as the portal began to seal itself. I took one last look at this amazing, fearful, and empty place. The light blinded me and filled me with life and power as I stepped out of the nexus and into a changed world.

CHAPTER 12

THE BLURRED, JUMBLED room was like an unfinished painting, its colors running down the canvas. I blinked and shook my head several times before the room came back into focus. I expected the nexus to disappear, but it still lingered, illuminating the chamber.

"You're alive," I said, staring at Prastian and Behast, relieved to see their confused faces.

"Of course," Behast said, "You weren't gone for more than an hour."

"I wasn't?"

"No."

"What did you see?" Prastian asked.

"Your deaths, along with the princess's." I breathed a little easier. That meant she was still alive. "I'm just glad you're all right."

"Can you tell if the Great Barrier is down?"

I reached out with my magical senses, but I shook my head when I found nothing. "It's too far. I don't feel a great magical disturbance. Stradus told me he felt something when the barrier was first put up, yet there's nothing now." I wasn't alive then, but someone was who might know the difference. "Premier, is there a way you can tell if the barrier is down?"

Premier closed his eyes. After a few moments he opened them and said, "No."

"Then how do we know if it's down?" Prastian asked.

"It's down," Premier said. He didn't state why, but there was something he was hiding from me.

I glanced at Prastian. He subtly nodded as he got the binding potion ready. He would act as soon as I made my move, or Premier did. "Remember your promise, Premier."

"I remember."

Premier and Baal took one step closer to the exit. Behast drew his sword, I summoned my magic, and Prastian readied himself to throw the potion. He would only get one chance. The light in the chamber dimmed.

"I didn't actually expect you to succeed," Premier said. "The nexus should have broken or killed you like it did everyone else." He pulled out two vials and cradled them in his hand. "As promised, the cure for your friends."

"Give them to me."

Premier didn't budge. "Assuming you get out of here alive, it looks like the princess has another reason to thank you, but that reunion will be short-lived as you will soon find out." He grinned and dangled the potions in the air. "Alexandria will be left alone. However, you said nothing about Southern Shala."

"Get ready," I said not moving my lips, and in a low enough tone for only the elves to hear.

"Thank you for giving me a chance to return home, Hellsfire. There's going to be plenty of old scores to settle, plus a lot of new opportunities. There's one last thing you should have realized." Premier stared past me at the nexus. The light in the room darkened further. "Catch!"

"Now!" I said.

Prastian threw the vial at Premier and I tore my eyes away from him, holding my hands out. As my eyes followed the potions, the nexus sealed completely, plunging the chamber into darkness. I had no idea where the potions were so I lifted my robes out, praying my robes would catch them.

My robes thumped as the potions landed in them. I let out a breath of relief and secured them in my purse. I formed a huge fireball in my hand, illuminating the room. I was about to fling it at Premier or Baal, but they were already gone. The broken vial of binding potion was where Premier once stood.

We rushed out into the corridor to find them. The elves used their long ears while I scanned for any sign of magic. They could have been anywhere, as they knew the tower far better than we did.

The elves didn't hear Premier or Baal running up the stairs. With Baal's heavy steps, they should have. I moved down the hallway. Shadows crept along the walls and ceiling. They must have gone down one of these corridors, but which way?

My magical senses pricked me, and I felt something very old and powerful. It wasn't Premier, but it could be anything in this ancient tower. I remembered Renak's words about Premier. I peered down the darkened hallway, feeling the presence coming closer.

"I hear something," Behast said.

"Me too," Prastian said.

Before I could illuminate the shadows down the hallway with my flames, a slimy tentacle reached out and seized my wrist. I tried to pull my arm away, but I couldn't. It began draining me of my magic, and I swayed like a reed in the wind. The fireball in my hand almost vanished. I kept the magic lit lest we be plunged into darkness. Behast yelled and cleaved through the tentacle. A monstrous bellow echoed from down the corridor.

A gigantic orange worm nearly filled the entire hallway. It scraped its belly along the floor, its open mouth shooting out dozens of squirming tentacles. The tentacles only went for me. I screamed at my body to run, but I stood like a statue, while they wrapped around me. Having my magic sucked away made me feel like a newborn babe. It was hard to maintain my tiny spell, which grew smaller each passing second until it was no bigger than a candle's flame.

Behast jumped in front of me, slashing at the tentacles, breaking their hold on me. Prastian let loose his arrows at the worm. They clanged off the creature's metallic skin. He changed tactics and shot at its gaping mouth. It screamed and closed its mouth, stopping the tentacles from coming through. It had no eyes or ears. Its colossal body rolled closer.

"We…must…go," I said before my spell vanished.

Unfortunately, Premier would have to wait, but at least I knew where he was headed. Southern Shala would have to be warned about Premier and the threat Renak had told me about. I still couldn't believe that the gods were at war. I prayed that in bringing down the Great Barrier I hadn't doomed the world.

Behast swept me up and carried me over his burly shoulder. Prastian drew his sword and cut back the beast's tentacles. They ran to the next floor, getting us out of the monster's reach.

I tried to stand on my own, but I couldn't. I leaned against the wall for support. Reaching into my purse, I pulled out my rejuvenation potion. My energy would be restored, but because of the nature of the creature's attack, it would be awhile. Behast said he would carry me and he did.

They jogged back up to the top of the tower, hurrying to get back to our friends. The top floor was the only place we felt relatively safe. I figured that Premier kept it protected. We backtracked the way we had come, keeping a lookout for any surprises Premier might have left, in case he did go up instead of escaping from the tower. We scanned every door, table, and stone, trying to see if something was out of place. I kept my magic in place, but the light was pitiful. It exhausted me to keep up even that minor magic.

Eventually, we reached the top of the tower. Enough light shone that I no longer needed to keep up my spell. I was able to walk on my own two feet. We checked our room, hoping that Jastillian and Demay were still there and safe.

The pair slept, still smothered by the blankets we had left covering them. Sweat rolled off their pale faces and their breathing was labored. I poured one of the potions into each of their mouths, then wiped up the drops that didn't go in. Their breathing eased, but that was all. It would take some time for it to work.

I kept an eye on the unconscious pair while Prastian and Demay searched the rest of the floor. I told them to get me if they found anything that made their hackles rise. They carefully checked everywhere, trying to find a potion, an enchanted weapon, or even a map of where Premier might have gone. They found nothing. Either he had stashed what was important to him or he had taken everything with him when he escaped. Renak was right. Premier was crafty. He had expected me to come here all along and he had planned things accordingly. I had thought him weak from his lack of magic, but I was wrong. Next time I saw Premier, I would waste no time in killing him.

I finally allowed myself to relax as the land of dreams called to me, the potion working its own magic.

When I awoke, night had fallen. I smiled when I saw a familiar face in front of me.

"He's awake," Jastillian said and smiled.

"You're all right," I said.

"We both are," Demay said, handing me a jug of water.

I took a long drink, letting the water cool my parched throat. "I'm glad."

"I'm not," Jastillian said, frowning. "I missed seeing the Nexus of the Wastelands and that slippery snake got away."

"There's always Southern Shala," Demay said.

"Aye," Jastillian said with bright eyes.

"I want to thank you for bringing down the Great Barrier to save us, Hellsfire," Demay said. "You didn't have to. From what my brother told me, you took a great risk in doing so."

"Thank you, lad," Jastillian said.

I stared at my pale, smiling friends. I placed my hands on each of their shoulders. "No, thank you. You both saved my life. Premier would have killed me if it wasn't for you two."

I walked to the window and peered outside. It seemed quieter, somehow, and brighter. The black clouds that had settled around Masep, and particularly this tower, had dispersed. The constant eerie lightning that raced across them had fallen silent. Those clouds weren't the result of the residual magic in the tower. They were the fault of the Great Barrier and the nexus Renak had used. I wished it was daylight so I could see how much it had all changed.

I peered at the countless campfires showing where the creatures were. What did they think about the skies changing? Were they fearful?

"Are you two well enough to travel?" I asked without turning around.

"Yes," Demay said.

"And to fight," Jastillian said, reading my thoughts.

"Good. We can't explore the tower and find a secret way out. The tower's far too dangerous if we don't know where we're going." I clenched my hand, feeling my magic swell up. "We're going home, and gods help whatever gets in our way."

It was a shame I didn't have more time to study what was in Renak's old stronghold. The knowledge, power, and history it contained could have taught me a lot. Even though my friends had already combed the top floor, I double-checked it, scouring for a clue they might have missed. Renak's old journals would have helped a lot. Both for information on the threat in Southern Shala, and for the other knowledge they contained. I didn't find anything, and the stronghold was too big and too dangerous to search it entirely. I wanted to see with my own eyes that Krystal was safe, and the Elemental Council had to be warned. Renak might have lied to me about my friends' deaths, but he was deathly worried about the gods' war.

We gathered our things and left the tower. My friends had their weapons drawn, and I cloaked myself in magic as I led the way. I glanced up at the sky. A gray overcast hovered above the city, but patches of blue and rays of sunlight poked out. It was far more than I had ever seen since my time in the Wastelands. The tower still had its magical gleam, but it didn't shine as brightly.

The ogres and wolves were still guarding the gates, but other creatures had filled the road, watching the entrance to the tower. The two ogres guarding the gate turned to face us and ordered others beyond to open the gates. The wolves barked madly. The ogres had their swords raised, poised to strike. The other surrounding creatures had confused looks on their faces. I stopped in front of the ogres, just out of sword's reach, and peered up at them.

"Move," I said, staring them in the eyes.

The ogres didn't budge. Their muscular bodies tightened, and they loomed over us. "Who are you?" an ogre asked.

"Move. I'm not going to ask again."

The barking wolves made it hard to concentrate. I glanced at them and released a hint of power in my eyes. They whimpered and cowered away. The ogres looked stunned, but held their ground.

I lifted my arm and flattened my palm, releasing the magic I had gathered. The air exploded, smashing into the ogres lifting them away. They plummeted into the crowd a hundred feet away.

I turned my head, glaring at each of the creatures near us. They stepped back, giving us a wide berth. All of Masep was silenced. The creatures stopped their conversations, their bargaining, their fighting, and turned their complete attention on me. They recognized me for what I was—a wizard.

We continued as the heavy tension closed in on us. We didn't talk, much less breathe. My friends walked back to back, making sure the creatures didn't try anything, and my eyes scanned the crowd for any sign of attack.

A trembling goblin, nearly frozen with fright, asked, "Youuuu gonna ruule nowww?"

I turned a fierce gaze on him. He leaned back so far I thought he was going to fall. I didn't answer him, but he had a valid question. I couldn't have these creatures under Premier's thumb again, or worse yet, running wild and threatening Alexandria.

I wrapped myself in the cold air. "Hear me!" I called, the wind carrying my words to all those in Masep. "Premier is gone. I am the wizard, Hellsfire. *I* am the one who defeated Premier in Alexandria."

I tensed as I held onto the spell, wondering what the creatures were going to do. They had left us alone thus far, but would they want revenge for their defeat, and were some loyal to Premier like Baal was? I might be a wizard, but not even I could take on all of them. I had thought I was going to retrieve the book. If I had it, I could have learned its secrets before I destroyed it—something that would have helped us. But the creatures did something completely unexpected.

They kneeled.

The ogres bowed, then the goblins, followed by the trolls, producing a ripple effect throughout the city. I stood there, basking in all the power I had over these creatures. I didn't need the book. Whatever Renak had done to them long ago was ingrained in them. But to think that one person could influence so many. It was no wonder Renak, Premier, and other wizards became corrupted. I could stay here and rule. I could show all those in Sedah that an ignorant farm boy like me could be something great, and have my own kingdom. I needed no one and I would never be bullied again.

Then I remembered my friends. Their eyes gleamed with questions, doubts, and even fear. They didn't say a word, but they reminded me of what I had to do. I didn't want to be like Renak or Premier. Besides, what would be the point of ruling without someone to share it with? I never wanted this power. Even though I was born with it, I had a responsibility to it and others.

"Arise," I said to the creatures. "I have not come to rule."

They slowly rose. I said nothing. They glanced at each other, unsure of what to do. They dared to talk amongst themselves. Their whispers grew to shouts and their shouts into a raucous roar.

"Enough!" I yelled, my voice piercing the city. "I came here to deal with Premier and I did. He won't trouble you anymore."

My words had the intended effect. Relieved, twisted, disfigured smiles passed throughout the crowd. They probably didn't like Premier any more than I did. I thought long and hard about what I was going to say next. What I hoped Krystal would have wanted.

"I'm going to give you your freedom," I said to the gathered crowd. "You will rule over yourselves from now on. No one will ever tell you what to do."

The creatures roared again. A few of the goblins jumped up and down. After some time had passed, I put a hand up. They all stopped.

"You will *not* go past the mountains into Northern Shala," I said. "If you do, I will be back. And I am far worse than Premier." I let the fire flow out of my eyes and scowled at them. "We're leaving. Do not get in our way."

I let go of the air spell and almost fainted. I was using far too much sloppy magic to show how powerful I was. I should have used a simpler spell to demonstrate my power to them. I continued to look strong for fear of their attack, and let the fire seep out of my hands.

The creatures parted before us as we marched through the city like a strong breeze through a dense forest. They stood still, gawking at me, waiting until I passed before they talked amongst themselves. After all these years, they could finally have their freedom, but would they know what to do with it? Do any of us? They made no move against us, but my friends and I never dropped our guard.

When we reached Masep's gates, there was one brave soul who dared to question me.

Kemek blocked our path. There were no other goblins around him. "What you say true, Great One?"

"Yes," I said. "As long as you stay on your side. Perhaps one day we'll get along, but now's not the time, Kemek."

His eyes nearly came out of their sockets. "You know my name?"

"I'm a wizard. I *know* everything. I even know of your secret city."

Kemek gasped and tripped over his own feet.

"I won't harm you or your people as long as you spread word of what I said here today."

He trembled. "You-you strange, Great One."

"Call me Hellsfire."

"Hells...fire? Hellsfire." Kemek sounded out my name as if saying it would strike him down. "You strange, but me like you. Me make sure goblins don't go to human place. Don't know about nasty trolls or dirty ogres."

"Maybe one day we'll meet again. Goodbye, Kemek."

Kemek kneeled. "Bye, Great Wizard."

We departed Masep. I thought the creatures would accept their freedom and leave us alone.

But they didn't.

CHAPTER 13

NOW THAT THE Great Barrier was down, I was better able to access the Wasteland's earth magic. The land was still sickly, but I felt patches of the creatures all around us. There were thousands of them in their separate groups. None of us felt safe. Without our disguises, we were more exposed than ever. Despite what I had done in Masep, the creatures could attack us at a moment's notice.

We hurried as fast as we could towards Alexandria. We made better time, since we didn't have to hide or take detours. While the majority of the creatures avoided us, I sensed two large groups at the fringe of my senses and powers. I thought it might be coincidental, until I realized they were headed our way.

Because of how damaged the land was and how far away they were, I couldn't tell exactly what followed us. The smaller group had to be either trolls or ogres because of the way their footsteps stomped on the land. They traveled the terrain well, bypassing any crevices.

The smaller, numerous group could only be goblins. They circled around us, not caring how many they lost in their hunt. Their group shrank over the next few days, but it was more than enough.

The others and I tried to lose either group, but they tracked us. We pushed ourselves faster, barely getting any sleep. Soon, the creatures were only a day away. They were so close that my powers let me know it was ogres in that small group. They were the ones we were going to have to fight first.

Jastillian and Behast thought we should hole up in a cave, so that the ogres' size and numbers would work against them. We decided against it, as none of us wanted to be trapped in a cave and have it be our final tomb. Out in the open, there was still a chance for one of Alexandria's patrols to see us.

We stopped and prepared for our final stand. We still had a few hours of daylight left before the creatures came at us. We decided to use the terrain to our advantage instead of them using it to theirs.

There was a rock outcropping up a small hill, providing cover for the elves to shoot from. It faced north, where the ogres would be coming from. The ground in front of it was loose enough for us to dig ditches. In front of those, I could cast my own trap.

By the time night fell, we had prepared our defenses. I had constructed a magical trap, powerful enough, I hoped, for Alexandria to see.

I sprinted back to the others. Prastian and Demay hid behind the rocks, their arrows pointing into the darkness from whence I came. Behast and Jastillian stood behind ditches the two had dug.

Our defenses were adequate at best. We would have liked to prepare more. There was nothing we could have done about the fast approaching goblins coming in from our western flank. If we had time, we would finish off the ogres, then fall back to higher and rockier ground.

"How many are there?" Behast asked.

I bent down and placed my fingertips on the ground. The ogres' vibrations traveled through the earth to me.

"Far too many," I said, glancing up at the night sky. The large clouds blocked out a lot of light. The ogres had better eyesight at night than any of us except Jastillian.

A low rumbling came from half a mile away, accompanied by the ogres' screams and growls.

"They come," Behast said.

Behast and Jastillian moved to the spots they had picked out earlier, and I went back to the elves. Hiding behind the rocks, I sat cross-legged on the ground. I closed my eyes in a trance, letting the earth mana guide me until I reached where my trap was. Earlier in the day, I had gathered in mana and channeled it through a large area, storing it until I was ready to unleash it. I was exhausted from the spell, but if it worked, the ogres' numbers would be greatly diminished.

The ogres stomped across the ground. They were so many and so heavy that the vibration of their footsteps traveled up my arm. If only I could have accessed more of the land's magic, then I could have done a devastating spell. As it was, I had to work with my best magic—fire.

Dozens of creatures ran through the wide circle I had laced with my magic. There seemed to be an endless number of them. Before they reached the border of my giant circle, I ignited my spell.

A wall of fire erupted from the circle, halting the ogres and entrapping them. The circle of fire bloomed, lighting the night sky until it could be seen for miles around.

I brought the fire crashing down into the ogres. The fire consumed them, burning away their flesh. They shrieked a chorus of agony as I broiled them. I had killed the ogres before, but never this many at once. I held the fire for as long as could before I let it go, exhaustion almost overwhelming me.

I opened my eyes and glanced up at Prastian and Demay. Their green eyes were mesmerized, tiny flames dancing inside of them. I stared in horror at the carnage I had caused. The landscape was now illuminated by my dying fire. Small fires fed on the ogres' dead bodies, some of them twitching involuntarily. Three ogres, their backs on fire, tried to get away, but they collapsed and smashed into the ground.

My chest heaved and sweat drenched my clothes. I needed to rest, to gather in more magic for the upcoming goblins.

"It's over," Demay said, helping me up. "Let's go before the goblins arrive. Maybe the fire and the ogres' corpses will buy us some time. If we're lucky, they might feast on them."

"No," Jastillian said, peering to the dying fires. "It's not over yet."

We stared into the distance. Looming shapes burst through the ring of fires. I tapped into the earth mana. More ogres were coming.

"By the gods," I said. "How many are there?"

"Positions!" Jastillian said just as the first wave of ogres approached.

Prastian and Demay loosed their bows as soon as the ogres were a hundred yards away. Because there were so many, their arrows always struck true. Ogres stumbled to the ground. As many ogres as were killed, more took their places.

As tired as I was, I summoned my inner fire and clapped my hands together. A huge fireball burst from my hands, colliding with a group of ogres. I did it again and three caught on fire and veered away, screaming. Others leapt over fallen bodies. The corpses piled up, but the ogres kept coming. We needed to slow them down.

My mind strained to conjure all the earth mana in the area. The broken mana was reluctant to heed my call, but I risked permanently damaging the area. When the ogres were fifty yards away from our trenches, I emitted shockwaves through the area. A dozen ogres tripped and fell. Broken rocks flew into the air, one ripping through the mouth of an ogre before landing in another's eye.

As the ogres struggled to climb the trenches, Jastillian and Behast struck the ogres down. They moved down the line, guarding each other's backs as they cut and sliced the monsters.

The ogres breached the trenches and Jastillian and Behast fell back. The ogres roared when they saw me and sprinted my way. Prastian and Behast continued to shoot their arrows, but their quivers were dangerously low.

"Kill the wizard!" an ogre shouted.

A dozen veered away from Jastillian and Behast and stomped towards me. The warriors slashed at them, but they pushed the pain aside. Behast clipped one in the knee. The ogre glared at the elf, but his hatred deepened when he met my eye. He clawed his way toward me before Behast finished him off. Whatever else Premier had taught them, he taught them one important thing—kill the wizard first.

The ogres were twenty feet away, but my minor spells weren't slowing them down. I used the air to slice and rip into their heavy flesh. Their dark gray skin peeled away until black blood oozed out. I scrambled backwards, needing time to gather in more mana. I thought I could get some distance from them, but then an ogre leapt out from behind a dead companion, almost on top of me.

The ogre raised his rusted sword to strike me before I could conjure enough magic for a defense. His dark eyes shone with triumph, knowing that he would be the first of his kind to kill a wizard in a thousand years. Death replaced that look when Jastillian's axe cleaved through the monster's chest from behind.

Soon, the ogres had surrounded us. We five were pressed against each other, fighting back to back in a small circle. Prastian and Demay had long run out of arrows and now wielded their short swords. Together, the brothers struck down an ogre three times their size. All my current spells were weak and easy. The earlier spells had taken their toll on me and I needed more time to gather in energy. Time I wouldn't have.

No matter how many died, the ogres kept coming. I flung smaller spells to give us some breathing room, but it wasn't enough. None of it was enough. I felt that black fire boiling up inside, aching to be released. I knew if I let it take over, the ogres would die, but my friends might as well. I didn't know if I could control it, as exhausted as I was. And the goblins were still on their way.

I stood in the middle of a protective circle. The noose around our necks tightened as my friends were pushed back into an ever-smaller circle. I could barely move to change the direction of my spells. I needed more power, more time, more space—anything!

Jastillian had taken a slash to his right side, and was trying to fight a huge ogre with a club while protecting the wound. Prastian's left arm bled yet he still tried to take down his ogre with one useless arm. Neither of them could last much longer, and I had nothing more to give. My vision was already blurring—another couple of spells and I would black out.

High screeches pierced the night air, and the sounds of death surrounded me. The goblins had come. There would be no escape now. The goblins worked their way into a frenzy and rushed into the surrounding melee.

I had no choice. It was time to unleash that dark and uncontrollable magic.

I waited until they were in range, until I could see the dark mass of them running at us. Jastillian was on his knees, and Prastian could barely lift his sword arm. But I had to make sure I could hit as many goblins as possible. The front of the horde was almost upon us, backing up the ogres. I readied myself, feeling the black fire build. The goblins shrieked their battle cries...

And fell upon the ogres.

The lead goblin leapt unto an ogre's back, driving his sword into the beast's neck. The ogre toppled over. The goblin jumped from that ogre and slashed one to his left, distracting him as another goblin ran him through.

Everywhere I looked, bands of goblins brought down ogres. Those without weapons fought with their sharp teeth and nails, mobbing the ogres and rending them apart.

The ogres turned from us to fight the goblins. Jastillian leaned against me while Behast held Prastian up. Demay took point, dodging and shoving through the melee, leading us to the rocks, where there was some cover. I leaned against a boulder, fighting the black power that still roared for release. Demay and Behast were busy with field dressings, patching up Prastian and Jastillian, while their own blood ran down from smaller wounds.

It was all over in a few minutes. When the last ogre fell, one of the goblins raised his sword and snarled in victory, the other goblins echoing his roar. He turned to face us.

It was Kemek.

Drenched in black blood, he walked toward us, along with a dozen of his kind. Behast stood at my side while Demay guarded the others. I was wary of what the goblins wanted, even though most of them were finishing off the wounded ogres. They may have killed the ogres, and I may have understood the goblins better because of my earlier disguise, but they were still Wasteland creatures. What did they want and why were they here? Did Kemek and his band want the glory of killing a wizard?

Kemek's head came to my chin. He pushed his helm up and stared at me with defiant eyes. I waited for him to make his move while I summoned what little magic I could. However, he bowed, and all the goblins in the area did the same.

"Great One," Kemek said. "We came to warn you of stupid ogres, but we too late."

"I see," I said. "Why did they attack us?"

"They stupid!" Kemek threw up his hands. "Trolls stupid too, but not attack. Ogres mad they no longer favorites." He puffed his chest out and said, "We goblins are!" The goblins around him roared in joy.

I gave a little nod to Kemek and the others around him and said, "Thank you."

The goblins stood a little taller and grinned so wide, I saw their rows of pointy teeth.

"I have a favor to ask you, Kemek," I said. "I need you and your people to escort us to Alexandria. You must make sure there will be no more attacks from the stupid ogres or trolls."

I stared at him as he scrunched up his face in thought. He wiped blood from his face and licked it. "Hmmm...we go, if that what Great One want. But smelly humans may attack us. We want no more goblins to die. Lost many to get here."

"They won't attack you. You have my word."

Kemek nodded. "Me believe you." He lowered his voice and said, "Since you know about secret city."

I went back to the others and told them what had transpired. They agreed on traveling with the goblins back to Alexandria.

For the next week, we journeyed with the goblins. We still rotated watch throughout the nights in case the goblins tried something.

As we sat at a campfire one evening, one goblin eyed the elves and asked, "Why you no eat meat? Me not seen you eat meat entire time even when we offer you ogre meat over fire." The goblin took a bite of leftover raw ogre meat. "You strange."

"Boghak!" Kemek said.

"It's all right," Prastian said, putting a hand up. "Not everything in the land eats as you goblins do."

"We know," Boghak said. "Smelly humans and dwarves," he said, motioning to Jastillian with his head, "like to burn meat before eating. But no eat meat at all? Me no understand that!"

The goblins around the campfire nodded in agreement.

"Hellsfire doesn't eat meat," Prastian said.

"But he Great One. He better than us. You elf. You no better than us. Why you not eat meat?"

"It's just the way the gods created us."

"Me not trust those that don't eat meat." Boghak scowled at the elves.

"Me don't trust those that don't cook their meat," Demay said.

Boghak snarled and so did the other goblins.

"Enough!" I said.

The goblins sat back down and bowed their heads.

"We are how the gods made us," I said. "We may have our differences, but we have to learn how to live with each other. If we don't, many will die."

"The Great One is wise," Kemek said.

"I wish you'd all stop calling me that. It makes me uncomfortable." I sighed and rubbed my hands through my dirty hair. "I am just a man, Kemek."

Kemek shook his head. "No. You more than that. You magic-man!" The goblin looked sad as he said, "First magic-man in long time to be good to goblins."

"I could still be good to you. We could be good to each other."

"What you mean?"

I tapped his dented armor. "What if I could get you and your goblins better weapons and armor? Ones that were in better condition and fit?"

"You'd do that?"

I nodded.

Kemek lifted his helm up. It had slipped again. "Me would love to have better sword to cut down ugly ogres and trolls with." His beady eyes stared intently at me. "What would me have to do?"

"As I said before, I don't want any creatures to go past the mountains, but I want you to give Alexandria information on what is happening in the Wastelands. Show them safe places to travel, where food and water is, be their guide, things like that. It would be an alliance between our two peoples. We both do things for each other."

"Me no know about *all-i-ance*. Me hate smelly humans. Me not trust them." Kemek sucked the marrow off a bone, then his tongue swirled around his mouth. His eyes wandered to the other goblins, examining their weapons and armor. "If you there, me could do what you want."

I nodded. "All right."

"Me can't get all the goblins to agree. Too many tribes. Too many that not as smart as we." Kemek and the other goblins chuckled.

"I understand."

Later on that night, before I went to sleep, Prastian came over to me. In a hushed tone he asked, "Are you sure what you did was wise, Hellsfire?"

"What do you mean?"

"You committed resources of a land where you have no say."

"But now Alexandria won't have to worry about things as much, at least when it comes to the goblins."

"But what if the princess and her father object to it? If they would prefer to do what they trained a thousand years for and kill them?"

I opened my mouth, then stopped. Prastian had a point. Both those in Alexandria and the goblins had it ingrained in them to slaughter each other the way they always had. "I thought of an opportunity and seized it," I said. "I think it would be a waste if they decide not to work with the goblins."

"I agree," Prastian said. "The information Kemek and the others can obtain here will be invaluable, but it will be difficult to convince King Furlong. He won't want to arm potential enemies. I wouldn't want to either."

"I can at least try. I believe working together will curb the hostilities more than each staying to their own land."

"You may be right, Hellsfire. Good night."

"Good night."

By midday, we heard the noise of thunderous hooves. Prastian and I ran to meet Alexandria's patrol before they attacked the goblins.

"It's good to see you both again," Captain Rebekah said, halting her horse. She and her men eyed the horde behind us, and her hands tightened on her reins. "Sorry to see that the others didn't make it. Stay back and we'll fight the creatures." She turned to two of her men. "You two escort them back to Alexandria."

"No!" I said. "Leave the goblins alone. They helped us return. All of us. They're our...allies."

"How can you ally yourself with the Wasteland creatures?" one woman said.

"You're no better than Premier," another rider added.

"Quiet!" Rebekah said. "King Furlong's not going to like this. I don't like this."

"Please," I said. "You must not attack them."

Rebekah glared at the goblins. She paused, but then eventually nodded. "All right. As long as they stay there."

"But Captain, that's a huge force threatening Alexandria. We should send for more reinforcements and crush these creatures."

"No," she said. "If what Hellsfire says is true, we'll let them live for now."

"But—"

"I said no! You, go back and send word that they've returned. Hellsfire, I suggest you hurry and get the others, and tell the creatures not to make any sudden movements and to be gone as soon as possible."

"I'll stay here and talk to the good captain," Prastian said.

I ran back to the others. Now that it was daylight and I was running towards them, I saw what Rebekah's people saw. A large dark force of armed goblins looked intimidating to a weakened city and smaller force. It could just be the beginning of another attack.

"We'll go back to the city on our own," I said to Kemek as soon as I arrived. "Thanks again. Thanks to you all."

All the goblins bowed to me.

"Give me one of your rocks to your secret city."

Kemek gasped. "You know about rock too?"

One of the goblins hesitated. She only handed me a rock after looking to Kemek. I closed my hands around it and chanted, imbuing it with power. I cast a one-time notification spell on it. The smudge-colored rock glowed briefly when I handed it back to Kemek.

"Don't lose this," I said. "When you come back here, I want you to slam this rock down on the ground. It'll notify me of your location. Don't come too close to the city." I remembered both Prastian's words and Rebekah's reactions. "And give it some time before you return."

"Me will. Bye Great One." Kemek bowed then barked orders to the goblins.

I waited, watching the goblins jog back into the Wastelands until they disappeared over the horizon.

Jastillian clapped me on the back as we walked back to Rebekah and her men. "That was a fine adventure, lad. I expect many songs to be sung about us. When I get back to Erlam, I'll have plenty of things to write down. I'll keep the scribes busy for ages." His brown eyes shone. "But first there's Southern Shala!"

I wanted to tell him that we should wait and rest, but he was right.

Southern Shala had to be told about Premier, and warned of Renak's words.

"We have to tend to our wounds," Demay said, "And we all need baths. We stink."

We all chuckled at that response, glad to finally be out of the Wastelands.

When we reached the others, we doubled up on horses. I sat behind Rebekah.

"Prastian told me what you did with the goblins," Rebekah said. "The king's not going to like it. The princess might not either."

"Did he also tell you that attacks may lessen because of it?" I asked. "Despite what you may think, the creatures in the Wastelands aren't just monsters. They have their own culture and rules of society."

Rebekah snorted.

"And they also have their faults just like any of us. Sure, they're more savage than most, but Premier was controlling them."

"So you say," she said. "But you haven't seen the things we have. In either case, it's not me who you're going to have to convince." Rebekah spurred her horse into trotting faster.

We arrived back at Alexandria three hours before sundown. Outside of the city gates was Krystal. My heart and face lit up at the sight of her. I knew that what I saw in the nexus wasn't real, but I still hadn't been completely sure. Renak's words about his spell being twisted and to watch Premier mulled over in my mind.

Krystal's eyes lingered on me for a moment, and she gave me a brief smile. "It's good to see you again. All of you. Thank the gods you made it. I was worried for your well-being."

"Your Highness," I said. "It's good to see you too."

"I look forward to hearing what happened, after you get cleaned up." She did her best to hide it, but her nose scrunched up in a way I found adorable. "I'll see you in an hour."

We trotted past her. I couldn't help but turn around and stare at her. She grinned, and I returned it. My cheeks flushed with heat. I couldn't wait to be with her and sweep her in my arms again.

I took a bath and had my wizard's robes washed. I scrubbed myself clean from all the grime, dirt, and blood. I worked hard to get rid of that Wastelands smell, the camping with goblins, and the black blood that clung to me from slaughtering ogres. The once clear water blackened until it was like soot. My robes were returned to me, and I shaved. I ran my fingers through my damp hair, then rushed to the small, quiet audience chamber, as there was much to report to the king.

Everyone was already seated around the table. I hovered near the door, watching King Furlong, his daughter, and Prastian engaged in animated conversation. There was plenty of fresh food on the table. It seemed hardly anyone had touched the food, despite how much was piled on everyone's plates. My eyes lit up at the fresh bread, fruit, and cheese. Even the platters of meat smelled good, but I felt I would barely be able to take more than a few bites. I took a deep breath and strode over to the table.

"It's about time you got here, Hellsfire," King Furlong said. "We have much to discuss."

I bowed and took a seat next to Krystal. "Sorry to keep everyone waiting."

The king stared at me as if he didn't know where to begin. I loosened at my collar before taking a sip of wine.

Finally, the king spoke. "You let Premier escape, Hellsfire. You didn't take away his powers or retrieve the *Book of Shazul*. He may threaten us once more."

I shook my head. "He gave me his wizard's word that he wouldn't bother Alexandria anymore."

"He already tricked and betrayed me once. How do you know he won't do so again? You can't be so naive as to trust him."

"That's not how it works, Your Majesty. If he breaks his word, his power would leave him."

The king considered this. "You should have killed him when you had the chance. You were too lenient. I know this was your master's last request, but some people don't deserve a second chance."

I nodded, not wanting to argue about this subject anymore, and because I also partly agreed with him.

King Furlong's face darkened. "Now, what's this I hear about you brokering an alliance between Alexandria and the beasts out there?"

I squirmed in my seat when even Krystal's stern gaze settled on me. "I thought it best, Your Majesty. In return for weapons and armor, they could work with your people and scout the terrain. They could feed you information so you would know well in advance if another wizard ever used the creatures again to attack your city. I already made them promise to stay away from Alexandria, but I thought it would be better if they did more."

"You would have me arm our enemies, Hellsfire?" The king's voice grew louder. "What if they decided to attack us with those same weapons?"

"They don't have to be the best of weapons, Your Majesty. They'll take anything. And these goblins won't attack you again. I made sure of that. They're one less threat to you."

"From what I understand, this is just one small group of goblins, and they're not loyal to Alexandria, they're under *your* command."

I started to respond but he cut me off.

"You may have control of the goblins, but what of the ogres and trolls? They easily kill goblins. What if they take those weapons off those dead goblins and use them against us? What then, Hellsfire?"

"I...didn't think about that, Your Majesty."

"Quite right," he said. "You're *not* our ambassador. You should remember that and not make promises you can't keep."

"I know," I said and bowed my head. Out of the corner of my eye, I looked to Krystal for understanding. Her face was impassive. "The creatures aren't what you think they are. They're rough and primitive, but they have their own culture and rules."

"Ridiculous," King Furlong said. "They're savage beasts and nothing more."

"You're wrong, Your Majesty," I said. "Even Jastillian could reassure you there's far more to them than that. You must realize that. I did what I thought was best for you and your city. Just give them a chance. That's all I'm asking. Please, Your Majesty."

The king stared at me, weighing me and my words for several long seconds. "I'll consider it, but I make no promises," he said.

"I understand, Your Majesty. Thank you."

King Furlong leaned forward in his seat, his blue eyes piercing me. "But that's not all you've done. Tell me how, after a thousand years, you brought down the Great Barrier."

I told him about the nexus and how it worked. I didn't give him the specific details of what I'd faced while in there, but I did tell him about Renak and what he told me. I also explained why I did it. How I had to save my friends' lives and that the barrier was destroying the land and would eventually ruin all of Northern Shala.

Afterwards, the king said, "I'm thankful you saved Jastillian and Demay. I would have mourned deeply for their deaths." Furlong smiled in their direction. His stern face returned when he talked to me. "But did you think this through, Hellsfire?"

"What do you mean?"

"Renak may not have lied to you about a threat that could destroy the land," King Furlong said. "You may have just misunderstood what he said."

"Armies," Jastillian said.

"More than that," King Furlong said. "Armies of wizards."

I shook my head. They wouldn't come all the way up here to attack. What could possibly be of importance in Northern Shala? Then I met Krystal's eyes and remembered the scroll she had given me. If they knew of Alexandria's secret vault, they might want that, and Masep still contained plenty of hidden secrets.

"What about what Renak said about the gods' war?" I asked.

"There has been no evidence," the king said. "You can't trust him."

"That's because the barrier has been up."

"Now that it's down, there have been no earthquakes or thunderstorms. Surely, a war with the gods would cause great devastation."

I crossed my arms, thinking the king might be right. Maybe Renak's seer just misinterpreted what she saw. No, the look of worry and fear had weighed heavily on Renak.

"We don't know that they have armies of wizards or that they seek to rule here," Prastian said, bringing the discussion to the point at hand.

"That's exactly my point," the king said. "We have no idea what dangers are down there. Hellsfire may have released unknown dangers to the land, real, more tangible threats than a vague notion of a villainous wizard."

"Or he may have opened up new opportunities," the princess said.

King Furlong slowly nodded. "That is a possibility. Jastillian and Prastian, I take it you both will go down there?"

Jastillian smiled. "Of course, Your Majesty, it's a great opportunity. I've already sent word back to Erlam about it. My mother will send a more proper expedition."

"I've sent word back too," Prastian said, "But I don't know if I'll go. King Sharald may decide to send someone else."

"But brother, we should go," Demay said. "I've always wanted to see what was down there."

"We'll talk it over with our king."

"And Hellsfire, do you also plan to go to Southern Shala?" King Furlong asked.

I glanced at Krystal. I didn't want to leave her so soon, especially after what I had gone though. But the Elemental Council, if they still existed, needed to be warned about Premier. I also wanted to see if they could help me with my power. I didn't understand the black flames, and if anyone could help me, they could. And I had promised I would look into Renak's story.

"Yes, Your Majesty," I said. "Bringing down the Great Barrier's *my* responsibility. If danger's down there, I should be the one to face it."

"With our help," Jastillian said.

"Agreed," Prastian said, and all my other friends nodded.

"Very well," the king said. "The five of you work well together, but I'll need to send my own people down. I need someone who can be a representative of Alexandria."

"I'll go with them," Krystal said.

King Furlong turned his head and stared at his daughter.

"I should be the one to go, Father," she said. "Because of our recent battle, we're spread thin. Our diplomats and ambassadors have been sent to other lands to reassure our allies that Alexandria still stands. We could wait for them, but it might be a while."

King Furlong cupped his hands under his chin. Silence reigned in the room as he thought about her proposal.

I plucked a grape, wondering why she wanted to go so badly. Why was it so important to her that she go and leave her people? A brief grin passed over my face as I considered the possibility that she wanted to go to be with me because she cared deeply about me—about us.

The king broke his silence. "You will not go. We will wait until the others return."

Krystal bowed her head. "As you wish, Father."

The princess's violet eyes danced in the candlelight. I knew she wasn't going to let this rest.

"I hope you'll be able to share with me what you learn down there," King Furlong said.

"Of course we will, Your Majesty," Prastian said.

"Aye," Jastillian said.

"When will the five of you leave?" the king asked.

"A few days' rest would be perfect, Your Majesty," Prastian said. "We still need to heal from our wounds."

"Very well. We'll see to your supplies and horses."

"Thank you," Prastian said.

We were dismissed, and everyone went their separate ways. I wanted to talk to Krystal alone to find out what in the gods' names she was thinking. She gave me a tantalizing smile and raised her eyebrows. I returned the playful smile before she disappeared into the castle.

I yawned, finding myself more tired than I ought to be because of the food and drink. Night had fallen, and it was growing late. I made my way back to my room and found the princess waiting for me.

"Hi, hero," Krystal said.

"Hi, beautiful," I said.

She took a step closer and wrapped her arms around me, squeezing me tightly. "Thank the gods you're back and safe," she whispered into my ear. "I went to the temple and prayed for your safety every day, and sent constant patrols."

I returned her hug, grasping her like a child would a parent, never wanting to part from her. Her warmth felt so good, and I melted into her arms. "I was worried we wouldn't make it when I was so close to returning to you. But then the goblins came and saved us."

Krystal pulled her body back. "So you've said. Do you really believe the Wasteland creatures aren't that bad?"

"They're...different."

"Then tell me. All of it."

We sat down on the bed and I obeyed. I told her how it felt to have two souls occupying the same body. The cravings I had and the memories I experienced. How hard it was to control, and how I forgot who I was at times. I explained in detail how there were different tribes and how the creatures all had their own rules. I let her know all of it. I even told her about the secret goblin city.

"You didn't mention that to my father," she said.

"I promised not to. Besides, according to Jastillian, it's too far away to be a threat."

"He should still know."

I shrugged. "I'll leave it in your hands. What are you going to do?"

"I'll discuss the situation with my father. What you proposed wasn't a bad idea, but there'd have to be limits. I don't want to arm potential enemies. If we limited the weapons and armor that went out, supplied them with food instead, or repaired the ones they had, it might be possible."

"Thank you."

Her hand squeezed my thigh. "There was another thing I wanted to know about."

"Sure."

"What exactly did you face in the nexus, and what did Renak tell you? You were holding something back."

I glanced away and bit the inside of my cheek. I looked back at her and sighed. "I'm not sure if I should tell you. It's...personal."

She put a hand on my cheek and forced me to look at her. "You can trust me."

I took her hand and kissed it. "I know."

I delved into details about what I saw and experienced while inside the nexus. I told her how happy I was when I saw my parents, how terrified I was when I thought she had died, and how she gave me strength to beat Renak. I could barely meet her eyes while I talked. It felt good, getting it off my chest, but I also felt like I was exposing a hidden part of myself.

But Krystal never judged or mocked me. She sat and listened intently, reaching for my trembling hand and stroking it.

"You don't have to worry anymore," Krystal said. "I'm here and safe."

"I know," I said, clutching her hand tighter. "Thanks for making me feel better, but the whole thing still upsets me. Renak said something had been altered with his spell, but he didn't have time to figure out what it was." I sighed. "And if that's not bad enough, I believed Renak when he talked about the threat from Southern Shala. Your father's wrong. It's not armies Renak was scared of...it's something else entirely."

Krystal intertwined her fingers with mine. "You'll handle whatever's down there. You just did the impossible by going to Masep *and* returning. I just wish I could go with you."

"I don't understand that. Why do you want to go to Southern Shala so badly?"

"Have you ever had a childhood dream, Hellsfire?"

I tried to remember. Everyday life had been a struggle growing up in Sedah, poor and without a father. I had wanted more out of my life and to not feel powerless, but nothing specific beyond that. I shook my head.

Krystal gazed away with a wistful look on her face. "When I was younger, I used to read stories about Southern Shala. I'd imagine the land down there and how it was before the war. It was full of possibilities, wonders, and magic. There were wizards like you." She playfully nudged me with her elbow. "Along with beautiful unicorns. I've always wanted to see one since I was a little girl. Think about it, Hellsfire, we would be the first to do so in a thousand years." Krystal focused back on me and shook her head. "It's just a silly childhood dream."

"No. It's not. I wish you could go with me." I did. Not as Princess of Alexandria, but as a woman. If Southern Shala was like it had been before the barrier went up and before the war, it would be a great place to escape to and be as a man and woman. That could never happen. She had her duties and I had mine.

She gave me a mischievous grin. "I still might."

"But your father—"

"I'm sure I can get him to see reason. Besides, you'll protect me from whatever's down there, right?"

"Of course. But I still don't think you should go. I have a feeling it's going to be too dangerous."

She shook her head. "It's too great an opportunity to pass up. We don't have time to wait. Sharald and Erlam might be our allies, but we can't let them have any advantages over us. I'm the best qualified person to go. If there were anyone else, I wouldn't press the issue, but there's not."

I stared at her and smirked. "Are you sure you don't want to go because it's a childhood dream?"

She grinned. "Maybe. If I can't go, you'll have to be my proxy. I'm going to need you to act in an unofficial, official capacity. When you meet the council or anyone else, try to work something out for the good of Alexandria."

"Are you sure about this? I'm not very good at negotiating."

"You negotiated with the goblins."

"But your father thought that was a mistake."

"My father may not trust you," she said. "But *I* trust you."

I smiled. "I'll do my best."

"That's all I ask. If you have problems or questions, follow Prastian's example."

"I will."

"Good," Krystal said. "We can worry about that later. We have a few days before you leave." A hunger dwelled in her eyes. She grabbed me by the collar and whispered into my ear, "I've missed you, more than you know."

"Me too," I said, finding it hard to speak. "The only reason I made it back was because of you."

Krystal's face burned red and she gave me the biggest smile. We closed the small space between us until there was nothing left, and kissed. Our tongues swirled while her hands roamed the back of my head and mine explored her lower back and rear. We both moaned, on our way to a rapture that only the two of us would ever enter.

A swell of magical energy bubbled up inside of me, feeling like the light I had experienced inside the nexus. It exploded outward, showering Krystal with its power. It wormed its way inside of her. Her face froze. Her fingers dug into my scalp and she screamed. All the color in her face drained, while her eyes screamed for help.

CHAPTER 14

I LET GO of the princess. Her face contorted with horror and pain.

"Krystal!" I screamed.

Her soft skin faded and shriveled, the veins turning black. It was worse around her lips, where I had kissed her. I hurried to lay her on the small bed. Her eyes were still open, but they stared at nothing. I leaned in to see if she was breathing, but she went into convulsions, thrashing her limbs. My wizard's sight saw that somehow the nexus's energy had entered her. It coursed its way through her body, filling over every pore, bone, sinew, and muscle.

I reached into my purse for a healing potion, but her flailing arms smacked it away. The vial crashed, the glass shattering on the floor. I grabbed her arms, trying to still her, but when I touched her skin, the magic inside of her blossomed and she screeched in pain.

I was killing her.

I let Krystal go and closed my eyes so I could concentrate on my magic, and not see how much agony she was in. I tried to block out her tormented moans and conjure white mana. Whenever my magic brushed up against her, the magic inside of her consumed it before it could work.

The bright light inside of her that I loved so much dimmed. Her wavy hair became brittle and her bones became visible under her shrunken flesh. She was dying and there was nothing I could do.

A bright green light flared from her chest, permeating her clothes and skin.

The magic from the necklace struck the curse with a clash of power. The two energies battled each other, the necklace's magic hammering the curse back.

Krystal's body stilled, her arms and head becoming motionless. She didn't even breathe. I bent over her mouth, trying to hear her. There was nothing.

I clenched my fists and bit my lip. The magical fight within her must have been too much for her. She wasn't a wizard. Her body wasn't used to that sort of energy. Or the ancient magic of the nexus was too powerful.

Krystal gasped for air and opened her eyes. The black lines in her face faded.

I stared into her eyes and said, "Krystal!"

Her glazed eyes didn't move towards me. Instead, she closed them, and her chest heaved with deep breaths. I hesitantly placed my hand on her chest, thankful that the fabric blocked the touch of my skin. I was relieved to feel her heart beating normally. However, her skin was still pale and her hair brittle.

The light from the necklace dimmed, but the two magics still assaulted each other. Krystal's eyelids twitched as if she were having a nightmare. Every few breaths, her body shivered like she was caught in a snowstorm.

I kneeled next to the bed and studied her. One by one, I tried all the healing spells Stradus had taught me. Every time my magic touched her body, the nexus's magic strengthened and beat back the necklace's magic. Sweat ran down Krystal's face and her breathing became erratic. When I stopped, her breathing eased.

I stared at the broken potion on the floor. I didn't have any more healing potions, as I had used them all in the Wastelands. I would have to concoct some more. For the moment, Krystal seemed to be out of immediate danger, but I would have to do more research to help her. I placed a blanket over her and ran out of the room to find help.

I burst back into the room with three healers. Two of them examined Krystal. I told the head healer, Shanna, what had happened to the princess, and that they shouldn't remove the necklace.

"Thank you, Wizard Hellsfire," Shanna said. "That will be all."

"But—"

She put her hand up. "You have done more than enough here. We will see to the princess's condition."

I slumped my shoulders. "Just let me know if she gets better."

Shanna turned and left.

"What's going on here?" King Furlong asked, barging into the room. His eyes filled with worry when they saw the princess lying on the bed. His gaze turned on me and his eyes filled with anger. "What did you do, Hellsfire?"

"Please, Your Majesty," one of the healers said.

"Outside," the king said to me through gritted teeth.

We went into the empty hall. I stood erect, meeting the king's angry eyes, as I told him what happened to his daughter and how she almost died when I touched her, because of the nexus's magic.

King Furlong couldn't keep the malice out of his voice. He moved until he was inches from my face and said, "You almost killed my beloved daughter and the only heir to Alexandria! How could you?"

"I-I-I'm sorry, Your Majesty. I didn't mean to hurt her." I shook my head, remembering Renak's parting words. I realized the cause of the curse. It was that dog, Premier! "Renak said—"

"I don't care what he said! *You* should have known. *You* almost killed her because of your *magic*. How could you be so careless?" King Furlong scowled at me. "Wizards! You're so arrogant. You only do what's good for you, and you never realize that the decisions you make affect countless people. We're nothing but tools to you and your kind! You may have the powers of the gods, but you are not gods, Hellsfire!"

He made a visible effort to calm himself and put his royal mask into place. "I know of the...indiscretions between you and my daughter. I've let Krystal have her fun, but it ends now. You weren't the first, and you certainly won't be the last. Do not think you were ever more than that!"

I stared at the king. I hadn't realized that Krystal had others before me. I didn't know much about her past. As much time as we spent together, I'd answered all of her questions when she wanted to know about my life, but whenever I asked about hers, she changed the subject or took my mind off it by other means.

Why hadn't she let me know about her past? Was I just a brief fling to her? How did she feel about me? Her father had reminded me that she was a princess, and that even with all the power at my fingertips, I was only a poor farm boy. Could we ever be together, especially after all this?

The king sighed and rubbed his wrinkled forehead. "Perhaps this is for the best. Hellsfire, you've saved my kingdom and my life. For that, I am grateful." His face hardened and his voice deepened. "But stay away from my daughter or I will have you hanged. If my daughter dies, there will be no amount of magic that can save you."

I lifted my tired head to look at him. I couldn't think of anything to say. I nodded in agreement. The king went back to my room and his daughter.

I followed the king back inside. I stood near the door as he talked to Shanna. While the healer didn't acknowledge me, she spoke in a voice loud enough that I could hear.

"She's resting, Your Majesty," she said. "She's calmed down for now and we've given her some poppy to help her sleep. We're still not sure of the nature of her problem or how deep it runs, but we'll do all we can."

"Thank you," the king said. He glanced at me from the corner of his eye, and I took that as a signal to leave.

The princess didn't wake from her coma, and I never saw her during the days that followed. Despite the fact that I needed to get down to Southern Shala and warn the council, I waited for her to wake. I wasn't leaving until I knew she was better. I would have understood if my friends wanted to leave, but they waited for me. I ached to go into Southern Shala, but only to find Premier and burn him in total, agonizing pain for what he had done to Krystal.

Despite the king's warning, I yearned to get a better look at Krystal. I had to understand the magic and see if there was anything I could do about it. If Premier had altered Renak's spell into a curse, perhaps it could be changed back. However, Shanna or one of the other healers always barred me when I tried to sneak in at night. I pleaded with them to let me see her, even if it was just for a moment, because they could never understand magic the way I could. My words fell on deaf ears.

Frustrated, I went to the library to try to find something that would help. I received icy glares from the other castle residents using the library. When I took a break and went to the kitchens for some food, everyone I passed gave me the same withering look. I ate my meal alone, then went back to the library.

I couldn't study because of all the seething people around me. I took what books I thought would be useful and went to the one place people would never venture into—Premier's tower.

Book after book was useless. I had been afraid of that, since Alexandria, with their ban on wizards, kept all their books about magic in their hidden archive. There were a handful of spells I found in my own spell book, but I needed to test them on the princess. After another day of frustration, I gave up searching through the books and walked down to the marketplace to get my mind off of things.

When I reached the honey bread stall, the owner narrowed his eyes at me and crossed his arms.

I opened my mouth to tell him what I wanted, but the man said, "No honey bread."

"Why not?" I asked.

"We're all out," his wife said, leaving another customer and coming up beside her husband.

I peered in between them at the bread. The sweet aroma tickled my nose.

"It's right there," I said, pointing.

"Those are bad batches," she said. "We were just about to get rid of them."

"That's all right. I'll buy one anyway."

"No!" the man said. "We don't serve those who hurt our princess. Now leave, *wizard.*"

I sighed and gave up. "Fine."

I walked away. The surrounding people pierced me with cold stares. I put my hood up in hopes that I wouldn't be recognized by more than a few, but it was too late.

The crowd jostled around me until they became a wall. I tried to squeeze through them, but I had to push to get them out of my way. They began to shout obscenities. I ignored them and bored through the ever-growing mob.

The crowd fought back and shoved me. I became a feather in a storm. My first instinct was to use my powers, but I didn't want to hurt anyone. I also didn't want to give them any more excuse to hate me and my magic. A small rock struck my back, and then a hail of stones were showered upon me. They battered my body, but my thick wizard's robes took most of the impact. I shoved people aside. I had to get out of here and back to the castle before things got worse.

A fist-sized rock struck me in the forehead. I staggered, and stumbled to my knees. Bigger rocks were thrown. I kept my head down, trying not to unleash my angry fire. I understood how Alexandria's people felt. It was my fault their princess was close to death. There was nothing they could do about Premier, but there was something they could do about me.

I cried out when a heavy rock hit my spine. I couldn't take much more, and the city guard didn't make a move to help.

"Enough!" I yelled.

A backlash of wind exploded from me. People in a fifty-foot radius were shoved back, knocking into each other. The rocks they had thrown flew backwards into the crowd, striking those that weren't quick enough to duck. Rocks shattered against the market's wooden stalls.

I rose and pulled back my hood. I wiped the blood from the bump on my head as I surveyed the frightened and injured people. I didn't want to hurt anybody, but they'd left me no choice. Didn't they understand how much pain I was in? It was my fault the princess almost died. Not theirs. Mine!

I walked over the fallen mob, leaving the wounded people, and headed back to the castle.

For the next week, I holed up in Premier's tower so I wouldn't be bothered or threatened by anyone. I only left to return books and borrow new ones, and to retrieve meals.

My frustration mounted. I needed magical books like those in Stradus's library, but I couldn't go back there now. It would take too long to travel to the mountain without Cynder. Since the barrier was down, I could go to the wizards' school in Southern Shala or see the council. That would take far longer, but they should have any information that there was. But I wasn't going anywhere without seeing Krystal first.

While I was thankful that Prastian, Jastillian, Demay, and Behast visited me and gave me news, they were nervous to come into Premier's former tower, and they were anxious to leave for Southern Shala. Their patience wouldn't last forever.

There was one other who delivered news about Krystal—Ardimus. "How is she?" I asked him. I rose from the piles of books I had scattered on the floor. Everything Premier had used had been removed from the tower, so I had no furniture.

Ardimus looked as exhausted as I was, since he was always with Krystal. "She lives," he said, "but she won't come out of her coma. During the night, her condition worsens. She screams, tossing and turning uncontrollably. The potions the healers brew have little effect. Only that necklace you gave her does. It flares, and she's calm again. Until she's at it a few hours later. Her outbreaks are fewer and less intense as time passes."

"I wish there was something I could do. It's all my fault. Journeying into the Wastelands was one thing, but bringing down the Great Barrier was another. If I hadn't gone into the nexus in the first place, none of this would have happened."

Ardimus stepped around one of the piles of books. "You did what you had to do to at the time to save Jastillian and Demay. The princess would understand that."

I shrugged. Were their lives worth more than Krystal's? "Ardimus, you know the princess better than I. Do you think me being here is...wise?"

"I heard what happened in the marketplace. It's wise that you've not left the castle grounds since then."

I nodded. "So Prastian's told me. He also told me that being in the castle isn't helping matters. Nobles are trying to get me banished, but King Furlong won't make a decision until Krystal wakes up...if she ever does."

I sighed and scratched my face. "I don't know what to do, Ardimus. I feel like I've been nothing but a blight to Krystal and her people. Maybe they're right. Maybe I should go and leave her in peace. What do you think?"

Ardimus stared at me in silence while he considered this. "I think you need to talk to the princess before you do anything. I've known her highness since she was a little girl, and this is the happiest I've seen her in a long time. If you left without saying goodbye, she'd be devastated."

"But do you think we could ever be together?"

"This, I do not know. I have lived here and served Alexandria for many years, but I am not from this land. Her people are filled with pride, like those of most great cities. They love their princess and king more than in most countries I've seen. That's a good sign, but if someone harms or threatens the royal family, the people will be out for blood."

Ardimus allowed himself a small smile. "I know you mean no harm to this city, but I don't know if her people will ever accept you. You are a wizard." He paused. "Maybe if Premier had never come into our lives, or if harm had not befallen the princess, they would have accepted you, but now..."

I stared at one of the open books, but never saw past the words. An idea struck me. I glanced back up at Ardimus and asked, "Do you know where Alexandria's vault is? The one that's guarded magic over the centuries? If I had access to it, I might be able to cure the princess."

"Sorry, I do not. As much as the princess trusts me, I'm not allowed there. However, Alexandria *buries* her secrets deep, Hellsfire. Very deep."

I wondered what he meant, but nodded when I finally realized it. "Thank you, Ardimus."

"Be careful, Hellsfire."

"I will."

CHAPTER 15

I WAITED UNTIL the middle of the night when the keep was quiet before I enacted my hasty plan. There would be only one place the vault would be—in hidden tunnels underneath the city. When we had retaken Alexandria, we had used those tunnels to enter the keep. There were few alive who knew about them. Krystal had guided us through the maze of dead ends and traps. Now, I would be alone.

I could have used Jastillian and Prastian with me. Their heightened senses would have been invaluable, but I couldn't ask them. If I got caught, things would be disastrous for them and their cities. I had to do it alone.

I returned the books to the library late at night, when only three people were there. I slowly put books back until I was the only one in the library. I went to the bookshelf we had used to enter and I stared at a small group of stones on the floor. They had to be pressed in a sequential order for the bookshelf to open and reveal the secret passageway. I closed my eyes, trying to remember Krystal's motions all those months ago. I bent down and pressed the stones. Nothing happened.

I continued to push down on the six stones, but there were too many combinations. I wished I had paid attention to the princess's movements, but I was too busy worrying about the Wasteland creatures and Premier that night.

I mumbled a curse, worried that I would be stopped here. I tried again, and finally the bookshelf pushed outward and slid to the side. I glanced around to see if anyone had heard the noise. Seeing no one, I slipped into the hole behind it.

I pushed another stone near the opening and the hole sealed up. I turned around and peered into the darkness. I took a deep breath, remembering that I was doing this for Krystal. I had to cure her.

A small fireball ignited in my hand, illuminating the shadows enough so that I could see. I crept down the stone corridor, moving in silence and keeping my magic small so I wouldn't be noticed.

I retraced the way we had originally entered and bypassed spy holes in the walls. Eventually, the corridor slanted down under the keep, and the stale air became colder and heavier.

At the bottom of the incline was a small wooden door. I knew that if I went through that door and continued, I would find my way to the catacombs under Alexandria. I also knew there were deadly traps waiting down there. Without Krystal, I could set off those traps and die. She had once said there were no traps in the keep.

I paused at the door and glanced down the corridor to my right. I had no idea where it would lead. Was the vault somewhere under the keep, or in the city? Would they have kept the items where they could never be taken, or where they might be accessed in case of an emergency?

I made my decision and turned right, knowing that it would take me longer to go and explore the catacombs underneath the city.

I slunk along in the near darkness as I navigated the passageways. Once I stopped and peeked through of one of the spyholes beneath my feet. Twenty feet below was a guard. I left him and pressed on.

At the end of the corridor, I reached a dead end. On the floor was another small, discolored stone. I leaned against the wall and listened. No sound traveled through it. I put out my fireball and pushed the stone. The wall opened up to darkness, its tiny scraping noise blasting through my ears. I held my breath, fearful of anyone hearing it. I exhaled in relief when no one shouted at me.

I poked my head through the opening. When my eyes adjusted to the lack of light, I gasped at what I saw. A woman and a man cradled each other while sleeping on the lofty bed, their naked bodies pressed together for warmth. I left the bedroom and went back into the passageway, sealing the door.

I back-tracked and took another route. In the middle of the corridor was another stone. After I opened that one up and stepped through, I banged my head on an overhanging pan. I cursed myself when I realized I was in the kitchens. I slipped back into the passageway before someone saw me.

I spent the next two hours searching the secret passageways. My time was running out. When I put my ear against the walls, I began to hear servants scurrying about, getting the day ready for their masters.

I hurried to get back to the library before dawn broke. I was still about an hour away, and if I was lucky, there would be no one there this early in the morning. When I was four corridors away, a tiny bit of light shone near my knees. When I bent down, the opening was bigger than I thought. I cursed myself. How many other openings like this had I missed in the darkness?

I peeked inside the small hole and saw a rat scurrying away from me. I placed my hand on the top edge and glanced back down toward to the library. If I searched this place quickly, I could make it back in thirty minutes.

I squeezed myself into the hole and shimmied along. I ignited another fireball and focused on my breathing. I hated being in cramped places, but I remembered why I was doing this. Krystal.

The small tunnel turned upwards into the keep. I crawled with my forearms. Sweat ran down my face as the small flame in front of me burned. I ignored the spiders crawling by me and went faster. I understood the need for secrecy in having these tunnels, but I didn't understand the reasoning behind the way they were built. For all I knew, this opened up in the sewers.

The tunnel leveled out again and grew brighter. Dawn's light shone at the end. I had wasted too much time. I couldn't risk going back to the library in case there were people there. Whatever was at the end of this tunnel, I was going to have to face it.

I extinguished my flame and crept to the end. Two pairs of feet faced me across from the little hole I peeked out of with the shafts of their pole-arms resting next to them. Guards. They stood, unmoving in front of a door.

Whatever they were guarding must be important. This might be what I was looking for.

I had to take the guards out before they noticed me. I gathered in mana to render them unconscious. I inched closer to the end of the tunnel to get a better look at the surroundings. One of the stones beneath me clicked. Pink gas blew into my face from a tiny crack above me. I coughed and summoned wind to blow it away.

The two pairs of feet ran towards me and yelled, "Intruder!" Before I could disperse the gas or crawl backwards, I passed out.

My eyes opened to near-darkness, and the world tilted on its side. I blinked and moaned, feeling something heavy attached to me. I struggled to sit up, but shackles bound my wrists and legs. I remembered what Stradus once told me. He had said there were bindings that could be used to contain a wizard's magic, but I still felt mine. A stench forced its way into my nose and I knew exactly where I was—a dungeon.

I had been in Alexandria's dungeons before, but never on this side of the door. Thirty feet in front of me, near the dungeon's stairs, was a burning torch hanging on the wall. I summoned my magic to brighten it. Nothing happened.

I stood up and performed the spell again. Still, nothing happened. I opened my hand to test my magic. A small fireball bloomed. But why couldn't I perform any magic outside of this cage?

I stepped to the bars, and they glistened with a sheen of enchantment. I tried to shoot my fireball through the cell, but my magic dispersed when it reached the bars. I created more fire in my hand and flared it so I could see.

There were two empty cells on either side of me. These dungeons were small and couldn't hold more than a dozen people, total. There were no guards. I sighed and sat back against the grime-covered wall. How was I going to get out of this? What was happening upstairs? I stopped my spell. Eventually, the light from the torch burned out, plunging the dungeons into darkness.

A guard eventually came. He relit the torch near the staircase, then plopped a plate of stale bread and mush in front of my cell, along with a tin cup of dirty water. Then he left, ignoring all my questions.

I marked time by the guard's arrival. Three days passed, and all I could do was think. What surprised me was that I didn't only think of Krystal. I thought of my home in Sedah, my mother, and of Kathleen, my first love.

Would things have been better had I stayed home and settled down with her? If I had, I might never have unleashed my powers that fateful day. And even if I had, I still could have learned from Stradus how to control them, and then returned home. Krystal wouldn't be dying, Stradus wouldn't have died, and I wouldn't be stuck in a dungeon.

I banged the back of my head against the wall. Assuming I could get out of here, was it too late to return home now? Would Kathleen want me still? I knew she had been with Nathan, my childhood enemy, when I left, but that couldn't have lasted. I stared at my hands, illuminating the darkness with my fire. There was so much I could do now.

I could control and smother any wildfire. I could make sure we had a bountiful harvest in years of drought. I could make sure wolves couldn't get the livestock anymore.

If I went back to my old life, I wouldn't have to worry about watching people I cared about die, about fighting creatures bent on killing me, battling other wizards, or having an entire city hate me. I could worry only about myself, my mother, Kathleen, and my small town.

What were they doing right now? Would they take me back? Maybe I could return, but first I had to leave here.

I passed the time with these thoughts. Krystal's agony, and the hate-filled looks on the faces of Alexandria's people, continued to plague me. And I dreamt of dozens of ways I could torture and kill Premier.

"Hellsfire," a voice said, pulling me out of my slumber. "Hellsfire."

I opened my eyes and lifted my tired head. The torch was still out, but the cloaked figure carried a candle. He set it down and opened the cell. I sat up, expecting Prastian or Jastillian to have come to get me, but the person was too tall, and clearly human. It might have been Ardimus.

"Hello," she said, pulling back her hood.

"Krystal?" I asked. "Krystal!"

I wanted to reach out and hug her, but stopped when I remembered what had happened when I last touched her.

"It's all right," she said. She closed the distance between us. "Just be careful not to make contact with my skin."

She slipped under the shackles that bound my wrists and swept me into her arms. We crushed our bodies into an embrace and hung onto each other, afraid to let go. She was alive and well, and that's all that mattered to me. We stood there, the silence speaking volumes.

We pulled back at the same time, but the lower halves of our bodies were still intertwined.

"Are you all right?" I asked.

She cleared her throat and said, "Yes."

She lied. Her skin was pale and she had lost a few pounds. Her grip on me moments ago wasn't as strong as it once was.

She slipped back under the chains, and then the princess's gloved hand went flying and slapped me hard across the face.

"What was that for?" I said, rubbing my throbbing face.

Krystal's face firmed. "You're imprisoned for sneaking around in the castle using our secret passageways. Passageways you shouldn't have known about in the first place, or ever used again. I'm fighting for your life, Hellsfire. There are those who would see you swinging at the end of a rope both for trespassing and for what you did to me." I looked down, not daring to meet her fierce eyes. "I'm sorry. I was looking for that magical vault you have so I could help you. The books you had in the library were useless, and it's too far to return to the White Mountain."

She narrowed her eyes. "Damn it, Hellsfire! That's what you were doing? Don't tell anyone that. It'll only make things worse. Thank the gods you weren't anywhere near it."

"I wasn't?"

"No, and I'm not going to tell you where it is."

I threw my hands up in frustration, the chains nearly hitting my face. "I wanted to help you, Krystal! You were in a coma and you weren't getting better. It was *my* fault you were dying. The healers barred me from you and I had to do something!" I sighed, feeling exhausted. "I would never have forgiven myself if you died because of me. I should never have gone to the Wastelands or brought down the barrier."

Krystal's hands were on my cheeks. She stroked my face with her thumbs. "Don't. You did what you had to do. There's nothing to forgive. It was Renak's fault."

I smiled, remembering how she could always make me feel better and how much I missed her. My smile disappeared. "No. It wasn't him. It was Premier."

"Premier?"

"Yes, I've thought about it for days. Renak warned me about him. He was puzzled by what was happening to the nexus's light. Premier must have planned this—all of it! I'm sorry, princess, I should have foreseen."

"I know you made a vow to Stradus—"

"But I'm making a new one to you," I said. "The next time I see Premier, I *will* kill him. I would have killed him the second I saw him had I thought he would do this to you. Your safety means more than anything to me."

"I know."

We stood there, not saying a word. I was thankful that she was alive and would recover, but there was something else on my mind.

"Your father doesn't want me to see you anymore," I said.

She had a sad look on her face. "I know. I also know that if you touch me, I'll die."

"What are we going to do about us?"

Krystal held her breath. "Let's worry about getting you out of here—then we can focus on that."

I remembered the king's words about there being other men, and how I wasn't the first. Now would be the perfect time for her to cut any ties with me. As devastating as it would be, I wouldn't blame her. She had a kingdom to run and responsibilities to tend to. We'd had a lot of fun, but I always thought it could be more than that.

"As you wish."

"Good," she said. "I'll try to get you more food sent down here. For good or ill, this will be over in a couple of days." Krystal looked exhausted. She had come back from the verge of death, and now had to defend me to her people and her father. "I'll do my best to make sure you're set free."

"Thank you." She went to leave, but I stopped her. "And Krystal, I'm sorry...for everything."

Krystal placed her hand on the cell's bars, her back to me. She turned, then ran towards me, throwing her arms around my neck and squeezing me. She pulled my hood up and kissed me on the cheek with the fabric between us.

"I know you are, Hellsfire."

She pulled away, and I watched her go. I couldn't help but wonder if that was a goodbye kiss.

Three days later, six guards came and I knew it was time. They drew their weapons when they opened my cell. I left it and they surrounded me, then escorted me out of the dungeons. We walked up the stairs, and when we got to the top, the morning light blinded me. One of the guards pushed me from behind and we continued on.

Everyone got out of our way as they led me down the keep's halls. They stood to the side, stared at me, and whispered. It reminded me of when I left Masep. I tried to read their faces, but one of the guards said, "Eyes front."

As we moved down the stone halls, I knew where we were headed—King Furlong's audience chamber.

The chamber was crammed full of people. They stood a respectful distance from the king, but crowded along the walls. The king sat on his throne and Krystal stood behind it. Guards littered the place. Nobles in their fine clothing waited in groups. My friends were there too. They nodded in greeting, and I walked up to stand before the throne. All conversations halted, and the silence in the chambers was deafening.

"Your Majesty," I said and bowed.

The king scrutinized me, but didn't say anything.

I glanced at the princess. She couldn't help me now, and I couldn't read past her royal mask. Did she know the outcome? Would I be executed? Would I even allow the sentencing to come to pass? The king didn't have a way to shut off my powers. He couldn't stop my magic, not outside of the enchanted cells. He would have been better off leaving me there to rot.

I shook my head. If I didn't accept the king's sentencing, she would get blamed for it. I didn't know if she'd ever wanted us to be together and possibly something more, but I knew I did. I also didn't want her to remember me killing her soldiers. I would accept the outcome, whatever it might be.

"Wizard Hellsfire," King Furlong said in a booming voice. He leaned forward. "You have been found guilty of committing crimes against Alexandria. You have trespassed and you have been a danger to the princess. Those are very serious crimes, the latter often carrying with it the penalty of death."

Death it was then. I held my head high, praying that I would have one last chance to talk to Krystal, and that my mother wouldn't take my death too hard. From the corner of my eye, I saw a couple of the nobles smile in triumph. The fire inside boiled, threatening to burst out.

I clenched my fist and squashed my magic. Now was not the time.

"As you wish, Your Majesty," I said and bowed.

"I'm not finished," the king said. "You have also saved my life and rescued Alexandria from the clutches of the wizard Premier. I have taken that into consideration. Because of those things, I sentence you to banishment from Alexandria."

Banishment? My friends looked relieved, but my heart was in pain when I looked at Krystal. I would never be able to see her again. In some ways, it would be easier if I was to die.

I bowed. "Thank you, Your Majesty."

"Gather your things, Hellsfire. You are to leave as soon as possible." The king motioned to one of the guards, who came over and unshackled my wrists and ankles. "If you are ever found in Alexandria again, you will be sentenced to death."

"I understand."

King Furlong rose and left. Krystal gave me one last look before following him. All around me, people conversed in hushed tones. One woman and man shook their heads in disgust before walking away. Another woman gave me a stare colder than winter. One man pointed, his finger shaking in anger. Those standing nearby tried to calm him down.

My friends made their way over to me. Jastillian clapped my back and said, "I suggest we hurry, lad. If things are this bad in here, they'll be worse outside."

"Thanks for staying," I said. "I really appreciate it."

"I just wish there was something more we could do," Prastian said. "I have your belongings. The princess made sure to get them to me."

"Thank you."

We departed the room and went to the rooms the elves had stayed in. I got my potions and purse back. I guessed it no longer mattered that I couldn't test a couple of rituals on Krystal to see if we could ever be together again. While we were getting our things, Demay and Behast left to get our horses and supplies ready. They would meet us at the city walls. Prastian, Jastillian, and I then made our way out of the keep.

As we left, I kept peering down the hallways in hopes that I would see Krystal again. Prastian said I shouldn't search for her, despite how much I wanted to. I knew I couldn't touch her, but I needed to say goodbye to her one last time. Everyone I passed stopped and stared at me. Servants paused with their trays in hand, guards stopped sparring, and gardeners ceased pruning.

We walked down the hill towards the surrounding castle walls. I kept glancing back, still hoping to see her. I gave up when we were near the exit. She couldn't come to see me. There were ramifications if she did. I kicked the ground, scattering some small rocks. I guessed what we had was nothing more than fun, as the king said. Perhaps not saying goodbye was for the best. I had no idea what I would say to her anyway.

"Hellsfire," Prastian said. "Sharald could use a wizard's services, especially now that the Great Barrier is gone."

"I believe Erlam would pay more," Jastillian said, raising his bushy eyebrows.

"They would have to," Prastian said. "If you have Hellsfire study old, boring artifacts and sites."

Jastillian laughed. "The future is in the past. Give me those boring books. They're far less dangerous than the people you deal with."

Prastian was about to say something, but then stopped. His ears twitched. "I believe we have company."

Krystal held her skirts up with one hand while she ran down the hill to us. We bowed when she reached us.

"I wanted to see you before you left." She didn't look at me, but at Prastian and Jastillian. "I wanted to remind you that we will soon send our own expedition into Southern Shala, and since you'll be there before us, we will appreciate any information you can share."

"Of course, Your Highness," Prastian said.

My friends moved away and gave us privacy. Krystal and I stared at each other, but didn't say a word. There was so much I wanted to tell her. Things I should have told her before I left for Masep. It all seemed pointless now. I was banished from Alexandria, and I couldn't even touch her without killing her. I would never see her again.

The princess jumped at me and wrapped her arms around my neck, hugging me tightly. "I'm going to miss you, Hellsfire."

My body froze, knowing this was entirely inappropriate, but I also knew this would be the last time I would see her. I bit my lip and let myself be taken into her arms. I closed my hands around her waist and inhaled the sweet scent from her hair. "Not as much as I'll miss you."

We clung to each other for several long seconds, the only two people in the world. That warm feeling in my heart would never burn as bright without her.

Krystal let go and put a gloved hand to my face. I nuzzled up against it. "Take care, Hellsfire, and be safe. Goodbye, hero." She pulled her hand away and walked back toward the keep.

My fingers lingered on the cheek she had touched. "Goodbye, beautiful."

"Come on, lad," Jastillian said. "If we were in Erlam, I'd buy you the strongest drink in all the land. One you could drown your thoughts in."

"After you vomit," Prastian said.

Jastillian laughed. "Well, there is that. I'm sure you can handle it, Hellsfire."

"If you want something sweeter that doesn't leave a massive headache, there is a place in Sharald I can take you to," Prastian said. "It lacks the strength of the dwarven drink, but it makes up for it in taste."

"Thanks," I said. "I'll have to take you up on your offer."

As we approached the castle's walls, Jerrell and half a dozen guards blocked our path. I worried they were going to try something before I left. Prastian and Jastillian tried to step in front of me in case they did, but I stopped them.

"Hellsfire," Jerrell said. "Not all of us agree with the king's decision." Those with him nodded, but those still at their posts glared at me. "You fought with us and helped us seize Alexandria back from Premier."

"Thank you," I said.

"Take care, Hellsfire."

"You too."

I took one last lingering look at the keep. "Take care, Krystal," I said under my breath. I pulled up my hood and disappeared into Alexandria.

CHAPTER 16

ON THE WAY SOUTH, we stopped in the elves' home of Sharald. While Prastian, Demay, and Behast needed to report to King Sharald and we also had to resupply, we went there for another reason—information.

Alexandria was founded after the War of the Wizards to guard Northern Shala from the creatures in the Wastelands of Renak. Because the city was built after the Great Barrier was erected, its library focused on the history of the war and information on Northern Shala and the Wastelands. It held very little information about Southern Shala.

Sharald was an ancient city, far older than Alexandria. Even before the Great Barrier was erected, Sharald had established itself as one of the first major cities in Northern Shala. The first King Sharald had even met Renak once. Though we didn't know if any information we gained in Sharald would still be useful, it was still the best place to start.

We were still heading towards Southern Shala, but my plan was to go to Fairhaven, the city where the Elemental Council should be. They had to be warned about Premier and about Renak's threat, and they might have a lead on where the *Book of Shazul* was. I also wanted to ask them about a cure for Krystal. Even though she and I couldn't be together, I still wanted to see if there was any way to reverse the curse. Better yet, I could find Premier and torture the information out of him.

While I considered Prastian, Demay, and Behast to be close friends and had cherished their company, expertise, and advice, there were times when I remembered they were elves and how different they were from me.

When we traveled through the forests, because of their green skin color, the elves appeared to vanish. They walked with ease and surefootedly, too, barely making a sound among the leaves, fallen twigs, and brush. The elves were so comfortable with the forest that they had constructed Sharald around that idea. Unlike the humans or dwarves, who bent the land around them, the elves built their entire city around the forest so they wouldn't damage it.

We approached Sharald by strolling along the well-traveled path leading to the city, the soft grass brushing our feet. Occasional shafts of sunlight pierced the cool, leafy canopy above us. Trees a hundred feet high loomed above us, their limbs as big as my waist. Nestled in the limbs were homes and shops. Rope bridges with wooden slats were strung between them. I would have worried about the group of four elven children chasing each other across one of them, fifty feet above the ground, but I knew from my last visit that those rickety-looking bridges were pretty strong. Still scary, though, if you weren't born an elf, lacked balance, and hated heights.

I tore my gaze away from the homes in the trees and brushed aside the long branch of a cedar tree. Not all of Sharald's buildings were high above the ground. We traveled along a road that was wide enough for two carts to roll alongside each other and walked through the marketplace. An elf in front of a forge stopped hammering and wiped his sweaty forehead. Not far beyond the marketplace was the archery range. The small elves took aim with their bows a hundred yards away from their targets. All their shots struck the center of the target with repeated accuracy.

As fascinating as Sharald was, it was always their royal castle that I admired the most. I was probably the only one who could truly appreciate it, because I saw the powerful and ancient magic that had gone into its construction, and still radiated from it to this day.

The castle's magic struck me well before we reached it, growing more powerful with each step. I turned to my friends, wondering how they could be oblivious to such a thing.

The large dome-shaped building towered in the middle of the city. When we reached it, its potent magic enveloped me, washing over me like a morning's shower.

All people had a piece of mana inside them that they carried around. Elves primarily had green mana—the mana of the earth and land. That was the reason they were so good with the land. The dome beat with that mana as if it was the heart of the city and its people.

I gazed at the hardened vines and twisted branches that wound their way into the dome. Before we entered, I traced my fingers over them, wondering how such a grand place could be crafted. This ancient castle had been standing since the War of the Wizards, yet none of its branches were rotten or brittle, and none of its green color was lackluster. I slapped my hand across the intricately woven branches, feeling the sting of the blow but also how strong the structure was.

We met King Sharald in his library. The king had maps unfolded and scrolls unrolled, and books were scattered across the tables. We learned that from the time the king had received Prastian's message, he had been preparing for us. He and his elves had been scouring the archives for every bit of information about Southern Shala they thought might help in our mission.

"Where do we go?" Demay asked, scrutinizing the old map of Southern Shala spread on one of the tables "It's so big."

"We'll have to get through the Ennis Mountain range first," Jastillian said, crossing his arms. "I can guide us through part of it, but after the place where the Great Barrier once was, I have no idea where to go. We could get lost navigating those cave networks."

"Isn't there a pass we could try?" I asked.

"We could, but it's treacherous. Worse than the Daleth Mountains, and I've only been over partway. I have no idea how bad the other half is, or if it's guarded. The caverns would be better. No one would see us if we crossed that way, and it's safer."

"Good thing you came here then," King Sharald said, and smiled. He unfurled a map and placed a candlestick on one edge and a closed book on the other. Sharald motioned with his hand for us to come closer. We all peered at the parchment. Mountains were etched into it, and cave systems were tracked and labeled.

"The Ennis Mountains," Jastillian said, tracing his fingers over the edge of the map.

"Exactly," King Sharald said. "This map will guide you through the caves to Southern Shala."

"I suggest you head to Fairhaven," the king went on, thrusting his finger into Southern Shala's map. "It was once a major city."

I nodded. "That's where the Elemental Council and magical school was." It was where I intended to go to warn Southern Shala of Premier, but also to get some guidance and help. I held no allegiances to either Sharald or Erlam. My goals might part us, and while I would miss my friends, Fairhaven was the place I needed to go.

"Exactly. There were also a great many elves there once." Sharald looked at his elves. "Make contact with our lost cousins there. They should be bound to help their fellow elves. I want you to gather as much information about them and Southern Shala as possible. Make them allies if you can."

Prastian nodded. "As you wish."

"Thank you for your help, Your Majesty," I said and bowed my head.

He put a finger up and gave me a mock angry look. "What did you say?"

"Sorry. Sharald."

"Better." Sharald smiled. "It's been a pleasure, Hellsfire. This is a great opportunity to reconnect with people from the south. We have so much to learn from them, and them from us." King Sharald took a deep breath then coughed. His eyes bulged against his elastic skin.

Prastian rushed to him as support. "Majes—Sharald, are you all right?"

Sharald wheezed for breath. He stopped, then gave a grin that made him look thirty years younger. "I will be, cousin."

I stared at the king of the elves, worrying about him. Would I lose him too? I had already lost Stradus and Krystal and I didn't want to lose Sharald. He had pledged me support in helping Alexandria in the recent battle, and he understood me better than most. He didn't judge or want anything from me. I kept failing people who trusted me.

Sharald stood to his full elven height. "Tomorrow, you leave for Southern Shala, but tonight, relax. I'll see to your supplies. You have a long journey ahead."

King Sharald left. Prastian and Demay followed him. Jastillian, Behast, and I all dispersed and went our separate ways.

It wasn't long before Prastian found me again. He led me to one of the venerable trees around Sharald. There were five of these great trees around the city. They stood out like pillars. Smooth staircases were carved inside the large trunks. There were other ways to get above the city. You could scramble up the trees or climb ladders, but if you were carrying something heavy, or if you weren't born in a tree, this way would be easier.

We climbed those spiral staircases. I stopped every so often to gaze out the open windows to admire the city. I wondered at it, seeing the city on the ground disappear while the one up above came into view. It was like stepping into an entirely different world. There were no roads, only rope bridges connecting everything.

We didn't climb the entire tree. We exited when we were twenty feet from the ground. I grasped onto the rope bridge until my hands drained of color. I lacked the surefootedness of the elves, and the bridge seemed far too rickety for my size. Prastian strolled across the bridge while I tiptoed onto it, worrying about how my weight shifted the bridge with each step. I felt like a leaf being blown in a wind, the way I swayed. Prastian looked back with an amused expression on his face.

At the end of the bridge was an elven tree pub. Prastian stood outside, unable to stop smiling as he waited for me to catch up. The pub was carved into the large trunk of the tree. The sign of a mug and a frothy drink was carved above the entrance. Prastian opened the door for me and I went inside.

The first thing I noticed was the smooth floor. I sighed when I realized that it was sturdy enough that even a large human like me wouldn't fall through. The view from the windows along the sides reminded me how high up we were. I could spy other bridges and houses throughout the thickness of the trees. The sun radiated from the clear sky above.

In the pub were six other elves. Five of them were scattered around the room, drinking and talking in small groups. The sixth was the bartender, at the far end behind the carved wooden bar. She finished crafting her concoction and served it to one of the customers. We walked to the bar and she gave me a youthful smile, but her light green eyes held wisdom. Because of how slowly they aged, it was always difficult to tell how old an elf was.

"And what would you like?" she asked.

Prastian stood next to me and said, "Eliana, I want you to give Hellsfire a Forest Sunset, and make it as strong as you can."

Eliana's ears perked up. "Are you sure? I know he's a wizard, but he's still only human."

"I'm sure. I'll see you later. Take good care of him, Eliana."

"I will."

I sat down on the stool and hunched over the bar, watching as Eliana reached underneath and pulled out two flasks with elongated necks. One bottle swirled with green liquid as bright as spring's grass, with a minty scent. The other was like a bog, its dark green muck sticking to the bottle. I turned away in disgust. She poured the two liquids together and the thicker liquid crushed and overpowered the first one.

Eliana stirred the drink and pushed it forward. "Here you go."

I raised an eyebrow. "What's in it?" I tried not to wrinkle my nose at it.

"Elf secret."

"Why's it called a Forest Sunset? It doesn't look like one."

"Drink it."

"All right." I lifted the glass to my nose and stopped. The rancid smell made me want to put it back down. Eliana's eyes were intent on me as she waited for me to swallow. I trusted Prastian and didn't want to show any disrespect so I took a sip. Maybe it was one of those things that smelled bad but tasted good.

It wasn't. I couldn't stop gagging and I put the drink down, having barely taken more than a sip. It was like drinking mulch. I shook my head. Elves must have different tastes than humans and enjoy eating leaves.

Eliana laughed at me and took the glass away. She wiped up a few splatters that had struck the bar. "I'm sorry. I couldn't resist."

I wiped my tongue with the back of my hand. "What do you mean?"

"That wasn't a Forest Sunset, or at least it wasn't complete yet." She smiled as she reached onto the bottom shelf and brought out a small, red vial. She dripped one drop into the glass. "Watch."

The dark green muck swirled like a river, faster and faster until it lost its heaviness. The movement stopped. The dark colors exploded, blossoming red, then orange. The liquid settled down and I sniffed it. An orchard-like smell tickled my nose.

"Go ahead," she said. "Taste it."

I gave her a sour expression.

"Trust me. This time it'll be different."

"All right." I sipped at the drink in case she was playing another joke on me. It tasted like honey, and I guzzled it down. She was right. It *was* good.

"Easy there," Eliana said, touching my hand. "There's plenty more where that came from."

"Thank you," I said, wiping my mouth. "How come you didn't think I could handle it before?"

Eliana gave me a mischievous grin. "You'll see."

I took another sip, allowing the liquid to dance around my mouth. I wondered what she meant. Bubbles rose up out of the bottom of the glass. They hovered and circled around my head. I stared at them, but neither Eliana nor any of the other elves seemed to notice. The bubbles burst, and when they did, little animals appeared.

A tiny snake and a bird went at each other. The bird swooped down at the snake with its claws. The snake hissed and leapt up at the bird. When they clashed together, the bubbles vanished.

My eyes crossed from staring at the space in front of my nose where the bubbles had once been.

"What was that?" I asked. "I've never seen anything like it before."

"I didn't see anything," she said. "It's different for everyone."

"Can I have another one?"

"Of course, but this time drink it slower. The more you drink, the worse it gets. Sometimes, people drink so much they become lost in a hallucinogenic stupor, but it's far worse than any ale or wine."

I nodded. And Jastillian said the elves didn't have anything as strong as the dwarves. He was wrong.

I nursed my second drink, the newness of the hallucinations starting to wear off. I stared into my glass and thought of home. We were going to be passing through Sedah on our way to Southern Shala. It had been so long since I'd been there, and I had changed so much. I missed my mother, and quietly wished that I didn't have these powers so I could have had a simpler life—one with far less heartache.

Eliana pushed another drink in front of me. "Have another one and tell me what you see."

I glanced up at her. "All right."

That third one hit the spot. All sorts of weird things popped into view. It didn't matter where I looked. Eliana didn't help. She took out a coin and flipped it, making it dazzle like a sun from her hand. She even snapped her towel at me and it roared like a lion, nearly knocking me from my seat. Three Forest Sunsets and much laughter later, I had a visitor.

"Sharald," Eliana said as she cleaned a glass. "It's a pleasure to see you again. I haven't seen you this high in a while."

Sharald leaned against a chair and took a deep breath. "I much prefer the ground these days, but I came to find Hellsfire."

"Your Majesty," I said, rising. I leaned against the bar as the world tilted into view. "You didn't have to come all the way up here. I would have met you."

"Nonsense. I wanted one of Eliana's delicious drinks, and I could use the exercise. I may be old, but I still love being in the trees."

I struggled to pull out a seat so Sharald could sit beside me.

"How many of those have you had?" he asked.

"Four."

"Six," Eliana said.

The king laughed and smacked his hand on the table. "Thankfully, Eliana's place is near the great oak, lest you break your neck climbing down one of the ladders. But I understand your need to drink so many. Eliana, can I have one Winter's Chill please?"

"Of course." Eliana fixed him a drink. A big mug was set in front of him. Frost hovered above the top. The king took a drink and sighed.

"Excellent, as always," Sharald said. He wiped the blue residue from his mouth with the back of his sleeve. "How have you two been doing?"

"I was just keeping Hellsfire some company here."

"And I appreciate it," I said.

She smiled with her eyes. "Any time, Hellsfire."

"Can you please give us some privacy?" Sharald asked.

"As you wish," Eliana said. She motioned to the other elves in the building. All of them left, until it was just the king and me.

"I wanted a chance to talk before you left, away from prying ears," King Sharald said. "I'm sorry to hear about your banishment from Alexandria and about what happened with Princess Krystal."

I stared at my now empty glass, wishing I had another. "Thank you."

"I wish there was something more I could do for you." Sharald took another sip of his drink. "This reminds me of something long ago."

"What do you mean?"

"I wasn't born to rule. I was third in line, but my older sister died and my older brother abandoned his duties. It had all fallen to me." He reached for his drink, but then stopped. "There was also a girl involved, before my late wife."

"And you chose the throne over her?"

Sharald sighed. "In a way. It was the toughest decision I'd had to make at that time. It wasn't long after that I met my wife—a few short years later. I didn't think it possible, but I loved Liliana far more than I ever did Kaleena. I had thought my heart would never mend over the hole Kaleena's departure left. I know it doesn't seem like this now, but you never know what the gods have in store and where it will take you."

I didn't quite believe in what the king said. The pain cut so deeply that I could drink Forest Sunrises until nothing I saw in front of me was real. I nodded, yet couldn't find my voice.

The king looked at me with caring eyes. "After the expedition into Southern Shala, I do not know what your plans are, Hellsfire, but you will always have a home here."

"Thank you, Your Majesty."

He raised his mug. "To lost loves."

I raised mine. "To lost loves." We clinked our glasses together.

"I do know some available elves," Sharald said, leaning in closer. "Eliana's pretty and single. Plus, you can have all the drinks you can handle."

I glanced at the door and frowned. "Thanks, but I don't think I'm ready yet."

"In time, you will be."

Eliana and the others eventually came back while the king and I sat and drank. While he had heard the report from Prastian, he wanted to know what the Wastelands were like from a wizard's point of view. He said it reminded him of when Stradus told him stories when he was younger.

After more drinks, we eventually left Eliana's bar. I would like to say I helped the aging king, but he helped me. He steadied me on the bridge and held my arm as we walked down the oak's stairs. I burst out in laughter when a few of the leaves brushed against me, tickling me. The leaves laughed as they did so, and followed me no matter where I went. The king also chuckled, but more at my state.

"Hellsfire," King Sharald said when we finally reached the bottom. "If I wasn't here, I don't know how you would have gotten down."

"It was the leaves, I tell you. They wouldn't leave me alone!"

King Sharald shook his head. "If you say so."

Demay ran up to us. He stopped and said, "I was just on my way up to see you."

"What is it?" Sharald asked.

"What's wrong with Hellsfire?"

"I've had six Forest Sunsets," I said, holding my hand out. I peered at it, only seeing five fingers. "That's not six."

"He's had seven, and a Winter's Chill," Sharald said.

"Oh," Demay said. "And you're still standing? Anyways, we have visitors."

"Who?"

"The Princess of Alexandria."

I grinned at Demay and touched his nose. "Yeah, right. She's in Alexandria. What would she be doing here?" My smile vanished and I frowned. "I'm never going to see her again except in my dreams."

"I'm serious," Demay said. "She's *here.*"

I stared at my friend and blinked hard until the circling stars around his head evaporated. What was she doing here?

"Lead the way," I said.

We hastened back to the dome and I tried to sober up. The haze in my head didn't leave me. It only worsened with all the questions of why and how she was here.

When we returned to the castle, Krystal and Prastian were standing in front of it, engaged in conversation. With her were Ardimus and Rebekah. They stopped talking and approached us.

I stared at her with my mouth hanging open. She *was* here and I was so glad to see her. The air dried my mouth and my heart threatened to burst from my chest. I hadn't thought I would ever see her again. For a brief moment, I thought of the things we could do together, but then remembered that if I ever touched her again, she would die.

"Your Majesty," Krystal said, bowing. She gave me a brief smile.

"Princess, please. Sharald will do."

She nodded. "As you wish."

"What brings you here?" Sharald asked. "I'm pleased to have you, but this is unexpected."

"My father decided to send an expedition into Southern Shala now instead of later. I wanted to catch up with the others before they crossed the Ennis Mountains. Thank the gods I reached you in time."

"I thought King Furlong didn't want you to go?" I asked.

"I persuaded him to change his mind. This was too great an opportunity to pass up, and it's best that we all go together." She stared at me. "Hellsfire, are you all right?"

Krystal's violet eyes danced and started to leave her skull. I shook my head several times. "I'm fine, Your Highness."

"I'm glad you're going," Sharald said. "The more skilled warriors, the better." He nodded at Ardimus and Rebekah. "Let me have one of my elves show you to your rooms. After you clean up, we can discuss the plan we came up with over dinner."

Krystal bowed. "Thank you, Sharald."

Two of Sharald's guards escorted Krystal and her people. I followed them, making small talk and asking how their trip was. I waited to talk to her until she dismissed her guards and we were alone in her room.

"What are you doing here?" I asked, keeping my voice low in case the elves overheard me. "I thought your father forbade you to go."

"He did, but as I told you, I persuaded him, and I can be *very* convincing."

She stepped in close and ran a finger along my chest. I smiled, reminded of how much I missed her and how much she was right. "What happened to you, Hellsfire? Your eyes linger on things and you're having trouble standing up straight without swaying."

"You ever hear of a Forest Sunset?"

She chuckled. "And how many of those have you had?"

"Seven, and one Winter's Chill."

"That many! That would explain it. Why so many?"

"Heartache," I whispered. I grabbed her hand and intertwined her fingers with mine. "But I'm glad you're here now."

"Me too," she said, squeezing my hand.

"I'll let you get ready, and see you at dinner."

"Hellsfire, there's one last thing. I didn't only want to come to Southern Shala as a representative of Alexandria or to even fulfill a childhood dream."

"No?"

"No," she said. "If we get the opportunity, I thought maybe this council of yours or other wizards might be able to help us."

I cleared my parched throat. "I would like that. But what about your father? I'm still banished from Alexandria."

"One problem at a time."

I nodded. "There are a few spells I would like to try that I never got a chance to. They might work."

"All right. After dinner. I know this is hard for you, Hellsfire, but it's hard to be a ruler sometimes. You have to put the good of your people before your own desires."

"I never asked you to choose between me or your people, Krystal."

"I know that. Yet I have also learned that sometimes what's best for the princess can be best for the kingdom."

I met her eyes and we shared a smile.

During dinner, we told Krystal and the others what we planned. She agreed with where we should go.

Afterwards, I examined the princess and worked my magic. But all the rituals and spells I tried failed. My magic just couldn't penetrate the nexus's curse. Whatever Premier had done to alter the nexus's magic allowed it to feed off my magic, using it to strengthen its own.

Early the next day, we said our goodbyes to King Sharald and left. Since we were headed south, there was one place I wanted to stop that I hadn't been to for years—home.

CHAPTER 17

AS WE RODE into my hometown of Sedah, I was thankful to have a chance to be back and see my mother again, but I was also worried. We rode as fast as we could travel without exhausting the horses, but even stopping here for only a day was wasting valuable time. Premier's powers had already returned and with each passing day, he was getting farther away from us. And Renak's warning of the gods' war still loomed in my mind. I believed him, and if I ran into such a war, I would have to deal with it, and I might never see my mother again. She deserved to see her son, even if it was for one last time. There was also part of me that wanted to know if I could ever return home. Would being a wizard finally get people to respect me, or would they fear and hate me more?

The windmill marked the entrance to the dusty main road. We trotted our horses up the hill and onto the bridge over the gurgling brook. I smiled, remembering the hours I would spend at that brook, my feet dangling over the sides while I tried to catch fish.

Not long after, we rode through the farms on the outskirts of town. That old cow with the missing ear chewed on some grass as we passed. I was surprised she was still alive, but Mrs. Bishop loved that gangly cow.

On the left side was a flock of sheep, running away from the young boy chasing them. I recognized young Corwyn, who was yelling and screaming at the sheep as he tried to corral them. That would never work with Andrick's sheep. I smiled at how much taller he was, how his brown hair got in his eyes as he ran, and how frustrated he became at that chore. I remembered cursing those dim-witted sheep. I turned my head away when Corwyn stopped and stared at us, fearful of him recognizing me.

"Corwyn!" Andrick yelled. "Get over here!"

Corwyn ran away from us and the sheep, heading back to the other backbreaking work Andrick had for him.

I hadn't known how I would react actually seeing someone I knew that wasn't my mother or a close friend. While I had nothing against them, Corwyn and Andrick reminded me of unhappy past memories and experiences I had been through.

I had been shunned by many of those in town. Shunned because I didn't worship their one god, even though my mother did. There were only a handful in town who believed in the four gods. I chose to do so like my father did before me, in hopes of seeing him when I died.

I was also afraid. I had grown up being bullied by the children in town. Before I left, when my powers had just manifested themselves, I had unintentionally burned their leader, Nathan. Luckily, no one saw me do it, but I had always wondered whether he told them, and if they believed him about me. As much as he had picked on me, I had always felt bad about what I did to him. He was the first person that I had hurt with my powers, before I had learned to control them.

We passed through the surrounding farmlands and entered the town. At the edge of the northern entrance to town was the mayor's house. It sat on top of a small hill, above the rest of the land, which had leveled out. His was the first house people saw when coming into Sedah, and he liked it that way. I stared at the waist-high wooden fence surrounding it and smirked.

The princess rode alongside me and asked, "Hellsfire, what is it?"

"I was just thinking. You see that fence over there?" I pointed to the mayor's fence. "I broke that section jumping over it." I left out the part about how I was running from Nathan and his friends at the time. It had been repaired sometime after I left, but it also seemed a lot smaller. I would have no problem jumping it now.

"And that beech tree we just passed," I said. "I once fell out of it and broke my arm."

"You were very clumsy in your youth," Behast said.

Everyone laughed, and so did I. "I'm *still* clumsy."

We continued our ride. It was unsettling. Nothing was as big or as tall as it had been before. The people we rode by were shorter, especially viewed from horseback, and the buildings were smaller. I had been in villages between here and Alexandria, but having spent so much time in Sharald and Alexandria, I had grown used to the multitudes of people and the gigantic buildings needed to accommodate them all.

There was one building that could rival those I saw in the cities and could hold everyone in the town. It was also the one place I hated to go—the church. It was the oldest building and even now, I saw its looming towers across town. Luckily, I didn't ever have to go there again.

The sizzling sound of metal being dumped in water caught my attention. I told the others to wait while I climbed off my horse and crept towards the blacksmith. From his massive size, I thought he might be my old friend Dorian, but when he turned around, it wasn't him.

I was ready to leave when an old man came out of the shop muttering about how incompetent and ungrateful his workers were. He wiped his dirty hands on his apron. "Do you need some help?" Emden asked.

"No. I was just looking for Dorian."

"Bah. Did he forge something wrong?"

"No, I—"

Emden peered at me, his beady eyes becoming even smaller. "Do I know you? You look familiar."

I kept my head down and said, "Sorry to bother you, sir. I'll be going now."

"Mmmm."

Emden stared at me as I walked away. I turned and saw Kathleen exiting the baker's shop across the road. My breath left me. Before our eyes met, I looked down at my feet and quickly strode back to the group.

"Did you find what you were looking for?" Krystal asked.

I shook my head. "My friend wasn't there. Sorry to keep you waiting. Let me escort you all to the inn before I head to my mother's."

I led my horse by her reins, using it to block Kathleen from seeing me in case she recognized me. As we walked, I couldn't help but feel as if I was being watched, but I didn't dare turn around in case I was.

When we reached the inn, a stable boy came and took our horses away. Jastillian and Behast went inside to get rooms for the night while Prastian and Demay headed for the marketplace. I was going to visit my mother and stay with her. I walked Krystal to the inn's door. Ardimus and Rebekah hovered around Krystal, doing their best not to look obtrusive.

"Do you mind if I come with you, Hellsfire?" Krystal asked.

I stared at her, wondering if that would be a good idea. She didn't understand where I came from and how poor I had been. She couldn't. Hers was a life of privilege and battle. "Are you sure, Your Highness?"

She nodded.

I sighed. "If that's what you want."

"You two see to the supplies," Krystal said. "I'll be back later."

"But Your Highness—" Ardimus said.

"I'll be fine. Hellsfire will protect me until I return."

Ardimus and Rebekah shared a glance. Ardimus nodded. "As you wish."

"Good. Hellsfire, let's go."

We began our trek to my mother's house. I kept glancing around, watching for both Dorian and Kathleen.

"Why did you dismiss them?" I asked. "They're supposed to protect you. What if something happens?"

"Sedah's a nice, quiet village. I'm sure nothing will happen."

I raised an eyebrow and grinned. "Remember when I first met you?" I had rescued her from two men who had abducted her, in the forest just outside

Sedah.

She brushed aside a lock of hair. "I remember. You protected me then. Are you saying you can't protect me now?"

"No, but—"

"Good." She leaned against me, laying her head on my shoulder. "You worry too much, Hellsfire. All I want to do is meet your mother. I don't want to scare her with a bunch of hardened warriors at her doorstep."

"Says the woman with a deadly sword swinging on her hip."

Krystal gave me a playful bump with that hip and I returned it.

We strolled to my home, leaving the main road and taking a smaller dirt path. I fidgeted with my robes the entire way, worrying about what the princess would think. Bringing her to Sedah was bad enough, but I hadn't expected her to want to meet my mother and see my home.

My mother's longhouse was at the end of town. The last time I was here, it had been in dire need of repairs. Without my father, my mother and I had to do everything ourselves and there was always another problem to deal with. We didn't have the money to fix everything. I glanced at Krystal, trying to read her face. What would she think of where I came from, and what would she think of my mother? Would the princess judge us unworthy?

At the end of the small path was the longhouse. A large ash tree shaded part of it; its long branches had always kept our house cool in the summer. I opened the gate in the lavender fence that now surrounded it. That wasn't supposed to be there, although my father had wanted to build one. He also had planned to expand the house, as they wanted more children. We had never been able to afford that either.

Now, though, there was a new stone path leading to the door. The roof sported new shingles and the hinges on the door were no longer hanging at an awkward angle. It seemed that my mother had spent the money I had given her before I left. Money that came from the princess—a reward for rescuing her. Or maybe there was a new man in my mother's life? How would I feel about that?

Over the past few years, I had been worried about her. I was only able to see glimpses of her through a ritual—one that had nearly gotten me killed.

As relieved as I was over all the improvements to the house, I remembered I was bringing the Princess of Alexandria home. When I looked at Krystal and saw her exquisite sword on her hip, the price of which could feed my mother and me for a year, I thought once more that what she considered nice would be far different from what we did.

Krystal placed her hand on my arm. "We're not going to stand here all day, are we? I'm anxious to meet the woman who raised you."

So was I.

We walked to the door and I glanced down, seeing the small garden in front of the low brown building. Fresh tomatoes were ripe to be picked. I raised my free hand before I hesitated. Why was I going to knock? This was my home too, wasn't it? I opened the door and went in before Krystal, wanting my face to be the first thing my mother saw.

The inside of the rectangular longhouse was more cramped than I remembered. If I raised my hand and stood on my toes, I could touch the ceiling. To the left were two small rooms separated by a thin open wall. The beds were in those, and I remembered shivering during winter nights when the wind crept through the cracks in the wood.

To the right of the door was a round table. I put a hand on the smooth, grained wood. This wasn't our old table. I was sad that the initials I had carved into that table were no longer there.

My mother was beyond the table, standing over the kitchen counter as she hummed and chopped vegetables. A black pot was boiling on the hearth in the corner. The aroma of a home-cooked meal tickled my nose and I grinned.

When my mother realized someone was there, she quickly turned the knife in her hand and brandished it as a weapon. Her dark green eyes narrowed at me. "What do you want?"

I smiled. "Food would be nice."

"Hellsfire? Hellsfire!" My mother dropped her knife and ran up to me. She smothered me with a hug and kiss. I returned them, trying not to feel embarrassed in front of Krystal. "I was so worried about you," she said. "I heard what happened in Alexandria."

"You heard about that?" I whispered.

"Yes, from travelers passing through town. I was so worried about you."

"What did you hear?" I asked, concerned about what she might think of her son as a wizard, and what stories and rumors people had told of me.

"They said you were a powerful wizard and that you saved Alexandria from those vile creatures in the Wastelands."

I smiled. It wasn't as simple as that.

"I was worried when I heard of the monsters you fought, but I knew God would protect you." My mother pulled back and beamed with pride. "My son, the hero of Alexandria."

My face turned red from embarrassment, and also because that wasn't what the people of Alexandria would say. Suddenly, I remembered the princess. "Mother, this is..." I looked at Krystal. I wasn't sure how to introduce her.

"Princess Krystal of Alexandria," Krystal said. "It's a pleasure to meet you, Mistress Niall. Your son saved my life and my kingdom. He *is* quite the hero."

My mother pulled away with a sharp intake of air and froze. Her eyes glanced around the house, no doubt thinking the same things I had when I first arrived here. Two heartbeats later, she composed herself and bowed.

"It's a pleasure, Your Highness. Welcome to my humble home, but please call me Damara."

Krystal nodded. "And you may call me Krystal."

My mother moved away from us and cleared more space on the table. "I was just about to eat dinner. Are you two hungry?"

"Famished," Krystal said.

I pulled two chairs out and went to sit in the wobbly one. I wiggled my hips, but it didn't move. She had gotten this fixed too.

My mother went back to cooking, but I had to tell her that since my training, I no longer ate meat.

"Lucky for you, I'm making a vegetable stew," my mother said. "I want to know all that's happened since you left here."

I nodded. I told her about my former master, who she thought was the angel that had visited her on the night I was born, and about the training I went through to become a wizard.

"My son, the wizard," my mother said in a hushed tone as she poured stew into bowls and served us. She cut up a loaf of bread on the counter. "It still amazes me. I knew the Creator had a plan for you." She brought the bread to us, then joined us. "So you can control this fire you wield?"

"Yes, among other things."

"It's amazing to watch," Krystal said.

I grimaced, remembering that the last time I was here, I almost burned my mother. But I was a different person then. I could control my power now.

My mother reached out and held my hands as if reading my mind. "Show me."

I let go of her and focused on the low fire underneath the black pot. A stream of it rose into the air until it changed into a dog. It barked without noise, then ran towards me. Before it reached my face, I dispersed it.

"You were right," my mother said to Krystal. "It is amazing."

I blushed and took a bite of the vegetable stew.

"I'm proud you used this power to help the princess and others." My mother reached out and pinched my cheek. "Just like I taught you."

I sighed. "But I also made a couple of mistakes along the way." I glanced at Krystal. "And one big mistake I regret more than anything."

My mother reached out with her hands and grasped mine. She squeezed. "Tell me all about it."

I told her what I had done after the battle in Alexandria. How I had to venture into the Wastelands to stop Premier. How I brought down the Great Barrier, and he got to me before I could get to him, and more importantly, how I almost killed Krystal because of it. I could barely meet either my mother's or the princess's eyes as I sat in silence, the stew in my bowl having gone cold now.

I finally dared to look at their faces. They were the two most important women in my life, and what they thought of me meant a lot to me. I tried to make the right choices in my life, but I kept screwing things up. They didn't say anything, and I couldn't read them.

Krystal placed her gloved hand on my thigh and gave me a reassuring squeeze. "It's all right. I'm here now."

My mother's gaze settled on Krystal, and she smiled. "The princess is right. We do the best we can, but sometimes the outcome is...unfortunate."

"I would have made the same decision," Krystal said. "I don't harbor any ill will towards you for what you did. You couldn't have known Premier had altered Renak's spell."

"Thank you."

We almost forgot about my mother until she coughed and said, "Thank God you're all right, Krystal." She focused her attention back on me. "Hellsfire, you actually brought down the Great Barrier?"

I nodded.

"I didn't think such a thing was possible." She leaned forward. "Do you have any idea what's down there?"

"That's what we intend to find out."

"But what does it mean for the rest of us? Will there be an attack? Do they know the barrier's down? What will—" My mother paused. "Forgive me, Krystal. I'm babbling."

"That's all right. Hellsfire tends to do the same thing when he's nervous."

Both women shared a smile.

My mother poured Krystal more tea. "And you two, along with your friends, are going down to Southern Shala to find a cure for the both of you and to stop this mad wizard?"

I was about to correct her when Krystal said, "Yes."

"I'm glad." My mother smiled at us. "You know, you remind me of your father. He didn't do anything as grand as bring down the Great Barrier or venture into the Wastelands, but he was a hero."

"Was he a wizard too?" Krystal asked.

"No. He died in the Burning Sands before Hellsfire was born."

My mother fell silent and looked away. I expected her to drop the subject right there as she normally did when she talked about my father, but she continued.

"Elden's younger brother, Hayden, got him killed," my mother said. "Hayden dragged Elden back to the Burning Sands when he *knew* Elden had a family on the way."

I stared at her. I'd never known that. I wanted to ask her more, but didn't risk it, lest she stop her story.

"Elden and Hayden had always done unsavory work." She smirked. "Now while I had once found that attractive in Elden, I was able to pull him away from it so that we could start a family. Despite his brother's pleadings, Hayden stayed.

"When a job went terribly wrong, it was Hayden who begged for Elden's help. I warned Elden not to go, but he couldn't let his brother down. He said it would be for the last time. It was, but not in the way he expected."

My mother reached for some more tea. She took a sip, then continued. "Turns out there was a cult that tried to resurrect a beast in exchange for power. That dagger I gave you, Hellsfire, was instrumental in stopping it. You look more like him with each passing day." She paused, but never looked at us. My mother allowed herself a wistful smile. "But Elden did what he had to do to save lives. I don't blame him for that, although I do miss him terribly."

That smile vanished, and she focused on me. "You're brave, Hellsfire, but please be careful in Southern Shala. I don't want to lose you too."

"I promise I'll keep an eye on him," Krystal said.

"Thank you. And please, Princess, take care of yourself."

We finished our meal, and afterwards my mother said, "It's still light outside. I was going to go out into my garden and pick some vegetables. Would you care to join me?"

"Mother," I said. "She's a princess. She doesn't want to dig in the dirt."

"Nonsense," Krystal said. "I would love to."

My mother brought a basket and we went outside. We bent down and my mother showed Krystal how to tell which vegetables were ripe and what to do to get rid of the pests.

"I like this," Krystal said, squatting near my mother. She plucked a tomato and dusted it off before dropping it in the basket. "I never get a chance to do this. There's always something else to do. I'd like to learn more about gardening."

"If you're ever this way again, I'd love to teach you," my mother said and smiled. "Hellsfire doesn't have much of a green thumb."

The ladies chuckled.

"I'm better than I was, Mother," I said, puffing out my chest. "I had to be to concoct potions."

"Didn't you tell me you had trouble with those lessons?" Krystal said. She stuck her tongue in between her teeth and smiled.

I shook my head and grinned. "Women."

We picked all the vegetables and fruit we could, then went back inside. My mother washed them while Krystal and I cleared the table of our dinner. We chatted a bit more, but I wanted to leave before the sun completely set. There was still something else I had to do.

Krystal hugged my mother and said, "I had a very pleasant time tonight, Damara. Thank you for having me and for a delicious meal."

"Not at all. I enjoyed your company. Thank you for coming, Krystal, and for bringing my son by for a visit. I pray to God you two find what you're looking for. Please be safe while you're down there."

"I'll watch him." She let go of my mother and waited outside.

My mother hugged me and said in a low voice, "I know you're a man now, but try not to stay out too late."

I smiled. "I won't."

She licked her thumb and wiped my cheek.

"What are you doing?" I asked, trying to squirm away from her. "Wizards don't have their faces cleaned by their mothers." From outside, I heard Krystal chuckle.

"I know, but you'll always be my child, Hellsfire." Her face became serious, and she whispered into my ear. "You should realize that if you can't find a way for you two to be together, I want you to let her go. I like her, Hellsfire, I truly do, but she's a princess and has a responsibility not just to Alexandria but to all of Northern Shala."

I sighed. "I know, Mother. But it's going to hurt to leave her. I don't know what I'll do without her."

"I know what you're going through is painful, but it hurts her also."

"It does?"

"Yes," she said. "She hides it better than most because she's a princess, but she's still a woman. She's hurting more than she shows."

I glanced back at Krystal through the open door. "I'll...try. That's all I can promise. I'm not going to give her up without a fight."

"I wouldn't expect you to."

I let go of my mother and said, "I'll be back later tonight."

I left her and went to Krystal. She turned around and waved to my mother before we began our walk back into town.

"I really like your mother," Krystal said, interlocking her arm with mine.

I grinned from ear to ear. "That means a lot to me. She really likes you too. I think she always wanted a daughter, but was stuck with me."

Krystal laughed. She stopped and turned, placing her hand on my chest. "Thank you for bringing me here. I miss my mother, and I'm glad you shared yours with me."

I snuggled up against her. "Any time, but thank you for wanting to come. You're always welcome here."

"I'll remember that."

We strolled back to the inn, not as wizard and princess, but as a man and woman.

As we walked, I thought about my mother. Part of me was sad that she had managed so well without me. She no longer needed me to repair things, fetch water, or gather food. I knew she loved me, but it hurt to think that she got along fine without me to watch out and care for her.

However, a bigger part of me was glad she no longer needed me. Over the past couple of years, I had had too many close encounters with death. It was all because I was a wizard. Venturing into Southern Shala might be a death sentence I couldn't escape from.

I smiled and hugged the princess even tighter. I was glad not only to have seen my mother, but for Krystal to have met her as well.

I knocked and waited in front of Dorian's door. I was more nervous standing outside than when I went to his shop. How would my oldest friend react to seeing me, especially since I was a wizard now? How would his parents react? I'd never had a chance to say goodbye to him when I left.

Dorian's face was full of shock when he opened the door. Then his laughter boomed out, and he nearly crushed me in a hug. "I thought it was you Emden said was looking for me. But then I thought the old man had to be imagining things. What would a great and powerful wizard be doing in Sedah?" He had a mock-fearful look on his face, and he shivered. "Unless there are more creatures from the Wastelands here!"

I grinned at that remark. "I'm only in town for a day. I just wanted to see you before I left." I stared at my old friend and patted his arm muscles, which strained against his tunic. "You look good."

Dorian had always been bigger and stronger than me, as he was two years older and his shoulders were massive. But I had been a little bit taller and quicker. He always fought with me against Nathan and the other bullies in town. But not even Dorian could be with me all the time. There were times when I had to fight them alone. Those times didn't go so well for me.

"I see working at Emden's smithy has made you stronger," I said.

Dorian laughed. "The old man has me working hard." He finally let me go and said, "Come in, come in. My mother would have loved to see you, but sadly my parents went to bed." He lowered his voice. "It's a shame you didn't come earlier, you could have had dinner with us."

I stepped inside his home. He closed the door and offered me the chair with the plush, red cushion.

"Sorry, I was spending time with my mother," I said. "Otherwise, I would have been here sooner."

"Bah. Don't be sorry for that. I know what it's like, especially since I have a little one."

"You do?"

"Yes, and I'm married. Didn't Damara tell you?"

I shook my head, unable to talk with my mouth hanging wide open in surprise. I closed it and cleared my throat. "She would have, but I brought a guest with me."

"Who?"

"Krystal."

"That name sounds familiar." His eyes shone with recognition, but before I could say anything, his wife walked in.

"Who was at the door?" Rose asked, coming through the doorway. She cradled a baby in her arms. Her eyes widened when she saw me. "Hellsfire." She gave me a tight-lipped smile.

I returned it and said, "Rose. It's nice to see you again. You look great."

"Thank you."

Even though Rose had married my best friend, we could never be friends. Because I didn't believe in the one god or go to church like most people in town, she thought I was a blasphemer and that my soul was lost. But because of Dorian, we were cordial. At least, now we were. Rose sat down on the couch next to Dorian.

Dorian took the baby from Rose. He looked so at peace when he held him. "This is my son, Morrow. I named him after my grandfather. He's almost one. Would you like to hold him?"

Rose tensed as I carefully took the baby in my arms. I didn't breathe, afraid that I would drop him, even though he was so light. Morrow squirmed in my arms and made cute baby noises. I let myself relax. The baby stared up at me with glazed eyes, and we had a contest. I stared back, then stuck my tongue out. I won when Morrow laughed in my arms.

"He's so cute," I said. "He has your eyes, Rose. And I'm sure he'll be as strong as his father."

"Thank you," she said.

I made more stupid noises to get Morrow to laugh, but ended up causing Dorian to laugh and Rose to smile. I handed Morrow back to Dorian.

"I'll go and make you two some tea," Rose said. She went into the kitchen.

Dorian glanced to the side. "Can I see it?"

I raised my eyebrow. "See what?"

He spoke in a hushed tone. "The magic, of course."

I opened my hand and summoned fire from the candles. Streams of flame flew towards me, darkening the room. The fire landed on my palm. I enlarged the ball of fire. Dorian and Morrow gasped, staring at it with the same fascination on their faces.

"Here you go," Rose said, entering the room. Her eyes widened and she nearly dropped the tray.

I crushed the fire in my hand and extinguished the magic. I rushed to help her balance the tray.

"I'm sorry," she said.

"Don't worry about it," I said. "It's not your fault."

Her eyes met mine. "The stories are true. You *are* a wizard."

I reached for the pot, and she moved her hand away.

"Remember," Dorian said, "he also helped save Alexandria with his magic."

"I've got to finish cleaning." Rose quickly left the room.

"Sorry about that," Dorian said.

I shrugged. "It's all right."

"I'm still impressed by your magic, and so is Morrow. I'll admit, it seems...unnatural, but it's probably because we're not used to seeing it. It's also amazing. Can you do more?"

I nodded.

He leaned back and said, "Wow." He smiled. "What else can you do?"

I grinned. "A lot."

"Tell me."

It felt great to tell Dorian what I could do with my power, and even more wonderful when I saw his eyes light up with delight as I performed small feats of magic for him. I had always looked up to him because of his strength, and now he had a family of his own. Something I terribly wanted and might not get with Krystal. Still, there was always Kathleen. She would accept me back, wouldn't she?

Dorian had reminded me what it was like to live in Sedah. Over the past few years, I had gotten used to being around wizards, dragons, elves, dwarves, princesses, kings, and hardened warriors. Dorian brought out memories and feelings of a simpler life. A life where I didn't have to worry about evil wizards, nasty Wasteland monsters, or a city mob trying to kill me. A life where I could settle down and have a family, only having to worry about where the next meal came from.

Stradus had been alone, and so was Premier. They were the only two wizards I had ever known. Was it even possible for a wizard to settle down and have a family? From what I knew, wizards lived longer than mortals. How did they deal with the fact that they had to watch their loved ones grow old and die, and was there anything they could do about it?

Dorian leaned forward with his baby in his arms. "So tell me about this princess. I've heard many stories about what you've done in Alexandria. I want to know if they're all true."

I nodded and told him about how Premier had taken over the land and how Alexandria needed both Sharald's and Erlam's armies to help. Then I spoke about my more recent problems. Rose sat through my earlier stories, but then left to put Morrow to bed. That was kind of her, because what I had to tell was for Dorian's ears alone.

I let Dorian know how things truly were between me and Krystal, and how I was banished from Alexandria.

"You're in quite a bind, Hellsfire," he said as he ran his fingers through his hair. "I didn't realize being a wizard carried so many responsibilities, or had so many consequences."

"I know, and my mother says I should leave Krystal alone if we can't find a way to be together. Even if I find a way to break this curse, there's still her father and others who wouldn't want me to be there."

"So you envision a future with the princess?"

I met his eyes. "I'd like to."

"Well, I'm not going to tell you to leave her alone because I know you won't do that." He smiled. "You'll always be my friend, Hellsfire, but I have no idea what to tell you. You move in circles I can't begin to understand. Just be careful."

"Sound advice as always."

Dorian sighed and reached for more tea. "If your mother didn't get a chance to fill you in on all the town's news, then you probably don't know that someone else got married too."

I raised an eyebrow. "Who?"

"Kathleen did...to Nathan."

Dorian was silent, studying me to see how I would react, but I couldn't form any words.

"It happened six months after you left," he said. "And she has a daughter, not much younger than my son."

I choked on my tea and it squirted out of my nose. I put a hand up, stopping Dorian from rising, and wiped my mouth with my robes. Fond memories of Kathleen holding my hand or sleeping peacefully with her head in my lap as I stroked her hair clashed against memories of Nathan teasing me or punching me in the face.

The candles in Dorian's home burned brighter. How could she marry *him?* Anyone but him!

The raging inferno in me threatened to boil over. I could never return home. No matter how hard I tried, I had never had a place in Alexandria, and I had lost my place in Sedah. I closed my eyes and took deep breaths, trying to calm my fire.

I opened my eyes and said, "Sorry, Dorian, but I must go. It's getting late and I promised my—"

"I understand."

We rose and he showed me to the door.

"Thanks for letting me get things off my chest like old times," I said. "I really appreciate it, and for checking in with my mother."

"Any time. Don't wait so long to come over again. We still have more catching up to do. At least this time you said goodbye, unlike when you first vanished."

"I'll try to visit more, but we wizards are busy people."

"Busy saving beautiful princesses, I bet."

I blushed at his remark.

We embraced once last time. "You have a lovely family, Dorian. I envy you. Take care, my friend."

Before he could respond, I put up my hood and disappeared into the night.

It was late. I had promised my mother I would be home soon, but I needed to clear my head. There was only one place I could go for that.

The stars shone in force and the bright moon lit my way as I walked to Peaceful Pond. When I lived in Sedah, this place was my only escape from the troubles in the world. At least once a week, I went there to let nature soothe me. I wanted to run now and feel the freedom of the wind brushing against my cheeks. As bright as it was, I didn't. I didn't want to trip on some unforeseen rock. While I once knew the path, it had been years since I last walked it.

The pond also had a special meaning for me and Krystal. It was where I had first met her, and unlocked my powers. But those thoughts were battered aside by thoughts of Kathleen.

I reached the pond and stared at the dark waters. The moon glistened off its ripples. Fireflies danced about, leaving trails of light in the air. Crickets surrounded me, creating an orchestra. I wanted to make camp and lie out under the stars like I used to, yet I knew I couldn't.

I collapsed to one knee, kneeling in front of the pond. My anger at Kathleen's betrayal left me, and exhaustion overtook me. I ripped up a patch of grass, realizing I couldn't go home again. People had gone on with their lives. I knew it was selfish for me to expect them to wait, but I had. Things were different. *I* was different.

I heard my former master's voice in my head, telling me to get my emotions under control. He had taught me better than this.

I focused on the water in front of me. Trying to clear my head, I forced all my turbulent emotions into the spell I crafted. All the rage, pain, frustration, and longing went into that bubble. It rose into the air and ballooned with the emotions leaving me.

"You *are* a wizard," an awed voice said. "I had my doubts."

The bubble popped and I froze. I knew that voice. Part of me wanted to turn around, the other half was scared to.

"Hello, Kathleen," I said. I tried to stare at the black water, but her presence was too distracting.

The grass crunched underneath her feet as she stepped closer. She stood inches from my back. Her smell was intoxicating. It had always reminded me of fresh flowers after a morning's rain shower.

"I thought I saw you earlier. You did a terrible job at hiding yourself," she said. "No matter how many years it's been, I would recognize you anywhere, Hellsfire. Once I knew you were in town, it was only a matter of time before you came here."

I took a breath and readied myself for what was about to come, and for what should have been resolved years ago.

I turned around and faced her. We were a foot apart, but I didn't look directly at her. She didn't make a move or say anything. She waited for me to finish looking her over. I stared at her feet, then worked my way upward. She had gained a little weight from the pregnancy, but it enhanced her short, curvy body.

Kathleen's long, wavy, dark brown swirled around her. When she saw me gawking, her full lips smiled. She was just as beautiful now as she was back then. I was tempted to embrace her, but held back.

"I hear you're the Hero of Alexandria and a wizard now," Kathleen said when our eyes finally met. "I always knew you'd do something great." She brushed her hand across my arm.

I cleared my throat and said, "Thank you. I saw Dorian. He told me you have a daughter." I took a deep breath and my voice became icy. "And that you married Nathan."

Her hand fell from my arm and hung at her side. She looked down and nodded.

"Why?"

She glared at me with fire in her eyes. "He's a good man, Hellsfire. He loves me and he's there for me and our daughter."

I scoffed. "Good man? Have you forgotten how he used to treat me?"

"I remember."

"Then how could you be with him?"

"I don't need to explain myself to anyone, least of all you. You left me, Hellsfire. Me! I didn't leave you." Tears hovered in the corners of her eyes. "Yes, I started seeing Nathan to get back at you for how badly you hurt me, but I soon found myself liking him. And eventually, I fell in love with him."

I stared at her, whatever illusions I may have clung to vanishing. Kathleen and I could never be together again. There was nothing left for me here. There was no one I could turn to. People here couldn't understand my powers or black flames, my situation with Krystal or in Alexandria, and those in Alexandria could never understand my simple upbringing.

Kathleen quickly turned away from me. A quiet tension brewed in the air. The fireflies left the area and the crickets stopped. "You left me. Why do I matter to you now?"

Her words were like an ogre's maul to the chest. I staggered backwards, wondering how she could think such a thing. She was my first love. She would *always* matter to me, no matter what paths the gods laid out for us.

I reached out to her, and she weakly shrugged her shoulders. I clamped down and spun her around to face me. Quiet tears rolled down her face. She scowled as I struggled for words.

The anger lifted from her face. "Please," she said in a soft voice. I knew what she wanted—the truth.

"You were *better* than me, Kat." My eyes burned with pain and tears. "I couldn't get anything right and I had no idea what to do with my life. I didn't want to be stuck in this town, shoveling horse manure and plucking feathers. I wanted to escape and be something more. I always dreamed of people knowing my name and not believing it was evil."

Kathleen narrowed her almond eyes at me. Her whole body trembled with rage. "You selfish bastard! How could you think only of yourself? Why didn't you tell me of these things, or how you felt?"

Kathleen's fist flew up. I could have stopped it, but I deserved it. It struck like stone, and it had nothing to do with her physical strength. Her anger and pain caused the most damage. Her punched sheared through my body to my soul, tearing at my spirit. It took every bit of will to keep from falling over. It was second only to what I had done to Krystal.

Kathleen pounded on my chest. I stood there watching, feeling her energy burn into me with each and every hit. My mind and spirit reeled, but I stood strong. I had to, for Kat's sake. She had to get it all out. Afterwards, she collapsed against my bruised, sore chest, sobbing.

"How could you?" Kathleen asked. "You promised you would always be there for me. You lied!"

I cradled her and held her against my chest. She fit snugly under my chin like she always had. "It's all right. I'm here for you now."

She looked up at me, her face wet and red like mine. We stared into each other's eyes. My tears fell upon her sensual face, but she didn't care. Our faces were pulled together by a long-forgotten force.

In an ever-increasing movement, our lips drew forward. Her breath came upon me and our hearts beat deep with anticipation. When we kissed, every sensation was wrapped into one. It hit me hard, taking over every feeling and thought. The floodgates were opened, and we kissed each other harder, as if desperate for breath. Old and powerful emotions rushed back, flowing as if a dam had broken. Pure euphoria surged between us. She broke the long kiss and left me standing there, yet my body ached for her to go on.

We gasped for breath. There are some magics in the world that cannot be understood or overcome. That was one of them. Kathleen flashed me a smile I had seen a thousand times before, and her eyes gleamed with hunger. She wanted me to take her right then, like I used to. My loins were on fire. It had been so long, and I needed the release. She motioned with her eyes to a clearing with soft grass.

I grabbed her hands and stopped her from tugging on my clothes. I fixed my robes and said, "I...I can't." I barely got the words out.

Kathleen stared at me in quiet fascination. That startled me. I had never seen her take rejection well. She *always* got what she wanted. She made sure of that. It was one of the things I loved most about her.

"There's someone else, isn't there?" she asked.

I nodded.

"Who?"

I hesitated to tell her, but she deserved the truth. "The Princess of Alexandria."

"Ah, so there's more to the stories. I thought so." It didn't seem to bother her; she grinned like a cat. Kat ran her finger over my chest and headed towards my waist. I stopped her, but only barely. "How come you're here with me instead of with her?"

I shook my head. "I needed to clear my head a bit. Things aren't…right with us."

Kathleen cocked her head. "Are you two fighting? If you are, you need to apologize. You were always a bit too prideful. One of the things I loved and hated about you."

"No, nothing like that." I licked my dry lips. "She's been afflicted with a magical curse. If I touch her, she'll die."

Kat's almond eyes searched mine. "Oh, Hellsfire. I'm so sorry." She reached up and pulled my head to her shoulder, and she cradled me.

"You must care about the princess a lot," Kat said into my ear.

"I do."

"Then I'm sure you'll find a cure. You're nothing if not persistent."

"I wish I could have been there for you, Kat." My hand reached out to her serene face. I stroked my thumb back and forth. She put her hand up, clasped my own, and moaned like old times. "But I'll be here for you now. Anything you need, let me know. I'll come running. Promise."

She giggled. "Even though you were fast, you were a bit clumsy at times. Hmmm, but you are stronger now." Kat ran her hand under my wizard's robes, making contact with my skin. I moaned as her fingers explored my hardened body. She gave me another tantalizing smile.

I forced myself to take her hand out from under my clothes. I took her hand in mine and intertwined our fingers. "I don't know your daughter's name."

"Hope."

I smiled. "You should always have hope."

Kat grinned. "If you're a wizard, anything's possible."

I reached out with my hand and put it to her face again. We kissed one last time, but it wasn't like it was before. It was good, and desire and passion lurked, but the emotions that were in our first kiss weren't there. Love was there, and it always would be. We finally had the closure we'd both missed.

I broke the kiss. She eventually opened her eyes and fixed them on mine. "You must really care for this princess of yours," Kat said. "More than you ever did for me. Usually I would have to break it." She reached up and kissed me on the corner of my mouth. "Take care of yourself, Hellsfire. There aren't many wizards around these days."

"I will. Goodbye, Kat. Next time I'm in town I'll make sure to drop by to see you and your daughter."

She smiled, turned around, and left. I could have been a gentleman and walked her home, but I knew she'd make it back just fine and that she wouldn't want my help.

I walked back home, and I couldn't help but compare Kathleen and Krystal. It wasn't fair of me, but I did it anyway. Kathleen was right. I did care about Krystal more than I ever did about Kat, but it was hard. Her father, the banishment, the people of Alexandria, the curse, all moved to work against us. I wanted to tell Krystal how I felt, but with what had happened between us, I wasn't sure if I ever could, or if I should. It would make things harder on her.

Instead of being absorbed in my thoughts, I should have paid attention to my surroundings, especially after what Kat had said. If she knew I was in town, there were bound to be others. Others who weren't like Kat or Dorian. Others who wanted a taste of my blood.

Two men stepped out of the woods and blocked my path. I glanced behind me to see two more men.

These weren't mercenaries. Three of the four men carried a pitchfork, a hoe, and a shovel. Only one man brandished a sword. He stepped forward and the moonlight illuminated him. I gasped when I saw his face. There was a burn scar on the left side—a scar I had burned into him.

"Nathan," I said.

"Hellsfire," he said, narrowing his eyes.

We stared each other down for one long minute. Neither of us said anything. Nathan's three friends shifted uncomfortably, as years of past anger vented from the pair of us.

"What do you want, Nathan?" I asked, breaking the silence. "I have no time for games."

He pointed his sword at me. "Just you." He reached up with his free hand, tracing the bumps and scars over his left cheek. "*You* did this to me."

"I warned you, and if you don't leave now, I'll do worse." I glared at his cronies. "You've heard the stories about me. They're all true. I'm a wizard now. I don't want to hurt you."

They glanced at each other, then to Nathan. They lowered their weapons.

"Don't be fools!" Nathan said. "This is Hellsfire. He's not a wizard, but some kind of demon. We've beaten him before."

They regained their courage and raised their farming tools. The pair behind me stepped forward. I let the fire flow to my eyes.

"Don't," I said, my voice and my hint of magic stopping them.

Nathan roared. He ran to me, bringing his sword up. I lifted my hand and summoned a gust of wind. It barreled into Nathan, knocking him off his feet. He tumbled backwards and crashed to the ground. His sword bounced out of his hand until it lay several feet away. He tried reaching for his sword again, but I shot a small fireball, smacking dangerously close to his hand.

I never took my eyes off Nathan, but said to the others, "Leave."

They wasted no time running well away from me, heading back into town.

Nathan cursed then looked to his fallen sword, but didn't make a move for it. He slowly rose and faced me.

"What are you going to do?" Nathan asked.

I considered. I could kill him. I could hurt him for all the times he hurt me. I could do whatever I wanted and there was nothing he could do to stop me. As I remembered all those past times with his mocking face looming over me, the dark flames within me threatened to rise up. I wanted to give in to their promises of retribution.

Fear vibrated throughout Nathan's face. He thought I was going to kill him. He stepped back and turned his head, deciding whether or not to make a run for it. He stared at the fire I cradled, knowing that I could strike him from afar. He faced me and held his head high, realizing his fate was sealed.

There were so many things I could do to him. I could burn away his flesh, inch by inch; I could open up the ground until it swallowed him, squeezing him until his bones cracked and he died of thirst.

But I would do no such thing.

That wasn't the way I was raised by either my mother or Stradus. And I couldn't leave Kat without a husband and Hope without a father. For whatever reason, she loved him. Maybe not as much as she ever did me, but she did.

"Nothing," I finally said, dispersing my gathered magic.

"Nothing?"

I nodded and sighed. "I'm tired of this, Nathan. I don't even know why we're fighting any more. Do you? We're no longer children. It's time for us to grow up." I walked past him, heading for home.

"This isn't over!" he screamed. "Do you hear me? I'll get you, Wizard, if it's the last thing that I do!"

Nathan continued to yell and rant, and I let him. As long as he didn't threaten my mother, Kathleen, Dorian, or anyone else I cared about, he could come after me if he wanted to. I had hoped that Kathleen or his daughter would have calmed him some. They might have, if only I hadn't scarred his face. Nathan might have tormented me growing up, but my anger melted away when I saw him, replaced with guilt by what I had done.

Nathan's anger seemed to grow, at least while I was in town. When I looked at him, I saw a shell of a man, one tormented by the past. I didn't know what Kathleen saw in him, but I hoped for her sake and their daughter's sake, it was something different. I had far bigger things to worry about than what he did to me growing up—like Premier, the Wasteland creatures, King Furlong, and the *Book of Shazul*. More importantly, I had to worry about what I had done to Krystal.

Early the next day, I said goodbye to my mother and my friends, and we left Sedah.

CHAPTER 18

AFTER THREE WEEKS' travel, we reached the Ennis Mountains. I gazed at the border into Southern Shala.

The high peaks rolled on for miles, the bright sun beaming from behind them. Thick forests grew up the sides of the mountain, and a low haze settled around the top.

Ever since the Great Barrier had been erected, the caves hadn't been used as a regular travel route. I thought they would have been overrun with nature's growth or fallen into disrepair, but that wasn't the case. The cave entrances were bare of growth. The black holes opened their mouths, screaming for us to stay away. The largest ones looked like they could swallow us whole. Yet we had to go through them to reach Southern Shala.

We followed Jastillian along the seldom-used paths leading up to the entrance we planned to use. Weeds and brush had overgrown the way, but there was still enough room for us and our horses, though we once had to navigate around a fallen tree. After three hours, we reached one of the smaller entrances.

I got off my horse and stared at the hole. What would await us in that darkness, and beyond it, on the other side?

"Look at this," Jastillian said, bending down and examining the ground.

We huddled around him, and I peered at the ground. It was still wet from the recent rains, as it was shaded and cooled by the mountain's shadow. A circular mark was imprinted into it.

"What is it?" I asked.

"A track," Jastillian said. "Look at the grooves in the dirt. Half of it is missing, but I've seen this track many times far from here."

"The Wastelands," Rebekah said, glaring at it.

"Aye, and an ogre from the looks of it."

"Premier," I said.

"He can't be more than five or seven days ahead at most," Jastillian said. He paused and placed his hand under his chin in thought. "If we push it, we might be able to catch him right after we exit the mountains, or just before we leave them."

I stared at the ground, trying to spot other tracks. There weren't any. They could have been washed away, but why would there only be one left?

"Think he knows we're coming after him?" I asked. "This could be a trap."

"He couldn't have known we would take this route," Jastillian said and shook his head. "There are plenty of ways to cross the Ennis Mountains."

"Still," Krystal said. "We had better be careful."

Jastillian disappeared into the cave mouth, and we followed. I created fire in my hand, both to light the way and as a spell in case Premier was here. Behast and I flanked Jastillian.

The cave wasn't as musty or stale as the White Mountain's caves were. The fresh, moisture-laden air filled my lungs. The hooves of the horses echoed all around us. If Premier was nearby, he would hear us long before we found him.

Shadows stalked us from above. Their disfigured faces screamed out and I kept imagining Premier and his pet ogre out there, waiting for us. Stalagmites dipped down from the ceiling, threatening to pierce us like arrows. The slow dripping of water surrounded us. Bats hung from the ceiling in slumber, waiting until nightfall to attack their prey.

"I've been to these mountains many a time," Jastillian said, keeping his voice low. "I've been here looking for artifacts from the War of the Wizards and, like everyone else, a path to get through the barrier. I had chased rumors that there was a secret way through." He shook his head. "But I could never find one."

"Why are the caves so smooth?" Krystal asked, reading my thoughts.

"You hear that slight dripping sound?" Jastillian asked. "These caves were naturally formed by water over time. There's even an underground river in here. As more people started to settle in Northern Shala, they started to shape a few of the tunnels for supply routes. Not soon after, when the war started, they did it for their armies." Jastillian snorted. "That was also when they collapsed a few of the tunnels.

"I chose this route because the tunnels should be fine, and according to the map Sharald gave us, it will put us close to where we need to go. But it could possibly be a week until we're out of here."

Three days passed in the Ennis Mountains. Jastillian said we were close to where the Great Barrier had been, but I didn't see an end to this eternal darkness.

On the fourth day, we had to travel in single file as the ledge we were on thinned out. I led the horse by the reins, trying not to slip and fall into the abyss below. I stumbled. A piece of rock broke away, clattering down the deep hole. I peered over, staring into the blackness. I wiped the sweat from my forehead and backed away.

Not long afterward, we traveled down a long tunnel barely tall enough to fit our horses. I tugged at my shirt collar, feeling smothered, as though the mountain might cave in on me. Jastillian stopped us in the middle of the tunnel. Small rocks were lined up in front of his feet, stretching from one side of the tunnel to the other.

"This is it," Jastillian said. "This is where the Great Barrier is supposed to lie."

I studied the surrounding rock. I had somehow expected grooves in the wall, as if they had been eroded by a long-runner river, or bite marks outlining the area where the Great Barrier had been. It seemed impossible that something so powerful wouldn't leave a mark, but there was nothing. If there ever was anything marking the Great Barrier, it was gone now.

"I can't tell if it's still there," Prastian said. "And if Premier came this way, there are no signs of him."

"That's how it's always been," Jastillian said.

"Hellsfire, do you sense anything?" Krystal asked.

I reached out with my wizard senses, trying to find some kind of unseen magical force, no matter how small. I shook my head. "Nothing. If there was a residue of magic marking it, there's none now. I couldn't even feel a backlash of energy when I was in the Wastelands."

She opened her mouth to say something, but then her eyes rolled into her head and she collapsed. I barely caught her.

"Princess!" Ardimus said.

We all huddled around her and I cradled her in my arms. Her skin grew pale and her eyes fluttered. The necklace underneath her clothes flared. The green magic brightened her skin while it worked its magic. I held my breath for several moments, not daring to breathe until she moved.

Krystal slowly opened her eyes. Her purple eyes focused on mine.

"Princess, are you all right?" I asked.

"What happened?"

"You fainted."

She gave me a small smile, then pulled away from me. Ardimus helped her up. "I'm all right now."

"Princess," Rebekah said, handing her a skin of water.

"You need to see the council before it happens again," I said. "They'll be able to help you."

"I'm fine." She looked at me, but her words were also meant for the others. "My health is not my priority. That's not why we're going into Southern Shala. Understand?"

I bit my lip. Her health was *my* priority. Premier had to be dealt with, but the curse also had to be cured. I bowed my head. "Understood, Your Highness."

"Good."

Silence loomed while we decided on what to do. Because of what had happened with the princess, the tension in the air was thick.

Jastillian broke it. He picked up a rock and said, "I've been wanting to do this for decades."

"Let me try," Demay said, grabbing the rock from Jastillian's hand. "I think Hellsfire brought it down."

"Aye, me too. But if he didn't, it's going to hurt when you smack into the barrier." Jastillian grinned. "Trust me."

"Don't worry," Prastian said. "My brother has a hard head."

"Here goes nothing," Demay said.

The elf held his breath and leapt over the rocks. He didn't hit anything. He exhaled and gave us a big grin. "I did it."

Jastillian strolled to where Demay was. He stared down the tunnel and didn't move.

I went to Jastillian and clasped his shoulder. "Are you all right?"

"I'm fine, lad. It's just been a dream of mine to do this. As many times as I've been down here, I never thought it would come true. And it's all thanks to you." That gleeful look on his face vanished, and it became somber. "Now let's go to Fairhaven. We've got a lot to do."

Three more days passed while we navigated the caves. We didn't find any other signs of Premier, but we did find dead ends and collapsed tunnels. It might have been Premier's doing, but it also could have been that King Sharald's map was outdated and that the tunnels had changed over time.

After passing where the Great Barrier once lay, we were excited as we drew to our destination, knowing we had done something no other had done in nearly a thousand years. But we soon grew tired of the darkness of the caves.

I did my best to conceal my nervousness. The caves got smaller and the shadows closer. I had always hated enclosed spaces. I focused on my breathing and the task ahead to clear my mind. Even the horses were in discomfort. We stopped riding them and led them. They seemed to drag their hooves and keep their heads down. While we had enough oats and water for them, the lack of light and grazing weakened their spirits.

The elves had an even harder time. Much like plants, they needed sunlight. We mostly had my fire as light. There were rare cracks throughout the mountains that brought in the sun's rays. When we crossed those areas, we rested or even built our camps there, so the elves and horses could recover.

Even Krystal, Rebekah, and Ardimus weren't immune. Thankfully, Krystal didn't have another fainting spell, although I watched her carefully. We all desperately wanted to feel the grass beneath our feet and to sleep on the soft dirt instead of the hard ground.

The only one who felt at home was Jastillian. It was more than his excitement about going into Southern Shala. He was a dwarf, used to the lack of sunlight and the dim conditions of caves. The bright mushrooms in the caves or the flapping bat wings above our heads didn't bother him. He didn't watch his footing like we did. His feet naturally seemed to know where to go, while ours slipped, and we had to study the ground before placing our feet.

On our last day inside the Ennis Mountains, the bright sun shone from the tunnel's exit. We paused, admiring it, relieved to begin another part of our journey. We raced towards the end of the caves and out from the entrapment of the mountains.

I shielded my eyes from the brightness. I let my skin absorb the heat and sighed at the breeze running through my hair. I stared down at the landscape beneath us as the mountains sloped down, opening up to this forgotten land.

Southern Shala radiated with green under the midday sun. The tall grass was like an ocean, ripples splashing against each other like waves. My horse bent down to chomp on a small clump of grass outside of the caves.

I stared back at the Ennis Mountains, peering at the other cave openings carved into the mountains, big and small. We still had a week or two of travel if we were to make it to Fairhaven, but we were one step closer.

The others studied the map and the configuration of the mountains, and then Prastian and Jastillian led us down the mountain slope. We set up camp at the base of the mountains. After dinner, Krystal and I had the first watch.

As usual, I set up detection webs around the area and cast earth magic to feel what was out there. When I was done, I sat down on a log next to Krystal. We hadn't been on the same watch since before we crossed into Southern Shala. I always cherished the moments when it was just me and her. Even if not a word was said during our watch. It was just nice to be in her presence.

She stared at the stars and didn't say a word to me.

"Krystal, how badly has the curse been affecting you?"

She shrugged. "It happens occasionally. Sometimes it's worse, sometimes it's not that bad."

"Why didn't you tell me about it?"

She turned and cocked her head. "Was there anything you could do about it?"

I sighed. "No."

"Then you have your answer. The necklace protects me well enough and I can handle what the curse throws at me."

"I know you're strong, Krystal, but you still should have told me."

We sat in silence while I figured out how to approach what I wanted to say.

"The council will be able to help you," I said.

Krystal gave me an incredulous look.

"Us, I mean." I took a breath and said, "I want you to be all right, even if we can't be together again."

"Are you giving up on us?" she asked.

I shook my head. "Things were tenuous with me in Alexandria before. They became worse with what I did to you, and now I'm banished. Even if the council finds a way to break to curse, things will be hard. It might be easier if...we end it after we see the council."

"Even if the council has a cure?"

I couldn't look at her. That wasn't what I wanted. I wanted to be with her more than anything, but no matter what I did, I just made things worse. It hurt me to see what kind of pain she was in—pain I caused. I nodded my head.

"I see," Krystal said. "I don't think you should worry about this now. Think about the task at hand. If you worry about too many things, you'll lose focus."

"Until I can break Renak's curse and you're safe and unharmed again, you're all I think about." I pushed my legs up and bent my head down until they touched. "Your father told me that you once had...others. Maybe our time for fun is over. I understand. You're a princess. You're groomed to be a queen and Guardian of Northern Shala. I'm just a peasant from some poor town."

"Fun? Is that what you think we're doing? Is that why you think I enjoy your company?"

I took a deep breath. "I honestly don't know what we're doing, Princess."

"Don't presume to know what I think or feel, Hellsfire." Her violet eyes shot daggers at me. "Nor presume to know what I want." She rose and walked away.

I didn't understand her. I was trying to cut ties to make things easier for both of us and for the good of her kingdom. She should have understood that. She made decisions for the well-being of her kingdom every day despite what she wanted to do. That's what she taught me.

After three hours our watch ended, and I dropped into an unrestful slumber.

I stand alone in the darkness, but it's not the darkness that comes after night falls. It's the darkness I once saw in Premier's eyes. It's what happens in the absence of light.

The darkness swirls and moves as if it's alive. It pauses and stares at me. I step back to escape it, but it stalks and chases me. I run as fast as I can, but there's no retreat.

The darkness leaps and smothers me. I try to shake it off, but it clings to me like soot. It crawls over my skin until it flows into my mouth. I choke on its cold touch, thinking that it will fill me with death.

My body betrays me and welcomes its icy touch. Lurking within it is a mighty power, and it calls my name. It feels familiar, as if I've known it my entire life.

A blinding light bursts from nowhere. The blazing light burns bright until it's a fire. The fire flies towards me, and my body absorbs it. Its warmth comforts my skin until it too fills my body. The darkness withers and I yell in agony. I can breathe again.

But the darkness doesn't leave. It still surrounds me.

The fire that fuels my magic rips from me, trying to incinerate the darkness. It fails and the darkness renews attack.

The darkness leaps out and fills my body again. I stumble and fall to the ground. Instead of reaching out to my flame, I let the darkness consume me.

I woke up drenched in a cold sweat. The morning mist lingered in the air, forever fighting a losing battle against the sun. I gathered up my bedroll and went to tie it to my horse. I was in the middle of securing my saddlebags when the princess came over to me.

"Are you all right?" Krystal asked, concern in her voice.

"I just had a bad dream."

"It seemed more than that."

I opened my mouth to lie, but thought better of it. I knew I could trust her, but I hated feeling so vulnerable around her, especially with what had happened between us last night. I stepped in closer and kept my voice low and muffled so that the elves wouldn't overhear.

"There's another reason I'm going to Southern Shala," I said. "I also need some help."

"With what?"

"My power."

As quickly as I could, I told her my dream and how there was something lurking within my flame—a dark and powerful magic aching to be unleashed. Each time I reached into myself and needed more magic, it beckoned me, enticing me. She could understand more than most. She was there when it first happened.

"What do you think it means?" she asked.

"That's just it. I don't know. Stradus never told me about this before he died. And it didn't come up until then. There are no wizards to turn to in Northern Shala. I'm hoping the council can help me, and that what I'm going through is normal. You know I wasn't a wizard until I beat Premier. It's all still so new to me."

"And if it's not normal?"

"I don't know. But as someone once told me, I'm not going to worry about that now." I smiled at her. "I have more important things to focus on, like warning the council about Premier, Renak's threat, and finding a cure for the most beautiful woman in all the lands."

Krystal blushed and grinned. She briefly laid her hand on mine before walking away.

We consulted the map before riding out across the vast plains towards Fairhaven—the place where we would all find what we needed.

We fanned out as we rode south, trotting along the plains. We kept an eye out for any town or village, or even simple travelers who could tell us if we were close or if there was a nearby place we could resupply.

After half a day's ride, my temples began to throb. I turned my head away from the bright sun and put my fingertips to my temples, trying to massage them. The pain worsened, like a dagger pushing its way into my head. The reins slipped from my fingers, and I tilted until I fell. I smashed into the hard ground and the rocks drove into my back.

"Hellsfire!" Krystal said.

The others leapt off their horses and ran to me. Rebekah and Jastillian were the closest. I staggered as Rebekah helped me to my feet. Our horses spooked, whinnying and bucking. Before the others could corral them, they galloped away and took our supplies with them.

The pain struck again. I slipped through Rebekah's arms, but Jastillian caught me. The ground shook and trembled, buckling beneath our feet. The blue sky deepened. Its normal colors vanished, replaced by an angry red with black clouds in it. The thunder rumbled in concert with the earth, and the wind picked up, forcing me to shield my eyes.

"Come on!" Jastillian yelled through the rough wind. "Stay close!"

I tried to follow him, my ears throbbing. Rebekah held me upright as I tried to move my sluggish feet. Jastillian motioned to the others. I stopped and turned, trying to spot the princess.

A magical force smashed into me like a falling mountain, and my legs gave way. My head spun out of control, and my stomach tightened so hard I thought it was going to burst. Waves of rainbow auras seared my body. I screamed in agony.

We had to get out of this magical storm, but I couldn't move. My muscles were jelly. I spewed my stomach up, gagging and coughing, while the wind tore at my face. The others weren't as affected as I was, but they were still in trouble.

Jastillian and Rebekah propped me up. The elves, Krystal, and Ardimus all tried to get closer. We had to leave and get out of this together. I yelled for Krystal with my remaining strength before the magic overtook me and I blacked out.

CHAPTER 19

WHEN I REGAINED consciousness, my head pounded. I moaned. A fire roared near me.

"Glad to see you're awake," Rebekah said, helping me sit up.

Jastillian handed me a skin of lukewarm water. I swallowed, and sighed as it soothed my throat. I glanced around for Krystal. I didn't see her or the others anywhere.

"How are you feeling, lad?" Jastillian asked.

I rubbed my sore head. "Terrible, but I'll live. Where are the others?"

"We don't know," Rebekah said. "The storm worsened. We were barely able to get you and ourselves out of there."

My heart got stuck in my throat. "The princess?"

She shook her head. "The wind and hail kept us apart. We were nearly hit by lightning, and we had to veer off to get away. I backtracked once we were safe, but I couldn't find them or see where they went."

Despair and hopelessness surrounded us. Not a noise could be heard. They could be anywhere in Southern Shala. What other traps were out there? What other forms of magic did they have to deal with? Was this just the beginning of what Renak had warned me about earlier? They needed me. *She* needed me. And we had no idea how to get to Fairhaven. Neither did they. The map was on Prastian's horse. What were we going to do now?

"Do you know what happened, lad?" Jastillian asked.

"A spell. A very powerful spell." I cupped my fingers under my chin. "A ritual like that would have taken at least a dozen wizards to perform. But why would they create a trap like that? What kind of wizards are down here?" The stories my former master had told me, about the wizards he knew and the helpfulness of the Elemental Council, might no longer be true. Much time had passed and a lot had changed since the Great Barrier and the War of the Wizards.

"I'm sorry," I said. "I should have listened to myself. I sensed it before I knew what it was."

Jastillian placed a hand on my shoulder. "No need to blame yourself. You couldn't have known what would happen, wizard or no."

I grimaced. I didn't agree with that. I was supposed to be protecting them from any magic down here. I looked at my companions. "So what do we do now?"

"We need supplies," Rebekah said. "We have a few things on us, but our horses ran away with most of them. Afterwards, we go look for the others."

"If they're still alive," Jastillian said.

I stared into the surrounding night. I closed my eyes and focused. I still felt the bond between Krystal and me, no matter how faint it was. I didn't know if it was magic or wishful thinking, but I knew in my heart that she wasn't dead.

"They're alive," I said. "I can feel it."

Jastillian gave me a hopeful smile. "That's good, lad. If the gods are on our side, we'll rejoin them soon enough." The spark in his eyes matched my desire to find them.

"Agreed."

"Good. Now get some rest. We'll keep watch a little while longer."

I wanted to argue with him. They had done enough for me already. But I didn't, as I felt my body crying out for rest.

Without the map, we couldn't tell how to get to Fairhaven. We didn't want to backtrack east for fear of the disturbance we had run into, as we didn't know how widespread it was. We decided to head west.

We traveled for two long days. The water in our two skins ran out. We found neither river, stream, nor brook and resorted to sucking the dew off the morning's grass. Using my power, I could pull water out of the environment. Once a day, I was able to create a small handful of water for each of us. It left any nearby flowers and plants withered.

The dates, prunes, figs, and other dried fruits in my purse were gone. There was no big game for Rebekah and Jastillian. They took to hunting and trapping small animals like hares, snakes, and gophers. That kept the hunger at bay, but it wasn't a proper meal.

One day, we reached a sea of high grass and weeds. There was no way around it. They were tall enough that I couldn't see over them without leaping in the air. Since I was the tallest, I led the way, fighting against the grassy current. Unlike the water, this current had sword-sharp points attached to it. I pushed and stepped on them, breaking their stalks, as they were too flexible to be cut by Rebekah's sword.

I quickly put my hood up when the sharp blades cut me. I had to spit out the small bugs that jumped in my mouth. I wished they were bigger. Even though I didn't regularly eat meat, I would have eaten them.

"Tell me you see an end to this, lad," Jastillian said from the rear.

I jumped a bit, trying to scan the layout of the land. I shook my head. "Nope. It goes as far as the eye can see."

"Still don't want to change your mind about burning it? I'll owe you one, lad."

I chuckled. "The only thing I'd do would be to start a huge brushfire."

"I wouldn't mind."

"Shhh!" Rebekah said. "I hear something."

We all paused in our tracks. The two withdrew their weapons and I readied my magic. We turned our heads, trying to figure out what she'd heard.

Off to the left, the tall grass rustled. The air was so still that it couldn't have been the wind. The noise continued, heading right for us.

I gathered in surrounding energy, thinking about that storm trap and the wizards behind it, of Premier, and of Renak's threat. The rustling in the fast-moving grass was almost upon us.

Just when I thought a monster was going to appear, a dark shadow soared through the air in a graceful motion, briefly blocking out the sun. He landed a few feet from us and created a clearing for himself. He stared at us, his purple horn glistening. A red scarf was wrapped across his white neck, and his long, white mane and tail swayed in the wind. He stomped his hooves and neighed.

"A unicorn," Rebekah said in a hushed tone.

His black eyes gazed at Jastillian and Rebekah before settling on me. He seemed to be communicating with me, but I couldn't understand his language. The unicorn broke eye contact and turned and galloped away, the folds of grass welcoming him.

We glanced at each other, all with the same thought in our heads. "Let's follow him!"

We ran through the grass, pushing and fighting against the rough sea. The cuts and scratches on my exposed skin no longer mattered. Suddenly, I felt no more resistance, and I nearly tumbled. We were free of that accursed grass. However, the unicorn was nowhere to be found. I had heard they were faster than any horse, but how did he get away from us? We weren't that slow.

"There he is!" the captain said and pointed.

The unicorn stood a hundred feet from us. He stared at us and didn't move. He ran as we moved toward him, and we chased him across the plains. We never seemed to get any closer, but he never got any further from us. Finally the unicorn galloped over a small hill. We continued after him, but more slowly now, tired from the travel and our lack of adequate food and water.

I reached the top of the hill and leaned over, gasping for air. Sweat dripped from my forehead and I wanted to collapse from exhaustion. What were we doing chasing a unicorn? We had more important things to worry about. I lifted my head and saw, through my hazy vision, that the unicorn had vanished.

Jastillian and Rebekah finally caught up to me, and the pair was panting just as I was.

"Where did he go?" Rebekah asked in between breaths.

"He's gone," I said.

"Blasted unicorn!" Jastillian said, slapping his knee. "He led us on a chase. At least we got to see one, and now I truly know that they're far more intelligent than horses."

"What's that?" Rebekah asked. She lifted her hand to her eyebrows, leaned forward, and squinted.

"What do you see?" I asked.

She allowed herself a small smile. "A town...or possibly a city. I can't tell from this distance."

"Do you think that unicorn was leading us here?" I asked.

"The question is, why?"

"Either way, we have no choice," Jastillian said. "We need supplies and information. And a warm bed, food, and drink would be nice too."

"But we must be careful," I said, thinking of the trap that had disbanded us. "We don't know what's in there."

"Aye."

We headed for this city, relieved to find a place of civilization, but worried about what type of people lived in Southern Shala.

CHAPTER 20

AS THE SUN SET, we trudged our way towards the city. While we walked, I kept wondering if Premier had come this way too. He couldn't have known about the trap. He might have been forced in this direction. I clenched my fist in anger, aching to kill him for what he did to Krystal.

Off in the distance, we glimpsed groups of people heading toward the city, but it was going to be another hour before we arrived there. I kept glancing around as we walked. I felt as if we were being watched. I never saw anybody and I couldn't sense any magic, but I couldn't shake that feeling.

A wall surrounded part of the city, but it was crumbling from age and years of neglect. Fallen stones were piled on top of each other, waiting to be repaired. A group of small children played around them. They climbed on the rocks and poked their heads out between the holes. As we approached, one of the older ones looked up at the sinking sun and gathered the others together, leading them off home.

There were guards posted near the rubble where the children had played. They reminded me of those I'd seen when entering Alexandria or Erlam, except these guards looked tired and weary. Their rumpled red uniforms almost matched the color of Jastillian's armor, but theirs were a slightly lighter shade. They chatted to each other, slouching and leaning on their spears. As we approached, they halted their conversation and glared at us. We kept our heads down and avoided eye contact, hoping they wouldn't stop us. They didn't, but I still felt their eyes on my back.

There were stables about a hundred feet from inside the demolished wall. We passed them and went on to the marketplace. The stalls were closing, the vendors packing their wares to go home.

The flat wooden structures were dull and unpainted, and some of them were rotting. One stall had carefully placed bracing, keeping the structure from falling down.

I noticed that over half the people we saw wore red. They had red tunics, scarves, cloaks, and headdresses. I had gotten used to emblems and colors being worn by guards in other cities, but here it seemed that everyone wore the same colors.

We passed by a young couple. They whispered sweet nothings to one another, with their arms wrapped around each other's waists. The woman laughed at what the man said, but she soon had to stifle a yawn. A man walked his young boy home, holding him by the hand. But he seemed to drag his feet as he did so.

We traveled the dirt-covered streets, searching for an inn. I kept my wizard senses open, seeking to find any hint of magic in this crowded city. Even if I found a wizard, I wasn't sure how I would approach them or if they would even help us. Until I figured that out, we would pretend to be simple travelers.

We stumbled upon a bustling inn and went inside. The aroma of roasted pig flooded my nose, and the sight of a baked potato on a nearby plate made me salivate. I blew into my numb hands and rubbed them, letting the warmth of the place seep into them. I quietly thanked the gods that we had a reprieve, but I wondered about the others. How did they fare and what were they going through right now?

I surveyed the room, wondering who we could get information from without sounding suspicious. My gaze lingered when I spotted centaurs at the tall tables. Their half-horse and half-human bodies were astonishing. I had heard stories, but always thought them too strange to be real. It was as if the gods couldn't decide on what to make them.

At other tables, I spotted a few gnomes. They were similar in stature to dwarves, with similar strength. Physically, it was their noses that differentiated them—twice as big as a human's nose. From what I'd been told, they had far grumpier personalities too. A pair of them gambled and argued over the outcome.

Two human men in the corner caught my eye. They wore big, simply cut robes like mine, but theirs were different colors—a dark forest green and an earth-toned brown. Like most of the people in the room, they had red scarves around their arms. I turned my head away before they caught me staring at them. I also suppressed my magic in case they might be wizards.

We swooped down on an empty table on the other side of the room. It was up against the wall and gave us a good view of everything. Jastillian left to get us food and secure us lodgings, while Rebekah and I kept an eye on everyone.

I drummed my fingers on the table, staring at the gnomes and centaurs while becoming lost in my thoughts. We would resupply and stay here for a day or two, but then what? Where would we go? The others could be anywhere and they could be in trouble. It was all my fault.

"It's not your fault," Rebekah said, reading my mind. "You couldn't have known what would happen."

I clenched my teeth and shook my head. "I should have known. I'm a wizard. I'm supposed to be the magic against magic."

"I should be with her instead of here with you," she said. "I have faith we'll see them again. The princess and Prastian are very resourceful people."

Rebekah was right. Krystal, Prastian, and the others were very resourceful. However, that didn't mean I couldn't worry about them.

Jastillian returned and sat back down. "I talked to the innkeeper, and he hadn't seen anyone matching my descriptions of Prastian, the princess, or the others. He also said that we're about two weeks away from Fairhaven." Jastillian leaned in close and whispered, "I also got the feeling that we shouldn't go there."

"Why not?" Rebekah asked.

"The innkeeper seemed surprised that I should ask about it and made it sound dangerous."

"Did you find out why?" I asked.

"I tried, but I couldn't without rousing suspicion."

"By the Inferno," I said. "We need to find out why. The others may be heading there and may stumble upon whatever's wrong."

"First, we resupply," Rebekah said. "We have some coin on us, and it should be good here. Next, we ask questions, find out more about Fairhaven, then search for the others."

Our food and drinks were served, and we ate and drank until our bellies were full. We drank so much ale it sloshed in our stomachs. We had several helpings of everything. I ate plenty of vegetable soup and bread while the other two tore at legs of boar.

Afterwards, I leaned back in my chair, feeling guilty over how full I felt and how we would get a decent night's sleep. Were the others experiencing hardship, or had they stumbled upon a village? Worse yet, did they run across another magical trap? Or were they at another inn in the city? Before we left, we were going to have to scour this city just to make sure.

The door to the inn was flung open and a young guard scanned the room. His eyes widened when he spotted us. They lingered, then he glanced away and kept his head down. He made his way to the robed figures in the corner.

The guard gestured wildly. One of the men he talked to leaned to the side. He smiled at us and nodded. I did the same. He returned to his position, and the young guard blocked him again.

"I don't like the looks of this," Rebekah said.

"Shall we find another inn, or is it too late?" I asked.

"It's too late for that," she said. "We've already paid, and leaving would look suspicious. They would track us to the next inn. I know I would. We're exhausted. We need sleep. Let's go back to our rooms. I'll take first watch."

We left our table and headed for the stairs, wading through the sea of drinking, eating, gambling people.

The door to the inn swung open, and an ogre strolled in. This one was well-dressed and armed much like the armor and weapons Premier had given

Baal. For a second, I thought it *was* Baal and that Premier was going to stroll in right after him. Others in the room didn't do more than glance at the door before going back to their food, conversations, or games. But my two companions didn't.

Jastillian and Rebekah drew their axe and sword respectively. Half of those in the room pushed aside their chairs and stood up, drawing their own weapons. The rest of the people in the room got up and crept away.

The noise in the room ceased, and we three stood back to back, surrounded and outnumbered. I created a fireball and prepared to hurl as many of the simple spells as I could. Those warrior instincts of Rebekah's and Jastillian's were about to get us killed.

The two possible wizards rose from their table. They strolled over to us, and everyone parted around them. The green-robed one put a hand up, and the surrounding warriors lowered their weapons. I crushed the spell with my hand and reabsorbed the fire mana.

"You're a wizard," the brown-robed one said. The color of his robes matched his skin, but I couldn't see the features of his face with his hood up. All I saw were his unusual gray eyes, trying to assess me.

I nodded. "Are you?"

The two ignored my question as they whispered to each other. The green-robed one asked, "Where are you from?"

"We're from the south," I said.

"You lie," a woman said from behind.

Her skintight black leather body suit looked enticing, but the spiked mace she cradled said otherwise. It was pointed directly at me. She glared at me with fierce blue eyes. Magical energy surrounded her, and she poked me with it, trying to delve into me. I pushed it off with my will.

"You will answer my question," the green-robed one said.

The woman chanted and the green-robed one joined her. They worked in tandem, their incantation piercing harder, digging into my mind for the truth. I flared my nostrils and focused, mumbling a spell to dismiss theirs. I created a shield for the three of us. Their power cracked at it like a hammer, but my shield held firm. The gray-eyed one didn't join in.

"Hellsfire, what's going on?" Rebekah asked.

"They're performing a spell." The muscles on my temples flexed. "I'm doing my best to block it, but I'm worried about all these armed people."

"Don't worry, lad," Jastillian said. "We'll hold them off."

I latched onto my strongest mana and focused on that. The flame burned and all the light in the room grew brighter. Their attempts weakened, devoured by my fire.

"Enough," the gray-eyed wizard said.

The wizards ceased their magic. The gray-eyed one drew back his hood and smiled. It was a kind smile, despite his strange eyes and rough face. His smile widened when he met Rebekah's eyes.

"Forgive us," he said.

Rebekah nodded, but didn't lower her weapon.

"Malik, why did you stop us?" the green-robed wizard said. "We were just about to break them."

"No, you weren't, Dylan. This one's strong."

Dylan pulled back his hood, exposing a clean-shaven face and stern gaze. "He doesn't look like it."

"Things are rarely what they appear to be," Malik said. "You should know that."

Dylan spit in disgust. "Don't go quoting me the old rules. I know them all. What should we do with them?"

"Stop being rude for one," Malik said. He looked at me and said, "We know you had lodgings for the night, but if you would please come with us, Wizard…"

"Hellsfire," I said.

"Hellsfire. We'll show you and your friends around Romenia and place you in much more secure lodgings. There are also very important people who want to meet you."

"Who?"

"The Elemental Council."

My back stiffened and I gasped. They weren't in Fairhaven. They were here. Out of all the things I'd expected, this wasn't one of them. This changed everything. They could help us, but what made them abandon Fairhaven? Renak's warning floated through my mind.

I regained my composure and nodded. "All right. We'll go with you."

Rebekah and Jastillian put away their weapons. Everyone else in the inn did the same, yet their eyes never left us. The three of us exited the inn and followed Malik and Dylan. The woman with the mace trailed us.

The large city was oddly quiet. There were no night services at the smaller temples we passed, no plays went on, and even the women who solicited us did so with half-hearted attempts. Romenia was a dead city. There were plenty of people about earlier in the day, but they seemed to have vanished, tired from the day's activities.

"It's a beautiful night," Malik said, gazing at the night sky.

"I agree," Captain Rebekah said.

Malik focused his gaze on her and smiled. "I'm sorry. We've not properly introduced ourselves. I'm Malik and this is Dylan. The sorceress behind us is Adriana."

A sorceress? That explained why her magic felt different from the others. Stradus had told me of their kind and said that like different species of animals, we all shared similarities when it came to magic.

"This is Rebekah and Jastillian," I said.

"A pleasure to meet you," Malik said.

"Yes," Dylan said. "Pleasure."

Adriana remained silent.

I stared at the stars, trying to figure out a way to lead our conversation. Rebekah and Jastillian seemed content to let me, since I was a wizard, but I had no experience in these kinds of things. They might be better at it than me, but it was I who had to do it.

I needed to ask questions about them, the council, Fairhaven, and Southern Shala without giving away that we were from Northern Shala and that the barrier was down. I was going to have to do something I was terrible at—lie.

Before I could open my mouth, one of the bright stars I stared at grew larger. It hovered and floated to us. The three of us were stunned, but the others paid it no notice.

"Ahhh, Serena," Malik said, holding out his hand. "I wondered when you'd be back."

The star landed on Malik's outstretched hand. The glow disappeared, and a little person stood there. Her spiky red hair blended with her pink skin, and she wore clothing that barely covered her. She had a sweet, enticing, magical feel to her.

"A fairy?" Jastillian said in awe.

"Hi, Malik. Who are these strangers?" Serena took off, and that shining brightness reappeared. She hovered around Jastillian. "I haven't seen a dwarf in ages." She darted to Rebekah. "Pretty blond hair." Serena flew up to my face, her light green eyes full of wonder. "Who's he? He's cute. Very cute." She giggled. I had a hard time concealing my red cheeks in the darkness.

"Serena, leave him alone and don't try anything on him," Malik said in a stern voice.

"Awww, but I'm sure he'd like to visit my kingdom. He'd love it there! Humans always do." Serena glanced at Dylan and Adriana. "Well, most humans."

She swooped over to Dylan, who waved his hand as if Serena were a horsefly. Serena dodged it.

"What's she talking about?" Jastillian asked.

"She's talking about Fairie," Malik said. "It's a land that exists in another world. Although some consider it paradise, you lose all track of time and indulge in its beauty and...fascinations. When that happens the fairies there make use of your spirit and heart—among other things. You become lost in a stupor, never wanting to leave. Some say it's worth it." He shrugged.

Serena flew to Malik and stuck her tongue out at him. "It's not that bad, if you remember correctly."

Malik sported a sly smile. "I remember."

"How did you two meet, Malik?" I asked.

"That's a long story, best saved for another time. Serena, please sit on my shoulder and be quiet. We were just about to get to know our friends here."

We continued our slow walk through Romenia, heading towards the center of the city.

"Where are you two from?" Dylan said. "Don't say the south. We've been tracking you ever since you sent off the trap."

"Trap?" I asked. "Then that storm *was* a trap? What was it doing in the middle of nowhere? We almost got killed."

"That's what traps do," Adriana said.

"We're in the middle of a war," Malik said with a sigh. Dylan shot him a look. "But now's not the time for that."

"A war?" I asked, raising an eyebrow. That would explain the trap and why the people in Romenia seemed so downtrodden. Jastillian, Rebekah and I exchanged a look of concern for both ourselves and the others. As much as I wanted to find a cure for Krystal, learn more about my powers, and warn the people about Premier and Renak's threat, we had to find the others and discuss what to do first. I wanted to press Malik on the matter, but he must have read my thoughts.

"Please, Hellsfire," Malik said. "It will all be explained to you in good time, but we must know if you're friend or foe." He stopped walking, and he and Dylan faced us.

"Well?" Dylan said, staring down his nose at us. He and Adriana gathered in magical energy. Malik did nothing.

I glanced at the others. We had discussed not telling people where we were from, but they knew we were lying. We needed their trust, and to see the council. If I lied again, it could only get us into more trouble. I took a deep breath and made a decision.

"All right, I'll tell you," I said. "We're from Northern Shala."

Confused looks appeared on their faces, but they weren't as surprised as I would have expected.

"That sounds familiar," Malik said, scratching his cheek. "But I can't remember where I know it from."

"Where is that, and why is it named after the legendary Shala?" Dylan asked.

Jastillian stepped forward. "Because Shala was a hero to us, as well, and like the lad said, we're from the north."

Malik put a finger under his chin. "There's nothing north except…"

Their calculating looks changed to ones of incredulity and dawning realization. Even Adriana lowered her weapon long enough figure it out.

Serena flew to my face and asked, "You're from the land past the Great Barrier?"

I nodded.

"That's impossible," Adriana said.

"It was," Jastillian said, patting my back. "Until the lad here brought it down."

I cringed. It was bit much for Jastillian to tell them that part. The shock did work to our advantage, though. Their eyes widened with a momentary fear, their muscles tightened, and they all took a step back. Adriana clenched her weapon tighter and Dylan summoned his magic.

"We've got to hurry then," Dylan said. "Malik, go and wake them."

Malik shook his head and didn't move. He had a sour look on his face.

"Adriana?"

She glared at Dylan.

"Fine, but you *both* owe me." Dylan turned and ran in the direction we had been heading.

"Where's he going?" I asked.

"To wake the council," Malik said. "Someone has to do it. We were going to introduce you to them in the morning, but this is too important to let them sleep."

Malik rushed us to the center of the city, where there was a small castle. The top half had been blown apart; black, burnt marks streaked the remaining stones. There should have been towers in each of the four corners, but only one remained intact. We walked under an arch and past a few guards. A red banner, torn to strips, flapped in the night breeze.

As we traversed the curved corridors of the castle, I couldn't help but feel let down. I had expected to meet the council in Fairhaven. From what Stradus told me, they were in charge of a prestigious magical school. People came from every corner of the land to study with them and learn to use and control their magical abilities. The council also made and enforced the magical decisions for all of Southern Shala. They prosecuted those who used their powers for ill, and helped those that needed it.

My former master also told me that the school in Fairhaven was a beautiful and wondrous place filled with magical artifacts and mesmerizing enchantments. There was nothing like that in this drab castle.

We passed by a mural that incorporated the symbols of mana, but the colors had smeared down the wall as if it once cried. I put my fingertips to it, carrying away a smudge. I passed in front of a statue of Shala, but he was missing his left arm. He stood proud and was supposed to look heroic, but with only one arm, he looked ridiculous.

As broken and run-down as the castle was, it did have one thing remaining—magic. Residual magic crawled all over the place. Neither Rebekah nor Jastillian knew it was there, but the force was in every room and on every stone. It was in the mold in the cracks and on the cobwebs hanging from the low ceilings. It reminded me of Renak's stronghold in Masep, but not as disorienting or scary. The magic in Romenia didn't linger like a ghost that haunted the place. It was strong magic that was used daily, like that of Malik and perhaps the council.

It wasn't long before Malik led us to the center of the castle. Dylan stood with two guards in front of a large set of double doors with bright protective wards moving over them.

"About time you showed up," Dylan said, looking agitated. "Did you take the scenic route?"

"I take it they didn't like being woken up," Malik said.

Dylan glared at him. "Come on. We've got preparations to make if what these three say is true."

"Good luck, Wizard Hellsfire," Malik said. He spoke an incantation, and the wards around the doors vanished. "Go through that door and you'll get a chance to talk to the council. I must warn you, they're bound to be in a grumpy mood." He spoke to me, but his eyes settled on Rebekah. "I hope we meet again."

Rebekah smiled and nodded.

Dylan, Malik, and Serena departed. I turned my head, looking down the hallways to see if there were more guards, but I saw none. We could have left, and the two guards wouldn't have been able to stop us. We didn't, though. We needed answers and help.

We huddled closer, discussing what we should and shouldn't tell them. I forced my hand to stop shaking and placed it on the door handle. I took a deep breath. This was what I had come down here for. Although I'd expected to be in Fairhaven and have Krystal by my side, and not be in the middle of a war.

I was going to have to do this and be strong without her. I could do it as long as I remembered why I was doing it.

I pulled the doors open, and we entered. Torches illuminated a giant, hollow chamber—a perfect wizards' place. A low haze of magic settled around me. It was strongest here in the central chamber because of the council's constant presence. A huge stone table sat on an elevated dais, and behind it, three wooden chairs. There were no windows to let natural light into this artificial cave, nor were there any guards. Not that the council would need them, with all their magical might.

I stared at the chairs, wondering why there were only three. There should have been six chairs, one representing each of the six manas. Did they divide the council so that each side ruled from a strategic area, or so that they would not all be vulnerable to one attack? Or was it something more?

I clenched my fists in frustration. There was so much I was missing that I had to know. Without the proper information, I could foul things up. I took a deep breath and let my hands relax, reminding myself that that was what I was here to see the council for.

Three people filed out from an open doorway behind the chairs, their hoods draped over their faces. The three wizards were each clothed in the color of their strongest mana: white, red, and green. Their robes swirled with life, the colors crawling over the fabric. I had never seen such a thing before. Stradus was right. A wizard's robes become part of a master wizard. I briefly grasped the sides of my black robes. My robes weren't alive like theirs, and I was supposed to be some kind of chosen one. Yet Stradus's robes hadn't been like theirs either. He was a powerful wizard in his own right. How much more powerful were these three?

The life wizard and the earth wizard carried long wooden staffs to amplify and focus their power. The fire wizard didn't. They took their seats and kept their hoods on. I wasn't able to see their faces clearly, but I glimpsed their eyes.

All their eyes glowed with a solid color—the color of the mana they were strongest in—a sign of pure mastery. I extended my wizard senses, and the power and magic seeping from them almost dropped me to my knees. I had seen both Stradus's and Premier's eyes solidify like that, but only briefly while they fought. No magic was being performed here. It was their natural state. It was like a hurricane wind scraping against my skin, and there was no shelter for me to hide in.

"Wizard Hellsfire," the white wizard said, his voice calm, soothing, and full of life like the mana he'd mastered. Hearing him speak, I no longer felt as tired or nervous as I was. "You have an unusual name. Did you come up with it by yourself, or did your former master give it to you when you became a wizard?"

"It's my name," I said.

He nodded, misunderstanding what I meant. "It's good to see some of the old ways are still alive."

"It's a perfect name for you," the red wizard said, his voice full of anger, strength, and—well—fire. "I feel your fire, and it's strong. Most wizards these days do not take a name, Wizard Hellsfire. They merely keep their own and drop their surname."

I nodded. They knew my name and whatever information Dylan had already told them, yet they'd told me nothing of themselves. I cleared my throat. "What are your names?"

"You will show the council some respect," the green wizard said. Her voice was low, yet full of menace. Her deep, thick, commanding voice was as rough and jagged as the earth.

"Forgive us, Hellsfire," the white wizard said. His voice soothed and calmed me. "Some of us still need our beauty sleep." He pulled back his hood, exposing a short gray beard and frizzy hair to match. "I am Ardonis. Helios is fire and Nairi is earth."

The other two pulled back their hoods and nodded in greeting, though Nairi's nod was shallow. Helios was the youngest of the three. His pure red and orange eyes matched his hair and freckles. No longer hiding in the concealment of his hood, he wasn't as intimidating. He couldn't have been more than a few years older than I. That didn't mean he wasn't a force to be reckoned with, especially since he didn't carry a staff to focus his power. I was curious as to why one so young was on the Elemental Council and where the other three were.

Nairi was the oldest of the three. Her big-boned body made her the most imposing of the council. Her sagging face reminded me of an aged dog, and she looked as tough as one. Her green eyes glowered at me.

"Thank you, Council," I said and bowed.

"Now that the pleasantries are out of the way," Nairi said, "can we get to the point? We need to know if what Hellsfire says is true."

"We know you're tired from your travels," Ardonis said, "but we have to know if you're truly from what you call Northern Shala, and what you can tell us."

I stood firm and held my head high. "As you wish. But then you must tell us of what's been happening down here, and of this war of yours. And you must help us find our friends."

"We're not to be ordered around," Nairi said. "You tell us what we want to know, and then we'll see what we can do."

"No. That's not how this works. You help us. We help you."

Nairi didn't say anything. She didn't need to. Under my feet, the building rumbled. Bits of rock fell from the ceiling, striking the floor.

"Nairi, please," Ardonis said. "He's not under our command. He's a fellow wizard." The rumbling ceased, but Nairi continued to glare at me. "We'll see what we can do for you, Hellsfire, but no promises. Agreed?"

"Agreed."

I let the words flow from me, careful not to say too much. We told them where we were from and that we were explorers into Southern Shala, seeking to establish trade. They weren't interested in that. They were more interested in me bringing down the Great Barrier, along with my training and who my master was. Nairi chuckled when I told them about Stradus. She once knew 'the pig-headed dreamer,' as she called him.

When I told them there weren't as many in wizards in Northern Shala as there were here, I thought they would be sad to hear that fact. They said they were, but their voices and bright eyes betrayed them. They seemed excited. It worried me that it might be because of a desire to use Northern Shala's resources to help fund their war and not because the land was open once more.

The council wanted to question me specifically because they had felt no disturbance when the barrier fell. Nairi said it was completely different from when it went up. That she had nearly toppled over from the magic used to create it. She had always thought it would be the same way if it were ever to come down.

I then warned the council about Premier and of his plan for revenge, but they dismissed him as a threat. I knew they were the council, but they shouldn't have underestimated such a wily foe as Premier, and one who had had access to the remnants of Renak's magic. But as was soon pointed out to me, he was just one wizard against many, and an army as well.

Lastly, I spoke of Renak's threat and the gods' war. As with Premier, they didn't take that seriously.

"You can't trust him," Helios said. "He is the Great Deceiver."

Nairi waved her hand. "Is *that* what he told you? That he erected the barrier to stop some fabled war of the gods? He did it because we were about to crush him. Plain and simple."

Ardonis leaned back. "Yes, there is no war of the gods, and we've not heard of any person of immense power. If there was, we would have recruited him. Or the other side would have."

"But—"

"Please, Hellsfire," he said. "We have more important matters to discuss. I give you my word that we will take Renak's warning under consideration, but until we see tangible proof, we can't take this as more than another one of his lies."

I bit the inside of my cheek. They were the Elemental Council, but they didn't understand anything! They hadn't fought against Premier and seen that even in a weakened state, he had contingency plans. They hadn't seen the panic and fear that was in the legendary Renak's eyes. Whatever their war was about, it clouded their judgment.

I stopped talking shortly after that. My voice was hoarse and I wanted to know more about them. I was surprised they asked so many questions about me and the magic I had seen and done. They didn't press hard to find out much about Alexandria, Erlam, or Sharald, which I didn't understand. Those cities were far more valuable than I was. They had vast resources, armies, and supplies. I was just a wizard.

I glanced at Jastillian and remembered what I had been through and done. I was a wizard who not only knew of Northern Shala, but one who had journeyed to the Wastelands and brought down the Great Barrier. I recalled my former master's words about me being a chosen one. That might be why they were so interested in me.

But I knew I couldn't ask these people for help with my power, or Krystal's curse. I couldn't be indebted to them, no matter how much I wanted to help her. There would have to be another way. With Southern Shala open, I would find it. There were bound to be wizards not involved in the war.

Helios and Ardonis then led the discussion and gave us some information. Nairi was reluctant to do so, even though we didn't ask for much. We were stunned by what we learned about the people of Southern Shala.

Some called their current war the Second War of the Wizards; others called it a civil war. It began after the War of the Wizards. Things heated up in Southern Shala, or Tyree, as they still called it, because of the Great Barrier. After several failed attempts to get through the barrier or around the Coast of Delia, arguments broke out between two opposing camps. One side blamed Renak, because it was he who had started the war and erected the barrier. They said it was all his fault that the land was split in two. It wasn't long before those two groups became heated and blood was drawn. Then war was declared.

The west side of the land and the city we were in, Romenia, believed in Shala and what he fought for. They despised Renak for what he had done and said that those in the east, and particularly the other half of the council in the city of Ashton, were fools for believing in Renak. When I asked how that happened, they said that there had always been a few who sympathized with Renak. But they had started to believe the lies Renak spoke. As the horrors of the war passed and people's memories faded, they started to believe those lies.

I doubted things were so cut and dried and that this story was the complete truth, but this was what this half of the council believed. No matter the reasons why, the fighting continued to this day.

What shocked me was that the council had split, and no longer represented all the wizards. That was why there were only three of them here. Some wizards, witches, and sorcerers did their best to stay out of it, hiding if need be. They didn't want to be involved in another war. However, there were still many who followed the councils on both sides.

Aside from humans, the western army primarily had centaurs, ogres, and gnomes while the east had dwarves, goblins, and elves. There were a few stragglers in each race that backed the other side, which was why Jastillian didn't stand out too much, and his colors helped us blend in. If we had gone east, we would have been in big trouble with his red armor.

They said the few Wasteland creatures left over from the war had been given a choice. They could either die or try to assimilate into society. Most died, but a few were able to adapt. I shouldn't have been surprised after meeting Kemek and Baal, but I still had a hard time letting go of the childhood stories that said they were nothing but mindless, savage brutes.

I rubbed my eyes and stifled a yawn. We had been up half the night, trading information, and I was tired. I thought we were through, but there was still one more thing they wanted to ask me.

"Will you join us, Hellsfire?" Ardonis asked, leaning forward.

"Yes, we could use your magic," Nairi said. "With your expertise about Northern Shala and the fact that *you* brought down the Great Barrier, we could end this war quickly. You could lead us into Northern Shala—"

"As part of an invasion force?" I asked, raising my eyebrow.

"As a liaison," Ardonis said. "Or a guide or ambassador. You would be key, Hellsfire, and play a very important part in things to come."

I stared at the council. I couldn't believe what they were asking me to do. I didn't come here to be in a war. I came here to warn them about Premier and Renak's threat, to ask for help in understanding my powers, and to find a cure for Krystal.

"I'm just one wizard," I said. "What can I do?"

"The fire's strong in you, Hellsfire," Helios said. "Join us and I'll help you unlock your full potential."

Helios could have helped me with my powers. I sensed his eagerness and I knew I could have bargained with them. If I helped them with what they wanted, they would have helped me with Renak's curse. But that's not what the princess would have wanted. She would have never forgiven me for making such a bargain.

"I'm sorry," I said, shaking my head. "I can't do it."

"I can't say we're not disappointed," Ardonis said. "But as a sign of good faith, we'll give you any information we can find about your friends and help you search for them. We would hate for anything to happen to them."

I was almost thankful for that, until I realized the meaning behind his seemingly sincere tone. Would this war council use my friends as bargaining chips to get what they wanted? I stared into their colorful eyes and knew they would.

I struggled to control my magic as I thought of them using Krystal in that way. Something drew the dark fire closer to the surface. I couldn't tell whether it was being in proximity to the council or the fact that they were willing to use innocent bystanders for their foolish war.

I swallowed and closed my eyes, feeling a drip of sweat run down my brow. Now was not the time for me to lose control. But the dark flame within me didn't want to go away. It wasn't just feeding off my emotions this time. Something else was drawing it out. But what? Was it the council?

I steadied my breathing and tried to balance myself. I gritted my teeth and bowed my head. "Thank you for sharing information, Council. We would appreciate any help you could give us."

"Are you sure you don't want to reconsider our offer, Hellsfire?" Nairi asked, her intense, green eyes flashing.

"I—"

"He's tired," Ardonis said. "We all are. It's been a long night and our guests could use some rest. In the morning, things might be different."

"Very well," Nairi said. "We'll have our guards show you to your rooms for the night. Get some rest."

"Good night," Helios said.

"Good night, Council." I bowed my head, concealing my twitching eyes.

As soon as we left the chambers, the dark fire receded. I wiped the sweat from my forehead and breathed easier. I shook my head. It probably had to do with the lack of a warm bed, hard travels, my lost friends, and being in the presence of that much raw magical power.

A pair of guards escorted us to our rooms. The rooms were like the rest of the castle—grimy and in disarray. The torn curtains covered only half the window, and the dresser was tilted, both legs missing on one side.

Guards stood outside our doors, but allowed us to move freely to each other's rooms. Rebekah and Jastillian came and huddled in mine.

"You don't plan on joining them, do you?" Rebekah asked me.

"I thought about it," I said and paused. "I might have agreed, if they could help us find the others and cure the princess. But it isn't what she would have wanted."

"Quite right."

"What do we do now?" I asked. "We can't stay here, and I'm not joining their war." I sighed. "If only we had more information. We learned one side of the story, but I doubt they'll let us go to the other side to learn theirs. And they would be just as biased as these people are. I fear that by bringing down the Great Barrier, I may have broken whatever stalemate these people had." I ran my fingers through my hair. "What's our next move?"

Jastillian grinned. "We escape, lad."

"When?"

"Tonight. It's only opportunity."

"What about the council and the other wizards?" Rebekah asked.

"Hellsfire can handle them." Jastillian smirked and clasped my shoulder. I couldn't help grinning, even though I didn't agree with him. "You look exhausted, lad."

I did my best not to yawn. "No more than either of you."

"We still have a little more time before dawn breaks. Let's get two hours rest. I have a feeling we're going to need it."

Jastillian and Rebekah came two hours later. I struggled to break my coma-like slumber. I knew I should have been ready, but with a belly full of food and a warm, if lumpy bed, it was hard not to succumb to sleep.

Rebekah and Jastillian had taken care of the guards outside our rooms. We backtracked our way out of the castle. We knew we should have gone through a side exit, or maybe even a servants' exit, but we couldn't spend time searching the place.

Jastillian took the lead, his superior eyesight guiding us through the dimly lit corridors. I used air magic to try to listen for noises and avoid anyone wandering around. I had to use as little as possible lest the council or another wizard feel my magic.

As we crept through the darkened hallways, what bothered me the most was that we ran into no one. There wasn't a single guard or servant. No one was about. It was as if the entire castle was dead. There should have been more activity if this was the heart of their operations for the war.

We reached the entrance and peeked around the corner. We expected to have to deal with the four guards we saw earlier, but no one was there. I examined the area for magic and didn't find anything. We cautiously skulked forward into the moonlight.

I allowed myself a glimmer of hope. I thought we might not only get out of Romenia, but that by the time they realized we were missing, we would have too much of a start for them to catch us.

CHAPTER 21

WE WERE TWENTY paces away from the castle when soldiers poured out of the streets and alleyways, rushing to surround us like water from a broken floodgate. They cut us off from retreating back into the castle. I summoned my mana to the surface while my friends drew their weapons. We stood back to back, staring at a hundred soldiers.

I cracked my knuckles, feeling the flame dance between my fingers. How did they know we were going to escape? I held my breath as I waited for them to make the first move. Their stony faces stared at us, yet they didn't take a step forward. I didn't want to kill them, but I wasn't going to let them stop me from leaving.

The army parted, and out stepped three familiar figures.

"Going somewhere, Hellsfire?" Dylan asked.

Adriana had her mace drawn. The pair of them drew in magic. Malik did the same thing, although he looked disappointed.

"Are we not free to move around the city?" I asked Malik.

"That's not what you're doing." Adriana said, narrowing her eyes at us. "No one said you could leave."

"Since you couldn't stay in the rooms we provided for you," Dylan said, "we're going to give you less...comfortable ones." Dylan threw something at me. "Here, put this on."

I caught it and stared. It was an open metal collar. If snapped shut, it would lock. "What is this?"

"Put it on, Hellsfire."

I searched the collar and sensed an undercurrent of magic as part of its makeup. I didn't have time to figure out what it was, but I wasn't going to trust them. I matched his fierce gaze. "No."

The army around us shifted. I glanced at an ogre and glimpsed the bloodlust in his eyes that I had seen in others in the Wastelands. It amazed me that he had the discipline to hold himself in check here.

"Hellsfire," Malik said. "Please put on the collar and give us your weapons. We shall not harm you. I give you my word."

"What will you do to us?" Rebekah asked.

"I'm afraid that's for the council to decide."

I looked at my friends. They were willing to die fighting, but that wasn't our goal. That wasn't why we came down here. I let go of my gathering magic and sighed.

"All right," I said.

I put the collar around my neck and it snapped itself shut on its own, the metal clanging and the magic humming to life. The underlying hint of magic I felt in every living thing dimmed. I bent over and gasped for breath. It was as if someone had stolen my sight by wrapping a light bandage around my eyes.

I summoned my inner fire and grasped it. But when I tried to release it, I shrieked in pain. I tumbled onto the dirt ground.

"First time?" Dylan asked and smirked.

"What did you do to him?" Rebekah asked as she and Jastillian helped me stand.

"Don't," Malik said to me, with an apologetic look on his face. "That collar's designed to stop the flow of magic. You can't access the magic in the environment. You can access your own, but if you try to use it...well, you know what happens."

I nodded.

"Hand us your weapons," Adriana said.

Jastillian and Rebekah turned over their axe and sword.

"All of them."

The pair shared a brief look before pulling out their daggers and other hidden knives. Just to make sure, Dylan searched them for more weapons.

"I promise you'll get your weapons back once this is settled," Malik said.

Adriana took my purse with all my potions. She patted me down and found my hidden dagger.

"I thought so," she said. "Crafty wizard."

Malik, Dylan, and Adriana, along with a dozen guards, forced us back into the castle. When we got to corridors I didn't recognize, I wondered what they were going to do to us. Without our weapons and my power, we were at their mercy. This Elemental Council wasn't the same one Stradus had told me about. They could do anything to us to get what they wanted. And I knew they would.

With these thoughts, I panicked and reached for my power. I strained to release it, forgetting about the collar around my neck. I cried out in pain and my knees buckled as the enchantment of the collar brought deadly daggers of pain to my neck.

Rebekah and Jastillian helped me up and carried my weight. I breathed heavily and in a raspy voice said, "Thank you."

"What are you doing, wizard?" Adriana asked. "Do you enjoy pain?"

"Please, Hellsfire," Malik said. "We'll get this sorted out. Until then, I promise no harm will befall you or your friends."

Eventually, they led us to a dim stairwell. Adriana told two of the soldiers to stay and guard the entrance. The dank smell assaulted my nose as we continued downwards. We came to a group of small cells, empty of people. There was still a dirty bucket in the corner of one of them, and bits of wet, dirty hay on the floor. They opened the cell. Rebekah and Jastillian walked in first. When I followed them, Dylan pushed me inside, then slammed the door shut.

"Hope you enjoy these accommodations," Dylan said. "Since you didn't like the last rooms we gave you."

"How long will we be here?" I asked.

"Until the council decides what to do with you," Adriana said.

"It shouldn't be more than a few days," Malik said. "They'll need time. We'll have food and water brought down."

They abandoned us to our thoughts.

"What do you think they'll do to us, Hellsfire?" Rebekah asked, slumping against one of the grimy walls.

"I have no idea. This council isn't the one my former master told me about. They won't be merciful. He would be saddened to see what they've become. He believed in them once."

Jastillian growled. "How did they know we were escaping? We never even had a chance!"

"It's my fault," I said and sighed. "It was probably my magic. I should have been more careful."

"Don't blame yourself, lad. You did what you could. They just didn't trust us."

I shrugged, but I wasn't going to give up yet. I would see Krystal and the others again.

I sat cross-legged on the ground and grabbed at the metal collar around my neck. I knew it was enchanted, but because of how it restrained me, I couldn't feel the collar's magic and they hadn't given me enough time to study it before I put it on.

Despite Malik's warning, I needed my magic. We had to get out of here and find the others. We might have been outnumbered by wizards with far more power than I, but my magic would at least give us a fighting chance.

I closed my eyes and siphoned in my energy, wrapping myself in the manas until a raging storm boiled inside me. Instead of trying to perform minor magic against the collar, I was going to hammer into it, hopefully overloading it and breaking the enchantment on it.

My body stiffened and I started to tremble. The magic ripped my body from the inside as if I were poisoned. My veins blackened and threatened to explode from my body. The magic ached to go somewhere and the only outlet was me.

"Hellsfire," Jastillian asked. "Are you all right?"

I opened my eyes and tried to unleash the magic from my body. Instead of burning with fire, my magic smashed into an invisible wall. My neck felt as if someone had run a sword through it, and the pain spread to my shoulders, my back, and my legs, paralyzing them. My mouth gaped open with a silent scream. I crumpled to the ground.

"Hellsfire!" Rebekah said.

They rushed over to me, but I couldn't speak. They were wise enough not to touch me as the backlash of unused magic continued its assault on my body. Several long minutes passed before my muscles loosened and the pain lessened. I let out a sigh.

"Are you all right, lad?" Jastillian asked as he helped me sit up.

"No." I rubbed my sore neck above the collar, trying to massage my muscles. "I used too much magic in trying to escape this collar. Let me try something else."

"Do you think that's wise?"

"We have to get out of here for the others. It's my fault we're in here in the first place."

"We'll get our chance," Rebekah said. "We just need to be patient."

I agreed, but knew it would be better to get out of here sooner rather than later. I closed my eyes, and again saw the barrier. Instead of blasting it with a torrent of magic, I summoned a tiny portion and brushed it against the collar's magic.

The pain returned, merely the force of a mosquito's bite. I increased the flow of mana, searching for a crack or weakness in the collar. The more pressure I applied, the greater the pain. Sweat drenched my forehead and I bit down, grinding my teeth. I did my best to ignore the pain, but my body started to shake and my stomach wanted to heave its contents.

I finally released my magic, sinking to my knees and gasping. I pounded the ground, angry at myself for not succeeding.

Rebekah crept to me and forced my head down. She examined the collar. "If magic doesn't work against it, I think I might be able to pick the lock by conventional means. But there's nothing here."

"It's all right," I said. "We have far bigger things to worry about. I have no idea what the council's going to do." I put a hand to my mouth and yawned. "I suggest we get some rest...while we still can."

A guard served us breakfast and dinner the next day, but it wasn't until two full days later that one of the council members finally came to see us. We rose to face her.

"Wizard Hellsfire," Nairi said, walking up to the bars with her hands behind her back. "I'm very disappointed in you." She allowed herself a stiff smile. "Yet you're so like your former master." Her smile disappeared. "We still don't know what to do with you. Any of you."

"You can let us go," Jastillian said.

Nairi shook her head, her aged cheeks jiggling slightly. "We can't do that. We can't allow a wizard of Hellsfire's caliber to fall into the enemy's hands. And you've seen enough of our city to give them plenty of information."

"Your city's in shambles," I said. "And I have little interest in joining your war, be it on your side or theirs. All I want to do is find our friends and leave this godsforsaken place!"

Nairi's pure green eyes met mine. "We know. We also know you won't leave Tyree until you do find them. If you don't find them on our side, you'll find them on theirs. What would you do to get them back?"

I didn't say a word, for she already knew my answer.

"Anything," Nairi answered for me, before she turned and walked away.

The next day, Ardonis came to see me. "I wish it didn't have to be like this, Wizard Hellsfire."

I lifted my tired head and scratched my cheek. "If that were true, you would let us go."

"Maybe if you cooperated more, we would."

I crossed my arms. "I'm not killing anyone."

He rapped his long staff against the bars. "We never said you had to. All we wanted was a liaison between us and the north, as we said."

I raised an eyebrow at him.

"Give us information about what you call Northern Shala, and we'll do everything we can do to reunite you with your friends."

"We've already given you that information."

"No. We want more, especially what you've seen in Renak's castle, the magic you experienced there, and what was inside the nexus. We want to know everything you saw." His white eyes gleamed. "We know you held back."

Ardonis turned towards Jastillian. "We could also use your expertise. You've traveled the land and know of the major cities, countries, and kingdoms in Northern Shala. You've studied countless artifacts from the previous war. You would be invaluable." To Rebekah, he said, "We would love to work together with you and your kingdom to venture into the Wastelands. You know the area and the creatures better than any of us.

"We could and should all be allies."

We fell silent. That was a lot easier than murdering people for a war, but my hands would still be bloodied. I stared into the wizard's magical eyes, wondering why the council wanted to know so much about our land. But I couldn't read him. He was too experienced, and I lacked my magic.

I realized there would be only one reason they would want to know more about Northern Shala: war. They were going to bring war to our homeland.

Before I could answer in anger, Ardonis said in a soothing and sincere voice, no doubt amplified by his power, "Take your time and think about it. I would hate for anything to happen to you or your friends."

Three more days passed and we never saw the council. There weren't any more threats or promises, or attempts at persuasion. Only guards came in silence to give us food and water. It was as if we had been forgotten. And that was worse than not knowing what they were going to do to us or what they had planned.

CHAPTER 22

THE HEAVY CREAK of the cell door opening jolted me awake. A single wizard in brown robes stepped into my cell.

"Malik," I said when the sleepy haze around my vision faded. I cleared my throat. "Come to finally take us to the council?" I yawned and rubbed my eyes.

"Hurry, we haven't much time," Malik said. He rushed to me, holding a key in his hand.

"Why are you doing this?" I asked, grabbing his hand and staring his eyes.

"Because you shouldn't be here." He glanced at Rebekah and Jastillian. "None of you should. This war has gone on for far too long. Too many good people have died." Malik's gray eyes became hazy, then briefly glowed. "And I should have seen it. I am the Seeker."

"Seeker?"

"I'm able to find and see things—hidden things that people don't want to be seen, like the truth. In past times, we were like magistrates. More recently, we've become instruments of war. With you bringing down the barrier, the time for this war has passed." He paused and glanced up. "However it ends, it shouldn't involve you or your lands."

I released his hand and bent my neck down. He unlocked my collar and the magic embedded within every living thing flooded my senses. I smiled and unleashed a hint of my fire on my fingertip. It felt good to be whole again.

"We can't return until we find the others," Rebekah said.

"I know," Malik said. "While you've been in here, I've been spreading word and gathering information about other travelers from a foreign land. I finally found something. Unfortunately, all I have to go on are rumors from the east. If you want to find your friends, that's where you're going to have to go. Come on, your belongings are at the top of the stairs."

A bright little star hovered above the stairs. "The coast is clear, Malik," Serena said, breathing hard. She wiped her little forehead. "The horses are ready and the supplies are gathered. Is there anything else you'd like me to do for you, Your Highness?"

"No, thank you. You're dismissed." Serena glared at him and stuck her tongue out as he passed by. Malik smiled.

My friends retrieved their weapons and I my purse. I checked the bag, making sure the potions were still in there. There were no guards to be seen as we left the castle. Malik said he had taken care of them, bribing those he could and disabling and hiding those he couldn't.

Outside the entrance, four horses waited for us, their saddlebags full of supplies. There was a shadow in the night sky, coming towards us. I readied my magic. If they had unicorns and fairies, who knew what else they might have?

Malik laid his hand on my forearm and said, "It's all right, Hellsfire." A large barn owl swooped in and landed on Malik's shoulder, blending in with his robes. "This is Mr. Hoot-Hoot. Not much of a name, but I was young when we first found each other. He's my guardian. One of the few still alive. Most guardians die quickly in the war."

"Hello, Mr. Hoot-Hoot," I said.

The bird ruffled his feathers and cocked his head before hooting.

"He's scouted the skies for us," Malik said. "We have a small window before the guards change shifts, but we must hurry."

We rode out again, keeping an eye out for whoever might see us. The clouds blocked out most of the moonlight, making our departure easier. We trotted our horses in silence until we were half a mile out of the city.

Malik carefully led the way in the darkness. Neither of us used any magic to light the way, and he took his time as he navigated his horse across the plains. When the sun's morning rays illuminated the land enough so we could see, that's when we galloped, wanting to put as much distance between us and Romenia as we could.

We rode a good distance and were well away from the city by the time the sun shone directly over our heads. I let myself relax, feeling the warmth of sunshine on my face and the smell of fresh grass that surrounded us on the plains. I had missed being outdoors. It was much better than being trapped in a cell. I patted my horse's mane. We were finally getting somewhere. With luck, we would see the princess and the others and leave this accursed place.

Mr. Hoot-Hoot scouted the skies. Suddenly, he veered back towards us and landed on Malik's shoulder, screeching. Malik looked over his shoulder.

"What is it, Malik?" Rebekah asked.

"We're being followed. I thought we would have more time, but I was mistaken. If we had reached the forest, we could have lost them."

"Then let's hurry."

"We can't, Rebekah. Not on this terrain. Mr. Hoot-Hoot tells me they sent two squads of centaurs after us. If we had unicorns, we could beat them, but they're fickle creatures." His gray eyes flashed, and he handed Rebekah a piece of parchment. "Take this. Serena will lead you to a place called the Dead Zone."

"The Dead Zone?" I asked.

"It's a swamp, but it was once a beautiful area. Because of the war, the land was destroyed and changed. We call it the Dead Zone because magic can't be used there and horses won't go in there. There is a relatively safe route to get through it, but you won't be taking it. The map will guide you to another more unknown and dangerous route. Afterwards, go east, and within a week, you'll end up in Ashton.

"Jastillian, once there you must change your clothes. Anyone wearing red is considered suspicious. Lay low, all of you, and try to find the answers you need. I wish I could have helped you more."

"You've done enough already," I said.

"I've only done what was right. You've reminded me what I'm supposed to do, Hellsfire. I'm the Seeker. I shouldn't have allowed myself to be dragged into this war."

"What are you going to do, Malik?" Rebekah asked, looking concerned.

"Buy you some time."

Serena flew in between them. "You better be alive when I get back, you foolish wizard."

"Take care of them, Serena."

"Be careful," Rebekah said.

Malik smiled at her. "You too." He spurred his horse west to meet the centaurs, with Mr. Hoot-Hoot hovering above him.

"Be careful with him," Serena said, flying to Rebekah's face. "He has a fragile heart, that one, and if you break it, I will break you." She jabbed her tiny finger at Rebekah. She flew to me and said, "Come on, cutie. We haven't got all day."

Serena was quick. She sped through the land like an erratic shooting star, keeping ahead of our horses.

From behind us, I felt Malik draw in mana. He called to the earth's magic, gathering in tremendous amounts. I thought he would succeed and defeat them, but then I remembered the collar. They were bound to have other weapons to deal with wizards, and those were friends and allies he would have to fight. That would make things difficult.

The backlash of his magic faded the farther away we got. I prayed that he would only buy us time, and not get himself killed because of us.

Two hours later, we reached the forest.

We pushed hard as Serena led us along a trail which she said was the fastest way through the forest. We couldn't deviate from it and still hide our tracks. None of us knew the terrain, and we couldn't fight an army. The only place we were going to lose them was in this Dead Zone of theirs.

We pressed on, with only brief rests for the horses, until it got too dark to see. We couldn't risk one of them breaking a leg. I gave the horses and Serena the rest of my rejuvenation potions.

We broke camp two hours before dawn and ran our horses ragged. I felt my mount's labored breathing beneath my body. Serena couldn't fly forever, and I was out of potions. She took short rests on our horses' foreheads, rotating from horse to horse. She spoke encouraging words to them and rubbed their ears.

At the end of the second day, we burst out of the forest and slowed the horses. We dismounted and fed them oats and water. They wheezed, threatening to collapse. Serena darted up into the air until she vanished from our eyes. She flew back down and hovered in front of my nose.

"Whew...this is as far as I need to take you," Serena said, pulling her little tunic's collar up and wiping her head.

"Thank you, Serena," I said. "We wouldn't have made it without you."

"Don't thank me yet, cutie. You don't have much time. In two, maybe three hours, the centaurs will have caught up to you." She flew until she was two inches from my face. "Listen, if you ever want to visit my realm, I'll take you. Malik has it all wrong. It's not *that* bad of a place. It's fun, and you look like you could use a little fun."

My face turned red, and it wasn't from the exhaustion of riding hard. I was tempted to visit that place, but I had had enough exploration of new lands. All I wanted to do was be with the princess.

"Perhaps another time."

Serena folded her arms and pouted. Then she smiled, flew up, and kissed me on the nose. "I'll see you there, if you survive all this. Good luck!" She took off and headed back west. I stood there with a gaping mouth.

"What was that about, lad?" Jastillian asked.

I scratched my head. "I have no idea. I know very little about fairies. We haven't time for that now. Let's go."

We interrupted the horses' short break and galloped east to the swamp. I couldn't get thoughts of Krystal out of my mind as we rode. Looming over those thoughts were their war, the council, Premier, and Renak's threat. I spurred my horse to go faster, as if I were racing to reach Krystal and keep her safe from all of that.

My legs and butt were so numb I no longer felt the saddle. My vision blurred from the lack of sleep, but when we finally came into view of the swamp, I was shocked by what I saw with my wizard's vision.

The closer we marched to the swamp, the more my power left me. The place sucked in my magic, and even the flame within started to waver and disappear. The swamp pulled in all the surrounding magic, entrapping it. I rubbed my neck, remembering the collar and how I hated to be without my magic. The Dead Zone was like one gigantic collar, but without a key. And it was the only way to get to Krystal.

A low haze smothered the swamp. Tall, leafless trees stuck out from the water, never rising above the mist. Dark shadows flew by through the trees.

"What was that?" Rebekah asked and pointed. "Something moved."

Jastillian and I leaned forward and squinted.

"I didn't see anything," he said.

Rebekah gave the swamp a menacing look, but didn't respond.

We had a hard time bringing the horses to the edge of the swamp. They whinnied and stomped until they wouldn't budge anymore. We took the saddlebags and hid the saddles. We slapped the horses on their rumps and they trotted off west, well away from the swamp.

We ventured around the swamp, heading north to the alternate route Malik's map gave us. We hunched over and jogged, stepping lightly on the grassy ground and veering away from the bog, lest we leave any tracks. Half an hour later we came upon the path we were looking for.

At the edge of a swamp were two bald cypress trees. The swamp was littered with them, but this pair formed an arch barely as wide as my shoulders, their bare branches aching to embrace. We shared one last look before stepping inside.

My magic evaporated like someone blowing out a candle's flame. I gasped for air, trying to ignore the emptiness I felt. I couldn't. It was as if a part of me no longer existed. I had learned to live with my magic over the past three years. It was a part of me, and I of it. But no longer. Unlike with the collar, my magic wasn't even there to access but not use. The swamp simply devoured it.

My wizard's senses weren't as dulled as they were when I had the collar on. I still felt the swamp's magic, but the magic was wrong. Its pulse was unnatural, as if it were a hole tearing through this world. That hole sucked in my magic.

I clutched my chest as if I could hang on to my magic. It was a worthless gesture. I had to remember that the swamp's effect wasn't permanent, and that I was trudging through it to get to Krystal and the others.

The thin trees closed around us, entrapping us. Even though they didn't have many leaves, they, along with the low fog, felt like a cage. We couldn't see more than twenty feet in any direction.

As we walked, I constantly turned my head back because of the noise my feet made as they squashed through the damp swamp. It sounded like we were being followed. My robes clung to my body like moss. No matter how often I plucked them away, the damp fabric stuck to me.

As much as I wanted to, I couldn't take them off. The tall reeds we waded through cut and slashed at my exposed hands and face—to take off my robes would expose my entire body. The most I could do was pull my hood down.

We followed Malik's map, but it didn't show much of a path. There were landmarks that indicated where to go, but even then, we found ourselves occasionally wading in chest-high water. My arms grew sore from carrying supplies and equipment over my head. The only bright side was I didn't have to carry a sword, axe or armor. With each step, our feet disturbed the murky water until it turned deep brown. Panic seized me when I felt a creature slither underneath my robes. I froze, thinking it might be a snake. The creature swam out—only a frog. I breathed a little easier, and we continued onwards.

We ended the day at a safe spot marked on the map. The land was above the water and drier than any of the places we had traveled so far. We found a large, hollowed out tree big enough for the three of us to squeeze inside. We plopped our supplies and equipment on the ground.

Jastillian prepared camp while Rebekah hunted for food and I scrounged for dry firewood or kindling. The humid environment made it hard to find much in the way of firewood. I wished I had my powers. I could have easily lit a campfire and dried our clothes. Eventually, I found a handful of dead wood and made my way back.

It took a few tries, but Jastillian created a small, hot fire. Rebekah had brought back a snake and skinned it. We left it over the fire to cook and stripped off our clothes.

"What is that?" I asked Rebekah, staring at her pale skin. Between her breasts was a dark, finger-length mark that looked like a bruise or a lesion.

"What is what?" She narrowed her eyes, thinking I was staring at her chest. Then her gaze followed mine. "Leeches," she said, plucking it from her skin. It stretched out and then let go with a tiny sucking sound. Blood trickled from where it had attached itself.

I gawked at her and Jastillian, realizing that they had dozens of the little black things clinging to them. Then I looked down at my own bare chest and jumped back. There were slimy leeches stuck to me as well. I hurried, prying as many of the things off me as I could. Their tiny mouths clung to my body. Blood ran down my skin. I shivered, but not from my lack of clothes. I reached into my trousers, my eyes widening as I found another leech.

We took turns, tearing off the leeches we couldn't reach without help. When we were finished, we huddled around the fire, letting our clothes dry as they hung. I kept checking my skin, imagining the leeches still feeding on me. Jastillian and Rebekah couldn't help but smile at my expense. My stomach growled from the rations I was on. They offered me a piece of their snake, but I wasn't out of food yet.

After we ate, we put on our still-damp clothes and huddled together once more. We rotated watch, keeping an eye out for any troops roaming the area or any dangerous creatures lurking in the swamps.

I had a hard time sleeping, despite how tired I was. The swamp was more alive at night. Screeches, howls, and occasional growls surrounded us. I curled up in my robes with my dagger clutched in my hand. Normally, I would keep my fire ready, and it would also comfort me. But that option was gone. I squeezed the dagger's handle even tighter as I remembered the collar. I never wanted to be without my magic again.

Time was agonizing in the mucky bog. Two days had passed and we were still stuck in it. The map said we still had two more days to go, but I was convinced there was never going to be an end to it. Every tree we passed looked like the one before. The alligator that watched us from the water had the same predatory glare as the previous one two miles ago. Even the mosquitoes I slapped seemed to keep regenerating themselves.

As the cuts, scratches, bites, and welts piled up and the pain racked my magic-less body, one thought fueled me to continue—Krystal.

CHAPTER 23

WE TRUDGED ONWARD through the mushy terrain. I ducked a leafless branch and snapped a broken one. The three of us barely spoke anymore unless we had to.

In silence, my thoughts betrayed me. Was Krystal in danger in a war-torn land? What revenge was Premier after? Was this war just a small indication of the gods' war Renak had warned me about? There were so many questions and I had not one answer.

"Do you hear that?" Rebekah asked, stopping in front of me, yanking me out of my thoughts.

I paused, cocking my head from side to side. "I don't hear anything."

She grumbled and pulled out her sword. "Exactly. Ever since we arrived in this swamp, there's *always* some kind of noise going on."

A finch took flight, and a basking turtle dove into the water. That worried me. Animals tended to leave when something was wrong.

Jastillian reached for his axe and stared at an alligator that splashed the water and swam away. I unsheathed my dagger.

"Has Romenia's army finally caught up with us?" I asked in hushed tones.

"Possibly," Rebekah asked, squinting her eyes back the way we had come. "I know you and other wizards like Malik can't use your magic in here, but what if other people can?"

I shook my head. "That's not the way it works."

"If the centaurs almost caught up to us, they could also have sent something else—something more powerful. Isn't that how you wizards work?"

I bit my tongue and said nothing.

"We don't know much about this land or its magic, Hellsfire," she said. "There are dangers we were unprepared for."

"Then we'll just have to keep an eye out," I said.

We walked faster, but did our best to do so in silence. We paused every few steps, scanning the thick fog around us, but we couldn't see past our misty prison. Soon, only our squishy footsteps could be heard.

We jogged by a large alligator skeleton. The gleaming white bones were picked clean. We shared a look, as we found no tracks to indicate what had killed it. We discovered more bones the farther we went. Hidden in the reeds to the right were small frogs, and to the left was a long snake. No meat was left on them either.

After a few long minutes, something pierced the dead silence.

"Do you hear that?" I asked. It was a faint buzzing noise.

"Aye," Jastillian whispered.

We stared into the dense, enveloping fog. I slowly turned my head, but the buzz surrounded us.

The noise grew louder, and I put my hands to my ears. The sound burrowed itself into my head until I froze. It became a melodious note that hypnotized us, drawing us toward it.

"No," Jastillian said. He saw the trance Rebekah and I were in and shook both our shoulders. "Snap out of it!"

I blinked several times, letting Jastillian's frantic face come into view. "What is it?"

"I know what that noise is! They're Will of the Wisps!" he said in softened tone.

He pointed as tiny bright, beautiful orbs floated into view. As I turned my head, more of the lights popped into view, and the sound inside my head grew louder.

"They look like big fireflies," Rebekah said.

"No. They're far more dangerous. They're like tiny bugs whose noise freezes you until they can sting you. I've heard the pain's so unbearable that you have no choice but to open your mouth, letting them in. They eat you from the inside out. I thought they were just a myth."

"What are we going to do?" I asked, clutching my dagger tighter.

Jastillian lowered his axe. "Our weapons are useless. There are too many of them and they're too small. Cover up and don't move. They've already seen us. Whatever you do, don't make *any* noise. Noise and movement attracts them."

We put away our weapons, and I pulled my hood over my head and closed my eyes. I remembered my training as the wave of bright lights inched closer. Their buzzing grew louder until they washed over us.

The Will of the Wisps flowed under and around my robes and undergarments, picking, prodding, and probing my skin. I bit down on my tongue so I wouldn't cry out. They were like millions of bee stings, each holding their own tiny, sharp sword. My legs buckled and wobbled from the blinding pain.

As the cuts sliced deep and I bled, I tried pushing out the pain and ignoring it. It didn't work. The Will of the Wisps were relentless, tiny things. Yet their stings were like music, forming notes to go with their buzzing sound. I wanted to cry out and sing, but I remembered Jastillian's warning.

I dropped to one knee as the pain racked my body and the music drove nails into my head. Their sharp stingers darted into my lips, daring me to open my mouth and scream. I squeezed my eyes shut tighter as the thin layers of my eyelids were attacked, feeling as if my eyeballs were going to explode. I feared the deadly things would fly up my nose. I almost took off and ran through the swamp. There was one thought that saved me.

Krystal.

I remembered the first time I met her. How even though she was exhausted from running, she fought to free herself from the two men chasing her. My mind flashed forward to when we took back Alexandria from Premier. She was injured and in pain, but she led us through the tunnels and fought with us against the creatures of the Wastelands, killing as many of the beasts as she could.

Lastly, I thought about how she hadn't feared even Premier, and fought on against his magic for her people and her kingdom. She was stronger than I and never gave up, no matter the odds.

I wasn't going to die here in a strange land. There were still things I had to do. Thinking of Krystal dulled the pain of the Will of the Wisps.

But as the long minutes passed and the pain intensified, thoughts of Krystal became fragmented as the wisps yanked me back to the present. I wanted to scream and shout and run away. The wisps stripped away every defense. Just when I thought I was going to give in, their deadly touch lifted and the pain lessened.

I could barely keep myself from falling over. My legs were gelatin, and I put my blistered fingers to my eyelids, face, and lips. I felt open sores everywhere. Small drops of blood came from every part of my body. I opened my eyes and saw that Jastillian and Rebekah were alive and in just as bad a shape as I was.

The wisps left for much easier prey. The buzzing faded, but we didn't talk, as dozens were still in view. They were drifting away, but if they heard us, they would come back. We crept away in dead silence and continued on the path out of this swamp.

I concentrated on the path in front of me, tiptoeing over the soft ground. I even held my breath as I avoided fallen branches and piles of bones, my movements slight and delicate. I didn't want the Will of the Wisps to hear anything. I tried not to focus on the lights that surrounded us. There were still dozens in the area.

I stared at a group of a dozen or so from the corner of my eye. They hovered over a carcass that had been killed through other means. They made no move to attack it. That's when I carelessly stepped on a fallen reed. The retreating wisps all paused. We stopped and I silently prayed to the gods that they didn't come back.

The wisps floated in place for several long seconds. Suddenly, they flew back in our direction. I turned my head and hundreds of the tiny things descended upon us. I raised my hand, threatening to burn them all with my fire. Then I remembered I didn't have any magic.

My hand fell to the side. What were we going to do? I couldn't handle another attack from them. I stared at the wisps, letting the buzzing music creep into my head until it overtook me.

"Go, lad," Jastillian said, pulling his weapon free. "We'll hold them off for you." His booming voice drew the wisps closer to him, as if they had found their prey.

I opened my mouth to object, but Rebekah covered it.

"Leave!" she said. "I promised the princess that nothing would happen to you." Her dark blue eyes bore into me. "I keep my word." She forced the map into my hand and pushed me away. I staggered backwards and almost tripped. "Now go!"

I could tell from the looks on their faces that they wouldn't be swayed. I wanted to talk them out of it, but that would only attract the wisps' attention and there was no time. If only I had my magic, the wisps would die.

I swatted a tall reed, then took the cowardly way and ran down the path the map indicated. I kept my head down and pushed through the wisps. A few clung and stung me, but they were drawn to the noise Rebekah and Jastillian made. I swatted those on me and continued to run.

I stopped running and gasped for breath as the buzzing from the wisps faded. I hesitated, knowing that I should keep going, but I couldn't help but stare back at my friends. I owed them one last look, if nothing else.

Jastillian and Rebekah swung their weapons in a blur. Dozens of bright lights diminished and died, but there were far too many of them. The hardened warriors were growing sluggish. The earlier attack had taken its toll on them. They stopped fighting and covered up as best they could, no longer needing to draw the wisps' attention.

I knew I should go, but I glanced back. Jastillian dropped his axe and fell.

Rebekah covered him as they were devoured in the bright lights.

I tore my gaze away. They had made their decision, and I had made mine. I had to leave this place and find the others. I had to see Krystal again.

My feet turned to go and slipped in the bog. I froze. It was my fault everyone was in Southern Shala in the first place. I couldn't—wouldn't—live with my friends dying without trying to do something. We were getting out of this together.

I drew my dagger and charged, rushing back towards my friends. After all they'd done for me, I was going to save them even if I had to carry them out of the swamp. I yelled, drawing the attention of the wisps.

I kept trying to tap into my mana because there was no collar to block it off. It was still a part of me and I of it. The swamp drained my powers, but there should be a tiny portion I could conjure. Just a tiny bit and I could cast a minor spell for the fleetest of moments, and that would be enough.

But my magic never came.

As I ran closer to the pair and was consumed by the lights, I brought my dagger down into the bright stars, wanting to kill as many of the wisps as I could before grabbing the others and running away.

Instead, my dagger's blade glowed, illuminating the area with a blinding blue light. It ripped through our world and tore a hole in it.

The tear sucked all the wisps in the surrounding area into another world. Ones that had been stuck in my hair or had clung to my body were pulled off me. Bits of dead leaves and reeds followed them. The hole tugged at my hair and robes, trying to take me into that other world, but I was too heavy.

I stared into the hole, seeing the wisps and plants that had been forced in. I glimpsed another world where long green stalks with bright flowers as big as my body bloomed. Before I could see any more, the hole sealed up and disappeared, taking all of the Will of the Wisps with it.

I helped the others up, and we all gawked at the space where the hole once was.

Rebekah turned to me and asked, "What was that?"

I remembered to blink and said, "I have no idea, but it led to somewhere." I inspected the area. I tried to access my magical senses and my wizard's vision, but all I felt was the Dead Zone sucking in my magic.

"I've never seen the dagger do that before," I said. I didn't understand it. Malik said magic couldn't work in this swamp, but it had.

"Where did you get it, lad?" Jastillian asked.

"It was my father's. He got it in the Burning Sands." I scrutinized the sharp, beautifully crafted blade, staring at the words "I will be with you, always" in Caleea. I couldn't sense any magic from it, but I never could. My mother had told me about the dagger when I was with Krystal, but she hadn't mentioned it tearing a hole into another world or the magic it held. Either she didn't want to, or she didn't know.

I brought down the dagger again, getting ready to move in case another, far stronger tear opened. Nothing happened. I did it again, but nothing changed. I gripped the handle tighter, not understanding why it didn't work now when it had moments ago.

I sheathed the dagger, aching to check it again once we left this awful place. We ran away from the area, not wanting to see any more Will of the Wisps. Despite what had happened, I wasn't sure if I could access the dagger's magic again if there was more trouble.

Towards the end of the second day, we were finally free of the snake-infested, leech-sucking, mud-squishing, bug-biting, will-of-the-wisp-attacking swamp. And we rejoiced.

My power rushed back like an avalanche. I roared with power, barely able to contain it. I was alive, complete, and whole once more as the fire within burned as bright as the sun. My power wasn't what made me a wizard, but it was a huge part of me.

Happy to be out of the swamp, we hurried across the plains to set up camp well away from it. We were too exhausted to look for any game, but we did scrounge for calamine. We desperately needed some because of all our bumps, welts, and rashes from the swamp.

We ate our cold food, quietly thankful to the gods to be out of the Dead

Zone and one step closer to finding our friends. Would they be at Ashton, or would Malik's information be proven false? Since I was going to Ashton, I knew I had a duty to warn them of Renak's threat and of Premier. But after having my magic cut off and forced into a dungeon, I had to think of a better way to do so.

I took out my dagger and inspected it, using every sort of magical sense I knew of. Whatever magic I had briefly touched upon was gone. I sensed no trace of that power I had used in the swamp. There was no teeming of life, no magical glow, no buzzing of power. I even tried to tear a hole in the world again. The dagger didn't work.

I gave it to Jastillian. I thought that with his knowledge of weapons and history, he might have understood something I missed. He too found nothing. All we saw was a well-forged dagger, but I knew it had some kind of undetectable magic to it. I needed to take it to someone more skilled than I or ask my mother what it was all about the next time I saw her. I put it away until that day came.

CHAPTER 24

WE TRAVELED EAST towards Ashton, pushing ourselves hard. At the end of our first week out of the swamp, we stumbled onto a small town. We resupplied and bought horses for each of us. We asked around about any other travelers, but they hadn't seen any fitting the description we gave them.

As exhausted as we were from the traveling, we only stayed in the town one day. We needed to get to Ashton as soon as possible to see if Malik's information was true. I didn't allow myself to get my hopes up too high, but every night I prayed to the gods that we found what we sought.

As we rode, I wondered if this was what the gods had laid out for me. Was I always meant to bring down the Great Barrier, or was that just a coincidence? And gods help me, I still believed Renak about the war between the gods. While one half of the council didn't or couldn't find any proof, it didn't mean that it wasn't happening. The gods did things beyond our understanding.

At the end of our second week, we arrived at Ashton. But before we could even ride into the city, two patrols met us on the outskirts.

Twelve riders wearing blue armor and uniforms closed in on us. My friends drew their weapons and I summoned my magic.

Ashton's human soldiers had their swords drawn, and the elves trained their bows on us. I had worried a wizard might be among them but I sensed no magic.

A short, brunette woman rode out in front and said, "Lower your weapons." She glowered at us from under her helm.

We hesitated, unsure of what they were going to do to us.

"We have orders to take you to Ashton, Wizard Hellsfire," she said. "The council wishes to see you. All of you. If you please." Her words were kind, but the tone was menacing. She placed her hand on her sheathed sword. A faint hum of magic emanated from it.

I didn't want to see the council unprepared. Our plan had been to gather information in Ashton. We hoped our friends would be found here, but we didn't bet on it. We were to talk to the innkeepers, the bartenders, the stableboys, and herb sellers. We wanted to know if any information could be found, since none was to be had in the west.

There was also another reason we didn't want to see the council so soon. This side thought Renak did the right thing in the War of the Wizards. I could never get behind that, especially after visiting Masep and meeting Renak. He said he thought he was doing the right thing in protecting the land by stopping the gods' war, but all he did was divide it and slowly destroy it. Ashton's council might not hesitate to do things the way Renak would.

"All right," I said, letting go of my building magic and feigning a friendly smile. "We appreciate your assistance."

She grunted and motioned to the others. The rest of her warriors fell in around us while she led the way to the city.

I tried to make conversation with the woman, but she wouldn't answer any of my questions.

"The council will answer all your questions, Wizard Hellsfire," she said.

I sighed and let it go.

Around the city were many more troops than I expected. There were thousands of them. Their camps were like an ocean of blue, hovering above the plain's green. It worried me when we passed wagons full of supplies. This army was mobilizing, but to where? Was it a great attack against the west, or something else?

The woman forced us off our horses. She and her men also got off with us, and we walked into Ashton. I craned my neck at the tall lookout tower. The tower had been repaired recently—newly cut wood covered part of the bottom. Two soldiers manned it.

As we traveled the city, the groups of soldiers we passed through gave us a wide berth. Some of them stopped and saluted the woman who escorted us. Much like Romenia, the buildings in Ashton were badly in need of repair. As we passed one, a shingle fell from the roof and nearly hit a child. She saw it in time and dodged it.

The ordinary people who lived in Ashton scudded around the throngs of soldiers. They looked weary, keeping their heads down and avoiding eye contact. They had the same haggard look as those in Romenia. I wondered what it was like for these people who had been caught up in a war for generations?

The only people who didn't avoid the soldiers were those who were selling their wares. We passed by a boisterous man who quickly cowered when the four soldiers in front of his shop wanted to pay a cheaper rate.

There was one person who was unafraid of the soldiers. He didn't wear a scrap of blue, and he passed through the throng, laughing and patting soldiers on their shoulders or backs. He stopped every few seconds to strike up a quick conversation. He sauntered towards us, and as he smiled, the grim soldiers around us did the same. The stranger wore shades of a neutral brown that matched his rugged face and ponytail. A black eye patch covered his left eye. Two obsidian daggers hung at his sides.

He bowed to the woman in charge and said, "Hello, Paige." He smiled. "Beautiful day, isn't it?"

"I haven't time for this, Fortune," Paige said, but she did her best not to smile.

"That's not what you said last night," Fortune said.

Paige stopped marching, digging her heels into the ground and clenching her fists. Fortune grinned at her.

Paige turned and punched Fortune. Fortune looked more shocked than hurt, but he dropped into a fighting stance, grinning. None of the other soldiers moved to stop it. In fact, they seemed amused, and a few of the soldiers even placed bets. No matter how relaxed they seemed, though, they still had their gazes trained on us.

Fortune grabbed Paige's next punch. He twisted her arm behind her back and said, "You know I love it when you play rough."

Paige flashed a quick smile before elbowing him hard in the stomach. She used her heel to trip him. One could only imagine what kind of history these two had. When she drew her sword, I felt the magical enchantment that encompassed it. She pointed it at Fortune's neck, drawing a drop of blood.

"It's seems you've lost," Paige said.

Fortune shrugged. "I have a bit of a depth perception problem, what can I say?" He grinned. "I don't normally hit ladies, but then again, you're not a lady, my dear Captain."

Paige sheathed her sword, and her face became stern. "If you'll excuse me." She picked up the pace, and we started marching towards the center of the city.

"Wait!" Fortune said, getting up and rushing to her side. "I had news to deliver about the information you wanted from the South. I'm sorry it took so long, but my sources finally found something."

She raised her head, but she didn't stop. "That'll have to wait. I have to go see the council."

"Very well. You know I hardly have a chance to come into the city and see you these days."

"Not now, Fortune. I have business to attend to." She glanced at him. "Maybe I'll meet with you later."

"As you wish." Fortune bowed to her. "A pleasure to see you, as always, my dear Captain."

He rose and his gaze met mine. He winked with his good eye, then left.

I didn't have much time to ponder what that was about. Not long afterward, we reached our destination.

In the center of Ashton was a huge castle. The granite had multiple cracks in it, as if it were an old man. Bits of stone had fallen out, and one wall had collapsed. An open tower stood in front of the main entrance. Guards peered down from it, eyeing us as we made our way to the double doors below.

A goblin saluted and said, "Captain Paige. The council's waiting for you. I'd be on guard if I were you. They seemed agitated."

"Thank you, Whatu."

I gawked at the small green goblin. I didn't know if I'd ever get used to well-behaved, well-spoken, decently dressed, and almost nice-smelling goblins.

We ventured under the tattered blue banners hanging over the door and were escorted down the corridors. I felt a tinge of magic in the hallways and eventually saw why. We'd reached an area shielded by wards. Paige whispered the incantation to pass through them, keeping her voice low so that even the elves wouldn't hear her.

As soon as we stepped through those wards, the council's powerful magic was like a shining beacon. I gulped and glanced at the others. Rebekah loosened her collar, and Jastillian squinted his eyes as he stared down the hallway. Usually, I was saddened by how people couldn't feel the way magic worked its way into everyday life. At times like this where it could be overwhelming, I envied them.

The goblin had said the council was agitated. I was going to have to face them and their magic, agitated or no.

We reached the end a quiet and gloomy hallway. A pair of guards stood near a closed door. Paige motioned for the guards to open the door.

We stepped inside the chamber. Paige and the other guards stayed behind and closed it after us. The chamber looked remarkably like the one in Romenia. It had the exact same design, from the raised dais with its stone table to the three chairs behind it, and no guards. The council was already waiting for us. Underneath their hoods, the dark colors of mana stared back at us. I rode their powerful, magical auras, trying not to be swept away again.

We bowed to them. I knew I going to have to take the lead again, but what worried me was that I had had no time to prepare. After what had happened in Romenia, seeing this council was our last resort, not our first. We needed to plan *after* seeing what information we could obtain in Ashton. Paige's arrival had ruined any shot of that.

This was going to require a more delicate tongue than I had. The council already knew of me, but how much did they know?

"Hellsfire," the master of black mana said. She pulled back her hood, revealing a young but thin and frail-looking woman. The dark power that radiated from her more than made up for any physical weakness, and her black hair contrasted with her pale skin. "I am Bellona," she said, her voice like tar.

"I am Dorissa," the water wizard said, her voice as hypnotic as the ocean. She exposed a young and pretty face. Her eyes shifted from blue to green, and she had hair that matched. I began to get lost in her eyes.

"Humph, I'm Zephyrus," the air master said, his words as light as the air. He was the only one who had a wooden staff. When he pulled back his hood, he had a grizzled look with a long, frizzy beard.

I steeled myself against their fierce gazes and overwhelming magic. I had to tread carefully here, but I didn't know where to begin. They knew so much about us and I knew so little about them.

"How did you know about us?" I asked.

"You've caused quite a ruckus," Zephyrus said. "I heard you were quite the handful for the other council."

How could word have gotten here so fast? Their spies must have worked quickly, or they might have had other means of gaining knowledge. I shook my head. That wasn't important.

"No," I said. "How do you *know* about us?"

Bellona's dark eyes narrowed. "That is not important."

Before I could respond, Dorissa said, "From your friends, the elves."

Bellona glowered at Dorissa, but my spirits rose. "Where are they?"

Zephyrus said, "All in good time." He chuckled. "You're so bold. You remind me of a young Stradus. My old student taught you well."

"You knew Stradus?"

"He was an excellent student, when he wasn't worrying about the future or chasing girls."

I grinned, thinking about that Stradus. I would have loved to find out more about him over a drink during more peaceful and less pressing times. I took a step closer and asked, "Where are my friends?"

"Don't worry," Bellona said. Her eyes shone with intense darkness. "They are safe."

"We would like to see them."

Dorissa turned her watery eyes towards me. "I promise that you will, but we must know something first. Is it true what they say? *You* brought down the Great Barrier?"

I nodded.

"He has much power, this one," she said.

Zephyrus nodded. "Humph, that he does."

"But what are we to do with him?" Bellona asked, peering down at me.

Dorissa smiled, and I couldn't help but feel a little calmer. "He is to be our guest. If that is all right with you and your friends, Hellsfire?"

What shocked and surprised me was how nice this council was. I didn't expect that. They didn't grill me like the other council, did nor did they push and ask for my help. For a brief second, I thought that maybe they could not only help find Krystal and Ardimus, but that they could cure Krystal.

That thought was fleeting. This council *would* want something from me. In fact, they might want the same thing as the other council, but just be going about getting it in a different way. These were people who believed in Renak and continued a war in his name. There could be far worse things that they wanted.

"Thank you, Council, but there are more questions I have and important matters to discuss."

"There will be time for all that later, Hellsfire," Bellona said.

"But—"

Zephyrus put a hand up, and his words were amplified by his magic. "Later, Hellsfire. We know you're tired from your travels, and you should see your friends. Afterwards, we'll prepare a meal for you, and then we can discuss things like proper wizards. Not like those fools in Romenia."

I opened my mouth, then closed it. They were right. There would be time for that later. When I was refreshed, I would be less inclined to make a mistake. But I could sense there was something that this council wasn't telling me.

I bowed and said, "Thank you, Council."

They nodded, and we left their chambers. Captain Paige waited there with her arms crossed and a dozen men around her.

"If you follow me," the captain said, "I'll take you to your friends."

She led the way out of the castle. As we walked, half a dozen more soldiers came and trailed us. They didn't surround us, but they didn't go out of their way to not make their escort obvious.

Outside, Paige brought us to a row of three houses. They were well away from the castle walls, surrounded by guard posts. Outside one of the houses, five blue-clad elves circled three familiar elves wearing colors that matched their skin. They all heard us well before I saw them. They stopped talking and their heads turned toward us.

Prastian excused himself from Ashton's elves. He, Demay and Behast strolled over to us. I smiled, glad to see them here and safe.

"It's good to see you again," I said. "Have you seen the princess or Ardimus?"

"It's good to see you as well," Prastian said and smiled. "Come, my friends, we have much to discuss."

"We'll leave you alone," Captain Paige said, motioning to her soldiers.

"Thank you, Captain," Prastian said and gave her a short bow. "You've been most gracious to us."

"You're welcome, Prastian."

Captain Paige left and most of her men departed with her. A few of the soldiers went back to their posts around the buildings.

"It's for our protection," Prastian said, following my eyes. "As we're not from around here. They've been quite accommodating to us." He nodded at one of the elves.

Behast opened the door, and we all funneled inside. The house, which was really just a small room, became cramped. There was a stove inside, a tiny table and three chairs, but that was it. Beds were matted straw on the floor.

"Welcome to our prison," Demay said and spread his arms wide. "And now yours."

"Demay, lower your voice," Prastian said and grimaced. "He is right, though. This is a prison." Prastian smiled. "But we're glad you can join us nevertheless."

"Aye," Jastillian said. "Now that we're together, we can escape."

"But have you heard news of the princess?" Rebekah asked before I could. "We can't leave without her. King Furlong wouldn't have sent us down here if he knew there was a war, especially a war between wizards."

Prastian shook his head. "Unfortunately, we've not heard about the princess since we've been here. And we've been here almost since we got separated. We've been able to talk with some of the elves here. They've had them guarding us to try and coerce information out of us about Northern Shala and Sharald, but they've not been very good at it. They're too eager. However, we've been doing the same to them."

"How much did you tell them?" Rebekah asked.

"Nothing that wasn't common knowledge, that they wouldn't learn by sending scouts into Northern Shala." Prastian sighed. "I said enough to keep them satisfied...for a time. Thankfully, you three showed up. I was running out of things to tell them."

"What did you learn?" she asked.

"The elves here are unhappy. They can hear the forests calling them and would rather be there." Prastian's face saddened. "Instead, they get to watch the trees burn in their war."

"Can you get any of them to help us?" Jastillian asked.

"I've been trying, but it's hard. They may not like the war, but they're duty bound."

"Aye, I understand."

"We would have left already if we could," Behast said. "We had no idea that you were coming here. They've been bringing in thousands of soldiers. Whatever they're planning, they're going to act soon. We may be able to use that opportunity to escape."

"But what about the princess and Ardimus?" I asked. "Wouldn't it be best if we wait for them here? While we were in the west, we learned that you would be here. I had hoped it was all of you."

"It's too dangerous," Prastian said. "Princess Krystal and Ardimus would be safer out there than in here."

"I'm not leaving Southern Shala without her."

"And neither am I," Rebekah said.

"No one said you had to," Prastian said. "But before we decide whether to stay or go in Southern Shala, we *must* flee this city."

"I agree," I said. I looked around the room and asked, "So what do we do?"

"We wait and plan," Prastian said. "Since you're a wizard, the council will be more receptive to your words." He looked at Jastillian. "I'm sorry to say that most here won't be as kind to you because you're a dwarf *and* wearing red."

Jastillian laughed. "I expect nothing less."

Prastian's light green eyes stared into mine. "Tonight's dinner is going to be very important, Hellsfire. What we do next hinges on what you say and how well things go."

I knew the full importance of his words, but I wasn't going to let anything stop me from seeing Krystal again.

I met Prastian's fierce gaze. "I know."

CHAPTER 25

I HAD THOUGHT that after meeting with the elves we were going to be summoned for dinner. That didn't happen. Food was brought to us instead, and over the next three days, we heard nothing from the council.

Captain Paige and her troops escorted us throughout the city, but they never left us alone. We explored the marketplace, stables, bakeries, blacksmiths and temples. We appeared to be interested in their city and their land, but we used it as cover to try and talk to the people. However, they didn't trust us any more than the soldiers because we were foreigners.

What compounded our difficulties was that the elves Prastian had talked to, no longer came around. There were a few elves that guarded us, but Prastian didn't recognize them and they didn't talk to him. We couldn't get any information out of anyone.

Since persuasion wasn't working, I demanded to see the council. Captain Paige was angry at my outburst, but she was also angry at having been forced to babysit us. With all the watchful glares around us, we couldn't easily escape, but we were going to have to do something. We couldn't stay in Ashton forever.

The next day after dinner, Captain Paige came to retrieve me.

"The council wants to see you," Paige said.

I rose from the table. "It's about time." My friends stood, getting ready to join me.

"No. They just want to see Hellsfire."

The others and I shared a look. I opened my mouth and Prastian said, "I trust we'll see the council later. It must be something only between wizards. We're tired from this delicious meal anyway." He put a hand to his mouth and yawned.

"Come along," Paige said without any sort of warmth in her voice.

I left the others and followed the captain. A dozen of her men enclosed me, when we got outside.

We headed back to the castle. The dark corridors were a lot more ominous at night. My eyes wandered over the creeping shadows on the walls, feeling the oppressiveness of the magic lingering beneath the high ceilings. I rubbed my hands together and breathed in them. This meeting with the council made me nervous. Not because of their ideals about Renak, but because I would be facing them alone.

"Do you know what this is about?" I asked Paige.

She didn't look me in the eye, but for a second her face softened. "I'm sorry, Hellsfire, I don't. The council will tell you everything you need to know."

Her final sentence was the only part of her words I believed.

Paige opened the doors to the chamber and whispered, "Good luck." She quickly closed them, and I was alone with the council.

"Council," I said and bowed.

They said nothing, but stared at me with their colorful eyes.

"We've reached a decision," Bellona said. "You are to join with our forces and guide us into what you call Northern Shala. We will secure a foothold there, and then you will lead us into Masep so that we may recover those objects lost to us because of the barrier. With them, we will crush those fools in the west." She leaned over. "Do I make myself clear?"

I stared into the hypnotic gazes of their eyes, feeling my magic swell up within me. "I understand perfectly, council. But I will not help you."

"Even if it means the lives of you and your friends?" Zephyrus asked.

"Yes. I will not help you bring death to my homeland. This is your war, not mine."

"Hellsfire," Dorissa said in a calm manner. "We don't want to kill anyone."

"Then end it," I said. "For the gods' sake, you're supposed to be the Elemental Council!" I threw my hands up in frustration. "You're supposed to preside over matters of magic, not start wars. This is a new opportunity, a time for change and peace, not for more bloodshed."

"We want to end the war quickly, and with as little bloodshed as possible. With your help, we can do it."

I shook my head. "I'm sorry, but I can't help you."

"Very well." Dorissa clapped her hands, and from one of the side entrances a guard pushed in a long table with wheels. Strapped to it was someone I recognized.

"Ardimus!"

I worried he might be dead. I rushed to him and was relieved to see his shallow breathing. He had no bruises on him, but he tossed, turned, and sweated as if he were having a terrible nightmare.

I narrowed my eyes at the council. "What did you do to him?"

Dorissa clapped her hands again and out rolled another table. I ran to it, already knowing who was on it.

"Krystal!"

She was in worse shape than Ardimus. I lifted a hand to her pale face, wanting to wipe the sweat from her. My hand froze inches away from the goose bumps on her skin when I remembered the curse. She had been through so much, and it was all my fault. I clenched my fists to control the boiling fire within me.

I used my wizard's sight to peer into her aura and saw how weak and wavering it was. I had seen it that way before, when I had almost killed her in Alexandria. I gently shook her, doing my best to wake her, but she remained in an unrestful slumber. I glanced over my shoulder, and the council stared at me, making no move to stop me.

Krystal's eyes fluttered open, but she wasn't awake.

"Princess, wake up!"

I used my robes as a barrier while I held onto her chin and turned her face side to side, calling her name. Slowly, her violet eyes opened. She gazed through me until her eyes focused.

"Hellsfire," she said in a tired, raspy voice. "Is that really you?"

I lifted a finger and put it just above her nose. "Shhh, princess. It's all right. I'm here for you now. I'll do what I can to get us out of here, all right?"

She gave me a weak nod.

I undid the straps that bound her wrists, and then woke Ardimus. I didn't need to tell him to take care of her, as I knew he would do his duty.

I turned and faced the council. "Release them." The fire oozed from between my fingers. "Now!"

"We will do no such thing," Bellona said. I shivered, feeling death as it crawled over my skin. "The princess is vital if we are to journey into the Wastelands."

"What did you do to her—to them?"

"What was necessary," Zephyrus said. "Not long after you came into our chambers, she tried to negotiate with us. And while she seemed sincere, we needed to know the truth about what she said."

I glared at them. "You used your magic for mind torture."

"Mind magic."

"Call it what you will, but it was still torture. Stradus told me you once outlawed this sort of use." I stared at them, barely able to contain my anger. The council couldn't do this kind of mind torture. It took a sorcerer, but they were the ones who ordered it done. "You are no longer the Elemental Council I was once told stories of."

"Who are you to judge, Hellsfire?" Bellona asked. "You know not the things we've had to endure and what we've had to do. You know nothing!"

"I know you've changed." I paused. "And I know you no longer have the right to ask anything of us." I gathered in more magic, but I started to feel woozy. Tiny droplets of sweat ran down my face. I pushed everything aside and focused on the council.

"If you help us," Dorissa said, "I promise we will help you."

I crossed my arms, keeping my magic at bay. "You have nothing I want."

"We've seen what's wrong with the princess. With all our power, we can help you undo that curse."

I considered. That was part of the reason I had journeyed into Southern Shala. I glanced back at Krystal. She tried to stand proudly and regally as she normally did. She couldn't. She leaned against Ardimus for support and he held onto her so that he wouldn't fall either.

I looked into Krystal's purple eyes. She didn't move or make a sound, yet I could read her thoughts perfectly. She wouldn't want me to ask anything of this council. If I did, she would never forgive me.

My eyes left the pair, and I gazed at the council.

"I don't need your assistance."

My entire body clenched itself as I waited for the council to make a move. Fighting one wizard was hard enough. Taking on three of the Elemental Council was suicidal. As long as Krystal and Ardimus got out of here alive, though, that's was all that mattered. I would buy them the needed time.

"I wish circumstances were different and it didn't have to be like this," Dorissa said with a hint of sadness in her watery eyes.

I was going to reply, but my vision blurred. A wave of nausea struck me and I stumbled forward. I summoned more magic to my defense. I thought it was the council casting subtle magic, but I sensed nothing. They stayed seated, watching me with cat-like attention.

Something was wrong, but I couldn't pinpoint it.

"We have to get out of here. Now!" I said to Krystal and Ardimus.

I raised my hand and invoked a minor spell to use as a diversion while we escaped. When I tried to cast it, I collapsed to the floor.

The darkness threatened to consume me. I cried out to Krystal and Ardimus to run. I felt their hands on my back as they dragged me to my feet. They dropped me, and my cheek embraced the cold, stony floor. When I next opened my eyes, I found Dorissa standing over me.

I concentrated on summoning my fire to the surface, the dark flame within swelling up. The council would all burn for harming Krystal.

Dorissa leaned over me and laid a hand on my back. I gazed into the oceans that were her eyes. "Stop fighting it. The more magic you use, the faster the potion works and the more painful it is. Goodbye, Hellsfire."

CHAPTER 26

COLD WATER SEEPED into my face, filling every pore with tiny droplets of ice. It made my body shake and my mind reel. I opened my eyes to see a grinning Fortune and a relieved-looking princess standing over me. I glanced to the side and saw the others, as wet as I was, and they had their weapons back. I stared past them at the bars that glistened with magic. The same type of magic as the dungeon cell in Alexandria. I reached for my neck, feeling the open collar around it. My anger rose at the touch of the cold metal. The council had tricked us, then put us in the dungeons. More importantly, they had harmed Krystal.

"Are you all right?" I asked her. I used my wizard's sight to peer into her aura. It was more stable now, but Renak's curse was still intertwined in it.

"I'm fine. Thanks for asking." She pulled my arm and helped me sit up.

"You don't ask how *I'm* doing," Fortune said. "It wasn't easy fulfilling my part of the bargain."

"I hired Fortune," Krystal said. "He showed Ardimus and me around and has filled us in on what's been happening in Southern Shala. I also paid him to be on the alert lest we run into trouble."

I narrowed my eyes at him. "You didn't hold up your part of the bargain, Fortune. The princess and Ardimus were tortured by the council."

He shrugged. "I tried, kid."

"That's not good enough. They could have been killed."

"Hellsfire, it's all right," Krystal said. "We're safe now."

I took a deep breath. I was more angry at myself than Fortune. *I* wasn't there for her the way I'd said I would be. I couldn't protect her from all of this, or it seemed, from anything. I gave her a subtle nod.

"Be thankful I'm here now," Fortune said. "Rescuing you from these dungeons and retrieving your weapons was far easier than some foolhardy attempt to wrest you from the council. I expect the rest of the payment when we arrive in Alexandria."

"You'll get your money," Krystal said.

Fortune bowed his head. "Now that you're all awake, I can fill you in. The council and their army are gone. They've mobilized to Northern Shala."

"So that's what they were up to," I said.

"There's another thing," he said. "There was a reason they didn't kill you all outright." Fortune paused and looked up.

"Which was?"

"They were told not to. Someone wanted you all alive—especially you." Fortune pointed at me. "But I wasn't able to find out who." He reached into his pouch and pulled out a red apple.

In the short time I had been in Southern Shala, I had made my share of enemies—we all had. But who would want us alive? It couldn't have been Ashton's council, as they already had us. They wouldn't have worked together with Romenia's council. There was only one person who it could be. Krystal and I shared a look as I raised my eyebrows. She gave me a subtle nod. It could only be Premier.

"Let us hurry back to Northern Shala," Prastian said. "Our people must be warned."

"Agreed," Krystal said.

"I have your horses and supplies ready," Fortune said. "We'll have to go around the Dead Zone and away from the main roads the army is using. If we force march our way to the Ennis Mountains, we should be able to beat them."

"Then what are we waiting for?" Krystal asked. "Move out."

The others put on the cloaks that Fortune gotten for them. I put my hood up and we left the dungeons.

There were no guards nearby, as Fortune had paid them to be elsewhere. We hurried down the hallway, with Fortune leading the way.

"Wait," Prastian said, his ears twitching. "I hear something. Someone's coming."

We froze, and a familiar aura of power I hadn't felt in quite a while came down that hallway. Premier. I had a fleeting thought of attacking and finally putting an end to the untrustworthy wizard. He deserved to die for what he had done to Krystal. I glanced at my friends. Their people had to be warned. As much as I ached to kill Premier, Northern Shala came first.

"Is there another way around?" I asked.

Fortune shook his head. "This way is clear. I have no idea how well guarded the other areas are."

Loud footsteps stomped into earshot. We scouted around for side passageways. The nearest doors were locked. I reached for one handle, getting ready to use my power. My magic swelled inside before I stopped it. This close, he might feel my power, especially since I could feel his. I glanced back. The long, curved hallways didn't leave any room for us to hide, and if we ran, they would hear us.

We heard voices approaching. "I should have been notified of this earlier," Premier was saying.

"You were notified as soon as possible," Paige said.

"We had a deal. I fulfilled my part of the bargain. I expect the council to fulfill theirs."

"They did. We've been busy."

"Invasion or no, I should have been told."

"What's your hurry?" Paige asked. "They're not going anywhere."

"You don't know Hellsfire as I do. He's tricky, that one."

I whispered to Fortune. "Lead us out of here."

Too late. Premier and Paige came around a curve and saw us. "Hellsfire!" Premier's voice boomed out.

We stopped creeping away. My friends tore off their cloaks and freed their weapons. I summoned my magic. Captain Paige and the half-dozen men with her drew their own weapons. Premier's burnt face stared at me with cold, angry eyes.

"Going somewhere?" Premier asked.

"Fortune," Paige said, glaring at him. "I should have realized you were up to something."

He bowed. "Always, my dear."

"*You're* the one who wanted us alive," I said to Premier. "Why?"

"Revenge. You defeated me, humiliated me, and almost killed me. I was going to enjoy making you and your friends suffer for what you did."

"You already did." My hands balled into fists and my knuckles cracked. "You're responsible for the condition the princess is in. You broke your word, Premier."

"Not I," he said, granting me a taunting smile. "That was Renak's spell. I just...altered it a bit. The magic's all his. If it got that far, you were meant to die in the nexus." His dark eyes briefly stared at Krystal. "It's all your fault, Hellsfire. If you had died or never had come into the Wastelands, none of this would have happened."

Premier was right. This was all my fault. Every decision I made affected others. And I just made things worse. But I couldn't think about such things now. I had to focus on the present and not get distracted by him, of all people.

"What did you give them in return?" I asked.

"Information. They were quite eager to learn some of the things I knew from Masep, and were pleased that I agreed with Renak." I knew he was lying. He cared little for Renak. He was just using these people, much as he had used the Wasteland creatures. "There were things of interest they gave me, but then you showed up. And I also wanted you." He pointed his long finger at me.

Then why did they offer me the chance to lead them to Masep? They genuinely seemed willing to work with me. Then it dawned on me. They didn't trust Premier any more than I did, which was why he was here now instead of with them.

"Damn it, Premier!" I said. "This is bigger than you or me. Do you realize what you've done? What you've brought into Northern Shala?"

"I care not for the war or your land." He spread his arms wide. "This has always been my home. If you turn yourself willingly over to me, I may not kill your friends or your beloved princess."

I smirked, because I wasn't going to make the same mistake of trusting him again—wizard's promise or no.

"Why don't you surrender, and maybe I'll let *you* live." Before Premier could respond, I said, "Captain, you can't trust Premier. He's a lying snake. I beat him before and I *will* beat him again. This time for good. He still hasn't recovered."

I accessed my wizard's sight and glimpsed Premier gathering in mana. It was slow and carried nowhere near as much power as the first time I'd faced him. This time I had my friends with me—all battle-tested warriors.

The soldiers standing around Paige were different from my friends. Three of them were so young they had no growth of hair on their faces. They nervously looked at one another. The goblin with them had a shaky hand, and another aged man was missing his left hand. They couldn't possibly take on all of us. Not with the bulk of their forces marching into Northern Shala.

"Captain, please," I said. "I don't want to hurt you."

Her enchanted sword glowed brighter. "I'm duty bound, wizard."

"Paige," Fortune said. "Now's not the time to be foolish. I beg you. I don't want you to get hurt."

Before she could respond, Premier raised his hand and unleashed a funnel of fire towards me. I expected the tiny fireballs to ram into me, but only a portion of them flew my way. The rest attacked my friends, and a large portion of the magic aimed for the princess.

I dispersed the tiny flames and Premier smiled at me. He might not be able to beat me in his current state, but he could easily kill my friends. I was going to have to protect them and leave myself open for an attack.

Paige and her men charged us, and my friends met their attack. Premier stayed behind the melee, flinging spells not at me but at my friends. They weren't powerful spells, but they could do enough harm if given the chance.

I couldn't counterattack Premier. He didn't give me a chance. He kept hurling quick and easy spells at all of my friends while they fought against Paige and her soldiers. My friends heeded the soldiers more than the magic, as that was their instinct. I paid too much attention to Premier and his spells as that was my training, but I should have been mindful of everything.

I was yanked backwards as Paige's enchanted sword passed through where I had stood. I instinctively cast a fireball at her and her sword cut right through it.

"Paige!" Fortune said from behind me. "What are you doing?"

"What I must, Fortune. You of all people have never understood duty. You never chose a side."

The couple continued to argue and yell despite all the fighting around them. I looked over Paige's shoulder, worried that Premier would cast a spell at my friends. He didn't. He finally released his gathered energy at me.

I didn't have time to disperse Premier's powerful spell, as a crackle of lightning raced through the air. I could have redirected it, but it would have harmed someone else.

Paige didn't see it. Without thinking, I grabbed her, narrowly avoiding her sword, and threw her to the ground. The lightning grazed my back. I cried out in pain as it sizzled against me and seized my muscles.

As my body crushed Paige, I stared at her, seeing a hint of green in her questioning eyes. Those eyes hardened and her sword pressed up against my side, the sharp blade digging into me. The magic I brought forth to defend myself was absorbed into the sword. The sword's power grew and the blade brightened. There was nothing I could do to stop her.

Paige was going to kill me. All to fulfill a duty I didn't understand or agree with. And worst of all, there would be no one to stop Premier. He would finish off my friends and Krystal after I was gone.

"Stand down!" Paige yelled. The sword's pressure against my side lessened, and she squirmed out from under me. Fortune helped me up. I placed a hand on my back, feeling the tingling, painful sensation of Premier's magic.

Paige's soldiers and my friends halted. They didn't put away their weapons, but they did lower them.

"What are you doing?" Premier asked. "You were ordered to—"

"I was ordered to escort you to Hellsfire. I did."

"You know these were not the terms of our agreement. They were supposed to be bound and imprisoned, not free and armed."

"Not *my* problem."

Premier glared at her. "You don't understand what you've done. Foolish woman."

His eyes darkened until the two globes became pure black. His power swelled inside him. This was the Premier I had faced the first time. Paige readied her enchanted sword. Premier couldn't possibly take us all on.

Magic exploded from Premier and a gloom smothered the room, drowning out any and all light. The light from Paige's sword shone in response, but not even her sword could draw out that much of Premier's magic.

"Find him!" Krystal said.

We groped around in the pitch black of the hallway. I used my power to sense whether Premier was going to attack us, but I couldn't sense any magic besides my own. Thirty long seconds later, the darkness lifted and Premier was nowhere to be found.

"Find him," Paige said to her soldiers. "And alert the city." She faced me. "We're even now, Hellsfire. Leave Ashton and do *not* return here." She eyed Fortune. "This includes you." She stormed away.

"Paige!" Fortune said. "Paige!" He looked back at me and grinned. "Women."

"What about Premier?" I asked. "He has to be stopped. Paige will need our help."

"She can handle herself," Fortune said. "She knows how to deal with wizards."

"He's *my* responsibility. It's my fault he's here in the first place. He's weakened now, but you have no idea what he's capable of, and I still owe him for what he did to the princess."

"Hellsfire," Krystal said. "Fortune's right. Premier is no longer our problem, at least for the moment."

I grimaced. "All right." I would see Premier again and we would finish what we'd started.

"I suggest we hurry," Fortune said. "Paige won't be lenient for long."

We exited the castle and got our supplies and horses. We departed Ashton and rode hard and fast, moving like a flying dragon. Fortune took us on roads Ashton's army didn't travel, but they added distance to our ride. I wished I had more of my rejuvenation potions so that we could push the horses faster. We had to warn Northern Shala before Ashton's army reached them, but we couldn't ride the horses to exhaustion.

We made good time. A week after we left Ashton, we arrived near the Ennis Mountains, where we would cross back into Northern Shala.

But there was one last obstacle standing in our way.

CHAPTER 27

ASHTON'S COUNCIL WASN'T the only one who thought sending their army into Northern Shala was a good idea. Romenia did too, and we stumbled straight into their battle.

We got off our horses and crept toward it in complete silence. We stood on the crest of a hill, overlooking the struggle on the plains. My eyes followed two dozen of Romenia's centaurs charging into the fray from their right flank. They tried to reinforce the line, but galloped into a wall of pikemen. I winced as their bodies buckled like exhausted horses, but their human torsos cried out like a man would.

A dozen of Romenia's ogres bullied their way through, smashing through Ashton's weakened line. The tiny humans were crushed beneath their powerful blows. It took half a dozen men to bring down one of the ogres. With their strong armor and broad swords, the ogres were nearly unstoppable. They cut a swath through Ashton's line. If Premier had properly armed and trained his ogres, Alexandria would have fallen in no time.

A gigantic fireball crashed into the ogres. A green-robed wizard stood firm and hurled wind at them. One ogre was lifted a hundred feet into the air, limbs flailing. From behind the wizard, three dozen elves shot arrows into Romenia's encroaching army. The army scattered, unprepared for the elves' assault. The elves and wizard turned the tide, and Ashton's army counterattacked. Dwarves took the lead with elves providing them cover.

A red-robed wizard sprinted to the area to counteract the green-robed one.

Those two dueled amongst the intertwined blue and red armies. They cast spells and counterspells against one another, and struck at the opposing armies when they could.

Throughout the battle, about a dozen wizards, witches, and sorcerers were interspersed on each side. They struck where they thought their side could break through, and held where their line was weakest.

As I watched the bright and colorful manas blaze across the battlefield, a part of me marveled at how skillfully they used their magic. Then I glimpsed a gnome screaming out in pain as a wizard's fire devoured her alive.

Magic wasn't supposed to be used for horrors like this. Stradus had taught me it was supposed to be used to protect the people and the land. The two armies slaughtering each other here weren't fighting in defense of anything. It was because of a war centuries old. A war that no longer mattered, with the Great Barrier down.

They were wizards. Couldn't they see what they were doing? The ground ran thick with blood, but it also ran with something else. Because of all the fighting, the land's magic was twisted and weakened. It was the beginnings of what had happened in the Wastelands and in the Dead Zone.

Far too much of the land had been destroyed because of magic, and they were bringing their war into Northern Shala to continue it, not end it.

All because of me.

I ignored the ground troops, peering past them to the vital part of the battle. None of the others could see what I saw, but the magical fighting between the council was much worse and could be far more devastating.

Both councils and the majority of their wizards had linked themselves in a group. Elite guards surrounded them because of how vulnerable they were to attack. The groups hurled magical tidal waves of spells at each other, the power soaring through the air, trying to splash down onto the other group. Brilliant rainbow light shows fired back and forth. Each side vied to be the winner and push past the other.

They used their mana within and drew on the land's mana to strengthen one another. Together, they were able to perform complex spells that would have been too difficult or time-consuming to do otherwise.

"What do we do now?" Demay asked.

"Stay back, out of harm's way," Behast said.

"Fortune, are you sure you don't know of another route?" Prastian said. "Anything would be helpful."

He shook his head. "There was never any money to be made in the Ennis Mountains, so why would I go?"

"We'll have to risk getting lost in the mountains," Krystal said. "Our people must be warned."

"And we'll have to try not to run into the winning army," Jastillian said.

The others walked their horses away, but I stood firm. I stared at the horrors in front of me, seeing how the magic scorched and twisted the land when it was deflected away. Couldn't the council see what they were doing? They were wizards, for the gods' sake! They had a duty to perform.

I clenched my fists and gritted my teeth. This had to stop, no matter the cost.

"Hellsfire," Krystal said, laying a gentle hand on my shoulder.

"Yes?"

"Let's go, hero."

I placed my bare hand upon her gloved one. "This can't be allowed to continue."

She paused and stiffened. "What are you saying, Hellsfire?"

"This war isn't going to be brought to our homes. I didn't bring the barrier down just for this senseless slaughter to continue. It ends now."

She didn't say anything for several long moments. "I know you have great power and I've seen you do some amazing things, but you're only one wizard. How can you possibly stop all this?"

I pointed at the councils. "You can't see or feel the incredible magic being cast, but it's there. They're balancing each other out. Stradus once told me about how magic could be performed like this. The combined power would be immense, but all it takes is for one wizard to catch them off guard and tip the scales. That's why they all have guards around them."

"I understand all that, but what can you do from *here?* You won't be able to get that close."

"I know that, princess, but I have a plan." I gave her a smile. "It isn't much of one, but I need to *try* to stop them or at least slow them down. If I have the power I've been led to believe, I'll be able to do it."

Krystal looked like she wanted to object, but she nodded. "All right."

She departed and went back to the others. I took out my book of spells, trying to see what I could do. I couldn't perform many of these rituals because I didn't have the ingredients or the time. What I needed was a brutal spell—one that was quick and powerful.

I rummaged through the pages, but couldn't find anything. The frustration got to me and I crumpled the pages, almost tearing them. I flipped through the book again, praying to the gods that they could help or give me a sign, and my fingers found two pages stuck together. I pulled them apart and discovered the dangerous ritual I needed.

"Are you sure you can do this, lad?" Jastillian asked as the others came over to me.

"I have to, but I'll need your help. I'll be vulnerable. I need you to guard me, standing more than a hundred feet from me. It's dangerous. The armies will try to come after me."

Prastian nodded. "We'll do it."

"You're all insane," Fortune said. "You can't take on two armies, kid, no matter how powerful you are."

"You can always go," Behast said, glowering at him.

Fortune threw up his hands in frustration, then smiled. "If I go, I'll never see the rest of my money. Although I do expect double the payment."

"You'll get your money," Krystal said.

He bowed and drew his obsidian daggers. "That's all I ask, Princess."

"Good luck," Demay said.

The others walked away, except for Krystal.

She took the book from my hand and read the ritual. "Are you sure you want to do this? We could find another way."

"We'll never get this opportunity again, Krystal. A large portion of their armies are here. We can catch them unawares and possibly cripple them."

She nodded, but her voice was quiet. "You don't have to do this."

"I know."

She gave me a sad smile and crept forward until her body was snuggled against mine. "I could order you not to do it."

"I'm not a part of your kingdom, Princess. In fact, I'm banished from it, if you've forgotten." I gave her a playful smile.

She whispered into my ear, "You'll always be a part of Alexandria, Hellsfire." She pulled my hood down and kissed me on my cheek, using the cloth as a shield. "We'll keep you safe. Do what you have to do and come back to me alive, hero."

"I promise I'll do everything in my power to."

She smiled. "Good."

Krystal reached into my robes, and I squirmed as her fingers tickled me.

"What are you doing?" I asked while stifling a giggle.

"Reaching for your dagger. I read the ritual. You need help."

I did need help with one important part of the ritual. I was going to try to do it on my own or have one of the others help me. I didn't want her to do it or even see it. However, part of me was glad she was here with me.

I nodded. "If this doesn't work or you all are in trouble, I want you to leave. Make it back to Northern Shala...and tell my mother what happened."

Krystal's purple eyes became like steel, then softened. "All right."

"Thank you."

I pulled off my wizard's robes and placed them on the ground. I rolled up my sleeves, exposing my bare arms.

"Are you ready?" the princess asked, grasping my arm.

"Yes, but please don't overdo it." I grinned, and she returned it.

I winced as Krystal cut a small incision in my arm until the blood flowed. Afterwards, I drew a large triangle on the grass with my own blood. I began to feel light-headed, but I had to make sure the imperfect triangle was big enough for me to sit in. I used my torn sleeve to patch up the gash in my arm. I tightened it hard with my teeth until the blood stopped.

She performed another precise and sharp cut on my other forearm. I painted the grass with another triangle until a hexagram formed. My vision began to swirl from the loss of blood.

"Be careful," the princess said, catching me before I fell.

"Thank you." I smiled, my head leaning on her shoulder. "But I think you cut a little too deep."

Krystal returned the smile before tying up the gash in my arm.

"Be careful, hero, and good luck."

She turned and went back to Ardimus. We shared one last look, and I watched them leave until they were well away.

I sat cross-legged in the bloody hexagram and took a deep breath. This ritual was going to be dangerous, yet I chose it because it should also be powerful enough to cripple the two opposing armies. If I had as much power as Stradus always believed, it would rush out, reaching even the council. If I didn't, my plan would fail.

I closed my eyes and reminded myself that I was a wizard—an individual who brought magic together. I had a responsibility to the princess, to the people of Northern Shala, to the land, and to the gods themselves to use that magic wisely. The council and the others might have forgotten that over their centuries of warfare and bloodshed, but I never would.

I slid into a trance, blocking out all outside noise. The shouting, the fighting, the screams vanished until it was only me and my magic. My strongest magic roared deeply, taking over my very being.

The fire flickers into a spark. The sparks ignites into a flame. The flame shifts and burns into a shimmering fire. That great bonfire reaches into the sky, filling the entire area.

It sinks back down, moving with liquid grace, transforming into lava. The lava smothers and burns everything, darkening the sky with ash. It finally settles into a hole, becoming a lake of pure fire.

Out of the ground rises the most powerful of all flame. A massive volcano reaches to the heavens and explodes with violence. Lava belches great balls of fiery death everywhere. They crash into the ground, using it as fuel for the fire.

My mind was on fire as the blood around me boiled and melted the grass. Steam left my body, and I burned. My skin became the color of a cherry, my chest heaved, and I wasn't sure how much longer I could contain everything. My magic ached to be released, but I had to do it safely because of my friends around me.

A wizard always had the option of releasing all of their magic in an uncontrollable fury. But that was a final spell—a death spell, as the magic was tied into their soul. I was going to do the same thing, but the ritual allowed me to do so with some kind of control. However, there was still a chance I might not survive.

The hexagram burned brighter and higher until it encompassed me. The magic on the grass wormed its way inside and I screamed from the pain. Veins nearly popped out of my body, and blood poured from my ears and eyes. With every bit of strength and emotion I had mustered, I let the fire go. Without it, my body collapsed.

The fire blazed out of my body, incinerating my clothes and the surrounding area. A trail of fire lit the ground. It dragged along, burning everything that got in its way, evaporating grass and incinerating insects. It pummeled into the two armies.

The people gave high-pitched shrieks as they burned alive. Their armor offered them no protection, and their weapons were useless. An unnatural pork-like aroma filled the air as their flesh cooked. A few near the front lines were able to scramble away from the fire. Wizards nearby tried to douse the fire, but my fire consumed their water magic and the fire was too great for the earth to smother it.

The line of fire completed its journey, touching the Ennis Mountains. It rose and blossomed, shooting straight up to the skies. A gigantic wall of fire halved the two armies, so bright and high it could be seen for miles.

I thought about crashing down my fire on both sides of the battlefield like a tidal wave. I could end it now, kill thousands, and cripple their armies, but I would be as guilty as they. They deserved a chance to live.

I lowered the flame's power. The finger-like flames from my spell stopped reaching for fuel. They swayed back and forth, waiting for my next command. I had killed a great many, but I didn't want to kill any more. Not if I didn't have to.

My soul had completely transferred into the fire, and for all intents and purposes, I was dead. I wasn't sure if I could transfer my magic and soul back into my body, but that didn't matter. I knew that risk when I performed the ritual. The princess seemed to understand that too, and I was glad she hadn't pressed me on the issue.

With the flame as my eyes, everything was a wondrous mixture of wavy orange and red with a hint of blue. Past that, there was something more, and I was able to peer into people's manas.

Magic users had their strongest mana swirling inside them, filling every part of their body. The elves were dipped in green, and the dwarves and gnomes brown. The humans and the centaurs had bits and pieces of all manas mixed inside of them. What surprised me was what I found in the Wasteland creatures.

I expected them to have nothing but black mana lurking inside, and while that was their strongest mana, there was more. They had bits of colorful mana inside of them just like everyone else. Inside everyone there was tiny piece of flame. It blazed brightly in anger at what I had done.

As amazing as that was, they all paled before the princess.

Krystal was a blinding transparent light. It was hard to tear my gaze off her. In the bright rainbow, she outshone all. There was no color in her, only pure light. I had seen this before, back when I had fought Premier. I didn't have any idea of what it meant then, and I didn't know now.

Both armies halted, unsure of what to do. I was as tall as the highest peak. Everything around me was small and insignificant. I could crush them with a thought. My flames grew brighter and more intense, aching to destroy them. I had to fight my feelings and remind myself that they deserved a chance to live.

"YOU WILL STOP FIGHTING OR DIE." My voice boomed and crackled like wood being thrown into a campfire.

I leaned in closer. Pieces of my flames pulled from the wall and flew towards the council members. My fire peeled away their guards' protection, as their enchantments were not meant to counter a spell of such magnitude. The guards burned because they wouldn't move and the council didn't reinforce their spells. The council strengthened their own protective spells, yet they struggled against my fire. I tried to rein in my power, but it was too much even for me.

"END THIS WAR OR I WILL KILL YOU ALL."

"Why should we listen to you?" Bellona asked, her black mana growing. "You know nothing!" Her magic tried to combat my own, but my flame absorbed it.

That dark flame within me begged to be released. Her magic began to change my flames and they burned brighter and darker. I pulled the fire back from Bellona. She smiled in satisfaction, as if her defenses were working.

The earth rumbled. "We will not bend to a tyrant!" Nairi said. The Elemental Council was finally united, even if it was to ignore me.

But I needed to do more. I had to convince them to stop this war. Even if I could kill everyone here, there were bound to be more forces they could muster. Other leaders and armies in other cities that I would have to deal with. In the councils' pupil-less eyes there was no fear. Only strength and arrogance.

"YOU DARE TO CHALLENGE ME?"

"We will not challenge you," Helios said. His magic was the only one that didn't fight mine. He warped the fire around him so it didn't harm him. "We will kill your body, if you do not cease this, Hellsfire. Without an anchor, you will go up in smoke."

"YOU WILL DO NO SUCH THING!"

I couldn't believe they still defied me. Did they not realize how much power I possessed? They weren't bringing their war into Northern Shala even if all of them had to die!

But the council didn't yield. They executed their magic, casting spells and reciting incantations to lessen my flames. They even performed together, despite being far apart with my wall of fire blocking them. It was like they were whole again.

My fire burned slower and weaker. The cold feel of nothingness seeped into my skin. They assaulted me from all sides, each using their own specialties.

Nairi smothered my flames with the earth. The land rose and was torn asunder as earthquakes rumbled through the area. The jagged land was heaped onto my being. Where my flames were brightest, Helios soothed and dwindled them. He caressed them as if he was their lover. Dorissa and Zephyrus summoned the clouds. Together they drenched the area and me with raging rainstorms. Each drop was like a pinprick, and there were millions of them. Bellona, with her mastery of black mana, tried to extinguish my magic by crushing my soul. I shivered at her icy touch and did my best to shy away from her. I didn't fight against her, but against myself, against releasing that dark magic within. She unknowingly drew it out of me. Ardonis bolstered and strengthened the life of all the others.

The council's magic was far more powerful as one than by themselves. Even as the other wizards, witches, and sorcerers fought against me, their power was nothing compared to the council's.

I was a giant being attacked by an anthill. My fire died down until it was only as tall as a person. All the fuel I had consumed earlier ran out. The armies saw their chance. They ran to attack my body.

I ignored the magical assault and focused on them. My trail of fire shifted, blocking their paths and smiting them, but it also served to lessen my power as

I spread myself out. The centaurs and cavalry leapt over the flames. A few brave soldiers put their heads down, shields up, and charged.

Too much was happening for me to concentrate. The council gave me the most trouble, but I couldn't disregard the other wizards. The army pressed on toward my body and my friends would be overwhelmed with their numbers. With each passing moment, my power waned. I couldn't keep this up forever.

I ignored the danger to myself and focused on my friends. There was no reasoning with the council. I had to buy time for my friends to get away, since this plan wasn't working.

I released more of the fire I was into fireballs, shooting them at the armies. They splashed and burned the oncoming soldiers. A stream of fire funneled into a mob of goblins rushing for Krystal, Ardimus, and Rebekah. A wall of flame smashed into a group of centaurs before they reached the elves.

I started to lose focus. I was so tired. I couldn't even bring my small wall of fire down and destroy both armies anymore. I wanted to rest, but knew if I gave in, the only thing to comfort me would be the afterlife.

"Hellsfire!" Krystal yelled as she ran her sword through one of Romenia's soldiers and slashed the one behind her.

I renewed my attack against the armies and council. My fire blossomed and exploded with rage. I couldn't let her or anyone else down. This was going to end, one way or another.

My roaring red and orange fire mutated to a black-laced one. I let it all go, holding nothing back. I drew power from Bellona, her mana fueling my dark flame. Hundreds died, screaming as they burned alive.

The council and other wizards stopped their assault. Their armies no longer attacked my friends; their crisp husks littered the ground. The armies scattered while the council and other wizards used magic to try to protect themselves and everyone else. They couldn't. My fire battered and breached their defenses, consuming any magic they raised.

The black flames blistered and boiled, and I kept growing. The flames bucked out and incinerated everything they touched. In the councils' eyes, fear finally came, and part of me cherished it.

I gave into that unknown power, losing myself in it as if it were a river carrying me downstream. The power I released was the only thing that could stop this war. Since they wouldn't bow down to me, I made my decision to kill them all.

"We yield!" Bellona said. Her hands were up, straining to maintain her shield from my fire. She had long ago cut off her magic, but my black flames gobbled it like a starving man with an endless hunger.

"We'll call a truce!" Ardonis said. His staff and body glowed white, shielding him from the fire. "Call off your flames and we'll talk about ending this war."

They didn't promise to end the war, only to temporarily halt it. They might decide to enter Northern Shala with a combined force. I could kill the council and most of the armies here. My power urged me to end it and make sure they couldn't threaten Northern Shala.

But no. This wasn't the way I was raised. They deserved a chance. If they talked, they might see reason. I needed to get through to the council lest I make enemies of them and their people.

"VERY WELL."

I knew full well I might die if my soul and magic couldn't be transferred back into my body. My gaze lingered on the princess. She glowed as bright as the sun. Even if I died, I knew she could negotiate a peace and succeed where I couldn't.

But I couldn't stop.

My fire raged brighter and hotter. Instead of collapsing, the black wall of fire expanded. People scrambled to get out of the way before the flames engulfed them.

"WHAT'S HAPPENING TO ME?"

But I knew the answer. It was the reason I didn't want to tap into the power in the first place, and one of the reasons I had journeyed into Southern Shala. I couldn't control it. I was already weakened from the hard days of riding, and from the attacks. The blazing inferno became a wildfire.

My consciousness began to drift off into nothingness. If I died, the empty black fire would continue to burn until it had consumed everything. I had to extinguish it. I didn't want my name to be remembered with the likes of Renak.

Yet I didn't fight as hard as I could. Part of me delighted as I watched a wave of fire splash down on three humans, incinerating them. One wizard bought time, helping others run away. She stood her ground, casting her useless magic until my flames peeled off her skin.

Instead of resisting this power, I could have embraced it. Controlled it to do anything *I* desired. The fire whispered to me, its thoughts intertwining into mine. The Elemental Council was the best Southern Shala had, and not even they could oppose me with their pitiful magic. If a war was what they wanted, I would give them one. I would smite them from existence.

"Hellsfire!" Krystal said. Amongst the screams, shouts, and yells, hers was the only sound I heard. It overpowered the fire's promises.

Krystal sprinted from the black flames that surged to reach out to her spectral light. She looked back, and her violet eyes stared into my very soul.

"You've got to stop!" she said. "Please!"

"I'm…trying," I said, finding my own voice again. While the fire didn't lose strength, I did.

Since I didn't want to seize control of it, it subdued me. The darkness within the fire pulled at me, smothering me out of existence. I was left with two possible choices: succumb to it and change into something I feared, or get lost in it and have everyone here die.

The brightness within Krystal darkened as Renak's curse wormed its way through her. She stumbled and fell, the rocky ground tearing at her clothes and skin. The necklace's magic flared and pushed against Renak's magic until it receded.

Krystal wobbled up, but the damage was already done. The curse had slowed her down, allowing my fire to race towards her. It didn't burn her within its massive reach like all the others, but the fire ached to grasp and consume her.

Krystal turned around, seeing that she couldn't outrun it any longer. She gasped for air, and her sweat-drenched hair clung to her. She stared into me, reaching out with her transparent, glowing arm. "Hellsfire!"

A white, sparkling light shot out from her. It glided toward me, and I marveled at its beauty. It was like a tiny firefly. The closer it floated to me, the more it called out to me. I was no longer buried by the dark flames. I was stronger, but the flames turned against me. The dark fire attacked and smothered me.

The little light collided with the fire. The entire flame shivered when I felt it touch my soul. Memories of times spent with Krystal flooded my mind. I remembered the first time she kissed me, and how it caught me off guard. I was so drained from letting Stradus die and defeating Premier. I was a bit embarrassed, but the wonderful kiss also restored something in me. I thought about the first time she brought me to the top of one of the castle's towers. How soft she felt as she snuggled up against me and I wrapped my arms around her. We had watched the sun set with our legs hanging and intertwining over the balcony.

We had spent countless hours together in Alexandria. In those private moments when we were alone we were just a man and a woman, not a wizard and a princess, and I felt more alive, at peace, and as happy as I had ever been during those times.

That sensation burrowed into me now. It bestowed upon me an amazing strength and power—far more than the temptation of the dark fire. It latched on to my feelings for Krystal and amplified them. I became enraptured by it and it brought me to the euphoria I only felt when I was with Krystal.

"Enough!" I said.

The black fire vanished, and the normal flames dwindled down to nothing. There was one last thing I wanted to say to Krystal. I should have said it before the ritual. I should have said it while we were in Alexandria.

With my last bit of breath I said, "Krystal, I…"

Then the darkness engulfed me.

CHAPTER 28

I **APPEARED IN** a blinding bright, barren place, wearing my black wizard's robes. I glanced at my hands, seeing the welts, bruises, scratches, and scars gone. I sniffed my robes, finding them and myself fresh and clean. That could only mean one thing.

I was dead.

I always thought I would find my father in the afterlife. It was what I was raised to believe and what I hoped. I glanced around, desiring to see my absent father for the first time. I didn't find him—or anything. I didn't understand it. After you died, you were supposed to be reunited with your loved ones. This emptiness disturbed me. What if nothing happened when you died and it was all a lie?

"You're not dead yet," a quiet voice said.

I spun around and glimpsed nothing. Hope bubbled up inside of me when I thought it might be my father.

"Who's there?" I asked.

His laughter echoed around me, yet I couldn't see anything. "You don't recognize me? I'm hurt, my boy."

That voice and laugh sounded very familiar. "Stradus?"

"Yes." He materialized in front of me, wearing his sky blue robes and smiling.

I ran up to him and embraced him. His warm hug and the smell of wind in his robes reminded me it was him.

"I've missed you too, Hellsfire, and I'm proud of what you've done. I knew you had it in you."

"Am I dead?"

"Almost. You're in the world between worlds—a kind of waiting place." His back stiffened and his smile ceased. "You did something *very* dangerous, Hellsfire. I wasn't even sure you'd make it. You should be dead. There was only one reason you survived."

"Hellsfire," a small and gentle voice said in the void. "Hellsfire..."

"Krystal?" I said, peering around. Her voice sounded so sad and quiet, as if she had been sobbing for hours.

"I'm glad the necklace I gave you was of use as s*he* is the reason you survived," my former master said. "No matter how much power you have, she has more."

I remembered how bright she looked and how she extinguished my fire when no others could—both when I defeated Premier and just now.

"Yes," I said, nodding. "I realize that now." I looked into his eyes. "But what does that mean?"

He shook his head. "I wish I could help you, my son, but I can't. I'm dead and I have nothing more to give you."

"Please come back to me," Krystal said. Her voice reached out to me and tugged at my soul. It made my heart clench.

She continued to call to me, but with each passing moment, her voice faded.

"Please don't die," Krystal whispered. "You promised me."

Her quiet sobs filled my ears. I had caused her so much pain, and I continued to do so. The agony in her voice saddened me, but I was also thankful that she lived.

Stradus's eyes transformed until the pupils disappeared. They swirled with a deep blue. "She's calling you back. Now return to her before it's too late!"

A strong wind exploded from him and pushed me away. He faded from existence as I flailed and flew, out of control, through the empty void.

"Wait!" I said, reaching out to him. "I still have more questions! What else am I supposed to do?

"You brought the barrier down. There will be others to help you. Find those you can trust and remember what I taught you." He grinned and waved. "You'll do fine. Take care, my boy, and good luck!"

It was wonderful to see Stradus again, but it was time to let him go. I was going to have to accomplish things without his guidance. I was a wizard, and I had a duty to magic and to the land. I would always remember that.

I was ripped from him and the world between worlds and propelled back into the painful world I'd always known.

I slowly opened my eyes, finding myself in a comfortable bed. Buckets of sweat drenched my naked body. I moaned as I tried to move, my body weak and sore. I pushed back the throbbing headache, latching onto the fire inside of me. Although faint, it was still there. I started to lie back down when something else startled me.

"I'm glad to see you're finally awake," an older man said, sitting on a stool next to me. He was dressed in red robes similar to a wizard's. When he turned, I saw the fire symbol on his back. He was from one of the temples. He reached out with a damp sponge, but I backed away.

"Who are you?" I asked in a hoarse voice.

"Brother Elijah. Don't worry. You're safe now. I'm here to help, if you'll allow me."

I nodded, even though there wasn't anything I could do to stop him. He wiped my forehead with the sponge, cooling my heated head, then put a bowl of broth to my mouth. "Drink this."

"Where are my friends?" I asked.

"Brother Ardimus and Sister Rebekah are guarding the room. The others are out in the city."

"Where are we?"

"Romenia."

"Romenia!"

I strained to get up, but grimaced in pain. We had to get out of here as soon as possible. The others could be in danger.

"It's all right, Hellsfire," Brother Elijah said. He stopped me by putting a hand on my chest. He barely applied any pressure, but it stopped me from rising anyway.

"No, you don't understand."

"Ah, but I do. The princess—"

"The princess! Where is she?"

"Right over there," Brother Elijah said as he motioned with his head to the corner of the room. "As you can see, she's safe and unharmed."

My whole body stiffened up as I spotted Krystal in a makeshift cot. She slept snuggled in my black robes, curled up like a baby. She looked so peaceful that I didn't want to wake her.

"This is probably the first time the princess has had this much sleep," Brother Elijah said. "She's normally been where I'm sitting now for the past week."

"I've been out for a week?" I asked, shaking my head.

"It's been closer to two. We had to bring you back to Romenia. The princess has been right by your side the whole time. She only allowed herself to sleep when you were ultimately out of harm's way." Brother Elijah rose. "I'm going to bring you something to eat, now that you can handle solid foods again. You're probably starving."

My mouth salivated and my stomach growled at the thought of it. "Thank you."

I struggled to get out of the bed, as the blankets were so heavy and I was so weak. I shivered when my feet touched the cold stone floor. I flexed my fingers and toes, willing them to work before I trusted my body enough to stand on my own.

I shuffled my feet, attempting to get to the clean clothes lying across a nearby chest. My body ached and moaned every step of the way, but I wasn't going to be bedridden, and I wanted to hurry before someone came and caught me naked.

I dressed and tiptoed to Krystal, kneeling down in front of her. I leaned in close to her and brushed a lock of her sun brown hair aside. I hungered to lean in and kiss her awake, but couldn't. The best I could do was kiss her on the head where her hair was thickest.

"Rest, beautiful," I said. "You deserve it."

She deserved to lie on my bed. She was a princess and shouldn't be sleeping on a cot. Yet I had no strength to lift her. I grabbed my blanket and covered her with it.

"Sleep well, princess."

The door creaked open. Brother Elijah carried a large tray of food with cheese, fruit, bread, and a bowl of beans. I limped up to him, thanked him, then ravished the meal.

"I told Brother Ardimus to gather your other friends," Brother Elijah said. I nodded, but didn't pause in my eating. "They should arrive shortly."

I was tempted to ask Brother Elijah some questions, but refrained from doing so. I didn't know whose side he was on or if I was a prisoner because of what I had done. I rubbed my neck. At least I wasn't wearing one of those accursed collars or in one of those cells. All I knew was that Krystal trusted him enough to fall asleep, and that the others roamed the city.

By the time I finished eating, my friends had arrived. I was glad to see everyone had survived the battle. Even Malik was there. So were Fortune and Adriana. I left the room so Krystal could get some peaceful sleep. Ardimus and Rebekah stayed behind to guard the princess.

We traveled the familiar hallways, and Malik led us to a big balcony. I glanced at my pale skin in need of some fresh air and sunlight. I took a moment to revel in the sunshine, allowing the cool breeze to fill every pore of my body. I gazed at the animal-shaped clouds, thankful to be alive again.

Hundreds of people wandered below us. I picked out the armies from their two colors of blue and red. Most of the soldiers still stood apart from each other. An ocean of blood was about to be shed if they clashed. A few people intermingled between the two, but could the truce be maintained, or would violence break out again?

I also noticed that there weren't many wounded. I sighed and shook my head. That probably had to do with me. I was sure I'd left nothing but burnt-out husks on the battlefield. Hundreds, more likely thousands, dead, all at my hands. They were just regular people. They weren't monsters being controlled by Premier. They had wives, husbands, and children. Even the Wasteland creatures had those things. And now their families would have to survive without them because of me. They couldn't even give them a proper burial.

I felt remorse for them, but I had needed to do what was necessary. They were going to bring war into *my* homeland, to my mother's doorstep. I also had to watch myself even more. I had made a great many enemies that day. Finding people to trust was going to be even harder.

Things would have been easier if I'd died.

I leaned over the railing. None of the others said anything to me. I stared at three of Romenia's soldiers. They were chatting until the lead man stopped and quieted. He bent down and stretched his arms wide as a little girl raced up to him, and they crushed each other in a bear hug. Soon after, the rest of the man's family caught up to the little girl and they all embraced each other.

I allowed myself a small smile. Maybe there was a little hope after all. When I was ready, they finally told me what happened after the fire dissolved.

The two side's armies had enclosed my friends. My friends had guarded my body, but couldn't fight off the remaining armies or the council. Krystal, Prastian, Jastillian, and even Fortune were able to negotiate so that I wouldn't be slaughtered on the spot for my actions. But that was all. I and the others would still have to answer for what I had done. Now that I was awake, that would have to be dealt with.

"Do not keep the council waiting," Adriana said.

I took a deep breath. It was time to end this. "All right."

I turned and headed back down the hallway.

"Where are you going?" Adriana asked. "The council's chambers are the other way."

"I know. I will be there shortly, but there's something I must do first."

I went back to the room, wanting to see the princess. Seeing her would grant me the strength to face the council. I wished I could have had my wizard's robes, but I wasn't going to wake her to retrieve them.

When I opened the door, I expected Krystal to still be asleep, but she had risen and was talking to Brother Elijah. Her violet eyes met mine, and she stopped in midsentence. We didn't say anything; we just stared at each other.

Brother Elijah cleared his throat. He bowed to the princess. "If you'll excuse me, Your Highness." He nodded as he went by me. "Wizard Hellsfire." He closed the door, leaving me and Krystal alone.

"You're alive," she said in an astonished voice.

We closed the small distance between us. Tears hung in her violet eyes. I opened my mouth to say something, but only air came out. We reached out at the same time and embraced each other. Fresh tears fell from both of us as we clung to each other. I inhaled her scent. She smelled of horse, dirt, and grass. The necklace I had given her shone, illuminating the room with its green light.

We didn't loosen our hold for several long minutes. We were so close to each other, yet so far. We made sure not to touch each other's skin, but it comforted both of us just to stand there and experience the warmth from each other's bodies.

When our tears ran dry, Krystal broke the hold and said, "Thank the gods you came back to me."

"Only because of you. Krystal, how did you do that?"

She gave me a quizzical look. "Do what?"

I returned her look. "*You* stopped the fire. Didn't you see anything? A bright light emanated from you that flew into me!"

She shook her head. "It did?"

"Yes. Did the council or other wizards say anything to you?"

"No, but I got the feeling they were hiding something." She shrugged. "There could be a great many things they would hide." She stared into my eyes. "I don't doubt what you said, but what do you think it means?"

"I don't know who else to ask. Renak said that your ancestor, Alexander, was special in the ways of magic, but he didn't understand how or why. I think you may have inherited it." I wrapped my arm around her waist, reeling her in and grinning. "But I already knew that you were special."

She smiled back. Krystal wiped my tear-soaked face, then did the same to hers. She started to take off my robes. "You'll need your robes, if you're going to go in front of the council. We have to look presentable."

I raised an eyebrow. "We?"

"Yes. I'm going with you."

I didn't argue. "All right."

I put my wizard's robes on and inhaled the sweet aroma that lingered on them. "Smells as if a beautiful woman wore them and kept them safe."

She touched my black robes. "I'm going to miss wearing them. It felt as if a part of you were there, holding me." Krystal stepped closer, and I wrapped my arms around her and spun her outwards. I ached to kiss the back of her neck like I used to. "But I don't need them any longer." She broke the embrace and asked, "Are you ready to see the council?"

"Shouldn't we wait and get you a clean and extravagant dress?"

"Hellsfire, you're stalling."

"I'm just...nervous. I've been in a room with three of them, and the power they radiate is intense. Plus, I decimated their army, Krystal. What if they want revenge?"

"If they wanted you dead, they would have already killed you."

I ran my fingers through my hair and shrugged. "You're right, of course. But these people have long memories, and they will want something. I still can't forgive them for what they did to you and Ardimus."

"Neither can I, but you must push aside those feelings and work with them for the greater good. Or would you rather the war continue?"

"I'll try."

"You'll do fine, and whatever you decide, I'll be right beside you," Krystal said.

"I thank the gods for that every day."

She bestowed that special smile that was reserved only for me. "As well you should."

We ended up in the same stark chambers. The only difference was now there were six chairs instead of three. It also lacked Ashton's mana symbols in the background. The Elemental Council looked comfortable as they chatted with each other, but they probably didn't realize it.

"We summoned you, Hellsfire, not the princess," Helios said and gave a slight nod to Krystal.

Before I could open my mouth to reply, Krystal said, "His fate concerns me."

"Very well."

"You killed thousands of our troops," Bellona said, her already black eyes darkening. "And you attempted to kill us."

I almost said, "And you tortured the princess and threatened to bring war to my homeland," but thought silence would be best. I nodded, glanced away from their eyes, and clenched my fists.

"This is not the time for that," Ardonis said, his calming magic dampening our emotions. "We're past that. It's time we discuss the future."

Nairi crossed her arms. "Yes, yes. So we've been told."

"How did you cast that fire?" Dorissa said. "We've learned you've only recently become a wizard."

"Hellsfire, indeed," Helios said with a youthful smile.

"I don't understand, council," I said.

"Humph," Zephyrus said. "You don't even comprehend the extremely dangerous spell you performed. Youth today."

"Your name," Helios said, his red eyes flashing, "is perfect for you. The fire you created is called 'hellsfire.' It's when you master both black and red mana and combine them into one. I have trouble with it myself, but Bellona and I could easily perform it together."

"Oh. Thank you," I said. I paused. Stradus was right. He had chosen the perfect name for me. I stepped forward. "Does something else happen when you create this hellsfire?"

"What do you mean?" Ardonis asked, with an intent look on his face.

"Is there a...feeling or a presence there?" I wanted to tell them more, but couldn't trust them. I wasn't about to tell them how the flames whispered to me or that they caused me to take delight in things I wouldn't normally.

At that second, a visual of how my dark flames incinerated a wizard flashed into my mind. His defenses burned like his flesh. A small smile crossed my lips.

"It's because you're young," Bellona said, pulling me away from my sinister thoughts. "You cast a spell far too advanced for you."

"There's nothing more dangerous than a wizard who cannot control his powers," Nairi said in her deep voice. "Even Renak's creatures learned control."

The others nodded in agreement, but that wasn't it. There was something else behind the magic. Something more sinister and powerful.

"Thank the gods, you were able to get yourself under control," Dorissa said, smiling. "Or we might not be here now."

I stared at the Elemental Council, then glanced back at Krystal. Did they not see what had happened? *She* was why I'd stopped. There was no other reason—or were they omitting that fact on purpose?

"These are new times for us—for everyone," Zephyrus said.

"Indeed they are," Bellona said. "But before we get to that, we must know if you'll accept our sentencing. Will you abide by our ruling for you and your friends for your actions earlier?" The light in the chambers darkened as the Elemental Council peered down at me.

"No," I said. "I will accept whatever you have in store from me, but you will let the princess and the others go. They had nothing to do with the ritual I performed."

Helios turned his head and stared at the princess. "That's not true. They guarded you, and they are here because of you."

Before I could open my mouth, Krystal said, "We'll accept your judgment, council. We stand together."

I wanted to argue with her, but now wasn't the time. I also wanted to wrap my arms around her and kiss her for standing by me.

"Good," Dorissa said. "After much discussion, we have decided to let you go, Hellsfire."

I was surprised to hear that, but glad to be free. Dorissa had a kind smile on her face as if she genuinely meant what she said, but Bellona and Nairi did not look happy about that outcome.

"This also includes the princess, along with the elves, the dwarf, and even the troublesome Fortune," Dorissa continued. "We would like to send more diplomatic forays into Northern Shala. Perhaps we can trade and share information."

"Yes," Krystal said. "I would very much like that. There is much to be learned from one another."

"Don't forget Prastian and Jastillian," Zephyrus said. "We'll have to discuss things with them as well."

"There is one thing we would like to ask of you, Hellsfire," Helios said. "We would prefer it if you stayed down here to—"

"To atone for what you've done," Nairi said, staring down at me.

"Help us," Helios said.

"You've crossed into the Dead Zone," Dorissa said in her calming voice. "That is one of the more extreme examples, but there are a lot of other things that need to be fixed, such as our old capital of Fairhaven."

I understood the implications. If I left, there would be repercussions. It might even give them an excuse to attack Northern Shala and the country that harbored me. They most certainly had other reasons for letting me live, but whatever the reasons, I had to atone for all the deaths I had caused. This would also be a great chance for me to learn more about my magic and even find a cure for Krystal, if I had access to even half of their resources and knowledge. And there was still the looming threat Renak had warned me about. I had to identify and stop it.

I glanced at the princess. What would she think about me staying in Southern Shala? Would it matter to her? It's not like I could ever return to Alexandria.

I bowed my head. "As you wish."

"We would also like your expertise and guidance in Northern Shala as a fellow wizard." Helios glanced to the others. "So that other incidents may be avoided. You understand better than us what it's like up there."

"We also want what you learned in Masep," Bellona said, her black eyes intent.

I looked at Krystal. She gave a subtle nod.

"Very well," I said.

"Great," Ardonis said, clapping his hands together. "We look forward to getting to know you."

Krystal bowed, and I did the same. She turned and walked away. I stopped and realized this was as good a time as any to ask for a favor.

"Council, if I may," I said. "I have a request."

Nairi leaned forward and gripped her staff tighter. "You've already done enough, Hellsfire. We owe you nothing. You should thank the gods we let you live. Not all of us were in favor of that."

"Let's be reasonable and at least hear his request," Ardonis said, putting a hand up. "There's no harm in that." He smiled. "Go ahead."

"Can you help me break Renak's curse on the princess? Ask your price and I'll pay it."

"Hellsfire, what are you doing?" Krystal asked.

"What I must," I said.

Ardonis peered over at Krystal. "So that's what I see in her. How and why did Renak curse you?"

"It was Premier's doing. He twisted and altered the spell used in the Great Barrier to kill her if I succeeded in bringing it down." I stared at the council from Ashton. "He's tricky and not to be trusted."

The council's colorful eyes all rested on Krystal as they sized her up.

"Humph," Zephyrus said. "It would require a very delicate touch for a wizard to twist Renak's spell, and he must have known you were coming."

"Give us a few days and we'll see what we can do," Bellona said. "That's all we can promise you."

Dorissa smiled at her. "I knew you were a romantic at heart."

Bellona's face became sour.

I bowed my head. "Thank you, Council."

We left the council's chambers. As we traveled the quiet hallways, Krystal and I walked arm in arm.

"Would you really pay *any* price to cure me of this affliction, Hellsfire?"

"Of course, Princess."

She leaned her head against mine. "That's sweet. Do you think the council will be able to help?"

"I hope so. They're the Elemental Council. No one knows more about magic than they do."

"But the magic was created by Renak and twisted by Premier. We shouldn't get our hopes up, Hellsfire."

I untwined my arm and hugged her waist. "If they're not able to find a way, I promise I won't stop trying."

She didn't respond.

We spent the following week in Romenia, and the council was true to their word. They performed tests on both me and Krystal. We endured a lot as they probed us with magic, performed rituals, and concocted a few potions. However, in the end, they couldn't help us. They said that Renak's curse was too adaptable and strong. It wasn't only embedded in the princess, but in me. All of their powerful magic didn't affect the curse in the slightest.

They were the almighty Elemental Council, but not even they could defeat Renak. This might have been Premier's fault, but it was Renak's magic that was the source of it. Those council members from Ashton were awed by Renak's curse, even while it defeated them. I was surprised when the council said there might be others in Southern Shala who could help. Those who were more skilled in curses. They also told me that when Fairhaven was opened, something might be found in that abandoned city.

As disappointed as I was that the Elemental Council couldn't cure Krystal, I wasn't going to give up hope.

Captain Rebekah, Ardimus, and at least one of the others constantly shadowed and hovered over us. They were apprehensive that people might attack us in retribution. I was worried, too, not for myself but for the princess.

Krystal, Prastian, Jastillian, Fortune, and Malik sought to work things out, talking to the people as we went to the market, the temple's services, or the inns. They had a difficult time because of my presence. The regular people that lived in Romenia were more relieved that the war was over, but even they had lost people because of what I had done. I had a harder time meeting their eyes than anyone else's.

At the end of the week, it was time to depart. The council had given my friends enough supplies for the long journey back into Northern Shala, along with gifts. We were outside the city, with the horses loaded. The low sun shone over our heads.

"May I talk to you, Your Highness?" I asked Krystal.

"Of course."

I led her away from the others, and well away from the elves with their excellent hearing. Krystal pulled on her horse's reins and put the horse in between us and our friends.

As much time as we had spent together over the past week, with me clinging at her hip and her mine, we hadn't discussed the fact that I was going to stay down here. We both knew it, but I think it was too painful for either of us to talk about. At least, for me it was.

"I guess this is it," I said.

"How long will you be gone?" she asked.

I sighed. "I'm not sure. I have to help the council take down whatever defenses and traps are left and try to repair the land, but I'm also going to look for a way to break Renak's curse. And there's also Premier. I doubt Paige caught him. He's bound to be planning something nefarious." I met her eyes. "While the council may not believe me about Renak's threat of the gods' war, I do. There's a danger out there, Krystal. One that I'm going to have to deal with. They didn't see what I saw in Renak's eyes."

"I believe you." She dragged her fingertips along my side and gave me a sad smile. "Just try not to take too long, hero, and please be careful. We don't know what else is out there."

"I'll try."

Krystal dug into one of her saddlebags and pulled out a vial of blood and a lock of her hair. She put it in my hand.

"What's this?" I asked.

"I was told this could help you test your spells without me being here."

I stared at her. She thought of everything. I placed those items into my purse and reeled her in. She snuggled up against me as I grasped her warm body tighter.

A single tear trickled down her face, and her royal mask started to break. "Hellsfire, I—"

"Shhh." I mustered all my strength to use magic I wasn't trained to use. "Close your eyes."

I leaned in close enough to kiss Krystal. Her slow, rhythmic breathing rang in my ears. I concentrated and reached into my soul, grasping onto my feelings for her. The amulet I had given her glowed in response, and I gently blew. My breath scattered across her face, flowing all over her. She shivered in response as the feeling of a thousand kisses brushed upon her tingling body. Her knees buckled, and she nearly fell.

"That was amazing," she said. She laid her hand against my face. I nuzzled against it, wishing I could feel her skin.

Krystal's hand became limp and fell. She turned and mounted horse, wheeling it around to face north.

There was one last thing I wanted to tell her before she left. Something I should have told her earlier.

"Krystal, I love you."

For a brief instant, her entire face lit up with the grandest smile, and the jade hexagram's light blinded me. When I opened my eyes, both had vanished. Krystal didn't say anything for the longest time, her violet eyes drinking in the sight of me.

She sadly smiled and said, "I know."

The princess spurred her horse onward, galloping back towards Alexandria. I stared at her shrinking figure, feeling my heart drop into my stomach. Captain Rebekah and Ardimus sped by to catch up to her, and they gave me a cursory nod. The elves rode by and waved. Jastillian smiled as he passed. They might have said something, but I couldn't hear them. I couldn't hear anything.

Fortune and Malik came to me. Fortune slapped me on the shoulder, ripping me from my trance. "Come on, kid. I'll buy you a drink."

Serena flew from Malik and settled on my shoulder. "Don't be so glum, cutie. We'll have lots of fun while you're down here."

"He's not here for fun, Serena," Malik said. "We'll do all we can to help you with the princess's curse."

I stared at the now tiny horses, waiting for Krystal to turn around. She didn't once look back. Did she not feel for me what I felt for her? Then I remembered what she had given me. She wanted me to find a cure, so she must have some feeling for me. Memories of us together raced through my mind. It hurt to remember her laughter and smile, that fierce gaze she wore when she fought, and the way she never gave up. The most painful one was the memory of before I left for the Wastelands and what she would have asked her father, but never did.

I couldn't help but dwell on King Furlong's words. Was I someone she was just passing the time with? She never said she would wait until I found a cure. That scared me more than anything. What if I couldn't find a cure? Even if I did, what if I was never allowed back into Alexandria? What would she do? What would *I* do? Kathleen was right. I loved Krystal more than I'd ever loved her, and that was why not knowing hurt more than anything.

I shook my head. I wasn't going to give up hope of a future with the princess unless that was what *she* wanted. She was all that mattered to me. I would do everything in my power to break this curse Premier had twisted upon us and find a way back into Alexandria. I would sacrifice everything to do so.

But the recent war and the council's action reminded me that I still had a duty to perform. Krystal wouldn't have wanted me to shrink away from it. I was going to help repair and restore what I had to in Southern Shala, hunt Premier down, and find clues to the menace Renak feared.

I stared at my hand, feeling the dark flame within me. I was going to have to deal with it and learn to control it, lest it overwhelm me. It threatened to rise up, its shadowy promises weaving into my mind. It was getting easier to summon, but no matter how much it promised, it could never give me Krystal...or could it?

To be continued in

Reawakening

The Passage of Hellsfire Series, Book 3

To undo a mistake made a thousand years in the past, the wizard Hellsfire used his magic to bring down the Great Barrier that once divided the northern and Southern lands. In doing so, he nearly brought war to his own homeland, and he afflicted the love of his life, Princess Krystal of Alexandria, with a potent and deadly curse.

Since then, Hellsfire has been working in Tyree with its Elemental Council, to rebuild its war-torn land and find a way to break Krystal's curse. Now Krystal's time is running out. As the princess fights for her life, Hellsfire learns that the wizard responsible for the curse—his old enemy Premier—is heading to the Burning Sands to steal the mysterious Jewel of Dakara.

If Hellsfire can capture Premier and learn the secret of the curse, he can save Krystal. But the Jewel of Dakara holds its own deadly secrets, and the hunt will take Hellsfire farther than he ever imagined, and cost him more than he bargained for.

The past is never gone nor buried...

Author's Corner

Email: *marcanthonyjohnson@gmail.com*

Facebook: *http://www.facebook.com/MarcJohnsonAuthor*

Goodreads: *http://www.goodreads.com/marcjohnson*

Twitter: *http://www.twitter.com/Hellsfire*

Website: *http://www.marcanthonyjohnson.com*